The Robot and the Vampire

F. Eagles Pope

The Robot and the Vampire

By F. Eagles Pope

Tell-Tale Publishing Group, LLC

Printed in United States of America

Stargazer Imprint

This book is dedicated to the Clark County research librarians at Sahara West, Their guidance on vampirism and the technology of robots helped immensely.

PROLOGUE

THE caretaker to the graveyard felt uneasy. The year was 1554 and he knew that on this day the sun, moon and earth were in alignment. He was not a man of education. He certainly never thought about the morals of his existence, but he had learned a remarkable fact from the friars. It was also the day of the winter solstice, and the two events only coincided once every 456 years.

It was unusual for him to make his rounds so late in the day, but he was waiting for dusk and the night to follow. The lunar eclipse was certain to arrive on this Wiccan's eve, and all things were possible. He sat by the gravestones of the three girls who had been massacred so horribly by the evil vampire Drakonius many years ago. Yes, he had known them personally, Iphigènie, Athalie and Phaedra, all beautiful, all so young and innocent at the time. Their eyes had been gouged out, their innards torn apart. They were raped both before and after they died.

All three were buried one next to the other.

The landscape had changed considerably since their time. Now they grew poppies in the hills, the same hills that had once had a different fragrance, olive trees and tamarisk with their white, pink and red flowers. His gaze strayed away from the hills and to the northwest, to the castle of the Alucards, constitutionally a family evil, the cradle of vampirism.

It was they, the Master along with his British wife, who controlled the entire region. He had spoken with him only once and on that day the prediction was made that the three girls would be resurrected. They would rise again, not like the Christ on Easter, but into a life of vampirism, each given a specific trait by which they would be recognized into the sisterhood. Iphigènie was to have the quality of invasion, the capability to enter another human form's body. Phaedra would have the ability to transmogrify into a bat and transport herself long distances in an instant. Athalie was to be given the power of Achilles, the strength to throw the spear and thrust the lance with deadly accuracy.

The caretaker was waiting to see if all this was about to happen. Was it a mere fable told to townspeople enchained by certain superstitious impressions, from Alucard to maintain his power over them, to keep the mystery of the vampire going strong? Soon he would know the truth, when the lunar eclipse began to take place.

∞

At last night descended upon the cemetery, the shadow of the earth slowly forcing itself against the face of the full moon. There was no wind; the earlier sharp gusts of late afternoon had left the area. A strange quiet ensued. The normal everyday sounds of the neighborhood absented themselves. He stared down at his mud-encrusted boots. He was unwilling to make a sudden movement, but slowly averted his gaze from his footwear to the slab of stone that covered the grave of Iphigènie. Had it moved? Or was that just his imagination? No, the debris and dirt just to the side of the slab were disturbed, an awkward painstaking movement, slowly lifting the stone such that it was no longer set straight into the earth, but now tilted, lopsided. He changed his focus; stared once more at the moon, now less than half full, then again back to the gravestone which hesitantly cracked at the base, bits of stone falling loose, scattered crystals.

The movement of rubble and dirt was now faster, more of the earth uplifting, the slab falling to one side, the moon now a crescent, then suddenly a woman's hand struck through the opening that had been created where the gravestone so long stood embedded in the earth. His heart dropped, he withdrew one step, then two, but continued to watch as another hand and arm emerged from the depths of the grave pit. He wanted to turn and run, but his fascination held him rooted to his spot.

The muscles at the back of his neck clutched tighter at his flesh. Something was waiting. A membranous head emerged, with rotted teeth. The smell of rotten eggs reached him, a sulfurous lustre in the air. The caretaker shuddered. The other two gravestones began to move slightly. He sought instinctively to look away, but his curiosity got the better of him.

The apparition's hands tore at the membrane covering her face, the shreds of tissue and globs of phlegm and pus falling to the side. Yes, now he could see the emerging head and body was that of the once beautiful Iphigènie. However, mottled and ugly this head, the remnants of the lines of her face were still there. It was she. She moved toward him in recognition, extended her arms, rasped out his name in a whisper. The spoken words were slow to form. The sound of her speech took some time to reach him, as if traveling through the air in slow motion. Her arms reached for him, seeking an embrace.

The caretaker ran away, and never looked back.

The moon was now fully eclipsed.

2058

THE earth had traveled counter-clockwise nearly five-hundred revolutions around our explosive nuclear sun since the alignment of the three heavenly bodies had taken place on that particular winter solstice. In all that time, the immense solar flares and the power changes in the magnetic fields that the planet had endured registered dimly on the blind eyes of the three resurrected young women. No one could ever forget the unbelievable horror and mayhem they, and others like them, left in their tracks. It was difficult to judge when they would show up again. And in those nearly five-hundred revolutions no one like Vladg had yet been created.

Chapter I

At present the house where I live is quiet and I am propped up in bed, relaxing, waiting for Lydia to return from work. The truth of the matter is that I am her designated companion and have been so assigned since 2056. It is like being a designated hitter in baseball, you don't really get to play the entire game and yet you are an integral part of the team. So I have been on the job for two years and in that span of time I found she could get on my nerves now and again, but only as a person who holds a special place in your heart can do.

Lydia is the type of woman whose kisses either brought you closer to love or closer to death; mostly I didn't know which way she intended to go. Yet if anyone loved her I did. That is if I am capable of love.

Her mystery was involved with her heritage.

She told me she hailed from a little town in Nebraska populated by people from the Balkans. True or not I do not know. Her story was that she was of very mixed lineage; that these descendants of immigrants were saddled with old fashioned ideas; numerous customs and rituals, such as rites of passage that are passé in today's high tech world.

Don't get the wrong idea when I say in the Midwest minds are slower. Slower does not necessarily mean duller. Folks there just don't string ideas together as fast as back east. So I take this into account when she tries to talk about things above her head. That's the irritating part; she jumps my nerves more than my bones. And yes, I do have bones.

What was curious, deserves to be noted, is that Lydia spoke French. And I don't mean she spoke student French, no, her accent was first rate almost like a native Parisian. The problem for me was that I knew she had never been to Paris or even to Montreal and to speak refined French with the facility she had meant you didn't just visit as a tourist; that level of first class French takes years to accomplish. That was one mystery.

The other mystery was her husband. She didn't much care for him, said he depressed her because he was so weird, frequently leaving her in the middle of the night for no apparent reason. His job was in the Foreign Service, an ambassador-at-large or some such, covering all the Slavic countries, so he wasn't in town that often, which was to my liking.

She said I was exciting to her and made her laugh. This is strange because while I do have optimum self-sufficiency, I wasn't built with a sense of humor. True, every once in a while I could overdo my particular brand of snarky sarcasm, usually by making some mistake. This came about the other day because there are certain things I do not know, like the difference between a straight man and a stand-up comic. I told her that while I was watching C-SPAN-4, the majority whip of the Senate stood up and told the assemblage that after thirty years, Toyota was going back into the production of automobiles. Everyone on screen laughed, so I told Lydia I hadn't known that the Senator was also a stand-up comic. I meant it, but that's why she thought I was funny. No matter. She told me if I wanted to be her straight man I'd have to set it up better.

Speaking of cars, another form of mechanical device, I was a used model. Not in the traditional sense. I was never pre-owned, a fine but important distinction. Lydia was my first purchaser, but of course during that long period between my creation and her ownership, I was still very useful. I was first trained as a welder, but when school teachers were not in adequate supply, I was upgraded. Eventually I taught earth science and math to 6th graders. At that time, I did not yet have the sensual-sexual systems installed. However, I did possess a yellow card which allowed me to teach, but granted me no other rights whatsoever. Even so, I still don't think of myself as a synthetic man.

Just prior to my purchase, I was also programmed by Eiselman in the classics, so I asked Lydia why she insisted on trying to talk about things like Auguste Renoir, Goya, or William Shakespeare, things she knew next to nothing about.

"You don't always have a choice," she said. "I wasn't brought up in that New York culture, but I want to be interesting, to have significant conversations about love."

Why should this lack of logic bother me? After all, I wasn't married to her. I was just her companion.

As if I had spoken out loud, she said: "I wonder why that should bother you?"

That was Lydia, she had this knack of reading my mind when I least expected it. I knew I had to have a comeback, to say something clever, so I bent my immense shoulders over, and said: "We are not talking about love; at least I didn't think we were."

"Every one of us has a thousand variations on the theme of love, it is my basic difficulty."

See what I mean? Irrational.

"You know, Lydia, you've got a troubled nature," I said.

She didn't accept my criticism.

"For years love has made a mockery of me, so it isn't just my troubled nature."

I struggled to find some logic to her declaration.

"If love cuts you up so much, why don't you just abandon the idea? Ditch the attempt to find someone who loves you."

"Because of ancient desires, injured vanity, whatever," she said. "Then again, you never know, I might get a lucky break, so I persist."

Lydia only looks to be in her late twenties; so I didn't know what she meant by 'ancient desires'. On the other hand, she has what some of the long-lineage groups of humans call a meshuga way of saying things at times, as if her sentence structure is out of whack.

"I thought we were companions, friends," I said.

"Yes, but we are not truly lovers, only friends with benefits. That makes a difference."

Once she pushed this particular button I decided to let it go, and managed to change the subject.

"Would you like to have a drink?" I asked.

"Of course I do, always, but it's too early for blood," she said, "How about a Jack Daniels on the rocks?"

I figured she had meant a Bloody Mary, didn't give it another thought and made the J.D. for her. We sat together on the couch. I was getting ready for one of her 'significant conversations'.

∞

I don't want to give the wrong impression about Lydia. She really is talented; she has gifts, just not in a way that is measurable by the standards of most people. Early on she was trained in midwifery and later as a veterinarian. She knew all that was necessary of small animals. She was never capricious about the trials of creaturely existence, never refused a client who couldn't pay or didn't have the proper health insurance for their pet. She did seem to be a bit absent minded at times, but is that really such a big deal? She knew cytology and hematology quite well, and now that I think of it, she did seem to have an inordinate interest in the different types of blood of all the animals she treated. I suppose that is the way with specialists trying to master a field of science. Perhaps that's why she came off so alien when it came to the humanities. So when she began to talk about the complexities of love and existence I felt it was better, for her own sake, not to encourage her along these lines.

Well now that you have a fairly good idea of Lydia, I suspect you might wish to know a bit more about me. The undeniable fact is that I am a SEXTUS-IX, a Duplicant. And yes, I was created at Eiselman's Pyrell Corporation in 2033, born as a generally complete unit on March the seventh of that year, but without many of the features such as the sensual-sexual system already mentioned. Remember I said that I was used but not pre-owned. That's because the Pyrell Corp. needed to have their units earn their keep before a purchaser was found for them. We need to be sheltered, have to eat and sleep like humans, so the COO found jobs for us which were in the public interest.

We were given yellow cards which brought us into the labor pool, enabled us to contribute, and pay taxes of course. So we fulfilled a double need as there was a dearth of competent teachers, electricians, welders and plumbers. For the most part this system worked quite well as we paid our union dues in full on time, and never raised a rumpus in union meetings. Generally, I got along with humans quite well.

The various unions could object to very little in the way of our talent or productivity as we zipped through all the apprentice manuals and hands on work in record time. The teacher's union did try to raise a formal protest at first, but since we were not humans, only humanoid, they had no legal recourse. Certainly we were more knowledgeable than most teachers, did a better job with lesson plans, and were never sassy to the principals. Our ability with the pupils was at least as warm and inspiring as most human teachers and the parents took to us at the parent-teacher conferences. To the best of my knowledge the same held true in the other professions such as welding and plumbing. We were generously accepted into the fold, paid our health premiums but never had to make use of the health benefits. So we helped their financial base and never once took advantage of their bylaws.

Now in addition to my lack of street sense there are other areas of knowledge that I do not contain. The reason for this is that Eiselman did not believe in myths or magic, only in materials, realistic and logical thought which, undeniably, included all the emotional interactions. So I lacked study in wizards, witches, wiccans and werewolves, in demons and vampires, in fairies and leprechauns. The entire world of mysticism was alien to me, a world which I later found out to be very active and prominently intermingled with the world of abject humanity.

Speaking of which, you may want to know how much the basic Duplicant costs. At present the base price is two-hundred thousand New Dollars, but it is like buying a home or an RV. All you need is ten percent down and the rest can be paid out in installments over a period extending to as long as sixty months. Of course, all this gets you is the basic companion with minimal thought process abilities and maximum work skills and muscle power. All the other amenities, such as a sophisticated Like-Dislike system, or a Sensual-Sexual system are add-ons at a hundred thousand a crack for each feature. So someone with my abilities can cost upwards of a million New Dollars or more.

All this was done in order to meet up with the wishes and desires of Lydia, my purchaser. My updated education had to be accomplished in so short a space of time that much street lingo was left out. That's why I didn't know the difference between a stand-up and a straight man. On the other hand, Eiselman did fill me up with Yiddish expressions; that explains meshuga. The day-to-day common knowledge, most of which the ordinary individual absorbs in the course of development, I did not learn. Much later, I discovered this was to my detriment compared to humankind. My street life basics came at the expense of some pretty mysterious and morbid events, which we will get to later.

As you may know, Cyborgs are part human, part mechanical, but the term Cyborg has gone out of fashion as so many humans now add mechanical parts. Yes, humans are still evolving, not with the slowness of Darwin but with the rapidity of technology. Now we call these hybrids Humilicants and each year there are more and more of them. Droids, on the other hand, are entirely mechanical (albeit with nuclear fusion supported electronic mechanisms) and Clones are genetically exact reproductions. Duplicants differ from Replicants in that our life spans are about equal to that of the average human being although we never show signs of aging as we have an anti-senescence factor built right into our metabolic systems. So unlike other robotic figures I was totally humanoid, made completely from biologic materials except for certain added features you will hear about along the way.

Ever since the global legislation was passed in 2038 by the World Parliamentary Congress, twenty years ago, women were allowed to own Duplicants. Not that we had to look like their husbands, heavens no, we Duplicants are women's fantasies, their wishes and desires. That's probably why Lydia could read my emotions, since I replicate her feelings.

The way this came about was due to the resolution of the problem of nuclear fusion in 2025. Please don't get this discovery mixed up with nuclear fission. Fusion leaves less radiation in its tracks than the average X-Ray machine.

It took until 2028 to make a commercially viable pilot plant. The physics was known, but all these equations had to be worked out engineering wise. Once this was accomplished we were halfway there. The programming difficulty was to confine hot plasma long enough with the Lorentz force on a charged particle. Once this was done (the scientific term is called electromagnetic confinement) the method of achieving fusion energy for commercial purposes was close at hand. The next big step was to make the fusion engine small enough to turn the fan blades of a jet engine, add the hot plasma to the incoming air, and cause it to explode with enough thrust to lift a heavy jet aircraft and propel it through the air. The very first experimental aircraft was a success. The darn thing flew. Shades of Wilbur and Orville Wright! The total weight of the fusion engines turned out to be much less than the standard weight of jet fuel carried in the wings. As a consequence, the fusion-driven non-combustible aircraft was now lighter, safer and faster.

In a reversal of history, cars quickly followed aviation's lead. An even smaller motor was perfected to maintain the battery charge for electric cars which drove the vehicle forward at a clip that was steadier and faster than any battery operated car heretofore, actually achieving NASCAR racing speeds. This was the death knell to the internal combustion engine.

As soon as these changes took effect globally the world changed radically. With the availability of an inexhaustible supply of clean energy, this took care of the excessive CO2 problem and global warming was solved forever. For all practical purposes, this also defeated the terrorist menace as well.

What happened was that the large industrial nations no longer had any need for fossil fuels as their power supply and the grids necessary to bank and distribute the energy were quickly constructed. Now the oil cartels such as OPEC suddenly found themselves going broke. Their camels became as important as their oil reserves once again. Before you knew it, the war on terror problem was resolved as well by altering the financial systems of global banking. The sheiks were still immensely wealthy, of course, but they certainly had no extra funds to support the various terrorist movements.

Another point! In the period between 2020 and 2040 the percentage of gay men suddenly took an almost exponential increase from its bedrock level of 10% to more than 20%. This left women with a dearth of male partners. However, it did help to slow the population increase which had been hovering at the ten billion level worlds wide. The culture began a slow, but inexorable, change as the pool of available men decreased and the individual man became relatively more valuable to women.

Straight men (see how confusing the English language can be) liked the idea as they were able to choose from a greater group of potential candidates. Politicians finally got into the act and the marriage contract was redefined as one made between two humans of whatever gender. Match.com and others in the adventurous business of matchmaking saw an unprecedented uptick in their stock values. Naturally, Duplicants were excluded from marriage as we were not, strictly speaking, human, only humanoid.

There was, of course, some brouhaha by the moralists who saw the purchase and trading of Duplicants as a return to the days of slavery, but this issue was quickly hush-hushed when it became apparent that Basic-II Duplicants cleared up the illegal immigration problem. The reason for this was simple. They were better and more efficient at certain humdrum tasks such as gardening and housework, which illegals traditionally fulfilled.

The upgraded job Eiselman had done on me was easy to applaud. The bio-engineers programmed me in the classics from the Greeks through the 20th century artists, scholars and scientists. Once this was accomplished I was given lessons by the Institute of Sexual Arts. These lessons were both theoretical and hands on techniques. I enjoyed them very much and learned to insert and coordinate my genital apparatus according to the wishes of the female recipient. After ten minutes I was allowed to squirt and if the recipient wished to continue, she could push a bio-sensor button, placed adroitly within the tip of my left nipple, which restarted the entire program. (The joke amongst Duplicants is that we finally solved the philosophical problem of why men have nipples). Of course the female models consisted of many different body types; their personalities varied considerably in order to prepare me for the multiplicity of preferences of the possible purchaser.

So that's all referenced to my higher order systems. Now let's get back to the basic building blocks.

My construction is of all organic materials, my skin being an amalgam of resins mixed with real epidermal cells capable of their own regeneration. Everything about me is very humanoid except for my circulatory apparatus which resembles more of a lymph like substance than blood. I am tall, well over six feet and my body type is athletic. I do have the reflexes of a cat. I can evade a punch in 1/54th of a second, same speed as a roach you might try to swat with a folded up newspaper. My central nervous system, bone structure, plumbing and digestive tract are all cloned from embryonic lines that meet the requirements of the WPC criteria for in vitro reproduction. My muscular system is invigorated with ten times the ATP of humans. So my muscular strength and muscle fiber contractility are enormous.

Now my latest added feature is interesting. Lydia ordered a masculine scent which mixes with the perspiration exuding from my sweat glands and sprays a fine mist over my skin. It is not pungent but does give me a pleasant body essence. "Not exactly a love potion," she said, "but a helluva lot better fragrance than most jocks in the locker room."

Yes, Lydia shops Pyrell's catalogue for new features to be integrated into my systems as other women shop for shoes and purses. Generally, I was okay with it, but sometimes she made me feel like a pizza pie, ordering the extra toppings at her own whim and fancy. I almost told her that the fish smell oozing forth from her vulva after she had an orgasm was something I could do without, but I held myself back, having learned a bit of restraint since leaving Pyrell's, finally fully equipped, a few years ago.

So that's enough about me for now.

What you really need to know is that I have been with Lydia for well over two years and in all that time she has never once said the three words of love that every man, human or humanoid, wants to hear. I don't believe she is disappointed in me, after all I am a Sextus-IX, and there are not that many of us, not yet anyway, as there are hordes of Sextus-VI's still on sale.

Remember, Lydia had stated categorically that she did not love her husband, so he was not a man of whom I could be jealous, certainly not. After all, I am much better looking, taller, stronger physically, at least his equal intellectually and, of course, I have the advantage of youth, my appearance being that of a twenty-five-year-old. My construction design and featured software, aside from the effects of gravity, enables me to remain this way until the end of my natural life span. A nice addition, as I mentioned previously, is that Sextus-IX's do not fall ill to disease of any sort. When our time is up we simply drop dead.

So, you may ask, if Lydia has a husband why was she allowed to purchase a Duplicant. The answer is simple. Married women, worldwide, got together and formed a PAC. They then threatened to desert the major political parties unless they were no longer excluded. It seems that even the Sextus-VI was better at the cohabitation scene than the male human. As a consequence, these women wanted the 'right of purchase' which they presently saw as a prejudicial privilege of men and single women. This action had been the first split in the women's movement since the prior century. Married women (except for extreme right wingers who had lobbied against sex with Duplicants, although they were the largest purchasers of low level Duplicants for housework) quickly joined the movement and vowed to remain frigid with their husbands until this seeming injustice was rectified.

After a very short period of total abstinence by the married women of the world, married men joined in with their approval and as a consequence the WPC added an amendment allowing all women, regardless of marital status, to have the right to contract for purchase of Duplicants.

It should be noted that the men campaigned seriously for the production of the Sextus models, although their reasons for doing so were not spelled out with any specific details whatsoever. It was rumored that once men discovered that a Sextus could drive a golf ball straight, consistently, for over three hundred yards and rarely missed thirty foot putts they changed their tune, partnering with a Sextus on their free golf afternoons.

So now you're up to date on that little item. But I still need to say why there are so few female Duplicants. I myself have never been entranced by a female Duplicant. Perhaps this is because they are so rare and so well hidden in this country. Yet even a Duplicant can have his or her moments of softening or weakness about love.

It all has to do with Chairman Nancy Meadows, the head of monetary policy at the FED. She determined that if there were more female Duplicants available the frustrations that men have with their human women would be too heavily taxable. That's the way she put it in financial terms. What she really meant was that men's sexual fantasies could, in the large, not be fulfilled by human women, whereas a female Duplicant could more easily accomplish this task. So a strict restriction was put on Pyrell Corp. and other firms who manufactured high resolution Duplicants to delimit the production of females.

Even so, there evolved a growing black market in the purchase of female Duplicants manufactured in Eastern Europe, India and China, as well as some other Far Eastern nations. These countries did not strictly abide by U.S. specs and regulations.

As I said, I am truly in love with Lydia, although she looks upon me more as her boy-toy than as a man. I suppose this may eventually wear itself out, but as long as I consider Lydia a woman of beauty and distinction I am stuck with my somewhat adolescent affection for her. Of course she is beautiful with long auburn-reddish hair that slinks down to just above her waist. When she goes to the office she does pull her hair up in a bun of sorts, but even then she is gorgeous, a hunk I believe the expression is, with her pert cuppy breasts and long slim waist that is a thrill for me every time I wrap my arms about her. And she loves sex, all kinds and in all the standard positions as well as a few she herself invented which were not in my training manual.

She does have this tendency to bite my neck rather deeply, but at one lovemaking session she drew lymph and had to spit it out. She has since given up this maneuver. I do have the hickeys to prove it, but my epidermal cells are so regenerative that the evidence doesn't last very long and I cannot show them off very well to my neighbor, Rory, who is, after all, a mere Sextus-VI.

At Pyrell, all Duplicants, of whatever sort, are tattooed on their buttocks with a factory serial number, usually located on the upper outer portion of the left cheek. So I am labeled SE-9-44w6-3723. The w means white in color. I was the forty-fourth produced in the sixth production batch of fifty. The last four numbers are simply my birth date.

Once we are sold each client is given the right to name her purchase. My name was given to me by Lydia, and she calls me Vladg or Vladgey, sometimes using the diminutive as a term of endearment. Vladg may sound like an odd name, but I was glad to have it and not be called Robin or Robbie as some unimaginative women have done. All of those names sound robotic like to me. So Lydia calls me Vladg formally, but when we are making love she insists on Niner, which is a bit embarrassing since all Sextus-IX's have the same schlong length, although the form, girth and curvature, may differ in certain cases. In the erect state I am a good twelve inches, so I thought she lacked imagination in this regard, but she said twelver just didn't sound romantic to her. I have learned never to argue with Lydia on such matters, so I left well enough alone as they say in the jargon.

Her husband's name is Bram Alucard and he has an air of gluttonous self-sufficiency about him which turns me off. He is much older than she, must be in his fifties at least. He is a smallish man, not over five-seven, wears a trim moustache and a Van Dyke and sports a diamond earring; most unseemly for my taste and far too dapper for his persona. I don't believe he was born in the States as he has a thick accent in his English, although his grammar is without fault. He works for the Foreign Service as he is fluent in several languages, including all of the Balkan dialects. I suppose that is why the catchment area he serves for the State Department is between eastern Romania and western Macedonia, a desolate grim land.

At present he is posted in Bucharest and only visits Lydia on rare occasions, a few times each year for a week or so. During these times I am not allowed to enter her bedroom, but am reduced to the status of chauffeur and house valet of sorts.

My tactic, generally, is to avoid him as much as possible. Accordingly, our encounters are minimal, but when they do occur he tends to order me about asking me to perform menial tasks. Naturally I become peeved,.as my anger-frustration system is sensitive on this topic. Better said, my ego furnace gets stoked beyond belief. But I hold back, though I am seething inside. That's why I developed the habit of eavesdropping; I know, not one of my better characteristics. On one of these occasions I overheard him ask Lydia: "Are you unhappy, my dear?" "Oh yes. I am barren," she replied, "and I know that has disappointed you, but I have also had to learn to deceive Vladg and that is not in keeping with my fundamentals."

The best Bram could manage to say was: *"Very clever, my love, fundamentals eh?"* followed by a snort and a forced half-smile which did make her groan.

That's when I realized how important it was for me to make her laugh.

During his last visit things were even stranger. He seemed to be studying me, my every movement, even my facial expressions. If I didn't know better, it felt as if he were hypnotizing me which made me feel uncomfortable. So I looked at my watch in a kind of defensive maneuver; it read 9:07 in the morning. The watch was given to me by Lydia on the anniversary of her first year of purchase and she had it inscribed: 'To Vladgey, the best companion I ever had'. Naturally I treasured it and reading the inscription again buoyed up my spirits, but it didn't stop Bram, he persisted in staring at me with those beady eyes of his. He asked what subjects I was interested in, what books I liked to read and so on. Questions and more questions; I felt out of it. The oddest thing was that he seemed fascinated by my most least valuable feature, the last topping Lydia had added, my ability to spray a pleasant scent over my skin via my sweat glands.

I had no idea why he was so inquisitive, so interrogative, as he had not shown the slightest interest in any of my qualities during his prior visits. I told myself, when the time was opportune, I would ask Lydia if she had noticed anything different in his attitude toward me on this visit.

Entirely by chance I rechecked the time. Now my watch read 9:16 a.m. Apparently he had spoken with me for nine minutes. I thought it had only been for a minute or two. Where had the other seven or eight minutes gone? It was a mystery to me!

∞

Getting back to our JD on the rocks; we had nearly finished our drinks and were both standing now so I thought this would be a good time to ask her about her husband. Why had he shown such unusual interest in me the last time around? I thought this was a legitimate fear as it is well known that some men have been known to disable their wife's Duplicant completely on whatever whim strikes their fancy. Of course, this has legal consequences, not for the Duplicant, we do not have any civil rights as such, but it is a misdemeanor on the part of the husband to threaten or disable a Duplicant. Personal property and ownership laws are involved. That is the only protection we have. On the other hand, if the husband takes an axe (or uses some other malicious method of destruction) to a Duplicant the judgment is more severe, though still not registered as a criminal act. The punishment to the perpetrator varies accordingly from state to state.

So I jiggled the melting ice in my glass, took a last sip and was getting ready to ask her my big question when she began to do this thing of hers, a habit of sorts. What she does is to shift her stance whenever she anticipates someone's intention to confront her in some way. She begins by changing her posture, angling one of her slinky hips slightly off to the side and placing her weight on that one leg, then she half-lifts her opposite foot out of the heel of her pumps and plays toezy with the shoe, slowly moving it up and down as if the shoe itself is contemplating how to answer the question posed to her. Now what connection shoes have with a woman's brain I have no idea, but that is Lydia's way. I plunged forward, asked her what she thought had happened to the nine minutes; what was up with her husband, all those questions he asked me, the way he studied me with both eyes radiating so fiercely.

"You know Vladg," she began, speaking softly, "Bram is strange. This is no small item of individual psychology, but from time to time he likes to do life differently, to get a different mode of experience. Something new he can get his teeth into. So at the moment he is recruiting…"

"…Recruiting?"

"Yes, I can't tell you everything of course. I have taken an oath not to, but please don't get me wrong; we are looking at matters for which theorizing has no cure."

"Now what does all that mean?"

She was getting on my nerves again.

"It means I will not allow any harm to come to you from Bram, okay?"

"Yes, that's part of what I need to hear, O.K. But I still don't know what you mean by recruiting."

"All I can tell you is that you don't want to miss what is happening under your very eyes. Just because Eiselman did not program you in the medieval arts of mysticism and magic doesn't mean that you should fail to recognize the unfamiliar forms of existence."

"You say under my eyes, but you mean under my nose, don't you?"

"Have it your way."

"Well how would you feel if I said to you I can't disclose something you want to know because I had sworn an oath not to reveal the secret?"

"I would respect you for it. What I don't respect are those people who believe that if they do not recognize something it does not exist."

"That's most of the people in the world."

Lydia snickered at this.

"I had no idea you were so cynical about humans."

"I'm not really. I was being persnickety. It's just that I haven't met anyone lately who believes as you do. If Eiselman had no knowledge of the experiences you have in mind, then I can understand why the majority of people are the same way."

"Vladgey what you said was true. Most people don't believe in mystical things because it is not in their field of knowledge. What is not recognizable by their observations of a particular form simply does not exist for them."

"Well, you're not one of those people."

"No. And neither is Bram. Let me put it to you like this. It's just that all the familiar forms of experience have become disappointing to him. He is tired of the old way of living--"

"You're beating around the bush."

"Look at it this way. With the advent of Duplicants among us, he is trying to create a set of new things to enjoy, that's all."

"No, that's not all is it?"

Now she really hesitated. I could see she was trying to figure out exactly what her next thought should be, what she should say to me. She shifted her stance once again.

"It's like this Vladg. Our species has deteriorated into a fallen state. We find ourselves trying to support our lives with a series of made up events like animated computer games, ridiculous TV programs, 4D movies and the like. All these things are supposed to divert us from our real purpose, but it does not compensate us enough. That's why Bram is intent on his reforms, on recruiting Duplicants into our way of life."

"Now that is really ridiculous."

"No, it's not." *Every revolution was first a thought in one man's mind."*

"You're not making sense."

"Perhaps not to you at the moment. But it is a significant conversation, is it not?"

"I guess so."

I just nodded. I really didn't know what else to say, so started to the bar to put the dead drinks away.

"Niner," she called out, with that captivating pitch to her voice that could only mean one thing, "get us another, will you. You know where to find me."

I certainly did.

Chapter II

The reason Bram Alucard was driving to New York City from upstate was to visit with Eiselman at his offices in the Pyrell Corp's massive tower, built at ground zero in 2050. He was preoccupied with accumulated gripes; he hated slow drivers and as a consequence he drove too fast. He moved his car along at well over ninety, paying scant attention to the rolling foothills of the Adirondacks. He was equally unimpressed by the migrating flocks of birds visible through the sunroof or the verdant plant life streaming by as he whipped past Lake George and turned south toward Manhattan.

When it came to concealing his troubles not even his sepia brown eyes betrayed the wrinkles of agitation that rippled through him, yet the uneasiness was there, an impatience of sorts that declared him to be more human than he cared to admit, while he mummified his anger. This allowed him to hold death more gently.

Centuries ago his forbears had had the ability to transmogrify and fly, but this feature had never been part of his own makeup. His cousin Malignius had more powers; he could change almost completely into wolf. And then there was Drakonius, the Dhampire with a perverted nature, who loved mass killing. Bram hated him, despised his philosophy of total domination bent on creating a society of the living dead. No, he was wont to use Drakonius in his plans even though his powers of transmogrification were enormous. Yes, he was envious. This lack, this inability to fly bothered him, made him feel incomplete as a vampire, especially when he was forced to drive a long distance such as this.

He felt some satisfaction in his recent accomplishment though. This last visit with Lydia at home had been successful. He had put off subjection of the Duplicant to his dominant will until the time was ripe, although he had wanted to know for some time whether or not it was possible, whether Vladg was susceptible. As it turned out he had put Vladg under a spell relatively easily, a trance that lasted for well over six minutes. During that period of time he had learned most of what he wanted to know about Eiselman's habits, including the fact that he served English tea while he was conducting business with a new customer.

During his phone conversation with Eiselman he had explained his interest in purchasing a number of Duplicants, essentially for the Foreign Service, which was an outright lie. Actually he wanted his own platoon of soldiers; all committed to him and his private agenda which he thought of as the 2nd Reformation. Eiselman had been non-committal, told Bram that he never conducted big business over the phone, but would be pleased to see him in person. He was put on hold and Bram was transferred to a receptionist named Phoebe who made the appointment. This in itself irritated Bram as he liked to be in control of every situation, especially where large amounts of money were concerned.

By inheritance, Bram was an extraordinarily wealthy man, but like a good many of that class he could twist a dollar back and forth until he squeezed every penny out of it. In managing his purchases, he actually enjoyed haggling with the seller over an item or two and was quite proud when he struck a good bargain. So being a member of the upper crust didn't stop him from frugality. With one exception. When it came to women he wasn't stingy, especially in those instances where he had a hidden agenda, then he could be outrageously extravagant.

The financial aspects of the contract with Eiselman were merely one of the items he would have to negotiate. What he also wanted was to dicker for a full batch of Sextus-IV's, the same design purchased by the military. He thought that IV's would get things rolling enough to fulfill his purpose. He had read the advertisements, knew that they were on sale; probably he could pick them up for as little as seventy-five thousand apiece. It would amount to quite a large sum. If he paid $7,500 down on each unit that still came to $375,000. He could handle that amount, but the subsequent monthly payments would put an enormous dent in his reserve capital.

His mind wandered off to another topic.

He had heard that sometimes the brain pattern transfer operators who ran the Heringa-Wheel machine had programmed Duplicants with extras that were not within the scope of the purchaser's own brain projections. He would have to trust Eiselman to insure that no such monkeyshines would be permitted, and he didn't like it. Trust was not in his makeup. Indeed, he knew that Yiddish and some other cabala fetishes of Eiselman's had been inserted into Vladg's cortical associative tracts without Lydia's awareness or permission.

Yes, he had been impressed with Vladg. He could see that the Duplicant made a good companion, and unlike a Droid he did not need a cyclotron from time to time to energize his particles. He had had no trouble whatsoever subjecting Vladg to his will even though the unit was totally programmed with Lydia's idiotic notions. Of course, he released Vladg from his powers in deference to Lydia as soon as he saw that he had mastered him. So if he was successful with a Sextus-IX he should have no trouble with basic fours.

And that was the other point. It was an inviolate requirement for the purchase of any Duplicant that the buyer submit to the making of an electronic disc of their own brain patterns. The problem was he did not want Eiselman or anyone else to view his brain patterns. If he could somehow get around this requirement, he would be able to project the thoughts he wished each unit to have via his own inherent transfer powers. These powers were only slightly different from the ones he used when putting his slaves into a submissive trance.

He knew there was an extra charge for making the disc and transferring the thought patterns to each unit in question. Lydia had said the fee was nominal when she bought Vladg, so perhaps there was a discount for a large purchase such as he wished to make. Still if it was five hundred dollars per unit it would make the initial outlay a total of $400,000. Perhaps Eiselman would forego the transfer fees entirely since he would be doing the work himself. He did not look forward to it. Fifty different projection-transfer operations would be a strain on his physical health. It exhausted him just thinking about it. He'd just have to wait and see if Eiselman would be willing to forego the fee.

Driving monotonously along, Bram began to brood, to think over the fallen state into which his species had fallen in the last two centuries. Mixing vampire genomes with humans had at first been considered a triumph, but the program had backfired. Humans had gained somewhat in intelligence, height and energy distribution while his species had lost the ability to transmogrify, or to produce sufficient venom for induction.

In 1793, when he was born, and throughout his formative years, there was great affection between his father, a disciple of Count Dracula, and himself. In adolescence, however, Bram saddened him when he did not develop the ability to convert his body shape into wolf or bat. The natural desire is for a father to have a son who would take up where he left off and advance the cause along the same lines, or at least to maintain the same front. His father never said it in so many words, but he knew he had become a huge disappointment to both his parents. His British mother, Lady Lygeia, a vampire convert from whom he derived his humanness also had had great hopes for him, but his powers had fallen far below the classical vampire standards. After his father had been neutralized with a silver stake through his heart, the killing carried out by religious zealots, Lady Lygeia became totally bereft and died soon thereafter of grief and remorse. Just before her demise, she had given him a gift; she taught her son the secrets of alchemy and he became an apt student of the art. He placed high value on this useful knowledge as it alone had saved his life in many instances.

Formulating the right potion had allowed him to put many recalcitrant subjects under his spell. He still carried a great number of powders, concoctions and chemicals in his valise, and of course, he never failed to go without a live newt, a salamander, with which to make fresh elixirs for healing wounds. Actually he had been lucky this last century; except for the wounds of the Second World War fighting for the Free French he had not suffered from physical attacks, although there were many close escapes in his own predatory acts to convert human prey to vampires.

However, as a teen-aged orphan, aside from alchemy, Bram quickly realized that his occult abilities were actually quite limited to those items of suggestion and submission for simple control of humans and to anticipate and detect their unformed thoughts. Still, he now reasoned, his parents would be quite proud of him if he were able to succeed with this crucial project, given the meager powers he had inherited. And yes, he was able, at times, to produce enough venom to transform a female human into a vampire as long as he took his time and drew enough blood. But he was alone in this endeavor, there were never enough subjects to transform, never enough vampires created to help in the reform movement. One reason for this was his height. American women were not much attracted to men less than six feet, especially those who wore a cloak and grew a moustache and beard. However well-trimmed and fashionable these items had been in the prior centuries they did not seem to excite the modern woman. So he abandoned the cloak, but kept the moustache and beard as a tribute to his beloved father whom he resembled a great deal. Luckily, due to his mother's human genetics, he was not a member of the undead, he could cast a reflection in the mirror and he had no trouble staying awake and alert in the daytime, even though he tried his best to stay out of the sunlight.

Lydia had been born fifty years or so after him, a failure mostly, with a meaningless drool of a mother and a wraith for a father. Regardless of her questionable heritage, in the beginning he had loved her immensely, and hallucinated often about their relationship and the offspring that might be forthcoming. Nothing of the sort came about, no progeny, not even the semblance of a pregnancy. He cursed the powers that had made him infertile. As to Lydia, she had developed a crucial taste for blood, some mild mind reading powers of other's thoughts, but she was not a venom producer and was much too interested in love and passion to make a good wife. She hadn't yet learned that longing for human love can be a fatal mistake. If only he had been made aware of her lack of powers from the beginning, he never would have married her. Now he had to recruit and organize an entire group of Duplicates in order to fulfill his parents' wishes, to create what they themselves had failed to accomplish, a 2nd Reformation.

He slowed the vehicle, approaching the Holland tunnel. The GPS monitor told him to put the car on auto-pilot. He would have to be careful not to fall asleep as, except for the battery hum, the traffic was silent. He missed the horse and buggy medley of sounds, the clopping of the horses' hoofs, the wind flow against the carriage.

∞

Bram had to pass an electronic screening for weapons and other contraband before he entered the vast lobby of Pyrell Towers. All he carried was a small valise containing his bona fide papers from the government guaranteeing his immunity as a member of the Foreign Service, his passport and his pipe and tobacco pouch. There was one other item of importance. He felt in his pants pocket for the small vial of powdered crystals, the formula originally concocted by Lygeia and handed down to him as a sort of protective charm. He drew it out and held it in the palm of his hand. No problem, he passed through surveillance without a stir. Once inside the building he noted that security was present in abundance, both in the form of human officers as well as BASIC duplicants.

He didn't have to check the directory as he knew Eiselman's offices were on the 102nd floor. However, he did need water to make the elixir and he searched for a men's room. A uniformed human directed lobby traffic and pointed out the restroom's location to him. Once there he took note of the laser-video cameras, faked washing his hands, added a small amount of water, swirled the vial around as it sputtered and hissed, emitting a cloudy mist of vapor before the mixture settled down and changed color from a purplish hue to a reddish-brown tea color. As soon as the potion stopped percolating it quit emitting steam and began to cool down. Now he put the stopper back in and placed the vial once again in his pocket. The reaction would only sustain its hypnotic powers for twenty minutes or so. Bram hoped that tea would be served at the outset.

The public elevators were serviced by BASIC II's and he had to undergo a second electronic frisking before he was allowed to go up.

"I am a BASIC II, instructed to test you for weaponry or any explosive device. Please put your valise on the floor and open it for inspection and open it up."

Bram did as he was told. The BASIC was not surprised by the salamander as he knew that R&D used many types of animals in their development of different tissues and organs for the manufacture of Duplicants. He himself had been created with a variation of porcine skin for his outer covering.

"Please hold your hands above your head, spread your legs as wide as possible."

The BASIC ran an electro-magnetic wand over Bram's entire body and pronounced him safe to go up.

The operator only took him to the 100th floor. Bram got off there and picked up the wall phone which he had been instructed to use by Phoebe, the receptionist with whom he had made the appointment.

The private elevator, nearly noiseless, brought him up the remaining two floors.

He is punctual, and immediately greeted by Phoebe, a tall leggy piece with a firm step and a warm handshake. She is a looker, no question; a rapturous looking blond in a blue leather miniskirt, ultra-blue eyes, and a fashionable periwinkle colored blouse, with a scalloped neckline that subdues her cleavage but stimulates the imagination. Most importantly she has a long slender neck. Another feature that does not go unnoticed by him is the dimple in her left cheek. In Bram's experience, women with dimples were more susceptible to his spells, easier to put under.

Some humans do have pleasant attributes, Bram thought. He was sexually aroused but unlike humankind his sensual response was not genitally prompted. He felt the urge within his canines. They were already amassing venom drawn from the glands at the root of his gums; his erotic canines were coming to life, beginning to protrude, to elongate. The wish to sink his fangs deep into her throat, enticing him to drink sufficiently while he released his venom was overwhelming. He held back, repressing his desire. His canines slowly receded. There was no way he could cast a spell over her quickly enough, especially not in the daytime. In any event, the business at hand with Eiselman was too important for distractions, even one as choice as this.

The receptionist ushered him in to plush offices.

Eiselman rose to greet him and extended a warm hand. He too was well over six feet, very similar to Vladg.

Eiselman bade Bram to sit in one of the deep leather chairs.

"Please be comfortable. Would you like a cup of tea?"

"That would be pleasant, thank you."

"I'll ring for one of the Duplicants. Phoebe would be annoyed if I asked her to serve tea." Bram watched carefully as Eiselman turned to press a hidden button.

"I understand. Not in her job description."

"Precisely the point! It is nigh impossible to get human help nowadays. Don't want to offend someone as efficient as Phoebe."

"Do the Duplicants do a good job?"

"Yes they do well what they are programmed to accomplish" ...a Duplicant entered carrying an English tea set on a silver salver..."Put it down here, George," Eiselman said politely.

The Duplicant did so and then immediately nodded his head and left without a word. Like all Basic III's he had that odd characteristic of seeming to see and hear nothing, while doing just the opposite.

"Does he speak?"

"He was given seventy-five words in the factory as his basic vocabulary, along with a simple set of learning curves for experiential adaptation. Even with that skimpy start he now has over five-hundred words in his speaking vocabulary and a thousand or more in reading."

"Can he write?"

"Oh, no! We don't want them to write. Then they would start to keep a diary or a journal, you know something like that could get published and then where would we be?"

"I see. I notice he doesn't have any hair."

"Hair follicles are expensive to make. Anyway it's a non-functional accessory. Look at all the humans who are bald. It doesn't make them less human."

"That's true."

"Do you want to know what his biggest wish is?"

"Sure, why not."

"He wants eyebrows! Not that he thinks eyebrows will make him look human, heaven's no, his most ambitious desire is to look like a Sextus."

"So he is not a Sextus model."

"Certainly not, next to the II's he is our simplest and least expensive."

"I see."

"They are called BASIC-III's as they have adaptability to new situations, something BASIC-I's and II's did not have, still eunuchoid of course. We halted manufacturing of the I's years ago although the Chinese continue them in production to cultivate the rice paddies and such. Ever since the great urbanization of rural Chinese in 2030 there has been a shortage of farm workers in that country; the BASIC-I's fill the bill."

"I see."

"You probably came across the BASIC- II coming up in the elevator. They have some adaptability, but not nearly as developed to unforeseen situations as the III's."

"Yes, I see. Well to be honest I had wanted to purchase the Sextus Model, but if the Basic-III's are as adaptable as you say…tell me, do they have sweat glands?"

"Now that is a peculiar question, why do you ask?"

"Curiosity, no reason in particular."

"Well the question doesn't surprise me. If you like you can visit with Josh Wharton, our young man on the 47th floor. He is one of our up and coming production engineers…"

"Perhaps another time, not today…"

"Well you're certainly welcome to visit, nothing there is on the assembly line, every Sextus unit is put together by hand. Of course each floor has its specialty, eyes on 46; ears and noses are on 48 and so forth. Sweat glands, plumbing and defecation are together but I forget what floor they're on. I don't get down there very often anymore, swamped with paper work up here."

"I can imagine; hope you didn't mind my sweat gland question?"

"Oh no, I get asked everything and then some. It's just that I am amazed by the vast spectrum of questions customers present. And no, to answer specifically, Basic III's do not have sweat glands."

"Then how do they get rid of their waste? There has to be waste of some sort to everything that has a metabolism."

"Of course, you are right. Actually it is a very good question. You see the Basic III's have a different plumbing and waste disposal system. The sweat, the fecal products and the urine are filtered through a built in system and then compacted. Similar to the compactor placed next to your dishwasher, only in microcosm. Every night the Basic can pull out the compacted waste, rinse out the tray, put in a new filter and carry on for the next 24 hours. Usually we furnish them with enough trays and filters for a week at a time, just in case they are not located at home base."

Eiselman continues to talk as he pours…"Of course they don't have the muscular strength of the Sextus, nor any of the higher seven systems that characterize a human, at least not to any considerable extent. You can add certain features to the Basic, but then what have you got? It's still an intermediary unit. Tell me Bram… it's okay to use your first name is it not?"

"Certainly…"

"Milk or sugar?"

"A bit of lemon if you have it."

Eiselman searched the tray. "I'll have to ring for it."

This time, as he turned to press the button, Bram hastily poured the contents of the vial into Eiselman's teacup. Then he watched as Eiselman plopped in two cubes of sugar, stirred and took a sip. The elixir is odorless and tasteless; Eiselman doesn't seem to notice a thing.

"Tell me Bram, how many units did you have in mind and for what purpose?"

"My intent was to purchase a complete batch of Sextus-IV's, but before I give you a flat answer… David isn't it?"

"Yes, David."

"David I want first to know whether programming the units, other than the factory check-list that is built in, can be done by me or do I need to have a brain pattern disc made for the projection sequences and the subsequent programming."

"I get asked that question all the time. It is not easy to avoid, and too risky for my blood to transact business other than by the book. Is there some reason…I know that some people are afraid of being immobilized, scared of getting strapped into the Heringa-Wheel brain pattern duplicator…is that it with you?"

"Not a fear, I just don't want my brain patterns copied, that's perfectly reasonable isn't it. It's an invasion of privacy issue."

"Understandable! But I can guarantee you no one else will ever get to look at your personal disc. It is as safe as the gold in Fort Knox."

"Does that include the FBI or the CIA?"

Eiselman's gracious attitude changed radically as he answered, his facial expression becoming taut. He was suddenly all business.

"Making the disc is not just a requirement of Pyrell's but a federal statute designed to protect the system from the bad guys of the world, the crooked financiers and such, you know the old

Madoff types. I checked up on your profile and social history and you are none of these. If you were, yes, the CIA and FBI would possibly have the right to take a look at your disc. But otherwise, no federal agency has that right."

Bram was impressed with the thoroughness of Eiselman's due diligence toward a prospective buyer. He was careful with his answer while he waited for the potion to take effect.

"So you're saying I have nothing to fear in regard to prying agencies or investigators wanting to take a look at my disc?"

"That's right..."

Their conversation was interrupted by George's entrance. He set a saucer of lemon quarters down next to Bram's teacup and left as silently as he appeared.

"As you are aware, David, I am with the State Dept. They have assigned me a task in which a specific role is to be handled by Duplicants in several eastern European countries. But to announce the purpose of the missions involved ahead of time would be to forfeit the future objectives. Naturally, as an ambassador, I can not be directly involved, so the units procured should not have brain patterns resembling mine. This would be a breach of policy and I would become persona non grata to all the nations involved and likely get expelled."

"I see. Well as you may know we do deal with the Pentagon, so I am not unfamiliar with Federal requests, but this is the first time I have been sent an emissary from the federal government with no prior knowledge, not even a hint of the activity involved."

"But you do see the necessity of top level secrecy?"

"Indeed."

Bram read his mind and saw immediately that the man did not believe his story.

"I can't get around the mandate in the States. In Europe, predominantly at our factories in Holland, Bulgaria, Macedonia business is different. In general, the farther east you go, the less stringent will be the laws. In India you may purchase what you like, no questions asked, but the prices are prohibitive. They will sell two or three units at a time, no more, and then a personal disc of your brain patterns can be avoided. But here in the States it is a federal statute, one that, however obfuscated your proposition, can not be avoided."

"Not even for a considerable amount of money?"

"No amount would be worth the investigations and subsequent congressional hearings. The danger to my corporation, to the stockholders and to me personally would be prohibitive."

"I see. So what you are saying is to go abroad, purchase the units there, two or three at a time from different countries."

"I'm afraid that's your only option. Sorry I couldn't be of more help."

By now Bram can see that Eiselman's features have taken on a more stoic appearance, his manner of speaking had slowed down and his eyelids were slightly droopy. The potion was definitely working even though it had taken longer than he had expected.

"You are getting sleepy," Bram says in a modulated manner, an echoed tone of voice that is pleasant to the ear.

"Why yes, for some reason I am. Please forgive me; perhaps we can postpone this meeting to another hour?"

Eiselman tries to stand up, his weakness apparent, his balance failing him; he folds in two, and sits back down.

"I want you to listen to me," Bram says with an almost infinite tenderness of voice, "listen to my words, listen to my voice, listen to me." Then even softer, "I am now your master."

"Yes, master."

"You must take my instruction in all matters."

"Yes, master."

"I want you to sell me fifty Sextus fours, no strings attached."

"Yes, master. I'll see to it."

"Have your business manager draw up the necessary contracts."

"Yes, master."

"Have the units delivered to this address, two or three at a time." He hands Eiselman a slip of paper with the address of a small town in upstate New York.

"Now I want you to wake up. You will not remember any of this unless you hear me say the word Alucard, have you got that?"

"Yes, master."

"When I call, you will respond with the words: 'How can I be of service?'

"Yes, I will say: How can I be of service".

"Correct. Now awake. Awake!"

Eiselman rubbed his eyes, apologized for his sleepiness and stood up, this time having no problem with his equilibrium.

They shook hands, exchanged pleasantries and Bram took up his valise, heading for the door leading into the entryway. George was there and cast a stony suspicious eye at Bram, but before Bram could react he was once again met by Phoebe. The receptionist towered over him, a challenge he enjoyed immensely when he was successful in casting his spell. He removed one of his diamond earrings and placed it in her palm as she tried to shake his hand.

"This is but a token of unconditional friendship for your hospitality to me. Please accept it. She demurs, tries to give it back to him, but he encloses her fingers around the gem and in so doing, feeling the warmth of her hand, he gazes upward and gains eye contact. This one glance is all he needs to overpower her resistance. There is a flood of electrifying that will pouring out from his meditative eyes.

"I can't accept this, it's too valuable."

"Of course you can, I shall give you the companion to it when I call upon you this evening. Give me your address; I shall arrive promptly at six to take you to a formal dinner. Wear an evening gown."

Phoebe is flustered but subdued. The dimple in her left cheek indents and she smiles like a little girl with a new plaything. She has no idea why she feels so controlled by this strange middle aged, almost fatherly figure; it is as if she were adrift in a strange sea of wonders, scary but fascinating.

"I confess I don't know what to say. I haven't been out in a while."

"You must say yes."

She hesitates but a pulse of a second.

"Yes, I'd like that. Here's my card. You have to ring the downstairs bell and I'll buzz you up to the apartment."

Bram takes her card, fixes her with his eyes one more time and then releases her from his will. Immediately she is all business, pushes the private elevator button for him, and he finds himself descending to the hundredth floor, totally pleased with the results of the potion and the successful way he has handled Phoebe.

"Tonight will be different," he says to himself, his canines feeling the urge. He intends to stalk Phoebe and have the delicious experience of sinking his fangs deeply into her throat, to soak up her blood and inject his venom as deeply into her tissues as he can. She will become a slave who can keep him abreast of the goings on at Pyrell's.

Chapter III

LYDIA

I want to talk about Vladg, not just why Bram saw that I had a need for a companion, no not just that, but how Vladg came to be equipped with all my imaginative fantasies, my wishes and desires, and yes my passions. In order to truly grasp what I had projected onto him, you have to understand that human attachments hold a clear priority with me; some of my own failures, my grief at lovers lost, at time's farewells. Yes that is the disadvantage of eternal life, of having to watch others age and weaken, to make your goodbyes to the memories of youth.

I suppose my very first great love was Pierre, Pierre-Auguste Renoir that is. To the world he was called Auguste, but his first name was really Pierre-Auguste, and Pierre was my love name for him. Vladg wonders why I speak of him so frequently and know so little of his art, but you see I knew him personally; we were contemporaries many years before I became a full-fledged vampire. (Yes, I lied to Vladg about Nebraska. I certainly didn't want him to know my true age and at some point I will have to fess up as they say.)

Pierre was born in 1841 in Limoges, France and I in Belfast a mere two years afterward, so I've been around a long time. We first met in Paris at a gallery when I was in my early twenties. We were both searching. I was aspiring to become an actress and he a young impressionist painter searching for his true style, his work full of snapshots of real life, full of sparkling color and light. At the time I was too naïve, too inexperienced in the world of art to realize how he achieved his brilliant luminosity, but Vladg has taught me that Pierre's technique was to use small, multicolored strokes which created a sparkling effect. Vladg says the color of an object is modified by the light in which it is seen, by reflections from other objects and by contrast with juxtaposed colors. So after all these years I am finally learning the artistic secrets of a lover of old, of my true youth.

If you want to know what I looked like back then, check out his painting of the two women in a rowboat, I am the one on the right, the smaller one with my hat tilted fashionably to the side, at least it was all the rage back then. Fashion comes and goes, but I am getting ahead of my story, Pierre would not have liked that and neither does Vladg. Yes, like many of his women I became a model for his paintings, several of his early nudes are me, but certainly not all. And yes he did capture the luminosity of my skin, whether I was indoors or out in nature. And he did it in such manner that my skin vibrated with the atmosphere. What woman wouldn't go for that?

Pierre was an *homme à femme,* a woman chaser. Even in the beginning of our lovemaking I knew that something was wrong, that a certain confusion was evident. You see Pierre's agenda was to capture women by his art, he certainly wasn't that good looking, yet women, including me, were never the same when he left them, feeling the void yet unable to define the loss. That is always the big question isn't it? Does a man have a true love space in his soul to merge with a woman, or is it only a staggering charm that captivates, ennobling gestures full of technique but lacking the inherent space within that can only be filled up by the love of one woman.

After Pierre dumped me I stayed in Paris another twenty years, securing bit parts, often in Shakespeare's plays, but I never got to play Lady Macbeth which had been my strongest desire. What I knew of Shakespeare's genius was quite meager until Vladg filled me in on the true meaning of his works, the depth of the characters he created. So the wickedness of Lady Macbeth was always in me, long before I became a vampire.

When I was in my forties I met Bram. By then I had pulled the plug on Paris and returned to Ireland which had taken this long to get over the miseries of the potato famine of '46 and '47. Back then there was destitution everywhere; children left haggard and dying by the side of the road, death and disease tearing the people apart. So much cholera prevailed that the likely chance of a girl or boy living past the age of six was next to nothing. And you may have heard that immediately following my birth my father returned to his wraith-like appearance, his own ghostly nature and that was the male model I had to contend with growing up. My mother had become a shadow of her former self, suffered greatly from running off at the mouth, drinking excessive amounts of hard homemade Irish whiskey and generally making as much of a hullabaloo out of daily life as she could. So I wasn't exactly gifted with the greatest potential for success from the start. In my early years, my perceptions, all around me, were of such harsh circumstances, such dire misery, and such brutal treatment of my Gaelic brothers and sisters, deeply despaired of living, that I lost my faith. Yes, we Irish have always had our own beliefs, our symbols and idols that were different from other Catholics. All of this was in our Gaelic heritage. I was primed for a different destiny and the chance meeting with Bram at a pub where I worked as a serving girl turned out to be the turning point in my life.

To understand all this it is necessary to familiarize yourself with the spirit of the times. After my Parisian interlude, my failures at finding a true love and my lack of success as an actress I felt incomplete, not a whole person, and returned to my home in Belfast. The world was between wars, the Franco-Prussian war was over and the Russo-Japanese war of 1905 was yet to come. I mention this because while the rest of the world was fairly stable, Ireland remained poor as a church-mouse, the famine having left its toll. So a poorer choice of time to relocate could not have been made by me.

Spilled coffee grounds you say? Repercussions! Simply complaining of a mess you made yourself. Yes, it's one of those things you just had to be living through to know what it was really like. Sure, and you can sit back, ensconced in the comfort of the American way of life with unfocused consciousness and all the modern comforts and technology. But if you can hark back to the famine years and what they meant for a country whose population was being decimated, you might just have a bit of empathy for the position we were in. So that's why I weakened, actually came to welcome vampirism as the release from all my misery.

In Belfast I found a job as a barmaid in the Railway Saloon which had recently been renamed the Crown Liquor Saloon; it was 1885 you see and the twin spires had just been added to Saint Patrick's Cathedral, so all was not destitution but there were daily clashes everywhere between the Protestants and Catholics. It was this haggard and bloody scene that drew Bram's attention and he came to Belfast hoping to find a victim.

This was the setting in which Bram found me while I was at work in the Crown Liquor. Oddly enough, in the midst of all this wretchedness and sorrow what attracted me most to Bram was his sardonic sense of humor, not his power or money. He could wipe away my tears by forcing me to laugh at his morbid humor and paradoxical wit. It was our sense of what was funny that brought us together.

I still retained that singular void, the unloved feeling, not just for Pierre but by men in general. It was this very hollowness that allowed me to succumb to Bram's impetuous nature, to be enamored of him. Even when I saw my own blood dripping from his fangs I was enthralled. His passion was pure, no false idolatry; he cared for me for the richness of my blood and to attain his purpose, to transform me into a member of his species. There was no game playing on his part, no treachery of the sort seen so often nowadays by men cheating on their wives, even in the best circles.

He was the one who took me to America, not on a cattle boat like so many of the Irish, but on one of the new steamers that had just been built by a wealthy Englishman, a long time descendant of the Cromwell family who had butchered so many of the Irish Catholics in the fifteen-hundreds and brought in a horde of English Protestants to Ulster.

And Bram did the right thing, he married me before the Magistrate, you know he couldn't enter the Church as he might have melted straight away.

Right after the hitching-up we set sail.

I loved America when I got there, the pubs with their free lunch if you ordered a draft beer, the neat and tidy ways of the various groups that seemed, at least on the surface, to mix rather well. So my mood was one of optimism. Sure there were little enclaves of this and that ethnicity, but Bram got me right out of New York City where the Irish immigrants were shoved into settlements in lower Manhattan, conned by 'runners' speaking in Gaelic. These were supposed to be clean and healthy boarding house rooms with good meals but turned out to be filthy hell holes, vermin infested hovels with no running water. There I go again, spouting off, a trait I inherited from my mother. So getting back to it, Bram took me upstate, to a growing farm town called Oneonta, and ensconced me in a two story house with all the luxuries of the times. I was as far away from the cultural activities of New York City as if he had taken me out west to the frontier. It was in Oneonta that I first went to school, studying to become a veterinarian and doing some midwifery on the side. I loved it when the afterbirth let loose, all that dark red blood seeping over everything, the various fluids intermixing with the cries of the baby and the delightful gasps of the assembled. Of course I knew something they didn't, that the howls of the wolves in the forest meant a new life had entered their realm and might be soon ripe for the taking. It was all pretty exciting and wonderful.

Contrary to its promise, the dawn of the twentieth century became most bloody and hateful as it progressed with hallucinatory politics far surpassing any of the evil that our species might possess. Sure there was a decrease in child mortality and the scourge of epidemics was getting under better control, but this was not matched in the moral sense by the leaders of the world who butchered civilians on a monstrous scale with organized killings.

I didn't get to see much of Bram in the early part of the century. He was holed up in his castle in the Carpathian Mountains and I became an ambulance driver in the First World War. I spent some time in Paris after the war but most of the artists and theatre people I knew had passed on by then. That people dear to us should disappear into eternity simply because they died is an intolerable thought for me. Better to be a member of the undead. Perhaps I should tone this down, not give in to my great weakness, discussing the advantages of being a vampire.

To go on in a more sober vein, I returned to Oneonta for a time and then moved to New Orleans, where I found a considerable number of vamps doing their thing in the bayous and backwaters of Louisiana. The Kingfish, Huey P. Long was one of us and he spearheaded some things in the political arena that aroused the people. Unfortunately, he was assassinated in 1935 and not much else happened for a while. Bram came too, off and on. He seemed to enjoy the food and the life style, but unlike Huey he could not induce others to join with him in a united effort to take over the political stage. A certain number of Dhampirs did get into the corruption and caused their own mayhem, but they refused to be organized into one group. So Bram returned to France just as the Second World War broke out. The defensive barrier called the Maginot Line fell quickly to the Germans and Bram was unable to get back to Transylvania. What happened was he became a French Freedom Fighter. He was decorated after the war and applied for and was granted American citizenship. My route was totally different. I joined the Women's Auxiliary Ferrying Squadron (WAFS) and after my training with the famous Elizabeth L. Gardner was complete, I started transporting planes for the military from September 10, 1942 on to the end of the war. That is how I wound up in Santa Barbara, a gem of a town just ninety miles north of Los Angeles where I have stayed put since 2030.

The reason I mention this is that during the last century I usually had to move every twenty years or so. At one point I did move to Holdrege, Nebraska and was the veterinarian there for a period of time. So at least that part of my story was true.

California was less inquisitive about me. The people didn't seem to care much how old I was or how I looked. Since it had become socially incorrect to question the age of a woman and with the advent of modern plastic surgery for the masses, there were very few people who cared about my age one way or the other. Once I procured Vladg as my companion there was even less interest in my appearance and more questions about my relationship with him than any particular focus on me.

So now you are all primed to know how it felt when I went under the brain transformer-projector. It was almost like a religious experience.

This machine was created in the early part of the 21st century by two people who do not dilute the word genius when it is applied to them. One of the men was Jan Willem Heringa, the great grandson of the famous Histologist of the Binnen Gasthuis in Amsterdam, Holland. The other was an Englishman by the name of Matthew Wheeling. Heringa is an astrophysicist who won the Nobel for his work. Wheeling invented the nanometric-processor whose computer designs revolutionized the industry. (Vladg taught me all this.) Accordingly, the machine is called the Heringa-Wheeling Brain scanning projector, or just the Heringa-Wheel for short. Eiselman does hand out a manual of sorts to the potential buyer, but he doesn't want to scare them off, so the contents describing the machine do not offer the specifics Vladg gives you. I know I'm fairly brainy, but when it comes to certain scientific fundamentals Vladg has had to fill me in.

The machine itself is about eighteen feet in diameter, looks like two perpendicular Ferris wheels one running clockwise and the other counter-clockwise. The wheels are set one inside the other. At the center, each of the Ferris wheel contraptions has but one platform and when you first get into it you lie down supine, but the platforms flip you at regular intervals so sometimes you are lying prone in relation to the floor. This is why so many people do not personalize their Duplicants. They do not wish to go through the experience of the Heringa-Wheel and so they agree to have the unit feed its knowledge by a standardized disc of which there are many formats, some more expensive than others. But that was not for me, I wanted Vladg to share all of me that I could project, so I took the risk.

When you get into it, it is ten times as scary as an MRI. Similar in the way you are strapped in, yes, but with over one hundred electrodes attached to your scalp. The cables from these electrodes are attached to the head of the Duplicant who is positioned at a one-eighty from you, so you are head-to-head in a manner of speaking, attached only by the cables. The machine starts up slowly so that your body can get used to the large circular motion and doesn't flip you over in the first five minutes. But both the man-made cosmic and laser rays start reverberating almost immediately and run crossways between you and the immobilized Duplicant who is absorbing your thoughts which are now transformed into elementary particles (bosons, pions, photons) all having zero or integral spin which permit any number of identical particles to occupy the same quantum state; hence the successful transfer.

Sure they allow you to watch the wall-sized computer which is registering the transformation, like downloading, and then when you have decided the transfer is complete, you have to stay immobilized until the Duplicant uploads and then installs all the data. All this work has to be done while you are still strapped down, but you are able to communicate with Eiselman via earphones while one of his aides is making the disc. They are hidden from view behind a safe shelter of plexi-carbonate glass that resists all rays, as there are invariably a few rays that miss their target and ricochet back and forth for a time until they wear themselves out and the procedure can continue. This doesn't happen too often and as a rule the procedure goes forth without a hitch. Such was the case with me and Vladg, and from the moment of completion of the transfer of thoughts, a checkup was done on me as well to see that I had merely transferred, and not lost, my own thinking and fantasy apparatus. When this does occur, Eiselman explained in a preview session that the machine is simply reversed and the Duplicant now becomes the supplier to the human. Technically it is called re-induction. Of course, every once in a while this program fails as well, the human is left bereft of any brain function, and the Pyrell Corporation is libel. This has only happened once or twice in a decade, but it is a distinct possibility and that's what makes so many people steer clear of the Heringa-Wheel machine. So the truth is that most Duplicant brain function turns out to be made from standard discs. Vladg is one of the exceptions.

It is during the period of installation that Eiselman makes a back-up disc of your brain patterns, directly from the nano-metric processors of the Duplicant's brain. Now if the purchaser had chosen not to go through the H-W procedure, Eiselman would have simply taken a standard disc from his vast library and hooked it up directly to the purchaser's choice of Duplicant, all accomplished in a few minutes.

The entire H-W procedure takes well over an hour so it is not a short period of time to be strapped down, flipped and rotated. Naturally, I held back on certain personal items. I never let on my true age, nor my own conversion to vampirism, though I don't like to refer to it as an ism since it brings to mind all the horrors of the prior century, with fascism, communism, and so on.

All this to say Vladg has a very limited view of my true self but an extended view of my desires, sexual and otherwise. For example, he knows that I want to become a better veterinarian than I am, so Eiselman was able to instill the necessary scientific background into Vladg's cortical association tracts such that when I asked a question of him, Vladg could respond appropriately. This has worked in magnificent fashion for me and my love of histology and cytology has grown in proportion to the original work of Professor Heringa accompanied by Vladg's detailed and crystal clear teaching. When the science gets too much for me to absorb he is patient, and generally we adjourn for a time, have a bite to eat or a cocktail or two. Overall, the purchase was expensive, but I think it was worth it. From time to time I tend to add certain features that Pyrell's advertises. In Santa Barbara the culture is such that one has to keep your Duplicant up with the Jones's, for if you fall behind with one of the newer advanced features one of the other Sextus-IX owners will beat you to it.

To get back to Vladg, he is emotionally earnest *au fond*. A sensible person would understand that Vladg is not a one-time event. As soon as you are engaged with him in an activity or a conversation, something memorable happens. His talking points are invariably chaste and clean, he never uses offensive words in public, which is more than I can say for myself. He has some limitations if the conversation turns to mysticism and magical occurrences, but otherwise his repertory is sufficient for most social purposes and he himself seems quite satisfied with it. But remember this, Vladg is not an independent being, his life has been totally structured. He has, in fact, never been anywhere completely alone; he has always been accompanied by me or, before my time, by someone from Pyrell's overseeing his work as a teacher and such. So in a certain sense he was like an overprotected grown up, lacking confidence in his own sense of adequacy.

We were once invited to the home of the wife of the former Shah of Iran, not the Begum Soraya, but the last wife, the very elderly Farah Diba, the one who had her nose bobbed when she was young, which upset the Iranian people no end because they thought she wanted to look less Persian and more Anglican. Her surgery took place outside of Iran and this added to the general dissatisfaction with the Shah's reign and was a partial cause of the uprising that eventually resulted in the formation of a Theocracy and the rule of the Ayatollah Khomeini, born a *sayeed* (a descendant of the Prophet Mohammed). I guess the moral is if you are royalty and want to get a tuck or bob here and there at least get it done in your own country. I may be a vampire, but I'm still Irish don't forget.

Anyway, her house was located high up the mountainside and the view overlooking the Pacific and the outer Channel Islands was magnificent. The conversation that took place between Vladg and the elderly Farah on the history of Persia was so exciting and had such a pattern of rapidity that Farah said to me before we left that my companion knew the politics of Persia almost too well; she never once called the country by its more ancient name, Iran. I was so proud of Vladg as she remains royalty of a sort and Vladg came through with flying colors. I never told Farah Diba he was a Duplicant.

Things did not go so well at other social events. Most of the time Bram was not available, so I took Vladg along as my consort to a great many of the Foreign Service social events. We were once together at the Bulgarian Embassy in Los Angeles, and while Vladg is not programmed in that language, his French is excellent, though not quite as good as mine. Some of the dignitaries spoke of Vladg in a tone of envy as he had cornered the Ambassador, who was also fluent in la lingua franca and they held forth for a good ten minutes or so on the Balkan situation. One of the other members of the Foreign Service called Vladg an outright pest and said that Duplicants should be prohibited from attending diplomatic receptions. To his credit, Vladg did not react visibly, but I saw those immense shoulders of his set more firmly and I took it upon myself to hustle him away from the Ambassador and get him to the safety of the cocktail bar.

As far as the two of us together goes, I should mention that he has picked up many of my gestures, which are elaborate, and I have done the same, unconsciously, in imitation of his expressions and gesticulations, except for his tumescence of course.

Vladg has largeness of mind, he is a wide reader of newspapers and magazines and this enables him to discuss the principal political and scientific questions intelligently. So people in the loop take him seriously, they know he counts for something, but since he is a Duplicant they don't know exactly where to place him in the total scheme of things.

Vladg doesn't interrupt others when they hold sway, no matter how boring they may be to him at times. He simply, politely, excuses himself at the earliest pause in the conversation and makes a tactful retreat. Then he might whisper to me: 'That guy has his head up his ass,' or some such remark, and I will giggle and say: "I wonder what he sees from that awkward view?"

Yes there is affection between me and Vladg, not love. I can see why marriage to Vladg would be an inviting proposition, but it is illegal at present. And I still harbor the wish to have another human as my true love, but short of that we are special to one another. So that's about it on Vladg and me. I'll have to get back to you another time on my present feelings for Bram and what he is up to.

Chapter IV

Phoebe and Phoenix

What Bram had no way of knowing was that Phoebe had a roommate, an identical twin sister named Phoenix. Identical in every way except they were what is called mirror image twins. Phoebe was right handed, Phoenix left; Phoebe's left eye was dominant, with Phoenix it was her right. Same story foot wise, Phoebe always started walking left foot first, Phoenix the opposite. They were both into tennis and made great doubles partners as one could go to her left adroitly, the other to her right with greater dexterity and efficiency. And of course, Phoenix's dimple was on her right cheek, whereas Phoebe's, as mentioned, was on her left. Another big difference was the martial arts and fencing. Phoenix was deep into them. In high school she had actually won a city medal for intramural fencing competing with blunted foils; Phoebe was more into modern dance and ballet.

When it came to personality structure, Phoenix was punctual, Phoebe invariably late. Phoebe was generally submissive to others, while Phoenix was super-dominant, both with men and women. Not that she was butchy or desired to become an SM mistress, not hardly, just opinionated and assertive, very much so. Phoenix was older by seven minutes, and at times they joked about her being the eldest. In addition, they were true Gemini's, born on the cusp almost at the stroke of midnight,

As is often the case with identical twins, they liked to play games on their boyfriends, sometimes switching identities to see if they could fool the boys; comparing notes on how good a kisser one boy was compared to the other, little habit differences that amused them in a Disneyesque fashion. In this case, however, it was more than a game. Phoebe had told Phoenix how she had met Bram that afternoon at the office; that she didn't know what had come over her, but she had foolishly accepted a diamond earring from the man and had for some unknown reason agreed to go out with him this very evening. She admitted that she was baffled, actually afraid of Bram and practically begged her sister to be the one to return the earring when he came around to pick her up.

"You're asking me to do your dirty work with a weirdo? Suppose he's packing? He could ice us. Why don't we just call the Hood Patrol? They're always scooting around the place looking for something to do. I'd feel better with them here."

"Won't work! Once I accepted the earring that makes it an assignation in the eyes of the law. He could sue us for false arrest or some such. No. I have a better plan. I'll call Mr. Eiselman on the phone and get him to lend me George for the evening."

"George, a Basic Duplo, what good can he do?"

"George is reliable; he has never failed to carry out an order I've given him. Anyway, I think he likes me!"

"You've got to be kidding Feeb, Basics don't have feelings."

"I think George does. I spend a lot more time with him than Mr. Eiselman, and I'm sure he's fond of me in his way."

"Whatever. But you'll never get down to Ground Zero and back before six. The subway is full at this hour and street traffic is jammed full."

Phoebe pays no attention to any of this; she is on her cell gabbing with her boss.

"It's all settled Feen. I'm going up to the rooftop to hail an Air-Scoot with my strobe signaler, they come by every twenty minutes or so. It'll take me right to the roof of Pyrell's Tower and Mr. Eiselman said George will be waiting on top. Please Feeny, all I have is fifty, lend me the rest."

"You're going to spend a hundred bucks just to pick up a Duplo. Have you lost all your Betz cells Feeby?"

"We'll be back in a jiffy. Oh, wear a formal dress will you hon."

"Oh, all right, just don't leave me alone with this weirdo too long."

"I won't, Thanks, Feen."

She kisses her sister on her dimple and takes off like a whirlwind. It is already five o'clock and she knows time will be tight.

Thinking it over, Phoenix decides to act out the impersonation as a challenge and she begins to look forward to the encounter. After all, if Feeby's description was even half accurate, how dangerous could a little, middle-aged man like that be?

When Bram arrives at the apartment building, a few minutes before six, it is Phoenix who buzzes him up, welcomes him in. She is not exactly wearing an evening gown, but the neck line is low cut, showing off her cleavage, and the dress itself is a nearly transparent loosely woven micro-silk, a stunning flesh color with a coquettish slit cut on one side all the way up to the thigh. Her five inch stilettos are designed to match the dress and make her appear well over six feet.

Bram doesn't want his entrance to look mysterious in any way. On the contrary, his intent is to portray himself as gentlemanly as possible, but this benign plan is immediately thwarted by the girl now appearing before him. Bram certainly has many inadequacies as a vampire, but lacking powers of observation is not one of them. Unlike most of us he has a special gift, a photographic memory for observations that were emotionally significant to him.

He immediately spots the dimple on this girl's cheek, but it is placed on the right, not the left. This alerts him and it is as if the dimple becomes painted or holographed visibly before his eye. He summons up powers he has not called upon for some time, asserts his focus on reading her mind.

"What a silly gaunt little man trying to play Cupid, why would Feeb be fearful of him?"

Phoenix doesn't shake his hand but says: "Welcome to my place. Sit on the sofa for a minute. Would you like a drink? I'll get it for you, but then I have to freshen up a bit."

She is trying to stall for time.

Bram is furious. His imperial will acts up. Instead of sitting he brazenly walks right up to her, she towers over him such that his shoulder brushes up against one breast.

"Who are you?" he asks sternly, wanting her to know he is not fooled one iota.

At once Phoenix realizes she is under alien influence, the sharpness of his teeth, his eyes changing color, from brown to tawny, then to yellow, setting up a whirling turmoil in her mind; she has to take a step back, to gather herself, to prepare for anything. She takes a martial arts stance, but his eyes are boring into hers, she senses danger and for some reason clutches at her necklace, showing her silver cross.

Now it is Bram who takes a step back.

"Do you think that silly little knick-knack can stop me?"

Phoenix sees his canines grow out from their roots and this uncommon phenomenon in combination with his contorted face frightens her, she loses her advantage, knows danger is imminent, coils her fist, but it is too late, Bram has sprung at her like a wild cat and plunged his fangs into her throat; he does not drink blood at first but injects all the venom he can muster into her tissues. She tries to fight him off but cannot hold her ground against his attack, the rapidity of her circulation spreads the venom almost at once into her brain and nervous system. She falls into the darkness, descends into Dante's inferno, sees a storm of death, human beings wailing in pain and sorrow, only to be born again, sweating from every pore, their faces twisted and morose, the poison now reaching other tissues, her nipples quivering with desire, her pelvis feeling the urge to be impregnated, to have this man's penis inside her; she wants to have an orgasm and at one and the same time to feel him drink her blood, to feel her own strength ebbing away even as he gains her youth and energy.

And that is exactly what happens. Masks of weakness and masks of strength are exchanged, Bram's face takes on an almost cherubic color as he drinks his fill while Phoenix's color drains and her features become wan and pale, but she smiles grotesquely as his throbbing penis spurts and spurts into the depths of her pouch, stretching the inside walls of her passageway reaped by pleasure-pain, stamped with the indelible signs of evil and decay. She is in turmoil, panting hard, her pelvis slowing in its gyrations to shorter more angular movements, her vulva still throbbing with desire, for life is returning to her ever more ardent and exciting, different only in that she has found her master. Her breathing begins to settle down, the inner flames of lust and passion die down and she awakes from the eternal crater into which she had fallen, her face bleached a special tint of white by the unusual experience, but no dominant expression of her feeling is evident on her lovely features, now more voluptuous than ever.

All of this activity has taken place standing up. Phoenix's head is now resting, lolling loosely on Bram's shoulder like a rag doll, her weakness evident; she asks her master if she can be permitted to lie down on the couch. Bram, suddenly powerful from the ingestion of new blood, carries her to the couch and lays her down with the gentleness of a lover who cares deeply for his wounded mate. She is cold and he grabs a nearby coverlet to warm her, goes over to the kitchen bar and pours a brandy for her.

"Take small sips; don't drink it all at once. It will help your marrow to bring new blood into your veins."

"Yes, I shall drink as you say my master."

The two small slits in her throat, where his canines had entered her jugular, are still seeping a bit, and Bram gently wipes the trickling blood away with his handkerchief.

"I was in the cauldron of a volcano; I burnt to ashes and then rose again, reborn as your slave and mistress."

"Yes, I know. I was with you throughout your journey. I felt your devotion. I never left you even for a moment."

"I've never known that yielding to a man could give such pleasure…"

"…And such pain."

"Yes my master…and such glorious pain…my nipples were burning up…were you biting them?"

"Only to the degree that you asked, I would never wish to cause you a permanent deformity. Your beauty is unsurpassed. But I have something to ask you."

"Yes, my master, anything, ask anything of me. I am yours for eternity."

"Tell me slave, when is your sister Phoebe coming home?"

"Any minute now. She went to get George…"

"…The Duplicant where she works?"

"Yes. You must get away from here. I shall tell them I had a fainting spell. Here please take back the earring…"

She tries to hand him the earring but Bram will have none of it. Instead he removes its mate from his other ear and gives it to her.

"You must accept this as a token of my love. You are now my slave and soon you will have powers of your own…"

"Powers?'

"Yes, undreamed of power, for now you are a vampire and with it you have the gift of eternal life, as long as you retain allegiance to me and do not become human again."

"I would never wish that. But I have something to tell you. I believe that I am pregnant."

Bram is surprised and immensely pleased. In all his years with Lydia he has been infertile, never the semblance of a pregnancy of any sort, but he knows that vampire women do have the capacity to ascertain immediately whether or not they have been impregnated. Like snakes, because of their capacity to make venom, they are immensely aware of their bodies, the internal mechanisms of their glands, especially the workings of the organs of gestation, the womb, the ovaries, the fallopian tubes, all of these are ultra-sensitive messengers to a vampire when struck by sperm.

Bram is filled with delight, but remains incredulous.

"You're not one of these women who claims a child, then claims a grudge?"

"You have my oath; I am no such woman."

"In over a century no woman has born a child of my seed. Are you certain of this?"

"I am certain, my master."

"If this is true, then you may call me Bram, for I am not only your master but your eternal-mate. Unfortunately, I am married to an infertile woman, a convert to vampirism like yourself. We vampires have a right of passage. If you wish to be more than a slave, to replace her as my mate and eventually to become my wife you will have to kill her in order to do so."

"Not a problem," Phoenix says; her youth and human conceit returning to her.

"That may be more difficult to accomplish than you believe. She has a protector, a Duplicant by the name of Vladg who has many powerful features of his own."

Phoenix finishes her brandy. She is still very weak

"You mentioned that I would have a choice, to return to being human, how is that possible?"

Bram hesitates but a moment, decides to reveal the truth… that the mother of his unborn child deserves to know the secrets.

"There are two ways. First you must betray me by placing my life in danger of religious zealots; that is how my father was killed, by a silver stake through his heart…"

Phoenix shivers visibly when she hears of this.

"…And the second way?"

"The birth of your child, by giving up the child to the love of another human. But it must be done during the birthing, while you are undergoing the very pains that are declarative to entering life as a human or as a vampire. This act may result in the release of the devil's hold upon your soul and you will be returned to your God's hands."

"Thank you for telling me the secret."

"It is up to you, you may betray me if you wish."

"No, I will never do that, I swear."

"We shall see. I have a test for you. Are you willing to take it on?"

"Yes Bram, anything you ask."

"Not tonight, for it will take a while for you to develop the ability to make venom, but when that time is ripe I shall ask you to kiss your sister on the throat and then to bite her deep and inject your venom into her, drink of her blood as I have done of you. Only then will I believe your faith in me is greater than the love of your sister."

"Not a problem."

"You must not be casual about this. I do not want a human answer, but I ask you as a vampire. You must reply with an answer that befits your status."

Now Phoenix grasps the nature, the depths of what she has committed herself to.

"It shall be done as you wish, for now it is my wish as well my master."

"Now you sound sincere. I believe you."

Bram makes to go, releases her from his gaze. This alone allows Phoenix more freedom of expression, loosens her somewhat from his power.

"When will I see you again?"

"I own a farm in Oneonta, upstate. I must tarry there for a time on business, but I will call. Give me your tele-cell number."

She gives him her number and he plugs it into his contact list.

"I'll tell you when to come, for when you develop the ability to produce venom I shall be in need of your services. Normally it takes but a few weeks; I just don't know how long it will be in a pregnant woman."

"Anything, anything you ask of me I shall do, but please call me every day. I cannot bear the thought of facing the day without a word from you, the light is terrifying."

"You will adapt to that, it takes time."

"Please kiss me on the lips before you go. I do not want to be awake when my sister arrives, but put out all the lights."

Bram does as she asks, kisses her once on the lips, not passionately, but with great ardor. Then he makes sure the coverlet is spread over the two bite marks for he does not want Phoebe to see them. Then, having tucked her in like a child, he raises her limp hand to his lips and presses it as if she were royalty.

"You have made me very proud. I have not felt so fulfilled in over a hundred years."

Phoenix does not hear this last remark for she has once again fallen asleep.

Bram takes his leave as silently as he can, goes to the door and lets himself out.

In the lobby, on the first floor, he is lucky that one of the tenants is leaving for he learns that it is necessary to have a key to the inside door in order to enter the vestibule and leave the building after five o'clock

∞

The driver of the Air-Scoot had refused to allow George aboard, an item of protocol which Phoebe had forgotten: NO Basic Duplicants allowed! So the two had struggled with the enormous crowds on the subway; Phoebe getting jostled back and forth by youths in a swarm groping for a feel. Had it not been for George she might've been in a fix, but his strong arms pushed the boys away and after a time they left her and went on to rumble against another victim.

By the time Phoebe got back to the apartment, accompanied by George, it was almost seven o'clock. At once she spies her sister sleeping on the couch; she switches on some lights, but keeps them dim, using the rheostat.

While waiting for Phoenix to awaken she takes some Melba toast from the cupboard, slathers it with butter, adds guacamole and a slight amount of mild salsa and offers a piece to George. He looks at it sideways, gulps it down and does his best to smile. Phoebe is a total vegetarian and has no idea that Basic's need a high protein diet in order to sub serve their increased rate of metabolism.

After a time she tires of waiting, shakes her sister awake. She openly gasps at the pallor of Phoenix's features, at her transfixed look of languish, so at odds with her normal look of liveliness and sparkling energy.

"What happened, did Bram come? Was he here?"

Phoenix's voice is lower pitched than usual, but recognizable.

"Yes, he came over. Actually he's rather nice, gave me the other earring."

"And you took it?"

"Sure, why not?"

"It's not like you. So then what happened?"

"I told him you were working late and I'd be willing to go out to dinner with him, but he seemed to want only you, so that was that."

"Then how did you get rid of him?"

"We had a drink together, brandy, and then he left. No way to fool that man, he saw right off that I was different than you, so none of our usual stuff worked."

"Did he try anything funny?"

"Funny ha-ha or funny strange?"

"You know, like trying to hypnotize you, that's what he did to me, I'm surer of it now more than ever."

"No nothing like that sis." She tries to sit up, but her weakness causes her to fall back on the cushions. "I keep waking up and falling asleep again."

"Did he give you a potion of some sort?" George asks. These are the first words he has spoken.

Phoenix turns on her side, and in so doing the coverlet falls away from her throat.

"What on earth is that, those two red marks on your throat?"

"What red marks?"

"Wait I'll get a hand mirror; you can see for yourself."

She goes to the bedroom to fetch a mirror, comes back in a jiffy.

"Look for yourself; they're a lot deeper than hickeys."

"Gosh," Phoenix gushes, "I've no idea how I got them."

Though she is secretly proud that Bram has left his stamp of love upon her, she does feel a pang of guilt at telling a lie, for the two sisters are basically truthful to one another.

"Well I don't see how that could happen without your knowing it," Phoebe snaps, sensing something is amiss.

Phoenix changes the subject.

"George, why did you ask about a potion?"

"Because it is one of my duties; my job is to monitor the laser video cameras. Whenever Mr. Eiselman has anyone in the inner office it is my task to train the cameras on the visitor, to make sure that every single one of his words and movements are recorded."

"And?" the two sisters ask simultaneously.

"Two cameras, from different angles, caught him putting a vial of something into Mr. Eiselman's cup of tea."

"Really?"

"Yes. And I meant to ask him about it when he emerged from the office, but that is when Phoebe got into a huddle-if that is what you call it- with him and I had no chance to quiz him further."

"Did you report this to Mr. Eiselman?" Phoebe asks."

"Immediately!" George says, chagrined that he would even be thought of as derelict in his duties.

"And what did he say?"

"To my surprise he jotted down something, but he didn't seem to think that much of it, which upset me a bit. He was sleepy the entire afternoon, and as you know he went home early."

While George is talking, Phoenix seems to awaken somewhat from her lethargy.

"You were right Feeb and I was wrong. If George can be upset by something like this, he certainly has emotions."

"I was not programmed for emotion, no Basic is, but my association with your sister has changed me and also she has improved my vocabulary, taught me a great many words. I am grateful to be associated with her."

"Well I never knew Feeby to have much of a working vocabulary…but if you say so…"

"Ah, that's the old Feeny coming to light. See George what a pisser she can be."

"I don't know pisser in that light, I thought to piss was to void urine."

"Well this is just another meaning to the word; I wouldn't use it in Mr. Eiselman's presence if I were you."

"Just as you say Miss Phoebe."

"So what did you think of him, I mean for a little man he has a strong personality, don't you think?"

"Exactly." She wants to say much more, but does not know where to begin. She certainly doesn't want to tell her sister of the miracle, that she is pregnant.

"Boy are you close mouthed! Is that all you have to say?"

"I'm just tired, the brandy got to me and I'm sleepy as heck."

"But you're usually more of a night person, I'm the day person don't forget."

"Well, I'm going beddy-bye-bye. I've got to get up early for work."

She gets off the couch, clutches the coverlet to her throat, but she is still wobbly and has to measure her steps carefully in order not to fall.

"Okay, but where's George going to sleep?"

Their apartment is only a one bedroom and sometimes the girls do sleep together, but more often than not they take turns, a week at a time, between couch and bedroom.

"We Basics do need at least six hours in order to function efficiently the next day, that's in the manual. But I am designed to sleep standing up if necessary, or on the floor. The hardness won't bother me," George says.

"Oh no, we can't have that. You take the couch; I'll sleep with my sister."

This frightens Phoenix. She is afraid that her sister's warmth will induce her to carry out Bram's test before she is prepared.

"Not tonight please sis, I know I'm going to toss and turn all night. I guess this little episode has affected me more than I realized."

"Now that's a turnabout. You're usually the one that complains of my fidgety sleep, while you are dead to the world…"

"Don't say that!"

"Say what?"

"Dead to the world, don't say that. I'm as much alive as you are, perhaps more so."

"Well Miss Sensitive, what's come over you, it's only a figure of speech."

"I'm sorry, you're right. I know you didn't mean anything by it."

They kiss goodnight, Phoebe heads to the toilet to remove all her make-up and such while Phoenix plops in bed and falls asleep almost immediately.

After hearing how sensitive Phoenix was to Phoebe's remark, George is glad he didn't say more. It was on his mind to mention what a seedy little scoundrel Bram appeared to him to be, but he luckily withheld the thought, feeling it was not his place to offer an opinion on a customer of Pyrell's.

George's ablutions are taken care of automatically. All he has to do is throw his compacted waste into the trash and insert a new filter. He does all this while Phoebe is in the bathroom, sprays an automatic Lysol like mist over his entire frame, turns on his sleep program and lies down on the floor for the night.

In ten seconds flat he is asleep. When Phoebe returns, she steps over him, pulls two sheets and a pillow stored for the purpose in a bin below the couch, tries to get comfy, jams her fist into the pillow, all to no avail. She cannot go to sleep. She knows something is wrong with her sister; her story was too cerebral, too engineered, almost like it was rehearsed. And her voice was lower pitched. What was that about? And those marks on her throat, where did they come from? Why was Feeny so nonchalant about them? Phoebe goes on like this for a half hour or so, asking herself questions to which she has no answers. Eventually her guilt system takes over. She is absolutely sorry that she got her sister into this.

Now she falls asleep.

∞

Bram had left immediately for Grand Central where he intended to drop off the car at the Avertz Substation and to take the bullet train to his farm in Oneonta. Once there he would set things up with Eiselman to deliver the Sextus IV's two or three at a time. He did not intend to alert the population to the arrival of fifty Sextus IV's all at once, but to slowly absorb them into the community. This way was better for him as well, for he did not want to program more than a few each day, otherwise the brain projections would be too taxing on his powers.

All his plans were upset when his tele-cell went off unexpectedly. He was still on furlough and did not expect a call from the Washington bureau, but that's exactly who it was. He held the instrument in front of his face, which was awkward, but a requirement from Mr. Gregoriev, the Sub-Undersecretary for Eastern European Affairs. Apparently he did not like to speak to staff members *de profil.*

"This is Gregoriev here, can you see me?"

"Yes sir, I can see you clearly."

"Well you have to come back to Washington immediately. I have received a call from a certain Mr. Eiselman who claims that you have misrepresented the State Department's intentions at his firm, the Pyrell Corporation."

"I did only as…"

Gregoriev interrupts.

"I don't want to discuss this on the cell. I have called a meeting for two o'clock tomorrow afternoon. Be here!"

Bram is furious. If it wasn't for the fact that he needed a human resource to grant him diplomatic immunity, the protection it provided as well as the largesse it gave him to travel the world without applying for visas and such he would junk this job. He certainly didn't need the money. More bothersome than the call itself was the fact that Eiselman had got in touch with his boss. That meant that the potion had worn off some, that his influence over Eiselman was less than he had thought. And worst of all, the rest of his furlough was ruined. He had planned to hustle Phoenix up to Oneonta, to secrete her there and teach her some of the fundamental ways of vampirism as he had done so many years ago with Lydia. Now that too would have to be postponed.

His only alternative was to tele-cell her, to explain what he wanted her to do for him with the young man named Josh.

Chapter V

Josh Wharton wasn't that bad looking. At twenty-three he was no longer nerdy or pimply faced, didn't have acne or anything like that, it was just that he had no outstanding features. He spoke in a rather halting stop-and-go style and his social skills were admittedly minimal. He was sandy haired with light brown eyes, a slightly snubbed nose, surrounded by a sprinkling of freckles, but no strong chin nor striking cheek bones. And he wasn't quite as tall as Phoebe Winthrop with whom he was desperately in love. A genuine sexual problem, but not an incapacitating one.

At Pyrell's he wasn't in the loop, not in the fast track of executive decision making. He had been with Pyrell's special feature section of production engineering for almost a year now, right out of MIT, and in all that time he had never so much as gotten to water cooler gossip with Phoebe. Not that she came down to his section on the 47th floor that often. When she did visit it was usually because some celebrity wanted a freaky feature or two added to a Sextus-IX and Mr. Eiselman didn't want the order placed by in-house FAX where staff could get a look at the purchaser's name. Even when the customers were not that well known, it was up to him to design, engineer and program the request. So he wasn't just flipping hamburgers, his position with Special Features and Design Engineering was high level stuff, maybe not as newsworthy as the R$D section, but still valuable, and a moneymaker.

So why, until now, had Phoebe seen nothing in him worthwhile? He had even bought a pair of elevator shoes so that he could face her eye-to eye on those rare occasions when they did meet, all to no avail.

But today was different. He had to go up to Mr. Eiselman's office for a special consultation on a batch of Sextus-IV's and Phoebe had been really nice to him. She wore flats, had on a plaid skirt and a tight fitting cotton scooped neck sweater which accentuated her boobs and made his mouth water and his pup tent rise.

He had a monthly pass for the Air-Scoot, and while expensive, he felt it was worth it in time saved and avoidance of stares he still got from riff-raff on the subway. After work, on the rooftop where he waited for the Air-Scoot to bring him to his apartment in Lower East, Phoebe suddenly showed up. Now she seemed to be wearing a brown turtle neck sweater and a slightly different color plaid skirt. He would have sworn the sweater she wore earlier was maroon colored. Oh well, he thought, maybe I'm losing it.

What happened next was that Phoebe, who rarely took the Air-Scoot, came right up to him, actually jostled her shoulder against his. She wanted to know if he would like to have coffee with her in the cafeteria before he went home.

"You can always take a later Scoot," she said; "there's something I want to ask you."

"You're not making fun of me. You really mean it?"

"If I didn't mean it, I wouldn't say it!"

Josh jumps at the chance, decides to be assertive. His roommate, a frat brother from MIT named Billy Lakehomer, had taught him how to hold a girl's hand when walking, how to guide her along when heading to a nearby destination, so now he hooks his arm in hers and they go back down to the 80th floor cafeteria.

Josh is convinced that the sole purpose for the creation of this cafeteria was to bring on a suitable setting for employee promiscuity. The windows are slanted and tinted a soft plum color to allow some of the sun's rays in, just sufficient to create the right mood. Pictures of seascapes and sandy beaches adorn the pastel colored walls; all evoke notions of sensuality in his mind. He pays for coffee and cinnamon rolls and feels as if he is floating in seventh heaven.

They sidle into a nice window seat for two with a good view of stretches of the Hudson and Josh makes sure he doesn't slurp or spill or anything like that.

Phoenix, for this is not Phoebe, gets right to it. She had, in fact, rehearsed the opening sentence in her mind so that she would sound properly scientific.

"I heard you were the one who altered the sweat glands of the Sextus-IX so that they could emit a male scent."

As much as he is smitten with her, Josh is no dummy. This way of starting a conversation sets him back a bit. To him it seems more like an opening chess move than the romantic start he had expected. Billy had told him that you always begin with small talk: 'Small talk gives the appearance of dignity in case you strike out and is the safety net that will save the day'. Her opening gambit was something else. Whatever the game was, he didn't know how to play.

A vertical crease between his eyes gives him a thoughtful air, somewhat slakes down his reckless pursuit of love. His lower lip protrudes a bit, but he maintains composure.

"You know Phoebe, I can't talk about that stuff. Those are confidential matters between the client and Mr. Eiselman. I could lose my job talking to you about things like that. My work is everything to me."

"You're saying I mean nothing to you. I thought from the few times we met that you liked me."

"Sure I do. I'm not ashamed of it. You're on my mind a lot, but that doesn't give me the right to reveal trade secrets. You work for Mr. Eiselman. Did he give you permission to talk to me? Is that what this is all about?"

"No, I'm on my own. You see, I have a problem with sweating. I don't have to be jogging or anything like that. It happens a lot, especially when I kiss a boy. That's why I don't date, or very seldom. My sweat has this terrible foot odor, like I've been working out for an hour when all I've done is get excited over something, could be anything, even a suspenseful movie. If we were holding hands…she grabs his hand for emphasis…it could start right up."

"So what you're asking is whether the same system I used in the Sextus could be applied to a human?"

"Not any human, to me, I'm asking for me."

Josh has to think about this for a moment. At once he realizes that she doesn't particularly like him, but just wants something from him. On the other hand it is a way of getting his foot in the door, so to speak. It could be done, of course, but then there is the question of whether the process would be injurious to a human over the long run.

He takes a sip of coffee, careful not to slurp.

"Sure, it could be done, no problem, but if I were you I wouldn't do it."

"Why not?"

"Long term consequences, who knows?"

"But the sweat would still get out wouldn't it, I mean I would not want that male scent, but something feminine…you know, Dior like."

"Oh that's not a problem, we can take any liquid and transform it into a fine mist to be excreted from the sweat glands…did I lose you on that?"

"No I understood, but what if the liquid is viscous, can you still do it?'

"I suppose, that's for the chemists to determine, but hey, that's a pretty smart question. I never thought you had those kinds of smarts…"

"You thought I was a dunce?"

"Oh no, nothing like that, I mean…now I'm starting to sweat…"

In spite of herself Phoenix has to laugh. This boy is fetching in his own way, not sexy but terribly genuine. She has the information she wants. It sounds like the venom could be chemically reformulated into a mist that a Sextus IV could sustain.

"You're really nice," she says. "Let's get off that subject. Tell me about the Sextus IV?"

"What is it you want to know?"

"Well if I were to advise a friend who wants to purchase a companion, a protector say, what would you advise."

"Which? If you want a protector, like a bodyguard, you don't need a Sextus of any kind, a Basic-III will do. They're quick and very powerful. But if you want a companion there's nothing like the Sextus series. From the IV up to the IX they make the best companions, depending on the sophistication of the systems we put in."

"Well do the Sextus-IV's have sweat glands like we were talking about?"

"I thought we were off that subject."

"You're not very nice to say that to me," she pouts.

"Sure, sure they do. They have practically the same glandular systems as the IX, maybe not as extensive here and there, but yes they do. Now can we talk about us? I'd like to take you to dinner some time, perhaps an orbiting air restaurant, a 4-D movie or something, please."

"Those are expensive! I'll think it over. I'm sure you don't expect me to answer you right away, do you."

"No, that's okay. I can wait."

"I have to go. I hope I didn't make you late for supper. You live with your folks don't you?"

"No, they're in Indiana, Terre Haute to be specific. I have a roommate, Billy, but I can get a place of my own if that's what you mean."

"Silly. What are you implying?"

Josh knows he has gone too far, moved too quickly, that what he said was too impulsive.

"Sorry. Nothing. A guy has to have hopes you know."

"Sure thing." She touches him fondly on the shoulder, makes to go, but suddenly asks, "Who is the biochemist that works with you?"

"Henry Beasley," Josh sputters out before he realizes she has got another bit of information from him that he had no business revealing.

Then she is gone before he can say anything more. He had wanted to ask her for another coffee klatch but she had taken off so fast there was no chance. He scratches his head. He has no idea what the encounter was all about, but senses that he had been outwitted, manipulated back and forth by an expert. He knows that he is intelligent, but he also knows that when it comes to women he is pretty stupid.

Chapter VI

Phoenix and Phoebe

When it came to fashion they were both trendy, but the smallish closet in their one bedroom hardly held enough apparel for one girl, let alone two clothes horses like the twins. The good news was that they didn't mind sharing stuff, as they had very similar wardrobe tastes. The bad news was that Phoenix had taken a turtle neck from Phoebe without letting her know and they had agreed that this was a no-no in case one or the other wanted to wear a certain garment or pair of shoes.

"I was looking for my brown sweater and I couldn't find it."

"I sent it to the cleaners. I wore it the other day."

"Oh. You didn't let me know. It's been cold and windy. I wanted to put it on."

"Sorry, sis. You're right, I should have mentioned it."

"Not a problem. When did you last wear it?"

"To cover up those marks on my neck…"

"I didn't ask you why you wore it, only when."

"Sorry, I misunderstood."

"You sure have been out to lunch lately…"

"It wasn't lunch, only coffee."

"I can't follow you Feen, what wasn't lunch only coffee?"

"Oh, you meant that I was confused, I didn't get it."

"Well what, where and with whom was only coffee? Anyone I know?"

"No one interesting enough, not worth your while to tell about."

"C'mon Feeny, give."

"Oh, all right. I had coffee with this guy who works at Pyrell's. Not a big deal. He does something with sweat glands on the Duplicates."

"You don't mean Josh Wharton, that innocent on the 47th floor?"

"The very same."

"Well I know I've talked to you about him, but I never expected you to date him. He's not your type. Mine neither."

"Well from what you said I thought he might be entertaining. I knew it would be cold on the roof there so I slipped on the turtle neck and went up. Turns out he's not so bad."

"You've got to be kidding."

"Well I haven't dated in a while…"

"That doesn't mean you should take advantage…that kid isn't grown up yet."

"I didn't say I was going to see him again. By the way do you know of a certain Henry Beasley?"

"Sure. He's in the bio-chem department, but he's married. What on earth's come over you? There are hundreds of single guys around, who needs marrieds?"

"I didn't say I wanted to hook up with him. I'm just interested in why I sweat so much, thought maybe he could explain it to me."

"Well we both sweat a lot. Remember what that dermatologist said when we went to him, that it had something to do with our higher metabolism, that we were doing cardio-vascular work outs and that if we wanted to stay in shape that was the price we pay."

"That was some time ago. Anyway, my sweat smells different than yours lately."

Phoebe thinks on this.

"You've got something there. And I have noticed your teeth are getting whiter. They're positively sparkling."

"I've noticed that too. The sun does seem to be bothering me a lot lately, that's why I've been wearing sunglasses so often. Is it sun spot time of the year? Any ideas on that?"

"Nope. But you do seem photophobic. Only thing I ever heard is that when a woman gets pregnant her face darkens and it gives the impression that her teeth are whiter, but your face is definitely paler lately, so that doesn't fit, and you're certainly not PG are you?"

Now Phoenix breaks down. She begins to weep. At first the tears stream silently down her cheeks, but then she begins to sob, making little sniffle noises, starting to sound congested.

Phoebe is moved beyond belief. She puts her arms around her sister, is moved to express her love and hugs her warmly.

"Oh Feeny, what's wrong? What can I do to help? I care more for you than anyone else. Honey I love you."

Phoenix begins to dry her tears, sputters some words between sobs.

"There's nothing you can do. I face annihilation."

"Annihilation? Whatever do you mean?"

"Yes, I face total destruction. It all comes from that little monster Bram, the one you were supposed to have the date with two weeks ago."

"That imp. You've got to be kidding."

"No, I'm not. He has complete control over me. Calls me on the cell, tells me what to do and I am compelled to do it. Absolutely compelled I tell you. Believe me sis I have no way of getting out from under, I am his slave. Sometimes I awake at night and think of him as my master, then the next day, in the daytime, it all seems silly, I feel more like myself for a while, but then he calls me and I seem to do whatever he asks. He's the one got me to go meet with Josh and I can't even remember why."

"Now that you mention it, he did have a strange effect on me as well. I accepted that earring from him and that's not something I'd ordinarily do."

"See what I mean! And there's one thing more."

"And that is?"

"I missed my period and I'm always right on time. No spotting or anything. Feeby, I do believe I'm PG."

"How can that be? You haven't hooked up with anyone in weeks have you?"

"No. Honestly I haven't. I had this awful dream when Bram was here that he had impregnated me, but that couldn't be. I'm sure I'd know if he raped me or anything like that, wouldn't I, wouldn't I?"

"Sure. Of course you would. But that reminds me of Elliot."

"That bum, what's he got to do with this?"

"Well a couple of times when I was hooking up with him, remember I told you how wild he got…"

"Yeah, you said he had all the natural endowments, but no idea on how to please a woman…"

"That's right his cock had length and girth but he could never found my erogenous zones. Anyway there were a few times when he tore thru his condom and I hopped right down to the pharmacy and bought that Ultra-Preg test. Luckily it was negative."

"How does it work?"

"You just dip the end of the instrument into a small plastic cup with your urine in it and it gives you a read-out. No markings to judge or anything like that, it will say: 'Pregnant' or 'NOT Pregnant'.

"That's mechanical. I meant 'how does it work really, you know, the chemical thing."

"I had to ask Mr. Beasley the chemist. He knows all this stuff. It's the hCG."

"What's that?"

"It stands for human Chorionic Gonadotrophin, a hormone that doubles every two or three days up to the max at seven to ten weeks when you get preggie."

"So it is a chemical…"

"A hormone…"

"Okay, but the two mix somehow, right?"

"My understanding is there's an antibody in the Ultra-Preg test that interacts with the hCG and they add an indicator of some sort that changes the urine color and that gives the read-out."

"So the antibody or the indicator could deteriorate over time."

"Sure."

"But Elliot was six months ago, would your stuff still be fresh enough to be accurate?"

"Good question, but let's do it anyhow. How long since you missed your last period?"

"Over two weeks now. I was certain I was pregnant, but now I'm not so sure."

"We'll find out one way or the other. If its negative and you don't trust it we'll go to Dr. Pollack and have him do another test. If it's positive in 99% of the cases it's right, so we'll go to Dr. Pollack and get you a D&C."

"Well I'll have to think about that. I'm not at all sure what I want to do."

"Whichever. Up to you, sis, I'll respect your decision whichever way you go."

"You'll go with me? I'll feel better with you there."

"You betcha. I'll even hold your hand."

This perks Phoenix up some, she tries to smile, but it doesn't come off well. Her features are still taut and strained.

"Can you pee into a cup?"

"Sure, I'm accurate as hell, just like a guy."

"Guys aren't accurate. They pee all over the seat. Who do you think made our toilet so messy…"?

"Elliot, the slob."

"Right."

"C'mon, let's read the instructions."

"You know Feeb, just doing something about it like this makes me feel better already."

Feeby gives her a winning smile.

"You got that right," she says.

∞

The next morning they do the test because the urine is stronger, more concentrated in the morning. It comes out negative.

"I checked the date and it's less than six months old, so the stuff is probably okay, but we'll do it over at Dr. Pollack's anyway."

"I do feel better. Maybe it was all in my head…"

"No. Something else could be wrong, I mean you did miss and you're always on time…"

"True, I'll call right now and after that I'm going to junk this tele-cell, get a new number that Bram doesn't know."

"How did he get your number in the first place?"

"He asked and I felt driven to give it to him, see what I mean."

"We'll both get new phones then. The only person I'm obliged to give my number to, beside you, is Mr. Eiselman. The rest can go fly a coop."

"Sounds good. Maybe that will get me out of Australia."

"Australia?"

"You know, out from down under where Bram has me imprisoned."

"Clever Feeny, you're coming back already."

Finally Phoenix manages a smile that is half-way decent.

Both girls head for work.

Chapter VII

Gregoriev

The interior subdivisions of the Harry S. Truman State Department Building are as drab and rectangular as its outer appearance. If Gregoriev had been the Sub-Under-secretary for Western European Affairs instead of Eastern, he might have had a bigger office. As it was he had little more than a cubby hole furnished as Spartan as the Federal government's budget allowed. Aside from the obligatory American flag and the picture displays of the 53rd President and the Secretary of State, the elderly Chelsea Clinton, the walls too were barren. One of the walls was painted an odd background blue color which is standard for use of the images generated by the Projecto-FAX which, when properly hooked up to a tele-cell, can FAX entire video recordings.

Gregoriev's personality, however, fitted right in to this austere setting. He was one of those people with a small glacier in his soul challenging you to try and thaw it, and if you did, he had a small volcano in his heart at the ready to erupt. Of course this did not prevent him from being meddlesome, inquisitive, moody, and scheming. Above all else he was passionless when it came to human entanglements.

This is what Bram faced at two p.m. in the afternoon. Not even the semblance of a cup of tea or coffee was offered. Gregoriev got right down to it.

"I don't appreciate receiving nasty messages from civilians like Eiselman who do business with the military. What on earth were you thinking of Alucard?"

Bram has had skirmishes with Gregoriev before. He knew how to handle Russian blood; the trick, unlike the Germans whom you can shout down, was to agree with what he presented but to anticipate, to disagree with what he had not yet mentioned. In effect, dialogue with Gregoriev was a chess match.

"I was thinking of what you had mentioned to me on our prior discussion."

This unseats Gregoriev slightly, he has no idea what Bram is referring to but his national pride refuses to give in. However, he has lived long enough in the States to pull an American phrase out of the hat.

"Don't beat around the bush. Why did you tell Eiselman that the Foreign Service was interested in purchasing fifty Duplicants for a special project?"

"Is that what he said?"

"Absolutely."

"Remember Mr. Gregoriev, with respect, you are the one who said Foreign Service Officers who are away from home for long periods of time might consider the purchase of a Duplicate companion for their spouse in order to boost morale."

"That has nothing to do with this. You are evading my question."

"Not at all. I did what you suggested some time ago. And as you forecast it worked out quite well."

"Quit trying to butter me up." Gregoriev enjoyed using this phrase as well. "You are facing insubordination…"

"Please hear me out. You also voiced the opinion that Duplicates might make good sub-consuls. I am merely trying to explain that I had a prior relationship with Eiselman from an earlier purchase. I took care not to mention your name, but only made a reference to the Foreign Service. That counts for something does it not?

Gregoriev grunts, gives not an inch.

"At the personal level all I wanted was to buy two or three Sextus IV's to work on my farm in Oneonta…"

"You own a farm? Where is Oneonta."

"Yes, yes I do, and it is in upstate New York."

"How many hectare?"

"Over one hundred acres."

"Yes acreage, that's the reference used here, but what has that got to do *with 'the price of eggs'?"*

"Nothing, I never mentioned any special project, but when I considered purchasing the duplicants from the factory in Amersfoort, Holland, I may have mentioned that I was with the Foreign Service. But all that I am guilty of was to try and bargain the price of the Duplicants down by mentioning a competitor."

"Then how do you explain the fluid or whatever it was that you put in his tea? Hah, how do you explain that?"

Bram is taken aback momentarily. At once he realizes that Eiselman must have forwarded a copy of the laser-video to Gregoriev via the Projecto-FAX.

"Make no mistake. It's in your best interest as well not to know what I am about to tell you, but first show me the video. I assume that is what gives you the notion that something is amiss."

Gregoriev snorts.

"Not a notion, plain as day for all to see."

Gregoriev rings for his secretary, a woman as far removed from Phoebe's type as can be. She is the classical expression of a bespectacled shrew working efficiently in a boondoggled bureaucracy. She plugs the projector in. The way the projecto-FAX works is unlike the ordinary projector. What it does is to extract the significant figures in the disc, project them onto the far wall, the one with the bluish background, and bounce them forward, a foot or so, as life size holographs. Eiselman's figure appears first, closely followed by Bram's. The images are clear; one can see the surreptitious movement, that Bram is caught pouring some type of liquid into Eiselman's cup.

"There. You see yourself. Explain that and what it is?"

Bram decides he has to take the risk that Eiselman will respond appropriately when he hears his name, otherwise all is lost.

"I'll answer the second part first. It is a love potion. On the other hand, it is not for me to explain, but for Eiselman. Let's get him on the tele-cell. Allow me to talk to him and you can observe. Fair?"

Gregoriev mutters something under his breath but asks his secretary to get Eiselman on the screen. He is either too lazy to do it himself or doesn't want to show he has to look up the number.

As she dials, Bram takes special care to memorize the private number so that he can get straight through to Eiselman if it ever should become necessary.

Eiselman appears on the far wall and Bram immediately says, in a low pitched tone: "Alucard, Alucard here."

The response is immediate.

"Yes. How can I be of service?"

"Tell Mr. Gregoriev that you asked me to put a love potion in your tea."

"Yes, a love potion. I do remember now."

"You wanted to captivate your own receptionist, remember."

"Enough. Enough," says Gregoriev. Say goodbye to him."

Bram hangs up after making an excuse to Eiselman that he has another caller on the line. "In view of circumstances I shall tell you something rather confessional, as long as it's understood you won't turn it against me."

"No promises. I don't operate that way. Just tell me, what is this love potion you two were talking about?"   Bram had caught the jump in signal transference from Gregoriev's brain when the words 'love potion' were first mentioned. This enabled him to read his boss's mind, to learn that there was a red-headed woman in the building Gregoriev wished to seduce. On transfer, the image of the redhead flashes quite clearly to Bram's visual cortex. At times like these, when everything worked correctly, he felt impervious to fear, as if all his plans would eventually work out to his satisfaction.

"You see Eiselman was aware from a previous conversation, the time when I purchased the Duplicant for my wife that I had learned of the secret powers of love potions on one of my visits to an old castle in the Carpathian Mountains. He asked me for the potion so that his member could give off emanations that would excite his secretary, the beautiful Phoebe."

"Emanations…?"

"Yes, vibrations that project outward when you point your erect penis…please do not be embarrassed…at the woman whom you wish to seduce."

"Can this be true? There exists such a potion?"

"I ask you again to treat this conversation as if it were between a priest and a penitent…"

Now Gregoriev's little glacier begins to thaw. Bram had read his mind correctly; he is very much in need of a love potion.

"I am an atheist, but even so, I swear to you that I will never reveal the secret. You can bring me this potion?"

"It has to be made up fresh. Certainly I shall do this for you if you wish. But once you uncork the vial, you must use it within twenty minutes. Your fly need not be open that is unnecessary, just turn to the woman who has given your member the necessary stimulus to induce an erection and she will receive the jolt that compels her to come to you. But please, this must remain secretive. I do not want others to come running to me for this elixir of love, nor shall I ever mention to another individual that I provided a sample for you.

"You will do this before you leave?"

"Leave? I am still on furlough…"

"Not any longer. I am posting you to Holland. In fact to Amersfoort. As you mentioned the Under-Secretary is interested in the development of a few Sextus IV's as sub-consuls. He thinks this will save us a good deal of consular time and money. In Holland the Sextus is called the 'Royaal' and the Basic is termed the 'Basisch', but it makes no difference, they are essentially the same models as produced here."

"But Holland is in Western Europe, you have no jurisdiction to send me there."

"Hah. The Ambassador to Holland herself has asked me to intercede in this matter…"

"But I don't speak Dutch. My linguistic abilities are in the Slavic tongues and the French language."

"Not a problem. All the Dutch speak English."

For a moment or two there is a heavy silence, then Bram asks, "Should I buy the best models available?"

" Absolutely not, purchase the weakest ones you can get. The Dutch Ambassadress and I don't want this to work. Don't ask. We have our reasons."

"Understood."

"Since you have shown such alacrity in dealing with Duplicants, you are the perfect candidate for the position."

Bram is smart enough not to ask if Gregoriev is marginalizing him because of the mess-up with Eiselman. He doesn't know for sure if Gregoriev believes the story he told, but it doesn't matter. What Gregoriev is willing to do is to get him out of the country. ut the issue to rest as long as he becomes a supplier of the love potion. What Gregoriev does not realize is that there is no such thing, but Bram is sure of the placebo effects. He laughs to himself. He can just see Gregoriev pointing his fly at the redhead, his secret love object.

The chess game was a draw.

Chapter VIII

Bram and the Twins

As soon as Bram left Gregoriev's office he made a decision. He needed to see Phoenix immediately. It was already after five and he figured the girls would be home from work, but that didn't bother him. He was certain he could handle both at once if it came to it.

He decided to pay for an Air-Scoot shuttle back to Manhattan even though he felt the price to be exorbitant. He even paid the extra fifty to land directly on the rooftop of the twins' apartment. The Air-Scoot is designed to hover about a foot above the roof such that, if a passenger in a hurry wishes to disembark fast, they can request a hover landing. Bram does just that, grasps his valise and quickly jumps off the last foot or so onto the rooftop.

Right after he gets out of the Scoot he tries to call Phoenix on the tele-cell but is told that service for the number dialed has been disconnected. This unnerves him some, but he hustles over to the rooftop entry, adjoining the skylight, runs down one flight of stairs, finds the freight elevator and takes it to the twins' floor level. This doesn't help much because the door to gain entrance to the girls residence floor is one of those heavy metal security doors that opens easily if you are on the inside going out, but is locked tight from the outside going in. He leaves the stairwell, goes back to the elevator and takes it down to the main floor.

He manages to get out the card Phoenix had given him, knocks on the door labeled: Building Manager and Custodian.

The door opens just wide enough for a bald top to peek through, like a turtle's head pushing out of its shell.

Bram shows the card, explains that he is in a fix; that he got to the top of the building via Air-Scoot, but was closed off from the downstairs' entryway and couldn't call up to the girls' apartment.

Now the door opens wider, the manager is still chomping down on some morsel, his false teeth click-clacking as he speaks.

"Yeah, we keep the inner door locked after five. I'll have to unlock it for you if you want to buzz the girls' apartment."

"Can't you just take me up in the elevator?"

"Nobody goes up 'less they got permission from a tenant," he says suspiciously.

"Oh, all right, just unlock the entryway door for me and I'll do the rest."

The manager stares vaguely at Bram, says: "Not for nothin'. I interrupted my dinner to answer your knock, that's worth something ain't it?"

Finally, Bram gets it, hands over a five. The manager snaps it up and puts it away so fast that the exchange is hardly visible to the naked eye.

"Okay. For another fiver I'll key the elevator for you, let you go straight up."

Luckily Bram has another five. This one disappears as fast as the first.

∞

In the elevator Bram takes several deep breaths, tries to control his anger but feels the glands at the base of his canines beginning to enlarge. His facial features take on a morbid countenance, his fingernails elongate, becoming claw like, his tongue protrudes, he starts to pant, a vestige of the transfiguration into wolf.

He knocks loudly on the door of the twins' apartment and is greeted by the sound of two voices, neither one is female.

"Who is it?" the gruffer of the two voices asks. This is not a voice Bram recognizes.

Now the whites of Bram's eyes begin to take on an amber wolfish color. He is furious, akin to a maddening road rage.

"This is Bram Alucard speaking! I want to talk to Phoenix. I don't care about Phoebe, just let Phoenix come to the door and speak to me."

"No way," the softer voice says. To Bram this voice seems vaguely familiar.

The second voice goes on.

"The girls aren't here, go away. I've already put in a call to the Hood Patrol."

Now it comes back to him, he had spoken on the phone to this voice. He was sure it belonged to Josh Wharton, the young engineer on the 47th floor whom he had induced Phoenix to cultivate for information.

"I know you Josh Wharton and the vibes inside tell me the girls are at home."

Bram is dissimulating. In this case it is much more than vibes. His sense of smell has actually become equal to that of the wolf; even through the heavy door he can smell the essence of Phoenix, not just her perfume, but the strong scent of her womanhood. This tells him that she is still pregnant.

Bram hears a huddle of whispered voices, the name George is used by Josh and Bram now knows the identity of all four inside.

It is George who speaks next.

"It is in your best interest to leave at once. Otherwise the consequences will be dire for you."

"The least you can do is to have Phoenix return my engagement present; that is only fair."

"What engagement present?" Josh asks.

"The diamond earrings I gave her."

Now Phoebe cannot help herself. She impulsively shouts out, "You first forced me to accept one earring and then you gave the second one to my sister. That's no engagement present."

"Then give them back!" Bram replies forcefully, fully aware that once the deadbolt is released he can handle the chain latch easily.

Again there is a huddle, a murmuring of mixed voices. This time he can definitely recognize Phoenix as one of the four. Now his thinking is more positive. He sums up all his power, concentrates on the voice of Phoenix and urges her to return the earrings.

Now Phoenix tells her sister that she would feel less guilty about keeping the earrings if she returned them, that this would rid her of Bram's influence once and for all.

"All right," Phoebe says, "but let George give them back to him. NO way do I want him to confront you."

"All right," Phoenix says. "Do you mind George?"

"Not at all. My program states this is the right decision to make."

"Some programs don't have good judgment on decision making," Josh says. "I don't think we should do anything. Not till the Hood Patrol gets here. This can be a fatal error."

Phoenix's eyes are becoming humongous. She is beginning to receive brain pattern messages from Bram.

"It's the right thing to do. I'll feel better if we do this right now."

"Why?" Josh asks. "We can always send them back to his address by FED-UP."

"We don't know his address and it's more dangerous to ask him for it; that lets him talk and gives him a chance to influence us. No, it's better to just hand them back. No one is stronger than George…"

"You are keeping me waiting," Bram growls. He sets his valise down. "If you open the door now your suffering will be trivial, if you make me wait too much longer, it will be fierce beyond belief."

By now his face is grotesque, his fingernails have become claws, they stick out at least two inches from the pulp of his digits and his fangs are over three inches long. He concentrates inwardly, summons up all his powers.

"All right," Josh says, "I'll undo the deadbolt and set the door ajar, you got the earrings George?"

George nods.

"Okay girls. Put on your ophthalmic sunglasses, you don't want to be blinded by these magnesium-lights. Ok. Now get ready with the mirrors and focus the heavy wattage lights right on the doorway. If he makes a move to force an entry, you train the lights right on him, he'll be blinded for a few seconds at least."

As soon as the deadbolt is released and the door set slightly ajar, Bram sticks one pointed claw through a link in the safety chain and slides it off the slot. Then he pushes the door wide open only to be greeted by a series of lights and mirrors. The special mirrors, placed in a series, had been set up by Josh in such a clever way that they re-reflect the light back to the focus, and now they stun Bram. Momentarily he is blind.

George drops the earrings on the floor; he is ready to do battle.

The girls scream, but do their job, keep the powerful lights focused on Bram and the mirror system operational.

Bram ducks the first swipe at him by George, who unlike his slow movements in his role as a servant, now has the athletic agility of a professional boxer. His second blow finds its mark, a left hook square to Bram's jaw which sends him flying over the couch.

Bram regroups, gets on all fours, springs at George and claws half his face away, then sinks his fangs deep into his throat, releases some venom, but keeps a goodly amount in reserve for Josh. Josh grabs a sturdy lamp, holds it in two hands, and swings it with all the strength he can muster, the metal base hits Bram on the side of the head, blood hemorrhaging from the wound immediately. Bram has to release his fang-hold on George. He takes a step backward, is about to faint but recoils, charges into Josh and knocks him sideways. Then it is Phoebe who comes to Josh's rescue, she has a huge Japanese kitchen knife in her hand, slashes at Bram who raises his left arm to ward off the thrust but the knife finds his thumb, slashes through, slices it completely off at the base.

This awakens Bram to the possibility of his own demise. He knows he can bleed to death, that his mother's human genes have enough influence to allow him to succumb to his wounds. His fangs retreat; his claws once again regain more of a fingernail appearance. The whites of his eyes have faded from their strong amber color, but still retain a yellowish hue. His appearance is no longer wolfish yet not quite human looking.

And now George, with the flesh from one side of his face stripped away like a hang-down plant, slams into Bram, reeling him backward. Bram is stuporous, benumbed, falls to his knees, is beginning to lose consciousness when it is Phoenix who goes over to him. It is one of those unaccountable desire-repulsive intrusions affecting her mind. She is not naïve, she knows the danger, but seeing him this way, he appears so small, so helpless, she takes pity on him. His plight reawakens her repressed thoughts. She now remembers all that had transpired a mere two weeks ago, how they had joined together in the upright position, how exhilarated he had become in the belief that he had created a living being inside her. Now he will be so disappointed by what she must tell him, the truth about the pregnancy.

Bram is barely conscious, but even so he knows that Phoenix is still pregnant. His heightened sense of smell picks up her scent, one that continues to give off a maternal and child essence.

"I had to break my promise to you. Yesterday we went to my Gynecologist. He did a pregnancy test and it came out negative. That releases me from my oath."

Bram has such little strength that he has to whisper. Blood from his severed thumb continues to seep even though he has encircled the stump and applied pressure with the index and thumb of his other hand. The penetrating wound at his temple is still pouring blood down the side of his face. Even so he manages to say:

"You can't mean that, that you will forego your oath."

Phoenix still doesn't know why she finds this man so seductive. He is so different from the juggernaut jocks she has been dating. Yes, she knows he is a married man, and a very strange one at that, realizes he is a vampire, but that doesn't seem to make a difference to her. By some caprice she has fallen into his web and the sheer excitement of eternal life has stirred her desire.

At once she blows these thoughts away, steps out of the well of evil, returns to the situation at hand.

"Yes, I am so sorry. I know it means a great deal to you after all the travails you've gone through."

"I have a large handkerchief in this pocket, can you use it to bandage my head wound.

She does as he requests, twirls it into a makeshift bandage, ties it tightly around his head, but in so doing notices that this is the selfsame handkerchief with her blood spots on it, the one he used so tenderly to wipe away the blood oozing from her neck bites.

"This handkerchief… you haven't laundered it, why not?"

"I kiss the blood spots on it every day; it brings me closer to you."

In spite of herself, Phoenix is moved, but she doesn't let on.

"It doesn't master, I mean matter," she says. "Just don't think abandoning my oath was an easy decision for me to make, it wasn't."

Bram is too weak to read her mind, but he knows this is more than a Freudian slip; it gives him hope that he still retains some power over her.

"What kind of pregnancy test did you use?"

"Oh, the standard, that hCG thing, why does that master, I mean matter. There I've done it again."

"Don't talk to him," Josh interrupts, "don't give him any information."

Bram realizes what Phoenix does not. The test could not possibly have come back positive; the hormone she is producing is not hCG but vCG, the vampire variation. This means much to Bram, increases the possibility that, if it is a boy child, he will inherit true vampire powers, perhaps even the ability to transmogrify.

While Phoenix tends to Bram, Phoebe nurses George.

"Mr. Eiselman will be angry at me. I promised to return George in good condition."

"Don't worry about it. I'll get the boys from engineering to come over tomorrow. We'll have him fixed as good as new in no time."

"Really Josh?" Phoebe says. She begins to look at Josh in a new light.

"I feel my faculties waning, Miss Phoebe," George says softly, his voice beginning to trail away.

The Duplicant's face is seeping yellowish lymph. Phoebe pastes the loose skin gently back into place. The lymph acts like glue and just replacing the tissue makes George look somewhat better. Unfortunately, he has lost so much lymph, that his systems are beginning to shut down. Of a sudden his waste receptacle pops out of his right side, the tray holding the filter slides open and all the waste, urine, fecal matter, sweat, phlegm and abdominal juices create a horrid mess, first dripping, then pouring out in a torrent onto the thick lush carpet the twins had recently installed.

"How vile," Phoebe says.

"Disgusting," Phoenix says.

"He can't help it, he's shutting down," Josh says."

"It's the effect of the venom," Bram says.

"I am soo sawrry to…to leave you like this… my systems are failing…," George

says, his words draining off at the end.

Then he becomes immobile and stiff, his arms positioned forward, elbows slightly bent, positioned like a sculpture in the last gesture he had made. ks made by the others are lost on him.

"Please," Bram says, "someone find my thumb."

The three exchange quizzical glances.

"It's the Christian thing to do," Josh says, "even for a vampire."

They all get on their hands and knees, avoiding the mess on the rug, start crawling around, searching for the thumb.

At this point there is a loud repetitive knocking on the door which has remained completely open since the beginning of the fracas. It is the custodian accompanied by two uniformed Hood Patrolmen.

"What's this? What's this all about? We can't have domestic scenes like this. This is a classy place," the custodian says, his false teeth click-clacking as he speaks.

"This man sitting on the floor over there forced an entry," Josh says. "The girls didn't want him here, didn't want to see him at all. He's the one forced the door open."

One of the patrolmen speaks up. He seems to be the one in charge.

"Who unlocked the dead bolt?"

"I did," Josh says.

"That's all that counts. You made the move to let him in. Then there's nothing we can do. If you're dumb enough to do that, we can't find any legal reason to claim forced entry. Right Bill?"

"Right," Bill says.

"Next time make sure you stand on your legal rights. Now we have to charge you five hundred for the trip over here and the time spent."

"That's a rip-off. I won't pay it."

"Then we'll have to take you in, right Bill"

"That's right," Bill says.

Bram is bleeding less, still lethargic, but no longer stuporous.

"Bring my valise over here," he demands of Bill. "My diplomatic papers are in there."

For some reason Bill does as he is directed by Bram.

As Bram opens the valise the head of the salamander peeks out

"Oh, how cute," Phoebe says.

 Josh makes a face.

"What are you doing with a salamander?" he asks.

"What salamander?" Phoenix asks. She has not yet seen it.

"Why do you keep a salamander in your valise," Phoebe asks.

"I always keep a live salamander in there; it has properties to rejuvenate tissues. You must know that they can regenerate an arm…"

"I do remember that from biology class," Phoebe says. "Those newts are cute. You won't harm it, I hope."

The two patrolmen stare at one another in disbelief. Now they are sure these people are whacko.

Bram pushes the head of the salamander back in, slips out his papers and identification, hands them to Bill who takes them over to his partner. While the patrolman is scanning the papers, Bram, pointing to Josh, says: "And this man is under my jurisdiction, so he too has diplomatic immunity."

The two patrolmen exchange glances; they don't want to have anything to do with a federal employee of high rank.

"All right, no charges will be filed," the first one says.

"We're leaving," the other one says to the custodian. "The rest is up to you."

The custodian grumbles, tells the twins to be more careful who they invite up to the apartment. He knows he can not say much more since he had conned money out of Bram. He closes the door and takes off.

George has remained standing in the middle of the room, silent as a statue.

"I guess I owe you one", Josh says to Bram, "but that doesn't mean I can forgive what you did to Phoenix."

"Please find my thumb for me, and we will be even."

It is Phoebe who finds the thumb which had somehow fallen between two sofa cushions. She is skittish, holding the thumb, but hands it to Bram whose head wound has finally stopped bleeding.

He asks Josh to rinse off the severed end of his thumb with lukewarm water.

Bram takes the salamander out of the valise, clasps it gently in his good hand.

"I didn't think vampires were animal lovers." Josh says, handing the cleansed thumb back.

"I'm not. Please give me that kitchen knife."

"You got to be kidding," Josh says, "you're not getting any weapons from us."

"I need to cut off one of the arms, just to get the tissue fluid, then I can reattach my thumb."

"No way," Josh says vehemently.

"Then just give me a little of George's lymph…I have to make a paste."

Josh shakes his head.

"Not from my Duplicant you don't."

Bram is exasperated. He bites off an arm of the salamander (under the disdainful eye of Phoebe who mutters *'how vulgar'* mixes the newt's leaky fluid with some of his own dripping blood, sprinkles an alchemic powder from one of his vials into the mix, stirs it with his pinky, and applies the concoction both to the stump and to the severed part of his thumb. Then he presses both ends together.

"Do you have tape of some kind, even Scotch Tape will do?"

Phoenix nods. She wants to help; goes to a drawer and takes out some electric tape, picks up a paper towel from the kitchen. She returns to Bram, dries off the laceration as best she can with the paper towel, wraps the tape around the wound as neatly as possible.

Bram continues to hold the thumb firmly to its stump with his right hand.

"Will you take him down to the trauma center?" she asks Josh pleadingly. "He's so weak he can't hurt anyone."

"Oh, all right," Josh says against his better judgment. He wants to make points with Phoebe and it would not do to alienate Phoenix although he still bears somewhat of a grudge against her for the way she had deceived him. Josh knows that he had been made a fool of, that was his bad luck, but the episode had brought him into closer contact with the twins and this he recognized was his good luck. Now he had an outside chance with Phoebe which was better than none at all.

The three had gone over the entire episode, shared every detail. It was during this chatter, which Josh enjoyed immensely since the girls had taken him into their confidence that all three agreed Bram was undoubtedly a vampire and they had to set up a plan of defense, hence the mirrors and lights.

"Call me from the hospital, let me know if he is ok," Phoenix says.

"Okay, what's your number?"

Phoenix tells him before she realizes that it was the wrong thing to do.

∞

Bram has to be hospitalized overnight.

Even before they send him off to the Neurology floor for observation he is given two pints of packed red cells. Bram is glad they had not transfused whole blood, he does not want to become more human than necessary, knows that even the red blood cells from an unknown source will minimize his powers.

Early the next morning he is given a third pint of packed cells as his hemoglobin is not quite up to snuff. He is once again checked for late signs of concussion and contusion. All seems well. He allows the specialists to take X-Rays but adamantly refuses both a cathode ray MRI and a magneto-encephalograph of his brain. He does allow them to take a neutrino CT scan which he feels will cause minimal damage and not awaken any suspicions that he is of a different species.

The hand surgeon, with his coterie of residents, stops by in the afternoon. He is just finishing up with Bram, explaining to the residents that it will not be worth it for the reconstructive experts to do any more work on the thumb, when Phoenix arrives for a visit. She is wearing a push up bra underneath a party girl pink dress with a sweetheart neckline and wedgies to match. She is not wearing earrings.

Bram introduces her as his niece; this raises a few eyebrows from the young surgical residents who are blown away by Phoenix's charm and beauty.

"You can explain things to me," Phoenix says, "I'm a receptionist at an internist's office."

The hand surgeon checks her out, decides she is worth a few minutes of his time.

"The thumb only has two digits," he expounds, "unlike all the other fingers which have three." Phoenix nods her understanding. "And as you can see the tip is still bluish, what we call cyanotic," Phoenix nods again, she loves medical stuff. "Notice that the first digit is warm" …he takes Phoenix's hand- to the pronounced exasperation of the residents who know he is a lecher -and touches her index to the base- "that means it is receiving blood, that the circulation is getting there adequately, at least for the moment."

"What will happen to the distal digit?" Phoenix is proud of the way she phrased her question.

"I'm afraid he might lose that one, only time will tell of course."

"Phoenix deftly removes her hand from the surgeon's grasp, sensing that he had held it for more than teaching purposes. Both Bram and the residents exchange knowing glances.

The hand surgeon goes on in a formal lecture style.

"Of course, the nerves will not regenerate for six months" he turns to one of the residents, embarrasses him by asking: "Do you remember what that process is called?"

By luck the student knows.

"Wallerian regeneration," he snaps off, as if it were common knowledge to everyone, but he sees the admiration in Phoenix's eyes and wonders just how he can manage to hit on her.

The surgeon goes on and on about repair of tissues, ligaments, tendons, nerves, bone fragments and by the time he is finished Phoenix feels she has to refresh her makeup, but the group ultimately leaves and Phoenix is finally alone with Bram. She sits on the edge of his bed, has to swing her fanny over a bit to make room. The starchy hospital sheets somehow roll up a crease in the elastic of her flimsy panties, rubbing it against the soft skin of her inner thigh. Annoyed, she stands up at the side of the bed, reaches through the material of her skirt, finds her panties and straightens out the elastic with a pull and a snap.

Now that she is more comfortable she can say what is on her mind:

"I brought the earrings. George had dropped them on the floor, and you failed to pick them up when you left."

"I wouldn't have done so even if I had two thumbs, they are yours for eternity…"

"Don't say that, say forever if you want, just not eternity, that makes me feel…you know, like I'm under your power again."

"I have no power now; I am weaker than you in every respect."

"Well, I guess that's true, just don't look at me with those penetrating eyes of yours."

"All right; but first let me thank you for coming to visit…"

"It was just to return the earrings…and yes a little bit to see that you were not suffering from a concussion, I mean that was some blow you took from Josh."

"It felt terrible I must admit."

"How did you do that? I mean spring so far. I must say it was a majestic leap."

"I don't know. I was half wolf at the time…when it gets like that I am almost unaware of what is going on."

Now it is Phoenix whose admiration shows.

"I do admit I have an affinity of sorts to you, not as a lover, I don't mean that, but you are a man who fights for what he wants to accomplish. That does sex me up a bit and that is exactly what I don't want to happen again, it is too dangerous for me."

Bram feels his canines aching for her blood; his glands are beginning to make venom in spite of his weakness.

"You are being honest Phoenix, and I appreciate that. It is so rare in a human nowadays."

"Well, pardon me for asking, but just how old are you?'

Bram smiles inwardly, admires her spunk a certain amount. It is a brazen question but he doesn't hesitate, chalks it up to her being an American woman.

"I was born in 1793…."

Phoenix gasps.

"My mother was English and my father of Slavic origin. These earrings were hers, and in all my years of living I have never offered them to anyone except you. Please take them back. These gems are precious, not just for their monetary value, but for their ability to protect you. The amethysts surrounding the large diamond will defend you from evil and the small rubies will warn you of insincerity in others."

Phoenix is moved beyond tears.

"All right, I will accept them."

Then, in her innocence, she goes to kiss him on the cheek and that is all the opening he needs.

He penetrates her soul with his eyes, sinks his fangs deep into her jugular, the venom immediately doing its work, he drinks only enough blood to reawaken his powers. Just at that moment the resident who had wanted to hit on her opens the door, but sees that Phoenix is in the grasp of 'her uncle' thinks this must be one of those sugar daddy things he has heard about and quickly closes the door. 'Damn, lost another one,' he grumbles to himself.

Bram doesn't release Phoenix from his grasp until he is sure she remains under his spell.

"I want you to go to Santa Barbara."

"Yes my master, Santa Barbara, I've heard of it, exactly where is that?"

"In Southern California; I will provide Sub-Orb tickets for you and enough money for you to purchase a new wardrobe for that climate and social scene."

"Where will I live master? What will I do?"

"You will reside with my wife, her name is Lydia and she is like you, a vampire. This is now your second impregnation with my venom. If you receive a third dose of venom, from any vampire, you will become a member of the undead, unable to see your own reflection in a mirror. I don't want that to happen, neither from me nor anyone else."

"Why master?"

"Because I believe you are still pregnant and I want you protected more than anything else on this earth, such as it is. Can you understand that?"

"Yes master."

"My wife knows midwifery. Long ago she has mastered the art of delivering babies. Now she has a small veterinary practice in Santa Barbara, it will give you something to do for nine months. You will be apprenticed to her as a veterinary assistant."

"Yes master."

"I know that you like medical work, it is even better with small animals than humans, they don't lie to you."

"Animals don't lie," she repeats in a monotone.

"Correct. Now I want you to awaken, to remember everything about Santa Barbara, but nothing about your pregnancy."

"Yes master."

"Awaken!" he orders.

Phoenix comes out of it. She is pissed as hell.

"I trusted you and you did it to me again. Why for heaven's sake?"

"Heaven has nothing to do with it. In a few days you will receive a Sub-Orb ticket to LAX. Lydia will pick you up at the airport. You will have ten thousand dollars in traveler's checks to purchase a new wardrobe. You like clothes don't you?"

"Certainly, and shoes, what woman doesn't? But that doesn't make up for the dirty deal you pulled on me when I went to kiss your cheek, I trusted you."

"Okay, you have a point there. I just didn't know how to get you to Santa Barbara without influencing you."

"You said you were too weak…"

"You said I sexed you up a bit…"

"You took advantage…"

"I will make it up to you, I swear."

"I don't need you to swear, I need you to stop pestering me like that."

"I said it was for the last time, but you have to wear the earrings every day. There are other vampires around and some of them are not as nice as I. Male or female they may try to drink all of your blood, not just the small amount that I took."

This threat, from others, is an unwelcome surprise to Phoenix. She now understands that to a vampire she exudes a submissive essence that alerts them to her desire to be obedient, to be torn apart at the roots of her psyche, a feeling she has had for most of her life, not one that has been engendered by Bram or anyone of his ilk.

"I see," she says contritely. "I see now that I cannot escape this new life. I shall continue to hate you Bram Alucard. I promise you I shall be more foe than friend for however long it takes. You have destroyed my humanness and that is unforgivable."

"You are growing up before my very eyes. Hate excites me more than love, remember that my dear."

"Will you at least accompany me to the airport?"

"No, I leave for Holland tomorrow. I will call you on the tele-cell from there and if you have any questions at all about your trip…"

"I'll have to give notice at the clinic."

"You have to leave at the latest in three days. That should give you enough time to explain things to Phoebe."

"My sister and I have never been apart, not once in all these years. Have you considered what you have done, separating us like this?"

"She can visit, the Sub-Orb flight is less than two hours."

"It's not that. It's the abandonment issue. I'm dependent on her, she on me. I'm not sure we can live apart from one another."

"What if you were married, what then?"

"We have talked about it, planned to live on the same street, a few doors down from one another. I guess that was an adolescent dream talking."

"Not necessarily. Perhaps that can be arranged. Don't think that such things can not happen, they can."

Phoenix shakes her head, she doesn't believe in anything at the moment.

"I'm leaving now Bram. Have a good trip to Holland. I'll wait for your call."

"You are not wearing your earrings."

"They don't go with this outfit."

"Remember you are prey, the earrings will protect you."

She puts them on.

"You win for now," she says. She stands up, at the edge of the bed, faces him directly… unadorned, unalloyed, unafraid.

Chapter IX

Vladg and Lydia

Lydia was at high voltage.

Another of those times when she was getting on my nerves; busily having one of her 'significant conversations'. She told me Bram had taken the Sub-Orb flight to Holland:

"Got there in two hours flat", she said, "Dulles to Schiphol and from there he has to go to some town called Amersfoort where they make Duplicants."

"So?"

"You know Holland has windmills."

"Lots of countries have windmills."

"These are the old fashioned kind."

"Cut the megillah! Why are you beating around the bush? When he goes to the Balkans you never seem to care much one way or the other."

"Because this concerns you as well. It seems the Duplicants there are in uproar. They're making a bid to enter society at a more significant level."

"And?"

"And they plan an insurrection of sorts…over lack of civil rights. The Royal Duplicants want to be allowed to vote, to marry and to get something more from paying taxes than their equivalent of your yellow card."

"Fat chance…"

"There's even a female Duplicant who is trying to run for Parliament as a member of the Green Party. She wants to stop the Black Market from selling female Duplicants to rich Arab Sheiks."

"So how does that concern me? I'm here in the States. I'm your companion. I've got nothing in common with Dutch Duplicants."

"God you are an isolationist aren't you? Don't you see that this has the potential to go global? And aren't you even interested in the fact that the Dutch are producing nearly as many female Duplicants as male ones."

"From what I've read they're not Duplicants like I am, but Dupes. All they do is sell flowers. The Dutch dress them up in 16th century garb for tourists and put them on display like animated dolls…"

"Not all of them…"

"Nope, the rest are servant girls, waitresses and maids, what the Dutch call bedieners and werksters, that's not for me. Historically they did the same thing to the coolies in Indonesia that they're doing now to the Duplicants."

"How do you know so much about this? You don't speak Dutch."

"I read history, you don't. And you don't watch TV. It's been on constantly. You know how the media people can report a story to death. Well ever since the terrorists have quit messing around every little uprising of Duplicants anywhere in the world has taken over as the story of the day."

"Well whether you like it or not it's going to affect you."

"How? What do you mean?"

"Bram wants you to go to Holland."

"I'm not Don Quixote, Cervantes has no holds on me and I'm not interested in poking my lance at windmills."

"You never poke Niner. But to be serious, Bram wants you to help him out."

"Help him out with what."

"With the Duplicants. He feels you can talk to them on their level since you are one yourself."

"Impossible. He just wants to get me away from you; he's planning something ugly…"

"Bram would never do that to me. He has always looked out for my welfare…"

"I smell something else brewing this time."

"You have no choice in the matter."

"If it were some other place, maybe. But I can't go to Holland; you know I'm weather dependent; I'll have hang-ups, periods of despondency, seasonal moods. It rains over there all the time. When it's not raining, it's overcast. I need to see the sun every day. I like it here in Santa Barbara."

"Nonsense! Holland is mostly below sea level, the change in atmospheric pressure will do you good. And the people are great conversationalists, you'll probably fall in love with a Duplicant."

"I don't want to go anywhere without you. I wasn't fabricated for that purpose.

I'm designed to be your companion, not your husband's. If you say you don't want me to do this my understanding is I don't have to."

Lydia's brow furrows, she is putting her thoughts in order, and then she does her thing. She shifts her stance, rolls her hip provocatively, and leans at an angle while she contemplates her answer.

"It's not forever, only for a few months. Please Vladg, go for me. He can make my life miserable if you don't go and I can't leave my practice at the moment. I've got two very sick dogs, one with diabetes that is going blind and the other with a lymphoma that I am treating."

"But who is going to be with you? I'll be worried as hell, you being alone…"

"I won't be alone. Bram is sending me a protégé of his, a girl named Phoenix Winthrop. Apparently she wants to become a veterinary assistant and will be apprenticed to me. Bram arranged the whole thing."

"I don't trust it…"

"You mean you don't trust Bram?"

"Have it your way."

"That's silly. I've taken care of myself for more years than you know and nothing violent has ever happened to me."

"Is that a hint of some sort? It's the umpteenth time you've said something mysterious about your age like that."

"I don't want to go into it right now. Someday I will tell you. The timing is off at the moment."

"So you're going to leave me in the dark. Are you already a thirty something pretending to be younger? Is that it?"

Lydia giggles like a little girl who has just been handed a surprise lollipop.

"Something like that," she says, then she goes on in a more businesslike manner.

"Listen Vladg, this is important. I've booked you on a Sub-Orb-Flight to Holland from Los Angeles…"

"Why do I have to fly sub-orbital? I don't care how long it takes…"

"But Bram does. Time is of the essence."

"Isn't that dangerous, getting so close to escape velocity, suppose the rocket-plane leaves the atmosphere; that happens now and then. You'll be without a companion forever."

"I can always buy another one, you're insured you know."

"That's heartless…"

"I was just trying to make you feel a little bit of sympathy for what the Dutch Duplicants are going through. Like I said there's a female Duplicant over there named Hikey van something or other, one of those unpronounceable Dutch surnames. She is fighting for your civil rights. You may not know it, but the Royaals are very closely aligned with the Sextus in their makeup. You should support them. Have you no solidarity?"

"I'm not political, you know that. I wasn't programmed that way."

"Not a valid argument. When it serves your purpose you admit that you have learned a great deal from me and other humans for which you had not been programmed. Now when it comes to a class conscious effort on your part you claim lack of programming. That doesn't compute."

"Oh, all right. Maybe you have a point, but when I said I learned a lot from you it was mostly sexual…"

"Mostly, but not all. And that Bulgarian Ambassador, you said you learned a lot from him as well, on how different cultures run their governments and such."

"Okay, OK. You win. When do I have to go?"

"As soon as Phoenix gets here…"

"When will that be?"

"She's coming on a Delta-Am flight tomorrow. I've got the flight number right here somewhere," …she digs through a gigantic purse, searching, finally comes up with a slip of paper on which she has written the number.

"The idea is for me to drop you off at the Sub-Orb after we pick up Phoenix. That way you'll get a good look at her and be able to let me know what you think. If you don't get good vibes, I'll not ask her to stay with me. She'll have to find a place of her own."

"And if she's ok?"

"Then she can have your room for a time. Santa Barbara is not the easiest place for a young girl to find a decent apartment. You don't mind do you, I mean her being in your room."

"I've got mixed feelings about that. When I come back from Holland I don't want to see my room all messed up with female junk all over the place."

"I'll see that she leaves it spic and span…sometimes you sound quite dowdy, you know that Vladg?"

"Look at it this way Lydia, my room is all I've got; it becomes relatively more important to me than it would to a human who has so many luxurious things. After all, you were just talking about Duplicants as a class, well what about the individual, me for instance. I'm not only getting tossed out of the house, losing my room to an unknown female who'll probably leave her dirty linen hanging from the bathroom door, but getting sent off to a land where I don't even know the lingo to be ordered about by a man who doesn't happen to like me."

"He likes you well enough. If he didn't, you wouldn't have been allowed to be my companion, so there."

"Do I have to pack tonight?"

"Whenever. As long as you're ready to leave early tomorrow. The drive will take us an hour and a half to LAX, then parking and so forth. You'll need to bring your yellow card for identification as a Duplicant; otherwise they won't let you on an international flight."

"This is all very sudden for me. Don't we even get a finale before I go?"

"Of course. That will never change. Bring the J.D. and we'll do fun and games."

"That's not very romantic for my state of mind. I don't need a nipple programmed squirt; I need an electronic renaissance."

Now Lydia realizes that she had sounded too shallow, too harsh.

"Renaissance? I'll give you an electronic resurrection! So there."

She stands on her toes, lightly presses her pelvis to Vladg's groin. It is a subtle but meaningful move. "I feel in my heart a wicked burning desire to have you close," she whispers into his ear. "Please come and enter me, Niner."

Vladg lowers his massive shoulders, encircles his arms around her slim waist and holds her tight.

"You mean it? You're not spoofing; you really want to make love with me, to feel my warmth mixing with yours, your bod against mine?"

"Of course, two dissimilar creatures such as we need a dollop of romance in their lovemaking. And believe me it shall not be for the last time."

"Okay, now I feel better about it. I'll fix up a batch of cocktails. Wear that satin negligee I like and I'll rip it off for you."

"You got it. Don't make me wait too long. I want to run a sex marathon."

Chapter X

Holland: Bram and Vladg

At LAX, Vladg and Lydia picked up Phoenix, and after introductions they decided there was just enough time for a short coffee klatch before his flight took off.

Bram had told Lydia that Phoenix was a convert, but had he not done so she would have recognized it immediately in any case. The scent of her sisterhood was too strong for Lydia to miss. Bram had purposely neglected to mention that Phoenix was pregnant, and Lydia did not have enough wolfishness in her to detect that Phoenix was carrying.

Vladg looked at her differently.

To Vladg, Phoenix certainly appeared to be stacked. She was shapely in all the right places, voluptuous every which way, in legs, mouth, hips and lips. The middle of her upper lip unfurled and protruded a little bit forward, making it attractively pouty. But he noticed right off that her complexion was sallow, her ultra-blue eyes saddened by a deep sorrow. Her gaze did not meet his eye-to-eye; rather it was cast slightly off, as if she was only half looking at him, giving but a part of herself to the conversation.

Vladg asked Phoenix all about her sub-orb trip, how the gravitational changes affected her, was she frightened of leaving the earth's atmosphere, did she think she would suffer from rocket-lag? He is about to go on when Lydia sees that Phoenix is overwhelmed by the questioning. She interrupts to say, "Vladg I've brought you a sedative from the office. It will take down your fear of flying. I only use this dose for large dogs, so it should work perfectly for you."

"How large?"

"Toy poodle size," she says with one of her sardonic grins and now Phoenix breaks out in a short gutter laugh in spite of her funk, as Vladg swallows the pill.

Her laugh makes Vladg feel better about the girl. He gives Lydia a prearranged signal which means he feels Phoenix is ok, that she is a genuine person, trustful enough to stay in his room. Lydia returns a nod of agreement and then it is time for Vladg to go over to the International gate for his Sub-Orb trip.

∞

At Schiphol, while waiting to meet Vladg, Bram appeared extraordinarily human, his brown eyes calm, his expression leanly composed. Not a wrinkle of agitation was visible on his face yet he had mixed feelings, somewhat sullen, somewhat agreeable. He left his seat and went over to the kiosk where every major newspaper of the world was displayed on the screens located at the front and sides of the kiosk, their projections appearing and disappearing at ten second intervals. Inside the kiosk a Basisch III with a sweet sounding voice served the customers. In the middle of her forehead she was adorned with a tiny LED light, glowing red, reminding Bram of an Indian princess.

"I am DiTA-248, your Data instant Transfer Assistant. Please place your Pass-Card on the Recordo-pad. Bram did so and as soon as the LED light on her forehead turned to green she said, "The price is standardized, all the newspapers cost the same. One New Euro each will be deducted from your Pass-Card. Which papers do you wish to purchase?"

Bram ordered Pravda and Het Parool, neither of which he could read or understand.

Now DiTA pressed the correct buttons from an index list inside her station and transferred the screens of his selected newspapers such that their titles, main headline and today's date were displayed directly in front of him.

"Please hold the scanner end of your hand held instrument in front of each screen for one or two seconds. Your choices will be automatically beamed to you. If you are visually impaired, I can enlarge the fonts."

Bram said the fonts were fine, no change necessary, followed her instructions to the letter and received the beamed newspapers into his T-cell. Then he went back over to his spot and extended his T-cell screen to a more preferred size, pressed the translation button, selected English and started to read. He was just getting interested in the uprising of Dutch Duplicants in Amsterdam and Moscow when he got a whiff of something disagreeable from a toddler passing by and his mind drifted off.

Before aircraft became nuclear, the gassy atmosphere from jet fuel at airports would permeate his nostrils and his nasal sinuses, depriving him of much of his vampire powers. That part of the 'old life' he did not miss. But now his thumb bothered him. It was still numb, yet prickly at times, the distal end bluish with very little feel to it, so he had to learn to be careful, how to hold his coffee cup and such.

Then too, he was miffed that his Oneonta plans had to be postponed until he could get back to the States. On the other hand, he wanted to see what the gripes were over here. Perhaps he might integrate the protesting Duplicant's into his grand plan if he should propose a mutual benefit, a symbiosis of sorts.

He watched carefully as the Boeing Sub-Orb landed smoothly on the nine-thousand-foot landing strip, one of the longest in Europe. Even with the reversed thrust of the rocket engines the runway length required to meet all safety contingencies of weather and mechanical problems made it prohibitive for many airfields to handle the Sub-Orb spaceship. Not a problem for KLM on this issue, they were able to influence the powers that be and buy up additional Dutch land as necessary without causing much of a political hassle from the people.

According to what he was reading, the situation was different when it came to Duplicants' civil rights. At the moment the highly articulate Royaal named Hikey van Westerveld wanted to run for parliament. She was campaigning to get equal opportunity rights for all Duplicants, both Basisch and Royaals; the entire country was divided on this issue.

Bram abandoned these thoughts to greet Vladg who was just now emerging from the tunnel. Vladg was nervous in that he didn't know precisely how to deal with Bram. Should he act as an inferior, as a peer, as a colleague? Just what should his demeanor be?

"Any problems on the flight?"

"No, your wife fed me a sedative before I left and it took the edge off. Actually, I kind of enjoyed the flight, you go up, then you come down, that's about it. The G's keep changing, but the automatic gravitational systems did their job, I didn't feel a thing."

"Yes, I thought the same. Well let's get your baggage and get going to Amersfoort. You don't mind driving do you? I'm not a very good driver and the Dutch are wild, so it would be a relief to me if you took over."

This attitude appealed to Vladg. It might set the bar for the rest of the trip. Bram wasn't talking down to him as he did in Santa Barbara when he was ordered to be the chauffeur, now he was asking more man to man. Of course, Bram was a member of the diplomatic corps, knew how to butter things up when necessary, but even so, it made Vladg feel more secure at the outset.

"I don't mind driving," Vladg says, "but I was talking to this Dutchy lady on the plane and she told me there is a monorail straight from the airport to Amersfoort, why don't we take that?"

"Because we will need a car in any case. Somehow we have to get in touch with this Hikey van Westerveld and she moves around a good deal."

"Why does she have a surname and I don't," Vladg blurt out.

This is an item that has haunted him for years, but he had never nerve enough to ask until now.

Bram is cool with his answer.

"The Dutch are gluttonous with names. It's peculiar to them. Some of them even have three or more middle names. I don't know why. It's got something to do with their history, pride perhaps. We can call you Vladimir Alucard over here if you wish, that's the formal name on your yellow card."

"That would be nice," Vladg says. Now he is sure that Bram has an interest in buttering him up.

They walk over to the mid-air baggage carousel to claim their luggage. There, out of habit, all the Dutch travelers look upward to find their suspended bags. All this is unnecessary as a Basisch III is employed as a baggage retriever. He is similar in many respects to George, except that he has an electronic eye flicker and wields an antigravity tractor-beam wand. He asks Vladg politely for his bag ID sensor which is designed to match his bags and no one else's. Vladg hands over the metallic alloy to the Duplicant who clicks once and one of Vladg's bags begins to fall like a dive bomber nearly to the floor, when it is grasped and slowed down by the luminous photon-molecules of the tractor beam. Then, concentrating intensely but with infinite care, the Basisch very adroitly swishes the beam toward Vladg and with the skill of a magician gently steers the bag right into his outstretched hand. Now, very relaxed, he clicks the sensor two times and the second bag is retrieved in the same manner.

"Sounds like castanets," Vladg says.

No one comments.

The Basisch returns the sensor to Vladg who wants to know if it can be reused on the return trip.

"No sir. Next time around they will discard the receptor attached to your bags and give you a wholly new initiator. You may certainly keep the other for a souvenir if you wish."

Vladg nods his thanks, tries to give him a tip but the Basisch says:

"Oh no, we are not allowed to handle money, no currency of any kind. It's a Dutch law."

"Does Ms van Westerveld intend to appeal that law if she makes it to Parliament?" Bram asks, catching the Basisch off guard.

The baggage Duplicant, obviously frightened, looks dumbfounded at Bram.

"We are not allowed to comment on politics," he blurts out, then hurriedly runs over to the next patron.

"Boy was he ever glad to get away from us," Vladg says to Bram.

"Yes, just so," Bram says.

Now they walk a short distance, each carrying one bag, to where Bram had parked in the rent-a-car lot. The automobile itself is called a DAF, an old name that has been revived. Ever since the battery problem had been solved by nuclear fusion, Holland started remanufacturing cars. Now it was giving Germany a run for its money as it had a better reputation in foreign countries than the Germans whose tourists were particularly scornful of anything and everything non-Teutonic.

They stow the bags in the trunk, Bram gets out a map that the rental agency had provided and they head out first on Hwy. A4 and rather quickly change over to Hwy. A10.

"I'll let you know when you have to turn on to A1 and after that it's all A28 and right in to Amersfoort on Kromme Street.

Most of the travelers from Schiphol had taken the monorail, but even so the traffic is heavy. Vladg has to be careful as the Dutch drivers are pulling NASCAR stunts to the left and right of him although they are only supposed to pass on the left according to the ANWB which is the counterpart to the American AAA.

"To hell with this," Vladg says, throwing the Netherlands' driving manual to the rear of the car.

"I don't want to say I told you so, but I told you so," Bram says.

Vladg grunts, goes into action, weaving in and out of the flow of traffic and giving the other drivers the finger as he passes them by. After a time his rage is dissipated and he slows down enough to renew his conversation with Bram.

"Why are we going to Amersfoort rather than Amsterdam?" he asks, getting his nerve up.

"Duplicants aren't manufactured in Amsterdam, only in Amersfoort which has a great production history for a variety of products."

"So where are we staying?" Now that Bram has answered his first question Vladg has gained confidence that he can speak to him on a more or less equal basis.

"The hotel is called the Golden Tulip; address is Rotunda 9. They put the number at the end over here. It's situated on the south-east side of the town, near the zoo. More importantly, it's right close to the van den Valk Duplo factory which is what they call Duplicants in Amersfoort."

"Is it a four star?"

"Supposed to be, but who knows. What Europe calls a four is only a three or less in the States. Let's just hope the beds are comfortable…. here, turn here onto Kromme Street, then we'll ask directions to the Golden Tulip."

Vladg slows down, comes to a stop, asks the first pedestrian he sees for directions. All he gets is blank looks. The man grumbles, steps off and moves away as quickly as he can.

"I thought all the Dutch spoke English?"

"Maybe he's just unfriendly."

Bram stops a tubby lady carrying groceries, cheese and bread sticking out of a wicker tote bag. Her English is poor but she knows the streets and with gestures and pointing Bram gets the general idea.

"Take a left here, then see that roundabout, it's a traffic circle they call a circuit over here, bear right, that's it, now go south, ok, there, that's the Guesthouse lane…"

"It says Gasthuislaan…"

"Same thing. Ok, now make a sharp right and there see it that's the hotel, the Golden Tulip."

They park in front of the hotel and a Basisch comes to help with bags. He is an exact duplicate of the one at the airport except he does not have a wand, but does have that electronic flicker in his eyes.

At the registration desk the reception clerk asks to see passports.

Bram hands his over, a special consulate passport and the clerk is impressed, but when Vladg shows his yellow card the clerk says:

"I'm afraid you can't stay here. We do not allow Duplicants as guests in the hotel."

"This Duplicant is with me, under my strict surveillance. In the States he can stay at any hotel as long as he is accompanied by a human."

The clerk's attitude is completely stoic. He is one of those people who is muscular enough, but has no two matching parts to his expressions. His mouth seems to go one way, the wrinkles in his forehead another and he squishes up his nose at odd times when he speaks.

"This is not the States sir. You are in Holland and that is our rule." Then in a flash of Dutch equanimity he says: "Of course, if he wishes to stay in the basement with the Basisch Units who are employed here, that is another option. However, the employees themselves will have to make that decision as I see that this unit has human form so he must be a Royaal and Basisch units do not take well to Royaals at the moment."

"This is preposterous," Bram says. "I am a special envoy of the State Department."

"That may be sir. You are certainly free to make a different choice of hotel," the clerk says, obviously enjoying every bit of the power scene. "Do you want the Unit here to take your bags back out to the car."

"No give us a few moments."

Bram crooks his arm into Vladg's, hustles him over to a seating area in the lobby.

"I'll be flipped," Vladg says. "This is my first experience with Duplicant prejudice. I guess I've been living a surreal life in Santa Barbara."

"What do you want to do? I know this is awful for you, but staying at this hotel is very convenient for me, to be near the van den Valk Factory. You see Vladg, I didn't tell you, but my last briefing, just before I left D.C., was not only with my boss, Mr. Gregoriev but also with a high ranking official in the Pentagon. This mission has military implications."

Vladg is brooding, but he is a realist, knows that it would be better if he were able to stay here in the basement with the Basisch Duplos.

"Let me talk to that Basic over there, the one that is still with our bags."

"Give it a go. I'll try again with the registration clerk, see if I can chat him up a bit."

"Lots of luck."

Vladg goes back to the Basic.

"Do you speak English."

"Just tourist English. I am limited to five-hundred words."

That's probably enough. I need a room and the day clerk over there won't allow me into the hotel..."

"Yes, I heard..."

"Can you find a place for me in the basement?"

"You can stay with me. Central shuts me down at five P.M. You will have the room entirely to yourself in the evening."

Vladg is very grateful, tries to shake hands with the Basic but notices that his eyes flash over to the room clerk, takes the warning, and withdraws his hand.

"Thank you," he says, motioning to Bram to join them.

"Do you have a name? Vladg asks.

"I am called Jan 237. All the Basics in this type of employment are called Jan plus an added number. That way the Central Monitoring System can more easily keep track of our whereabouts,"

"Is that what the eye-flicker is."

"Yes, but hush. They don't want us to talk about such things."

Bram joins them and learns that Vladg has negotiated a room.

They head back over to Registration, but have to wait again as the clerk is now busy with another guest, a good looking British woman, who smiles flirtatiously at Vladg.

"I must say you have gorgeous shoulders," she says, carrying on a bit.

"Madam, this humanoid is a Duplicant. We do not allow verbal exchanges of that sort in this hotel."

"Well fuck you, the lady says, traipsing off on her high heels. I'll go elsewhere! Come on Jasper," she says to her spouse, a dapper little man who obediently follows her out of the lobby.

Both Bram and Vladg chuckle inwardly. They do not wish to prolong the issue.

"We have made arrangements for my associate to stay with the Basic here."

The clerk makes a face, but acknowledges the resolution to the problem.

"Jan take this man up to 510. That is a very nice corner room," the clerk says. "It has a deep tub and a wide shower, the bed is ample and not unduly soft and you will, of course, receive a continental breakfast every morning if you so wish. There are three flat TV's in the room, one for each section of the globe, and you can program them for whatever languages you wish. All the phones are user friendly to all computers everywhere in the world and they will appear holographically following your instructions."

"Sounds adequate."

"However, I must warn you that all conversations between you and the Duplo Unit you call an associate must take place in the lobby, certainly in an open area that can be filmed. He is not allowed to go up to your room and you are certainly not allowed to go to the basement."

Bram is about to ask if this is a hotel or a prison, when he thinks the better of it, makes no reply.

"And the charge for my associate's digging's in the basement."

"No charge. We would be libel if we invoiced a Duplo for a room."

"So that's the reason."

"Yes, it is not out of the goodness of my heart, believe me. And he will have to eat outside the hotel of course."

"Of course," Bram says.

"I'll wait here till you come back," Vladg says to Jan, who is busy with Bram's bags.

Jan simply nods. He is intent on not expressing any emotion that might be construed by the clerk as a punishable offense.

"I'll call your tele-cell as soon as we both get settled," Bram says.

Vladg, rather deflated, nods in agreement.

∞

In their basement room, Vladg and Jan 237 are joined by Jan 276 and Jan 387. They are out of their hotel uniforms, but their clothes look frayed and seedy and, to Vladg's sensitive nose, smell of cleaning fluid.

Vladg sees at once that 276 and 387 are miles apart in their construction. 276 is almost feminine in appearance whereas 387 is very solidly built, more like a center forward in soccer, lithe and fast but powerful. He also wears a tool belt and many of the implements look razor sharp, obviously various sets of knives for different purposes.

Jan 237 motions everyone over to the microwave, turns it on to its highest power, points to his eyes. Vladg nods that he gets it. They all gather around the microwave to talk.

"We have never met an American Sextus before," 276 says. "Are you as stuck-up as the Royaals over here?"

"Well you have me at a disadvantage. I've not met a Dutch Royaal as yet; in fact you three and the Jan at the baggage claim at Schiphol are the first Basisch I've had the privilege to meet up with."

The way Vladg has answered, his tone and choice of words, are obviously pleasing to 276 and 387; they especially like Vladg's western twang when he says *'meet up with'*. They exchange glances which indicate they find Vladg *sympathiek.*

"Do the Sextus's in America think they are as *edel* as the Royaal's over here is what 276 is asking?"

"I don't know *edel*, "Vladg says.

"Tulip means well bred," 387 says.

"Who is Tulip?"

"That's what Jan 387 calls me," 276 says.

"Oh, I see. Well on that other, yes, we all have a few little extras that make us a bit edel, I guess you could say that. But that doesn't make us bad Duplos."

Now all three snicker, since they catch on to the analogy.

"I know of one extra I'd like to have!" Tulip exclaims.

"What's that?"

"A vagina. Look at my pelvis. Compare it to 237's. See mine is rounder and wider, his is longer and narrower."

Vladg has been quiet on this topic, but he does check out what *she* is saying on the pelvic structure; imagines if she wore a miniskirt her legs would look shapely. 'On the other hand', he thinks, 'she has no chest development whatsoever'.

Tulip goes on: "I'm sure they meant me to be a woman because I'm even numbered…"

"What's that got to do with it?"

Now Jan 387 explains. "You see Vladg, all the odd numbered Jans are masculine and the even numbered are meant to be more feminine…"

"Meant to be is right, Tulip interrupts, but to save on costs they didn't provide me with a genital apparatus. Now I have to go through life like this, neutered, no gender definition whatsoever."

"How about lipstick, blush, earrings, high heels and a head of hair, don't you want those too?" 237 asks.

"Sure, but Central would never let me be seen in public like that. A vagina they can't see."

"That makes sense," 237 says.

"The only feminine things I own are my maid's smock and cloth bonnet with the ribbons that fasten under my chin, they're provided by Central you see. Would you like to see my bonnet?"

"Sure," Vladg says. She takes it out, hands it to him. Her smile is affectionate, but suppressed; it is the best she can do.

Vladg fumbles with it, turns it admiringly this way and that, fondles the fabric, caressing it gently between his thumb and first two fingers, ties the ribbons together and returns the cap to her.

"Nice," he says, learning at once what it takes to please a woman at certain times.

Now he chooses to change the subject.

"I note that you wear a tool belt," he says to 387."

"Yes, I'm assigned to repair the entire tile and wallpaper work in the hotel, but when there is none to do I double in security, usually when I'm on the night shift."

"That is one of the issues we want Hikey to take up for us," 237 says. "Central has us doubling and tripling on jobs…"

"Yes, I do seamstress work," Tulip interrupts. "I can sew anything you put in front of me better than anyone else, but they have me helping in the kitchen and in the garden, tending tulips and geraniums when there is no other work to do. Sometimes they shift me without notice to graveyard to mop floors, clean vacant rooms, whatever needs getting done."

"Isn't that dangerous? Traipsing floors late at night with drunken tourists in the halls?"

"It can be pretty eerie," Tulip says, "but so far nothing wicked has ever happened to me."

"You hit the nail on the head," 387 says to Vladg. "I have been concerned for her, not being a regular day maid, subbing as she does at night."

Some sort of expression, akin to a feeling of ardor flashes between Jan 387 and Tulip 276.

Vladg notices this, wonders how these poor creatures, with their anatomic and sensory limitations can possibly make it in such a complicated world.

"If we could belong to the union, become members, we would have job descriptions. Central couldn't just order us willy-nilly to do what they needed done." This from 237.

"Tell me what you know about this Royaal that's fighting for you guys."

"You know we call Hikey 3-D."

"Why, has she been in a movie or something like that?"

"Heaven's no. Holland would never allow that, even if she is a Royaal. No, she is the Duplo-Dutch-Duchess, three D's, get it."

"Heh, that's pretty good English. I thought your range was limited to five-hundred words of tourist lingo."

"It was, that's the amount they put in our memory banks to deal with travelers and customers, but we seem to have learned on our own, something Central didn't think we could do."

"You should be proud of that."

Tulip 276 tries to smile, but her facial expressions are restricted by the limitations of her muscle tone.

"Can the Basics in America vote?" 387 asks quite suddenly.

"Not yet, neither can the Sextus. A bill passed the House but went dead in the Senate."

"We don't understand '*dead in the Senate*'."

"It just means the Senate hasn't yet acted upon it, but it will happen in time."

"And can your Basics get a room in a hotel? Can they eat in a dining room together with humans?"

"Oh yes, we don't have any of that nonsense. However, Basics can not fly on an Air-Scoot or Shuttle; yet Sextus can, so there are some differences. Sextus' still don't have voting rights; we are not citizens you see. And, of course we can not own private property."

"But otherwise a Basic can handle money, can purchase anything he wants?"

"Sure. Duplicants are big consumers. Sometimes I wish they didn't spend their money so frivolously, but it's a free enterprise system."

"Yes, that would be nice. I would like to buy things, just to feel what its like," 276 says.

"I thought the Dutch were called the Chinese of Europe. I'm sure the economy here would benefit if they allowed you to handle currency."

"We don't get paid at all. Everything we have is in the form of goods, hand-me-down clothing and food and shelter of course. We are constantly cleaning up with spot remover. "

"The nourishment is terrible. Mostly blood worst. I hate it. We have to magnetron all our food."

"What's a magnetron?"

"Same as a microwave. We only get enough food to support our minimal energy requirements."

"Really? That's it? That's all you get?"

"Yes. That's why Hikey van Westerveld is fighting for us. She is a very decent Duplo for a Royaal."

"I've heard. I'd like to meet her."

"She is in The Hague at the moment. Very difficult to get to see her no matter who you are."

"Well if the grapevine…"

"Grapevine doesn't compute…"

"Same as word of mouth. If you know how messages get to her, let it be known that the envoy I'm with, Mr. Alucard, wants to speak with her urgently."

"Certainly," 387 says. "We'll see what can be arranged."

Vladg's impression is that 387 appears to be the spokesperson for the group. He has more style, appears unafraid and is definitely outspoken.

Of a sudden, they all move away from the microwave, 237 shuts it off, Jan 387 and Tulip 276 scurry out of the room together.

"What's happening?" Vladg asks.

"It's almost five o'clock. Better to be shut down in your own room. Anyway they might get suspicious if the microwave is on for too long a time. I'm going over to the pad on the other side of the room to lie down. The place is yours to do with what you will as soon as they turn me off."

"When do you get turned on again?"

"I'm on a twelve on, twelve off shift. Promptly at five a.m. I will take up my duties as soon as I receive instructions."

"Tell me Jan, do you dream?"

"Only of duplo sheep," he says with a chuckle and then he goes over to the spot he had designated and in a few seconds he is immobilized.

∞

As soon as he was settled, emptied his suitcases and put away his clothes Bram had called the Consulate in The Hague. It was still well before five o'clock and he had no trouble whatsoever making contact. Actually, prior to this, he had spent three days in Amsterdam that he didn't want Vladg to know about. There he had met with some rather high ranking personnel at the embassy, both from the State Department and the Pentagon; they were interested in knowing more about the little uprising that Ms van Westerveld was staging and whether there were any international implications of interest to the United States. They had paved the way for him with their counterparts in The Hague.

Accordingly, he now had a time set up to meet with her at the embassy in The Hague, but this conflicted with his own visit to the van den Valk factory. He was wary of placing this responsibility alone on Vladg, who aside from his Sub-Orb trip had never traveled alone, but there was nothing else for it.

He calls Vladg on the Tele-Cell, pulls out and unfolds the screen to enlarge the image.

"Hello Vladimir, are you settling in down there all right?"

"Yes Bram, it is very Spartan, neat and clean, but not to my taste. For me a morgue would do better."

"Come now. It can't be that bad. Anyway you won't be there more than one or two nights. Can you manage that?"

"Sure, but what do you mean?" That desk clerk's bigotry was cast in stone. He'll never change his mind."

"Just don't agitate him. I've learned that he has a room right here on the third floor. Tomorrow, if he talks to you at all, be discreet. I intend to draw him over to our way of thinking."

"How are you going to do that?"

"Oh, its a little technique I use called the *'spell that quells'*. Never fails once I've cultivated a friendship."

Vladg doesn't get it, but he remembers the spell Bram had cast over him in Santa Barbara. He decides not to press the issue.

"Well, if you can get me a room, great. Whatever works. I can take a coupla nights here. No problem. I guess my simile to a morgue was uncalled for, but the truth is I am morbidly saddened. I don't know how the Basics here can deal with all the bullshit thrown at them."

"Well I'm glad to hear that you are interested in their plight as I have an assignment for you."

"An assignment?"

"Yes, tomorrow morning I will drive you to the Railroad Station here. I want you to go to the embassy at The Hague and meet with Ms van Westerveld. I've just finished talking to the people there and everything is arranged for your meeting with her at ten a.m. tomorrow."

"Do you think I can handle that?"

"You're the only one who possibly could. My understanding is she doesn't trust humans and is looking forward to a meet with an American Sextus. You will be a first for her as well."

"You know the Basics call her 3-D."

"What's that mean?"

"I'll tell you tomorrow. I assume we'll have breakfast at the Central Station."

"Yes, I had the same idea. I'll forego the Continental Breakfast they have for me here. Plan to meet me outside the hotel at around seven."

"Sounds good."

"Goodnight then and sleep well."

"You the same Bram, pleasant dreams."

Bram knew he would dream of Phoenix.

Chapter XI

Phoenix and Lydia

Phoenix and Lydia were having lunch on Stearns Wharf at Moby Dick's restaurant. Phoenix didn't have much of an appetite, poked at her food, but Lydia was eating up a storm, sautéed grouper with a Greek salad full of Feta and Kalamata olives plus freshly baked French bread, which she dipped into the sauce and munched on slowly as she listened to Phoenix's explanation of who the man was that charged into the office and proceeded to ask all the abrupt questions.

"It's my mom and dad, they were worried about me and that man who upset everyone the other day is a private detective from Goleta. They hired him to see if I was all right and, to be candid about it, to check you out, it's as simple as that. I meant to tell you, I was a little put off myself, I mean I know mom and dad are well intentioned, but now I'm in my twenties I think they might be a bit overprotective."

"Well I too was worried; the way he acted I thought it might be a police matter…"

"No, he's not police at all, strictly private. They just needed to know that you were what they call 'legitimate'. Mom and dad are not threatening people, not like your husband Bram, if I may say so. They just wanted to know I was ok, and that's all. As it turned out the man's a moron, pompous to boot, acting that way in front of the staff, asking all those questions about you, hinting you were a lesbian and such.

"Well lesbianism is not a crime in my book, but that's not what upset me. I thought you were angry with me for some reason and called the police."

"Just the opposite, it's not anger I feel toward you, it's more like a surrogate sister. I've learned from you that even though I am a vampire I can carry on a normal life style. You do, so I can. That means a lot to me."

"I'm glad to hear you say that."

"You know, I've talked to you about this before, Feeby and I have always been so close, I've never really been away from her till now, and I never thought that anyone could replace her, not saying that you fill the bill, but you come closer than any one else on earth. Bram says we are sisters of a sort following my conversion, and that's part of it, sure, but the rest is you, and that's why I was so sorry when that goon of a private eye came around with all of his charged up questions. So this is kinda-sorta a last-minute explanation that I should've given you beforehand, when I first knew of my parents' plan."

"What exactly do you mean by last-minute?"

"I have to get away. I plan on going to live with my parents in Nebraska!"

"I'd be horrified to lose you now. There's so much to work out, so much between us? Why the rush home? We must make time for each other."

"That is so…"

"And Bram led me to believe that you really wanted to become a veterinarian's assistant? You've already made a good start."

"Yes, thank you for saying that. I've been in need of compliments lately; my self-confidence has been shot to hell."

"Then stay here, you are just regaining your health…"

"I'd very much like to stay. In your way you've been very kind."

"Well then?"

Phoenix giggles.

"The most important reason for staying is the walk-in closet you've provided, something Feeby and I didn't have in our one bedroom in Manhattan. Now I've got plenty of room for all my clothes. It's majestic."

Lydia bursts into a spasmodic jelly laugh; she enjoys Phoenix's giddy style.

Phoenix waits till Lydia settles down, then she starts up again in a less frivolous vein.

"Really the problem is your husband Bram, he thinks I'm PG and if I am he wants me to do something awful to you and also to my twin sister, things I could never bring myself to do. So I thought living away from both of you would be a protection for all of us."

"I'm familiar with those rituals. Bram exaggerates. It doesn't mean that you have to carry them out. More importantly, I know you don't think so, but what if you are pregnant?"

Phoenix is not prepared to answer; it is a charged question. She takes her time, sips on her wine. She remembers the night with Bram when she was certain she was pregnant.

The waiter returns, hovers, Lydia suspects he is an eavesdropper, shoos him away.

"In that case I wouldn't have to go back home. It's bad enough that I bungled things in New York, but if I went back home PG my father would fall apart. He thinks Feeby and I are angels as far as sex is concerned. My mother knows better, she was pretty wild as a teenager herself, in that old school of coke and meth. But that was ancient times. She's totally straight now, has been ever since she gave birth to us and my younger brother Phillip."

"Well the New York part is a side issue. We can always deal with that later when the time is right. The main thing to concern us is the pregnancy, how to deal with it in terms of your parents, with Bram and your sister…"

"So what do we do?"

"We make an appointment for you with my OB-Gyn. If she says you are PG will you accept that?"

"I don't know for sure, but I have missed two periods now, so something's wrong. Still I have missed periods like this before in college when I was nervous about finals, or about a boyfriend who was cheating on me, you know those kinds of things. But yes this time I am baffled. You know what this signifies for us don't you?"

"For us? How do you mean for us?"

"Your husband is the only one that's been inside me in months. If I am pregnant, he's the father and that means the pregnancy applies to you indirectly as well, don't you see. He'll want you out of the way. He's told me the two ways that I can become totally human again. I've got to give him that; he was honest with me on this aspect when he didn't have to be. The first way is to give up my child to another Christian soul during the act of birth, while I am in labor, feeling all the pain. The second way means he has to die. I swore an oath to him that I would never betray him, but now I'm not sure. The third part has to do with you. If I wish to ascend to your status, to not be just a slave to Bram, I would have to kill you and also transform my sister into a vampire. I can do neither, especially now since we have been together in our sisterhood, I could never raise a hand against you. But the second way remains open to me, to betray him, and that I believe I could do, perhaps not alone, but with the right people, on religious grounds I might be able to do so. On the other hand I would be killing the father of my child; that would also be a tough decision, as they used to say, a Sophie's choice."

Hearing Phoenix go on like this was strange. A few minutes beforehand she had sounded so insecure, so lacking in self-esteem. Now she was firm and assertive. Lydia knew what this was like from her time in Ireland, trying to regulate an outflow of mingled emotions, multiple feelings, playing against each other, acting sober and solid when she was actually trying to control the wildness of her mind. She felt Phoenix was now going through something similar.

They finished eating and decided to walk along the wharf.

Lydia watched admiringly as Phoenix leaned her long Modigliani neck backward; saw how beautiful she looked with her straw sun visor, her blond hair pulled through the opening in the top, the brim encircled with a brightly colored silk sash and a half-veil that dropped over her forehead. Her light dress showed off the soft disappearance of her breasts and how the cotton fabric cloyed at the cleft in her derrière and clung tightly to the cheek lines of her full buns. At once she knew what a passionate man might feel toward a girl like this.

"Look," Lydia began, "I know how to handle Bram. Let me send him a hologram explaining things, that you want to go visit your parents, see what he says. Will you at least wait till he answers before you go?"

Phoenix thinks this over.

"All right, I'll wait one or two weeks, not longer."

"In the meantime we can get you to see my OB and then you'll know a lot more."

Phoenix is moved, gives Lydia a friendly cheek kiss.

"I don't want you to think I'm ungrateful. I really appreciate all that you are trying to do for me; it's just that the entire situation is so intense."

Lydia's cell goes off.

"Speaking of which we have to get back to the office for an emergency, that purebred cocker Spaniel is going to deliver at any moment and I think there's at least three in the oven."

Now it is Phoenix's turn to snicker; they take off their pumps, make a race out of it, dash for the car.

∞

H-mail from Lydia:

Dearest Bram,

I received your hologram telling me on no account am I to let Phoenix go up to Nebraska on her own. I am answering today as yesterday I couldn't write; things were so hectic at the office; I was overwhelmed with surgeries and deliveries. Now I am relaxed, sitting by the fire in the evening and have time to write. You know how damp and chilly it can get here on a foggy September evening.

First of all, you need not be overly concerned about Phoenix. She has agreed not to travel for the present. It's just that she wanted to spend some time in Nebraska with her parents. She has regained a beautiful skin color since you last saw her. She did have one untimely episode. While she was assisting me in the removal of a benign lesion from the left ear of a Doberman, she fainted dead away. She has also had a few episodes of vomiting in the morning hours so I am dead sure she is pregnant, suffering from morning sickness, but she gets adamant on the subject, saying that she has had two pregnancy tests and both were negative, so I don't know what more to say to her on this.

But, as I say, for the rest she is adjusting quite well to Santa Barbara. She is a quick learner and seems to enjoy the animals, although not their suffering as many of the dogs are quite ill at the moment, but I know you don't like to hear me talk about disease and dying so I shall change the subject.

We do take long walks on the beach and sometimes eat out at the fish restaurant situated at the end of the pier. I forget the name of it, but I think you know the one I mean. For the rest, we are very honest with each other, practically everything is all out between us. We have slept together, told all our secrets to one another and laughed and cried together. She has told me that you are the one who converted her, something you neglected to say straight out to me although you did mention that she was a vampire. I found this a bit strange because if she is indeed pregnant by you, then by the rituals that prevail she and I should be the fiercest enemies. So I will be waiting to hear from you on this.

In our strange world, age after age, haunting the living as we do, I have always understood your need for fresh youthful blood, but you have never, to my knowledge, sought sexual relief with a woman before. If this is so, you had no right to ask me to befriend Phoenix especially if she is pregnant. A new birth leaves little time to love the dead. My life may be simple and subordinate, but I still retain my imaginative dignities.

So please send me an H-mail with your explanation and also let me know when you are returning Vladg to me. By agreement he is my companion and our sexual honey is at least not between me and another human, so there.

As always I am yours, just uncertain of you at the moment,
Lydia

H-mail from Phoebe:

Hey Sis, howzit out there now that you're a California girl.

I just want you to know how much I miss you but I do understand that an apprenticeship to a veterinarian is something you want very much, there certainly was no future for you in being a receptionist to a dentist, and I am beginning to think the same way as my duties here are starting to bore me as well. It's just that I don't seem to have any career goals in mind that I care that much about. I guess I'm a bit ashamed to say it, but I had counted on marrying a man to whom I could devote my life, have children and be happy. You know the old fashioned idea of being useful to your husband that is such a downer in the minds of most of our friends. Oh well.

You'll never guess whom I'm dating. It's Josh, remember from that terrible night with the mirrors when George got half his face slashed away by that awful Bram, well since that time I felt so sorry for George that I followed all the work Josh and the others in his department did to repair him and then, after you asked about the movie date, one thing led to another and we started to hang out, first strictly as friends, but then he appeared so sincere and his eyes responded to mine. I mean this guy is really intelligent, and he is devoted to me, none of the other jocks I'd been dating are a patch on half his ass if you know what I mean. I don't think mom and dad would appreciate me saying things like that but sometimes profanity and slang seem to express my feelings better than all the correct phrasing they tried to instill in us.

Oh sis, I love you so. Do you think it would be all right if Josh and I sub-orbed to L.A. and air-scooted over to SB for a day or two. He wants to go out to the channel islands and teach me to SCUBA but I don't know if I've the nerve for that, maybe we could just do a little snorkeling first. I'm sorry to go motoring off at the mouth like this when the whole idea of coming out there is to be with you.

As far as Bram is concerned, I haven't heard a thing. I did ask Mr. Eiselman about him and at first he stared rather strangely at me, but then said that there had been no follow up as yet on the purchase, that the contract was on hold.

As far as the apartment goes, I am in a bit of a bind. I may have to pick up a roommate to make ends meet, but I've never lived with anyone else but you and don't know if I could do that. Josh wants to move in, and that would solve the financial end of things, but I don't think mom would like me doing that and for that matter I'm not sure I want to either. I always thought the first man I'd live with would be the man I marry, but there are so few first marriages that work nowadays I don't know what to do. Could use your advice on all this,

Exes and ohs and luv, luv luv,
Feeby

H-mail from Bram:
My dear Lydia,
Yes, you are right in almost all the things you say. I have been unfaithful to you by my involvement with Phoenix. But don't forget it's been years since you referred to me as your master. In the last few decades you have become more and more human, making me feel, at times, that you care more for your animals than you do for me. Perhaps that is overly sensitive on my part, yet that is the way I feel about our relationship at the moment.

Certainly you must admit that you have been barren, and I have often enough told you how important it is for me to have progeny. Only through the birth of a male child will we be able to continue the lineage of vampires in our sect that has such a proud and noble tradition. Our ascendency amongst the human element can only be achieved by our descendants, our children; everything depends on them. You have failed in this regard and for a long while I believed that the fault was mine. Now I know this to be untrue.

Yes, Phoenix is pregnant with my seed. And as you pointed out, the rites of ascendency, to be at my side as you were for so many years are indeed at play. However, I doubt that she has the will power to kill you in the appropriate manner befitting our species. Even so, I give you fair warning, should you try to harm her while her internment is at hand, I will personally see to it that you are put to death myself.

I have waited long enough for this child, and as you will be with her for the entire gestation period, she certainly will need all of your care. Soon she will no longer be able to deny her pregnancy as her bodily changes and then the kicking of the baby will force her to face reality. So here is my proposition. If you take good care of her, all my threats will be at an end. Also, please watch out for sleepwalking, as it is a well-known characteristic of vampires to sleepwalk during pregnancy.

If all goes well, I do wish you to be Anti-godmother to the baby. That is quite an honor and if you give assent I will forgive your haughtiness and accusations and forego revenge. This offer is in your best interest.

Another point. I do not begrudge you the sexual intimacies with Vladg you had so desired. Nor have I ever expressed a scintilla of jealousy in this regard. You must admit, unlike some Dhampire sickos in other vampire lines, I have never demanded the right to be present, to watch any of these sexual exhibitions of yours. Now, however, things have changed with me, and that means things will change for you. If indeed sleeping with Phoenix is a sexual activity on your part, I absolutely forbid it. I know that in the sisterhood, blood is sometimes exchanged between lovers, but this would give you some fetal blood from my child and that is a transgression, a violation of our laws.

As to Vladg's return, you should contact him yourself to see what he is up to.

Your Husband and Master,

Bram

H-mail from Phoenix:

Dearest Feeby,

God I miss you so. Sometimes I can't believe I'm out here, life is so different from New York, I really miss the hustle-bustle, something I thought I'd never say. But the sea is serene and the weather for the most part is pleasant, except that they have three different kinds of fog out here. I don't remember the specific names, but it can get damp and gloomy and Lydia's house is way up on a mountain. It has a hearth and we have a real wood fire of an evening. Lydia, as I told you on the tele-cell, is real nice, gentle and compassionate, a very talented veterinarian and I learn new stuff from her every day. The theory I need to learn is a bit hard on me at the moment as I seem to have a good deal of trouble trying to concentrate on my studies but the hands-on stuff I'm good at. Lydia says I have the knack for it and I was immensely pleased to get a compliment from her as my self-esteem has been pretty low lately.

I did have one fainting episode while I was assisting Lydia on a minor surgery, there wasn't much blood or anything like that, but I suddenly fainted dead away. Nothing was found wrong with me and it hasn't recurred since. But I've missed two periods in a row, and still don't think I'm pregnant as all the tests say the opposite. Lydia took me to her OB, a very nice and gentle woman I'd guess to be in her mid-fifties who also thinks I'm PG even tho the tests are all negative. So I am worried. I was going to ask you Feeb, are you getting any brown spots on your forehead? You know how we always get the same thing around the same time, well I have taken to wearing a half-veil which hangs from my hat over my forehead when we go out. It masks the spots. It's probably just the sun out here doing its thing, but I thought I'd ask.

On mom and dad I've decided not to make the trip I talked to you about on the cell. Ever since I had that fainting spell, I just feel that it would not be the smartest thing for me to do. And if I am PG and was in the air and something went wrong it would not be good for the baby either. Listen to me go on, as if I were a mother already and I'm not even sure I'm eating for two. Lydia has asked me to quit drinking wine and I've got into the habit of taking her advice, 'so there' as she says.

On Josh, I think it's wonderful. He's not really that nerdy and like you say he is sincere. You know, the jocks we've been dating were overrated. None of the ones I was close to, including that basketball giant, were that great. What was his name, oh yes, Rudy Windsor, he was so taken with himself and when we went out he got so much attention from fans asking for his autograph, and yet the Knicks are still in last place. And that's the way I felt with him too, like I was in last place. At least with Josh you will be first place in his mind. A man like Josh will never be unmindful of your needs, and what your joys and sorrows are. Rudy wanted me to be 'up' all the time and if I had even a slight bit of a downer he got on my case. And to be honest, even with that long cylinder between his legs, he wasn't that great in the sack either, too quick in his come and too selfish, tho I must say he was very athletic in bed, but sometimes I wasn't sure he cared one way or the other who he was with as long as he got off. I know this sounds utterly crude of me, but here in California they let it all hang out, and saying what you mean is closer to meaning what you say than in New York where they rationalize everything.

Yes, yes. Please come out, you'll love SB, it's very highly acculturated for a Southern California town, the architectural designs are interesting and varied and the food, while not meeting the standards of Manhattan, is fairly good as well, especially the variety of fish dishes. So please come, let me know about the brown spots,

Luv, luv, luv and miss you, miss you, miss you.

Feeny

Chapter XII

Hikey and Vladg

At the Central Railroad Station in Amersfoort, Vladg and Bram were having a breakfast of freshly baked croissants and strong coffee brewed from a mix of ground Indonesian and Brazilian beans.

"Good coffee."

"Yep," Vladg says, then hesitantly, "You know, Bram, I'm nervous. This train ride to The Hague will be my first."

"Not to worry; should be a pleasant journey. You pass easily as a human and no one on board is going to ask you for a passport. You have your Euro-Rail Pass don't you."

"Sure."

"Remember, Lydia and I have packed you with all the extras you need for domestic stress. If you start to sweat nervously your fragrance will settle you down and anyone sitting near you will be pleased. After all, the Dutch railway cars don't smell that good by themselves."

"Okay. I think I can manage the trip, but what happens when I get there? I've never been anywhere alone, with no one to meet me at my destination."

"Just take a cab to the American Embassy. They know you're coming and Hikey wants to meet you. I hear she is delaying her call for a work stoppage by the Basisch, at least temporarily."

"You're sure you can't come along, I thought it was urgent that you meet her as well."

"No I have to go to the ADD at the factory."

"What's the ADD?"

"The Advanced Design Division, it's similar to the one at Pyrell's, surely you must know that."

"Oh yes, I thought the letters might stand for something else over here."

"Understood. Let me know when you come back and I'll try to be here to meet you, if not take a taxi back to the hotel."

"All Right."

"Good luck. You'd better get going. Dutch trains leave on time."

Vladg took a deep breath, waved goodbye to Bram and hopped onboard. In a few minutes the train zoomed out of the station and Vladg felt the liberty of being on his own for the first time in his life. It was a double feeling, both exhilarating and nerve wracking.

∞

There were only two short stops. The next one was The Hague.

There was no trouble getting a taxi, everything was labeled clearly with icons enabling tourists to get around easily. Vladg followed the arrows to the exit and got in a short line, queuing up as the British say. A black Mercedes pulled up after a few minutes and he directed the cabbie to his destination.

At the embassy he was greeted warmly by the Vice-Consul and promptly ushered into the board room which was dominated by a superb piece of furniture, a curved conference table that was nearly ten feet long, apparently designed to meet the special requirements of the embassy dignitaries.

To settle himself down, he started off by asking about the table's construction and learned that the legs were of black walnut; the table top consisting of a mix of woods, Northern sycamore and Southern yellow-pine imported from America. The natural resins of the woods, combined with whatever varnish had been added, gave off a mirror like reflection to the table top in the few places where the clutter of official papers and laptops did not obscure the wood. Hundreds of cards, what looked like six by eights, were spread over the surface of the table top as well. The Vice-Consul mentioned they were not just write-ins from the Green-Link Party, to which Ms van Westerveld was a delegate, but from all the people of Holland, north and south, protestant and catholic. The cards contained a list of their individual grievances and demands in support of, or in opposition to, the Basisch Duplicants and were all signed and dated by the protesters.

The Vice-Consul first introduced Vladg to the Dutch Minister of Labor, a froggy type with bugaboo eyes, supposedly a socialist; he was followed by a two star from the Pentagon with a ramrod straight posture and an empirical stare; then the American consul, Ms Bradford, a deceptively simple looking woman with penetrating eyes and, as it turned out, just as deep an intellect. Finally he got to meet Hikey van Westerveld and the Vice-Consul took his leave.

What was so conspicuous about Hikey was the size of her head.

On first sight he took this to be a deformity, but much later he learned it was a design flaw, a simple computer error of measurement that had increased the diameter of her skull by two inches. She certainly needed the room; a mind like hers required space.

She wore her North Sea blond hair in a spiky mess on top of that gigantic head. She dressed with originality and had a flair for colors. As a companion to the wealthy widow, Mrs. Cynthia van Westerveld, her clothes were bought in the best shops. She was keen on make-up, using cosmetics like a weapon, with that clean and smart business look reminiscent of a Texas woman.

If not beautiful, one could call her a handsome woman, rugged, in that outdoorsy way that some women have who love horses and look as though they could go off galloping through the woods on a moment's notice. She was big-boned with broad shoulders for a female Duplicant, exceptionally large brown eyes that seemed to grow more prominent when she got excited over a hot topic of discussion.

Her mouth stretched wide when she smiled and her nose too was rather large, designed apparently after one of the Dutch master's paintings, perhaps a whim of Mrs. van Westerveld. But it was her broad forehead that was powerful and captivating. So here was a woman with that back-country look that never quite left her, but one who made the most out of modern fashion and style.

Needless to say, Vladg was smitten.

∞

Before we all sat down, Ms Bradford took me to the side, very private like. She was placed in this high level position for her thoughtfulness, and thoughtful she was. She wanted me to explain Bram's absence. I told her that I was his representative, that he had a conflict with another Foreign Policy matter for the State Department, but wanted me to say how sorry he was that he could not attend. She seemed to accept this apology gracefully enough and I was relieved. I really didn't appreciate the position Bram had put me in, forcing me to act as if I had been a designate of the State Department when the truth of the matter was that I was simply a pawn, being moved about by Bram and even Lydia to an extent.

Ms Bradford wanted to know if it was really true that Duplicant's were being considered for consular positions. I told her I wasn't certain on this that nothing was stamped in stone. She said she had made a decision, that Duplicant's would be welcome to do testing of job seekers for positions with the State Department; to help fill out immigration forms for applicants and to grant visas and such, but no higher consular duties. I simply nodded, she knew I was a Duplicant and yet she was taking me immediately into her confidence with good cheer.

"I intend to send a formal note to Mr. Gregoriev on this, but you may relay my thoughts to Ambassador Alucard." Now I felt more ill prepared than ever for I had no idea who Mr. Gregoriev was, Bram had not filled me in sufficiently, so I just nodded again and then we took our seats.

The meeting was interactive so I can't say that Ms Bradford conducted it, but without her guidance it certainly would have been chaotic as all the personalities were strong and held tightly to their convictions.

The General started right off by asking Hikey what her intent was in threatening a work stoppage of all the Basic Units. Hikey parried this immediately by wanting to know what interest the United States military had in the internal politics of Holland.

"I guess you've been misinformed," the General said, obviously taken aback by her retort. "Actually it's the opposite. Our intent was to purchase Dutch Basics for our standing army, as they can be monitored and the ones at home are not built that way. But if you, Ms van Westerveld, have some control over them that is powerful enough to influence their behavior, than we would rather not buy one single unit. You would be interfering with the military policy of America, not we with that of Holland."

"I was not misinformed General…Spader is it?"

"Yes, Spader…"

"I was informed by the people of Holland. Have you read one single card on the table outlining their grievances?"

"I haven't had a chance…"

"Well your statement that I was misinformed is another example of keeping us in the dark about activities that should be…"

"Not at all," the General said, exerting rank to interrupt. "The activities of such a purchase between two friendly countries are often done in secret. That does not imply anything clandestine."

"I disagree. You want to buy Dutch Basics to fulfill a human role in the military, but you don't want to grant them the same rights as humans."

"But they're not human…"

"Are you saying that the young men and women you recruited to serve in the military all these years are not human?"

"Of course they are!"

"Then why is it that you now want Duplicants to do the job for you but refuse to grant them any of the privileges that go along with service, with the same dangers and risks that humans took before we appeared on the scene."

"Because this is different. Now we're in peacetime…"

"But you intend to train them for combat in case a war breaks out…"

"That's the purpose of the army, we need warriors and my understanding is that Basics could make good ones…"

"Then give them the privileges they deserve! It isn't right that Duplicants are awakened every morning, electronically monitored, then get up to go to work and find out that life is an illusion, or that they should be so grateful to their employer for being allowed to continue so ritually in their habits that they shouldn't ask for anything more."

Now Ms Bradford breaks in.

"All right. This is a fundamental point. We don't have to decide the issue today, but we certainly can make recommendations to both countries based on what we come to terms with here."

Now the Minister of Labor, Meneer Bastiaans, gets into the act.

He begins by first puffing out his chest, then clearing his throat like a frog croaking for attention. Before he speaks he looks to the left and right to see if he has gathered sufficient recognition. "I agree with the Mejuffrouw van Westerveld. The Labor Ministry should not be kept in the dark on these foreign purchases. How are we to plan our labor force if we do not know the numerical data, what the potential may be?"

"In this case," Ms Bradford says, "the purchase would fall out of your jurisdiction, but I see what you're saying, there may be other non-military contracts which do…"

"My very point," the Minister groans.

"What do you think on this issue Vladimir?" Ms Bradford asked quietly.

Now all heads are turned, their eyes focus on Vladg.

His mouth is dry. He is extremely nervous.

Vladg takes a deep breath, hopes it is not noticeable.

No one has ever called him Vladimir in public. Certainly no one has ever asked his opinion on so serious a matter as this.

Vladg begins to sweat and immediately exudes a misty-spray of cologne.

"What on earth is that scent?" Hikey exclaims, "I can't place it."

"Yes, what is that?" Ms Bradford wants to know. "It's pleasant, a very masculine essence, I'd say."

"Smells pretty pungent to me," the General says with his dry decisiveness.

"It reminds me of my after shave," the Minister says.

"I'm the guilty one," Vladg says. "My sweat glands are designed to add a fragrance to my perspiration so that I don't smell so badly."

"That's very interesting," Hikey says. "I sweat like crazy; I could use some of that stuff myself."

By now the mist has died down and it is incumbent upon Vladg to say something. He gets up his courage. Making eye contact with the General, he says, "I know that the military back home has used Sextus IV's in the past. They are granted rank based on merit. Perhaps you could do the same over here."

"What of other rights?" Hikey wants to know.

"In the States the Basics are allowed to handle currency, in fact they are paid for their work, usually an hourly wage but in some cases a weekly salary. They are members of labor unions, if that is their choice, and they certainly pay taxes. Of course, they are not citizens, but neither are the Sextus of which I am one."

"I never would have known," the General says, obviously surprised. He turns to Ms Bradford. "You introduced Vladimir here as a substitute for Mr. Alucard. Since they had the same last name I assumed they were related somehow."

"I thought as much," the Labor Minister says. He slides his chair away from Vladg as if he had been contaminated. "Did you know this beforehand?" he asks the Consul.

"I didn't think it mattered much either way, after all you were aware of Hikey's origins, that she is a Royaal and my understanding is that the American Sextus and the Dutch Royaals are as alike as two peas in a pod, the same species so to speak."

"That doesn't make them human," the Two Star says, "they have no right to pass themselves off that way. It's misleading for one, a misrepresentation for another."

Now Hikey gets her dander up. "In the first decade of this century your Supreme Court declared corporations to be people, to have all the rights and privileges of humans…is that not so?"

"Yes, but that was mostly for tax privileges…on the products of the corporations…"

"Indeed, well following your logic I was manufactured by the Van den Valk Corporation, at the factory in Amersfoort, so I am as Dutch as anyone, designed following all the characteristics that Mrs. van Westerveld wished to have installed."

"That doesn't mean you are human…"

"It means I was created by humans…"

"Well so was I…"

"Well there you are. If you believe in creativity, Adam was fashioned by God out of clay, a single substance good for making pottery and not much else; if you believe in Darwinism we were made from more colorful materials as they developed and came on line, so we fit the bill both ways. If not human, we are certainly humanoid."

The Two Star's mouth drops, he has no rebuttal to this.

Now the Labor Minister speaks out. "Enough of this philosophical claptrap. Let's get back on task. We have to address the intention of Ms van Westerveld. In the past you have shut down the street cleaners, the baggage handlers and the sewage disposal workers. What is it you wish to get from the Ministry of Labor in order to avoid another work stoppage?"

"Recognition on a similar basis to that of the Basics in the United States that is all we want."

"And this means?"

"They should have the right to individual names, this business of calling them all Jan plus a number has to stop."

"And…?"

"The right to handle currency, a decent wage for work performed; the right to join a union if that is the individual's choice; admission to restaurants, theatres and hotels on the same basis as humans. We want transportation rights but we don't want to be relegated to the back of the tram, bus or subway."

"I have no say over transportation, which is a different ministry."

"As to my other requests?"

"We are socialists, but we are not the party in power. As you know the Prime Minister is a conservative. I'll have to see if he will allow this to be taken up by parliament."

"That's what I was told last year."

"This is a different year. The Finance Ministry is also on your side, I think most of what you wish to get can be attained. All the ministers will meet on your requests."

"All right, I will delay the work stoppage for three months. That should give you ample time to address the issues with the other ministers."

"Satisfactory."

"What about my purchase of Basics for the Army? Are you still going to try and influence them while they undergo basic training?"

"Will they be trained in Holland?"

"Certainly, we don't want to ship them out first and then learn they are non-trainable."

"Then I have no recourse but to refuse you. You have to come up with some proposition which will give them the sense that they are more than cannon fodder."

"How about rank? They have to earn it of course. But if we grant them rank on the same basis as human soldiers, will you go for that?"

Hikey appeals to Vladg on this question. By now having acquired a better sense of the situation and the egos involved, he has gained confidence, is less nervous. He nods his approval.

"Agreed," Hikey says, "no interference from me or the Green Party on this issue if you hold true to your promise."

"My word is law."

"Fair enough," Hikey says.

"Good work everyone," Ms Bradford says. I think we've covered enough topics for one day. Why don't we call it quits for now and meet next month to check on the progress of things?"

Everyone nods in agreement.

"I did have the caterers come to prepare a small luncheon in the dining room for all of you. If you have no other commitments the Consulate would enjoy your presence."

No one refuses.

Ms Bradford leads the way with General Spader by her side, followed by a famished looking Minister of Labor with Vladg and Hikey bringing up the rear.

"See," Hikey says, "after all that talk we're still in the back of the bus."

Vladg chortles, he likes her sense of humor, likes everything about her, so far.

∞

As soon as Hikey and I sat down together we held hands. It was electrifying.

The way this came about was because I held my fork in my left hand; she held hers in her right. So, while spearing a chunk of hearts of palm, I dangled my right hand at my side and she grabbed it and held on, not too tight but very warm.

I realized at once that my unaccountable taste for remoteness and solitude was at an end. I no longer wanted to bury myself in the woods; in fact, if I could learn to ride my wish would be to go galloping with her through the forest. I had to know whether my intuition was correct, so my first question to her was:

"Do you like to ride horses?"

"Yes, I do as a matter of fact. Sometimes I even go bareback, gives me a thrill."

"Does Mrs. van Westerveld go with you?

"Not anymore. Cynthia…I call her by her first name and she does the same with me… she's getting on a bit. She does everything else well but has had to give up riding. Actually she is the one who taught me to ride and when the grandchildren come to visit I take them on the trails. It's one of the activities I do with pleasure. We have two mares and a Gelding."

"Where is this exactly?"

"Our place is in the Veluwe, up north in Gelderland. It's forest rich and we have hills and sand drifts too."

"Hills in flat Holland, really?"

"Yes they're called push moraines made by the glaciers pushing up the sediment forming these hills. Some of them are really quite large reaching heights of over one-hundred meters."

Now she let go of my hand as she was getting excited by her explanation, but the warmth between the two of us remained, something my rational mind had difficulty to grasp. My understanding had always been that it was necessary to have physical contact, touch, for warmth to conduct itself between two beings.

Maybe I was going through a change of outlook.

She kept talking but I had lost track of her words. I was transfixed, her mouth was so wide and sensuous when she got going that it was unbearable not to kiss her, but I restrained myself, although my groin argued with my judgment. In order to get away from the sexual flood of impulses I decided to ask a significant question, something I had learned from Lydia.

"In what epoch did all this happen?"

"I believe it was during the Pleistocene period, you know when glaciers were all the rage, doing their thing, pushing the sand deposits in the Rhine and Maas Delta sideways, creating the hills."

"And the rest of the land?"

"The Veluwe has the prettiest landscape in Holland, small lakes, woodland and heather, and like I said Europe's largest sand drifts."

I didn't remember her saying that, but later I learned her mind worked so fast that sometimes she thought she said things out loud when in actuality she had only said them to herself. This didn't stump me, I had learned to live with Lydia's peculiarities and we still made out okay. But I wanted to get off this subject and on to something else, so I asked her about Mrs.

van Westerveld and how they got along. I needed to learn how their intimacy compared with mine to Lydia.

"You see," she began, "her husband held a rather high-up official position with the WPC in Geneva. Actually he was involved in how to integrate Duplicants into competitive society in the fairest way possible, a peace-time sort of Geneva Convention if you will. This was the basis of her interest, and eventually where mine sprang from."

"I see."

"They were very happy there and rode horses together a good deal. But he had a devastating stroke and after she became a widow she returned to the Veluwe. After a long period of loneliness and bereavement she spent the money to procure me. For reasons of her own, she did not go through the H-W experience so I am a standard disc Royaal, but she taught me a great deal and, actually, I am glad she did it this way."

"Why is that?"

"My take on it is that while the H-W types may know more at the outset, they are too heavily identified with the one whose brain they picked and this may limit their choices in life."

"Really? I am H-W induced by my mistress."

"See what I mean? You sound as if she owns you."

"I do not feel that way, but yes, perhaps I am overly fond of her, although she has many faults. We do have a sex life together."

Vladg has no idea that this was the wrong thing to say, but Hikey lets it go for the moment.

"Getting back to what I was saying. Mrs. van Westerveld is a member of the Green Party here in Holland, always has been, although her husband was in the Conservative Party. They got along well even though they had some pretty serious political differences. That was all before he went to WPC in Switzerland. Once they got out of Holland she converted him to her way of thinking. That's how he got to be such a fighter for Duplicants."

"Interesting."

"So that's my background, what's yours. Don't you have a nickname?"

"Sure. Everyone calls me Vladg. Tell me why they call you Hikey?"

"From the get-go I seemed to want to go for long walks, to hike through the woods for hours. Sometimes Mrs. van Westerveld would send someone out to see that I was all right. So that's how they started calling me Hikey."

"And your real name?"

"Inika, very Dutch."

"Inika, I like it.

Now they see that the luncheon is at an end, they are the last ones left sitting.

"Would it be too much to ask to have you drive me to the train station, I have to get back to Amersfoort."

"Amersfoort? They don't allow Duplicants to stay in hotels in Amersfoort. It's one of our most prejudiced cities. I ought to know, I was manufactured there."

"I'm staying with the Basisch, rooming with Jan 237. He's a bell and baggage boy and, by the way, he thinks the world of you."

"Yes, I've met him. He attended one of my organizing talks. It's amazing the minds these Basisch develop considering how meager their original input was."

"I noticed that too. They love education of all kinds, formal and informal. Too bad the gluttonous human kids don't appreciate school as much."

"That's why they're fat. If their minds were more active, if they had more gluttony for words and education instead of food, they wouldn't be so obese. I'm afraid the human element is really on the downturn. The average family in Holland has only one child and the population has diminished from fourteen to less than eleven million. If they keep going like this the same thing will happen as in Sweden, that country's population is so low they are begging for immigrants. Of course to qualify they have to be white and Lutheran, otherwise they don't fit the bill."

"Here you are, this is the station."

"Will I see you again?"

"Would you like to?"

"More than anything, yes!"

"You're not spoken for, back in the States."

"I'm a companion to Lydia whom I've mentioned, and as I said we do have sex, but I am not her lover…"

"You are a gigolo…"

"No, I am her imaginative creation, not her dancing partner. I am indebted to her that is all."

"Whatever. It sounds like a sexual circus to me. We've no time to go into it now. Dutch trains leave on time."

"Bram said the same thing; he wanted to get rid of me too."

"OK. This is my private tele-cell. Call me."

Vladg got out of the smallish DAF, his legs feeling cramped, his mind frustrated and his heart torn. He was perplexed, hoping he hadn't lost Hikey before they even got started. *Gigolo?* He had never thought of himself like that, but Lydia did provide for all his needs, and she did say that he had no class consciousness. Perhaps this was something he should think more about. Certainly the meeting had made him more aware of the plight of the Basisch and other Duplicants. And that consideration reflected on his life as well.

He got on the train. On the way up to The Hague his concern had been what others might think of him. On the way back he realized the Hikey thing had changed his perspective. Now his worry was how he reacted toward himself, not what others thought of his behavior. This change of attitude was something very new to him, something not in the manuals at Pyrell's or anywhere else.

He had just crossed the Rubicon without getting his feet wet.

Chapter XIII

Josh and Phoebe

Phoebe taught Josh a lot of things, but one of the most important was the difference between the two kinds of heat that mattered most in the love machine.

Their first date had been to a 4-D movie at the International Space Station where they held hands and mixed in a little topsy-turvy in zero gravity, but other than that sort of making-out nothing more along sexual lines had taken place. The way this date came about was strange in itself, actually due to Phoenix's feeling guilty. She remembered that Josh had asked her to go to a movie that time in the cafeteria when she had duped him, when he thought that she was Phoebe. So during one of their frequent sister-to-sister tele-cell talks she asked Phoebe if, to make up for things, she would return the favor and go to a movie with Josh. So that's what happened.

The dates that followed were not nearly so exotic, or expensive. Since Phoebe did not cook, they usually did dinners at local restaurants and once or twice Josh was invited up to her place where they had popcorn and cocktails. At first their conversations were stilted. They talked mostly about George and his progress, her work and of course how her sister was doing out in California. So the sexual progress was slow and this pace actually suited Josh as he knew he had a number of inadequacies as a lover. In fact he had only performed the sex act one time and that was with his cousin Merle who had more or less seduced him when they were both in early adolescence. He told

Phoebe about it and she said that that was just body heat, not love heat which was all that really counted.

"Body heat cools off quickly," she said, "love heat will last as long as there is a space for love."

"Is that why guys say: *'I'm no longer hot for her bod'*?"

"Sure, what that really means is they never experienced love heat in the first place, like I said body heat cools off fast."

After that, things did get a little hot and heavy, but nothing further transpired until he got the idea to become a voyeur of sorts at Pyrell's. Unlike most men, whose inferiority feelings had to do with the length of their penis, such was not the case with Josh. He felt his length to be average but that his penis was too narrow. It was its girth that bothered him, the lack of circumference in comparison to the shlongs in porno films which he watched so avidly, paying focused attention to this one area of concern.

What he decided to do during his lunch hour was to leave the 47th floor for the 54th, where the Sextus IX's were receiving hands-on sexual training as part of their developmental procedures. Needless to say, he was never allowed to take part in the training program that Pyrell's provided. Mr. Dunn, the sexologist, along with Mr. Beasley, the biochemist who analyzed the sexual fluids of the Duplicants for purity and quality, said it would be ok for him to peep as long as the models they employed for the purpose did not demand an extra fee for voyeurism. So for a time he was able to watch through a hole in the wall that Mr. Beasley had drilled out for him, but this came to a sudden end when he was discovered by one of the models taking a break for a snort or two of the new designer drug Ubiquitous which is a combination of the Yemenite drug *qat* mixed with hallucinogenic mushrooms. This particular sex-model, who was on a pleasant high, got a kick out of pinching Josh rather hard right in the fanny to let him know he was caught in the act.

Josh yelped and jumped away from the wall, embarrassed as all get out. After this episode, Josh was called on the carpet by Eiselman for potentially putting Pyrell in an embarrassing position of betraying confidentiality procedures to its clients.

"Even though no prospective clients were there to test out their purchases, they could have been," Eiselman said. "If this happens again, valuable as you are, I'm going to have to let you go."

Josh was chagrined to the limit, promised never to do anything like that again, decided not to explain that his great love for Phoebe was what prompted his peeping. Anyway, his friend Billy told him any such explanation would make things worse.

As it turned out, further complications were avoided when the Union of Sexologists did indeed insert an addendum into their stipulated contract with Pyrell's. They demanded an exhibitionist fee for anyone not clearly defined as a Duplicant, or, who was not a designated member of the teaching program. As a consequence, Josh was limited to studying the sex manuals and trying to learn from the Sextus IX's directly.

When Josh told all this to Phoebe she told him that she wanted nothing to do with training manuals of any sort, that it was her wish that they develop their own style and unique form of sexual bonding, one that was natural and flowing and in keeping with their own abilities, not that of some super standard set by Pyrell's.

As a consequence, Phoebe, who had much more experience in these matters than Josh, led him to her bed and he finally discovered the true meaning of love heat.

In time, Josh got over his lack of penis girth. Still, no matter how often Phoebe told Josh that they were an item, Josh felt that he needed to pass a number of tests each time they got together in order to meet up with her requirements. In his romantic imagination, Phoebe was so far above and beyond his reach, that merely being in her presence was a constant reminder that he was not good enough for her, that of a sudden she would meet some handsome tall jock who had no trouble unseating him from his perch.

So when he suggested that they go to Santa Barbara together, maybe do a little SCUBA, which was one of the few sport activities where he had managed some level of proficiency, he was totally surprised when she agreed to go.

"I'm dying to see Phoenix. I'll call and tell her we're coming out," she said. "I'm so-oo excited."

Then she kissed him passionately.

Josh had never seen such happiness on her face in all the time he had known her.

Chapter XIV

The Golden Tulip

On the return trip to Amersfoort Vladg was lucky to get on an express. Once he was comfortably seated in the speeding bullet train, he called Bram on his tele-cell. He managed to make a connection, but all the pics he got on the screen were some vibrating features of Bram's profile. It didn't matter much as he had always had difficulty interpreting Bram's facial expressions, so this shaky video anomaly was more than enough for communication by audio.

Bram agreed to meet him at the train station; said they had a lot of ground to cover regarding his participation at The Hague meeting. He also wanted to discuss his own trip to the factory, and what was going on in Santa Barbara between Phoenix and Lydia. None of these last two topics interested Vladg very much. For some reason, after he left Hikey he felt an antipathy toward Bram's interests in general and Bram in particular. Meeting up with Hikey-his very first encounter with a female Duplicant-the mystical forces affecting his spirit when holding her hand, had given him a wider range of feeling than he had ever experienced with Lydia, or with anyone else for that matter. But what had he achieved? Now it seemed he might have lost Hikey even before they began: *'Sexual Circus*; *Gigolo.'* The words stuck in his mind. He played back and forth with the deeper meaning: 'Why did she say it like that as if I were an acrobat of some kind?' Perhaps it was just the female passion for secrecy and game playing. 'No, that's not her, if it were I wouldn't be so taken, so infatuated'.

His desire to attract Hikey as his soul mate was clear to him, but how to do it? He had to show her that he was an honorable Duplicant. Somehow he had to impress her with his political savvy. Perhaps if he fought to advance the plight of the Basisch, then she might think more of him, then again she might just see him as an opportunist. He began to see the intricacy of the web he was spinning against himself; perhaps this was what Lydia meant when she said falling in love was like thinking in circles, an infallible sign of stupidity.

∞

True to his word Bram was waiting for Vladg at the station. He quizzed Vladg on every aspect of the meeting, wanted exact descriptions of all the participants and especially seemed interested to hear how his sweat gland feature worked.

"Did everyone at the table smell the scent you sprayed; how far do you think it reached?"

"Well we were all seated at this board room table, and it probably measures ten feet or so and yes, everyone got a whiff. Why is this so important to you? To be honest, I was a bit ashamed of the fragrance."

"It is of extreme importance, I can't tell you now, but I will later, after I make a purchase here at the factory. Then I must complete my contract with Mr. Eiselman back at Pyrell. I want you to go to Oneonta with me; there is much work for us to do there."

"You mean that little town in upstate New York. If it's just the same with you I'd rather stay here in Holland."

"I'm afraid that's impossible. You are essential to me in Oneonta, but I am pleased to hear that you don't particularly wish to return to Lydia in Santa Barbara."

Every fiber in his body told Vladg that Bram was up to something weird, something unusual, a scheme of sorts. Whatever it was, Vladg felt it would alter the direction of his life. Bram had that quality of secrecy mixed with single mindedness of purpose that was scary. It was obvious that he had no intention of returning Vladg to Lydia, at least not for the foreseeable future.

Vladg saw his immediate problem as how to remain in Holland to pursue Hikey. He had to come up with some sort of workable plan.

At the Hotel, Bram and Vladg were forced to continue their conversation in the lobby, as Vladg was not allowed to go up to Bram's room, and Bram was forbidden to go down to Vladg's diggings in the basement where all the Basisch were housed.

"You know this is really getting on my nerves. I just returned from a luncheon at the American Embassy where I was treated like a diplomat, and here at the Tulip, I can't even get a drink."

"Yes, I know what prejudice is like. You might be surprised at the extent of bigotry that I have faced at my home in the Carpathians."

"I believe it. At times you do seem sympathetic to the Basisch."

Bram smirks. It is his best effort at showing how he feels about Vladg's audacity.

"I have one more item of business to conduct with you. I want you to accompany me tomorrow morning to the factory to meet a certain Mr. de Boer, he is Henry Beasley's counterpart over here..."

"I'm sorry Bram, the name does ring a bell but I've forgotten precisely who Beasley is…"

"Hmmn. I thought as a Sextus IX your memory bank was indelible on these matters. Beasley is the biochemist at Pyrell's who assisted Josh Wharton in designing and implementing your latest system feature…"

"Sure, the one that mixes a male scent into my sweat glands and disperses the perspiration, we talked about it at the station."

"Yes, but I'd rather you did not interrupt me like that when I am talking business, I don't mind *otherwise*."

"Point taken. Okay, I'll be ready in the morning to go with you, but may I ask why you need me?"

"Mr. de Boer needs to examine you. I want him to learn the system so that I can replicate it in two or three Royaals that I intend to purchase for myself. This has nothing to do with the ones I bought for the State Department."

"So I'm to be a sort of guinea pig?"

"I wouldn't put it that way. Think of yourself as a model that others are trying to emulate."

Now it was Vladg's turn to smirk: 'Bram was a diplomat all right'.

"Fair enough," Vladg agreed.

"Good. No more business, what I say now is indeed an *otherwise*. I talked to Lydia recently; she wonders why you haven't called her."

"You've kept me too busy…well, that's not all there is to it…it's also the new things I'm learning here in Holland, how different life can be from the States. Even the way you and I interact is different."

"That is so."

"And I haven't told you enough of Ms van Westerveld and what she accomplished in the meeting. It looks like the Basisch that the Pentagon are purchasing for the Army will be treated with the same rights and privileges as human recruits."

"That's marvelous."

"Yes. She is a dynamic Duplo; no question she knows how to get things done. So I imagine she will make a cause célèbre out of the situation here at the Hotel."

"You told her you are staying here?"

"Sure, why not?"

"Nothing. I had wanted our stay here to be as inconspicuous as possible, but it's not a problem. Not to worry."

"Okay. You were going to tell me what's going on with Lydia and Phoenix. Is she taking good care of my room?"

"As far as I know she is neat and clean. Lydia likes her and apparently she is a quick study and a good apprentice as far as the work goes. There are other problems however, it seems Phoenix is pregnant and though she can work for a time, it is certain that she will need plenty of rest and fresh air during the last part of her pregnancy. So I doubt you will be able to get your room back for quite a while. That's one good reason for you to come with me to Oneonta."

Vladg grunts; says nothing further on this. His intuition tells him not to reveal just how taken he is with Hikey.

"Well, if there's nothing more, I just can't sit here without a drink after the day I've had. Jan 237 has some Dutch Gin and I could use a slug. So if you don't mind I'll get going, I need to hop into the tub anyway, I feel dusty."

"Not at all. Just remember to call Lydia, no need to worry her unnecessarily."

"I'll do it right off. See you in the morning."

"Yes, I'll call you. Have a pleasant evening."

"You too."

∞

In the basement room, Jan 237 has already been disconnected for the night so Vladg has the place all to himself so to speak. After he takes his tub, dries himself off, he knocks off a few gins, what the Dutch call jenever, a more viscous, heavier distilled liquor than ours. Feeling peppier, he picks up his tele-cell. He takes a page from Gregoriev's book, places the instrument so that Lydia can see his full face and puts the audio on speaker.

"Hi Lydia."

"Hi Vladg, I'm really glad you called…"

"So you're glad to see me?"

"I am, I am. Your face looks changed."

"It's been hectic. And maybe it's the change in air pressure, living below sea level like you said. The wind here is different too, kind of cascades around your face."

"I was getting concerned not hearing from you and with the nine-hour time difference I didn't know when to call."

"I know, it is difficult, it must be the middle of the night over there."

"Yes, but that's ok. Is everything going all right between you and Bram?"

"It's an experience, but yeah we're doing ok. I'm gradually learning what it's like to be on my own, you know, the independent bit."

"I'm glad you're getting exposed to things outside of me…"

"Speaking of which, I met someone, a female Duplicant named Hikey, she's enchanting."

"Oh, how so?"

"If I open up to you, you won't be obligated to tell Bram will you?"

"Not to worry. You can rely on me."

"Bram can be difficult at times."

"That's just what I wanted to talk about. My allegiance to Bram is on a downer. Lately he's been positively overbearing, governing our relationship from on high. Even his sardonic sense of humor is waning. In fact, he has been bullying me of late, ever since you've left. I don't know for sure what's going to happen, but honestly I think he's getting tired of me…"

"Does this have anything to do with Phoenix? Bram said she's pregnant and I got the feeling he might be the father; though I can't imagine what she could possibly see in him."

"Bram does have a convincing way about him with certain women; it can be very powerful…"

Vladg spots a querulous look on Lydia's face when she says this; she seems to be debating how to go on. After a long lapse she starts up again:

"I should have told you this long ago. You see Bram belongs to a certain Vampire sect…"

"I don't believe in vampires…"

"Listen to me Vladg. Try not to interrupt."

"Sorry."

"Years ago Bram converted me to vampirism and at first I was his slave, but then he fell in love with me and I became his wife, which gave me higher status. I never told him I loved him; admire yes, of course, love no. That may have had something to do with why I have been barren all these years. He had hoped that we would have children but that wasn't in the cards. So here we are, growing steadily apart and I am caring for the woman he impregnated."

Vladg is flabbergasted. This news is almost too much for him to bear.

"When you say '*all these years*' just how many do you mean?"

"Decades and decades. We have been together a very long time."

"But you look so young. You don't smell like an old woman, you don't act like an old woman and you certainly don't screw like an old woman."

"I'm chemically youthful."

"If you were a Duplicant I'd understand…"

"The problem for you is that you know nothing of mysticism and the lives of vampires. My mother and father were human, so I am not a member of the undead, I have a mirror reflection and I am as active in the daytime as anyone. Bram, on the other hand, is half human and half a direct vampire descendant. He needs to drink human blood during the night at least twice a month or he will lose all his powers…"

"Lydia, this all sounds like mishegaas to me, I don't believe any of it…"

"I acknowledge your skepticism but it's all true. Vladg, please believe me. I purposely saw to it that you were left ignorant of this part of our lives. I thought at the time that it was the correct thing to do, but as things have turned out, I am not so sure. In any event, now you know and you know why you could never be my true love. Actually I still pine for a man named Pierre, he was my only true love and I have not found his like since."

"You know Lydia this is all very hard for me to swallow. I wasn't schooled in the mystical arts as you say. My mind is rational and logical, perhaps a bit too pragmatic but I do have a sense of the creative imagination, it's just that vampirism doesn't seem real to me, even as a part of the spiritual world."

"Yes, I'm the one who should know how rational you are. I am truly sorry to have waited so long to tell you, but until this happened and it became necessary for your world to open up, I really didn't feel guilty about not telling you. Now I do."

Vladg cannot help wincing; he is pained in a strange fashion, as if he has just been given some new rules on how to do life.

"It's like being an adopted child and not finding out till you're a grown-up, the deception hurts. You may not have been the instrument of my creation, but you certainly were the imaginative force behind it. If our erotic happiness was not love, it certainly was fulfilling."

"I agree. I don't know what else to say except that I shall never be misleading to you again. You do mean a great deal to me and I hope you feel the same way."

"Well what has happened over here is that I have fallen in love with Hikey, the Royaal I mentioned to you a bit ago."

A warning signal goes off, red lights flash, Lydia is jealous in spite of herself.

"What's she got that's so attractive?"

"She has a face of great personal force that springs right out at you and a mind to go with it."

"That doesn't sound very sexy to me."

"She's sexy enough, but even more sensual."

"So she's not just a packaged beauty?"

"No. She has something unusual, an unreserved style about her that strikes me as positively attractive, even the way she speaks sounds melodic to me. As soon as we met I realized how much of me was unused, erotically I mean, untouched even…"

"That makes me sound like a total flop…"

"You were the one that said we were not lovers, gave me that bit about friends with benefits, remember?"

"You're right; I have no call to be jealous of your new love…"

"That's just it, I've screwed up already. I don't know what's going to happen, I mean I don't know what she feels toward me or whether I'll be able to stay in Holland. Bram wants me to go with him to Oneonta after his work here is finished. So I'm definitely in a pickle."

Now it is Lydia's turn to regain composure, to settle down. She does have Vladg's best interest at heart, but he had been her companion for so long it was difficult to think of him entranced by another woman, even if she was a Duplicant.

"Don't worry; I won't tell Bram you've fallen in love. We'll just have to figure out some way to keep you there…"

"The problem is I've screwed up. Hikey thinks I'm a gigolo because of my relationship with you."

"You told her we have sex?'

"Certainly, I was being honest."

"Honesty can have a sharp edge in love affairs when used at the wrong time, in the wrong place…"

"I'm learning, but now I feel so inept, as if the great gifts you have given me, my education, my intelligence, even my charm seem to be falling apart."

"Really Vladg, don't despair. You have a powerful system and I have an enormous desire to help you. Remember you are still virile, all your powers are substantially intact, it's just that falling in love seems to seep away one's strength in certain areas and to enhance them in others."

"We're talking about the secrets of love aren't we?"

"Yes, to manage the secrets well is an art, like other arts it needs to be cultivated."

"I'm a babe in the woods on this subject."

"I know. To some extent we all are, I've just had more time and experience to know what it's like. Just remember females play with a double deck, males have just one, but it is a full deck. So we don't have all the cards, just more than you do."

"Sounds pretty grim to me."

"Not that bad. It's just part of the art of love. True love can add riches to your life if you do not pursue it in the wrong places, with the wrong objectives in mind. At the moment we have to figure out how to keep you in Holland so that you can renew your spirit and recapture Hikey."

"Can you convince Bram?"

"I'll do my best. I have a few wild cards up my sleeve. Do you know about Brer Rabbit and the bramble bush?"

"No, what's a rabbit got to do with anything?"

"You'll see. Let me think on it. I've got to get a couple more hours sleep, big day at the office tomorrow."

"Sure thing. Sleep well, have good dreams."

"I'll probably dream of you now. Take good care of yourself. I do miss you."

"I miss you too. Goodnight."

"Goodnight Niner."

∞

Snail-Mail from Bram, delivered by diplomatic pouch to Gregoriev:

September 8th, 2058

To: Chief of Station:

I was pleased to hear in your last memorandum that the LP worked to your satisfaction.

Objectives at the Van den Valk factory accomplished. All Royaal IV's, factory rejects with minor defects purchased at bargain price per your instructions. Concerns of consulate over problem with Duplicants as replacement personnel mitigated for the present. Pentagon is due to purchase necessary and sufficient number of Dutch Basics as recruits for foreign duties.

Please advise when I need to return to Washington or if I may take a few days furlough.

Bram Alucard,

Ambassador-at-Large

∞

Bram's favorite adage is: 'If they're gay, they're prey'. He had seen immediately that just beneath the mask of the day-clerk's bigotry was a man who would easily succumb to a spell, whose sexuality was so diffuse and so needy that he should have little trouble seducing him. In actuality, Bram could kill two birds with one stone. He needed blood as he hadn't had a good drink in over a month and he was sure that by casting a spell the clerk would change his mind and grant Vladg a room in the hotel, regardless of his instructions from the hotel owners. He was getting ready to leave when he received a Hologram from Lydia:

Dearest Husband and Master,

I want you to know that when I said Phoenix and I had shared a bed I did not mean that we were sleeping together, only that we had slept together. I do not believe she is 'that way' in any shape or form, so there. However, I do object to your threats and propositions. They were insensitive and obtuse in every way imaginable. I have lived long enough not to be afraid of death; no matter how merciless and painful you may make it, so please desist with that approach.

Of course, I intend to do everything possible to see that Phoenix carries the baby throughout her gestation in the healthiest manner, after all I was a midwife for many years and it would be against my medical oath to allow anything to go amiss during her pregnancy.

However, I do want Vladg returned to me immediately! He is my companion, not yours, and you have no right to take him to Oneonta or to keep him entrapped in Holland where he seems to be most unhappy. And yes, I would be deliriously pleased to become the Anti-godmother to your child, as soon as my divorce is final.

Yr most humble servant and soon to be un-wife,
Lydia

Bram is furious. He makes a fist, hell-bent on slamming it into the open palm of his other hand, but he holds back, suspending his fist in midair when the violence of his action rekindles the numbness in his thumb. He is still pissed as all get-out, but this pause in the action helps some, now he settles down, regains a modicum of composure.

He has no intention of giving in to what Lydia wants. But he knows the State Department does not approve of divorce. His career could be put into serious jeopardy. He has to find a compromise Lydia might accept. What to do? How to respond to the bitch? Perhaps if he did not take Vladg to Oneonta but returned him to Santa Barbara she might change her mind on the divorce. On the other hand, if Phoenix could be induced to kill her in the correct fashion after the baby was born, that would solve everything. But if Vladg were present, he could easily circumvent and prevent any attempt on Phoenix's part to do away with Lydia. No, the best solution was to leave Vladg here in Holland with the Basisch. *'That way I would save face'.*

He decided to tell Lydia of his solution, no way was he going to allow her to push him around; after all he was still the master.

∞

It was in this mixed mood of accomplishment and defeat that he went down to the registration's clerk's room on the third floor. On the way down he runs into Jan 387, who is working the evening-graveyard twelve-hour shift doing security checks on all the floors. Bram explains to Jan 387 that he is going to visit the registration clerk and hopes to change his mind on some of the stringent rules of the house. Jan 387 wishes him success, bids Bram goodnight, and goes on with his duties. Bram thinks no more of this encounter.

Actually, he had called earlier, learned that the clerk's name was Peter Petrov, and promised to bring a bottle of Courvoisier Cognac along with him while they discussed the possibility of getting Vladg a decent room at the hotel. He did not bring a hypnotic potion with him as he thought the cognac would be sufficient to gain the slight advantage he needed to put the man under a spell.

At first things went fairly well although Petrov did have that defiant look about him with no two matching parts to his expressions. He offered Bram a Havana from a wooden humidor in which he kept his cigars. Bram refused politely as he did not smoke tobacco, but Petrov went through the cigar lover's ritual and got his stogie going. He did not blow his smoke directly at Bram's face, but he was careless with it and soon there was enough smoke in the room to make Bram hack and cough. Even so, the two chatted back and forth about a variety of subjects. He learned that Petrov had an interesting history. His great grandparents were not Dutch by birth, but came to Holland via Byelorussia and Indonesia when that country was under Dutch domination. Apparently they had secured jobs as plantation overseers to the 'coolies' as they called them back then. When the period of colonization ended the family migrated to Holland.

Having spent some time with him, Bram now began to doubt the man was gay. He decided to reassess his original opinion. Certainly Petrov was not the swishy type that made for easy prey. And, for a clerk, he looked fit and muscular.

Bram's plan of attack, however, remained the same. He simply poured cognac repeatedly into Petrov's glass while listening attentively to his story. As soon as the man was intoxicated he would jump him, sink his fangs into his throat and fill him with just enough venom to gain total power and drink his fill of blood. Once that was accomplished, the man's will strictly under his control, he intended to order him to check Vladg into a room as a normal houseguest in the hotel.

None of this played out the way Bram wished. The man didn't seem to be affected one bit by alcohol no matter how much he consumed and the smoke had weakened Bram to the extent that his fingernails failed to grow into claws; his incisors did protrude somewhat, but did not really grow into fangs.

By some prearranged signal within his psyche Bram jumped him anyway, only to find that he was falling and tumbling over backward, ending up sliding on the floor. A fist with a tremendous force to it had caught Bram square in the jaw, loosening one of his precious canines and bruising the side of his face, nearly giving him a broken jaw.

"I am a student of Tae Kwon Do," Petrov said. "I am sorry to have hit you, but all my instincts told me you were going to try something stupid."

"Well all I wanted was a room for my Duplicant."

"They're the same as coolies to me. I hate them, wish they were never manufactured. Do you feel good enough to get up?"

Bram said, "I think so."

"Thanks for the cognac. You can leave the rest of the bottle if you like."

Bram does so, gets up unsteadily, regains his balance and heads for the door.

"You'll probably sleep better than you have in years," Petrov says.

"I can do without the cynicism," Bram said, shutting the door with a bang.

∞

The next morning, on the way to the Van den Valk factory Bram tells Vladg he has decided not to take him along to Oneonta, that he believed he could get all the necessary work done there with the help of Mr. Beasley.

"You'll have to stay here in Holland for a time."

Vladg just nods, smiles inwardly, thinks of Brer Rabbit and Lydia.

Then Bram adds that he was unable to get him a room at the hotel.

Vladg nods again. No way was he going to mention a word more on the subject, not with the tremendous black and blue bruise Bram displayed on his face.

Chapter XV

The Factory and the Tulip

At the factory, Bram introduced me to De Boer.

Just shaking hands with the man was enough to make anyone nervous. His clasp was wet with sweat and, when he wasn't looking, I had to wipe my palm off on the side of my jeans; even then I couldn't get completely rid of the odor.

When he spoke there was a hint of artificiality about him. He was positively vibrating with enthusiasm at the prospect of unhinging certain of my parts.

I had never been examined by anyone not affiliated with Pyrell's and as I said this man turned me off instantly. It wasn't just his bald head and bushy eyebrows, set in an overly broad face to which I took an instant dislike; no, it was more the way his head twisted sideways when he spoke, avoiding direct eye contact. He would ask questions and when I gave an answer his eyeballs turned up in his head so that you could make out the whites. Ugh.

I was lying supine on an examining table in the testing lab. I had had to undress completely so that de Boer could test all my sensors and receptors. He pushed and pulled on my belly, then probed, pinched and picked at my tissues, especially my special sense organs. In order to follow the circuitry and collateral circulation to the major sweat glands under my arm pits and groin, he first unscrewed my belly button, and lifted it outward. Then he tilted it to the side sufficiently so that my immediate underneath features became visible.

"How often do you have to add the vial of male mist that circulates?"

"It depends largely on the weather, usually once a month. In Holland it is not that hot, but it is humid. Anyway, I am more active here than in Santa Barbara."

"So it depends on the type of activity?"

"That and how strenuous or how emotionally tense or excited I am. I notice my palms and soles sweat more when I'm tense, but my armpits perspire more when I'm excited. Don't know why that is."

"Interesting. Very interesting."

When he made this comment I caught his eyeballs doing their thing, rotating upwards in their sockets.

"Have you had to add a new vial of scent since you've been in this country?"

"No, not yet."

"Well, I'd like to test this new one out on you. Do you mind?"

"Do I have to?" I asked Bram.

Bram is stoic on this, nods his affirmation.

Now I start to sweat in earnest; the male scented mist begins to permeate the lab.

De Boer stops the process by removing the vial.

"Look here. This is the same type vial that fits just behind your umbilicus only this fluid is slightly more viscous, about the same specific gravity as Dutch gin. You're familiar with that aren't you?"

"I wish I had a slug right now. It might settle me down some."

De Boer grunts at Vladg's comment, inserts the new vial beneath Vladg's umbilicus, attaches the distal end via a micro-nipple to a vascular bundle entering his circulatory lymphatic system, and places the rest back neatly.

Unfortunately, Vladg quits sweating.

"Now's the time you need to sweat," Bram says.

"I'm not nervous now."

"Well then I'll take you to Transylvania with me. That's not what you want is it?"

"No, but saying that doesn't make me sweat."

I'm afraid we'll have to put him on the tread mill for ten minutes or so. In the meantime, I want to look at this fluid you've provided under the microscope."

"Oh, all right."

Vladg hops on, gets his circulation and heart beat up, and in eight minutes he begins to sweat. By ten minutes the sweat is strong enough to cast its mist outward. De Boer falls into a trance at the scope. Vladg has to quit running, stops and falls down right on the runner of the treadmill.

Bram smiles sardonically. He is satisfied that the venom works, at least in a three to four-foot radius. Not as wide a field as the less viscous normal scent, but sufficient for his purpose. Visions of the 2nd Reformation cross back and forth in his mind. Perhaps he will yet be successful in his parents' eyes.

∞

It takes almost an hour for Vladg to waken, perhaps ten minutes more for de Boer to come around. The three chat for another half hour and now it is Bram doing most of the interrogating. His purpose is to determine what type of trip each one had while under the hypnotic spell of the venom alone, without the loss of blood. He learns that de Boer could easily be cast into a vampire role, certainly as a slave, but the thought of drinking his blood is repugnant to Bram who also has taken a dislike to the man's body odor. Bram does have to admit that for a vampire he is somewhat prudish, certainly selective in whose blood he will drink. The blood of young females is by far his preferred choice, but sometimes, when such was not available he would relent and sup on older specimens.

Vladg's trip on the venom was less severe than what de Boer described. He had undergone much less fantasy production of fire and brimstone, of descending into hell the way de Boer experienced his journey. So Bram wasn't at all sure what this meant. Certainly inhaling venom was less potent than injecting venom. The difference between lymph and blood in the circulatory apparatus of Duplicant's and humans might give Vladg some immunity, some protection from the changeover, but it really didn't matter. As long as the specially selected humans were put under by the inhalation of his venom, that was sufficient. When the time actually came, he would be sucking out their blood while the Duplicant providing the venom would himself be unconscious. Certainly he would be able to control two or three at a time, turning victims into slaves who, once indoctrinated, would obey his orders and do his bidding precisely as he wished.

All in all, Bram felt that the experiment was a success.

Now de Boer's equilibrium and consciousness return to normal. He is focused enough to replace the new vial with the old male scent. He does so and Vladg is allowed to dress. While this is happening Bram takes out fifty-thousand New Euros from his valise, waits until de Boer is finished and hands them over to him. He watches carefully as de Boer opens a small floor safe, combination type. Bram cannot see the combination that de Boer uses, but he tells himself that if he acts in time, it won't be necessary.

De Boer removes a leather carrying case, perhaps 9 x 12 inches, and when he opens it Bram sees that it is velvet lined so that when de Boer replaces the vial of venom in proper position within the case it is safe and secure. When this is done de Boer deposits the wrapped bills in the back of the safe, twirls the combination a couple of times, and double checks that it is locked.

"Remember you only get the other fifty if you can duplicate my venom exactly."

"I have never missed copying the most obscure snake venom. Surely this cannot be more difficult."

"Good. When can I expect results?"

"A week or two should do it. We will need another test on your Duplicant to make sure the results are the same."

"Understood. And you will provide at least ten cc's of the new venom as well as the formula."

"When I receive the other fifty thousand, of course."

"Of course."

∞

On the way back to the Hotel it finally dawns on Vladg that what Lydia had told him about vampires might indeed be so. Maybe Bram does drink the blood of his victims? He does not know what Bram's experiment is all about, not for certain, but his curiosity is sufficiently aroused. In the recesses of his mind, he now knows he is but a key in the lock to Bram's ultimate scheme. Slowly he is becoming a believer.

As they approach the hotel, Vladg's heart beats faster, begins to pump with excitement. As they drive by he can see that several radical Basics, led by Hikey, are parading up and down in front of the Hotel holding their placards high and swinging them back and forth in a theatrical manner while they monotonously chant their slogans:

'Work for pay is what we say'. 'NO more monitoring'.

'Work for pay is what we say'. 'NO more monitoring'.

As Hikey marches about at the head of the group, she swings her placard in a smallish arc, with attractive clumsiness, emoting a planned kind of dainty anger that befits the scene. The rhythmic walking seems to accentuate her natural curves for she is wearing designer jeans that show off the roundness of her hips while a tight fitting blouse does the same for the slope of her bosom.

Vladg is so keen to see her, thrilled so by her very presence, that his impatience shows through. He jumps out of the car even before it has come to a complete stop, immediately runs over to greet her. He tries to hide his passion, refrains from grabbing her hand.

Still, her eyes indicate that she is glad to see him.

"How come the placards are in English?" he asks, striving to calm Niner down.

"Nothing like an American idiom to neutralize a Dutch phrase," she says. "The newspapers love to write up these things especially if they can quote a few phrases in English. It's a Dutch thing, any chance they can get to substitute a French or English word for Dutch, they'll do it. Somehow they believe it carries more emphasis."

"Well I thought you had promised in our meeting not to hold any general demonstrations until Parliament had a chance to get things moving."

"Oh, this is not a general anything. It is specific to this hotel. When I heard you were here, and Jan 237 and Jan 387 contacted me, I decided to go ahead. But so far it's not attracting much attention. Apparently something big is going on inside. See all those police cars…"

Now Bram comes over. He had parked the car and wants to meet Hikey.

She calls a temporary halt to the demonstration.

"Take a break everyone!"

"That was very considerate of you," Bram begins. "I'm sorry I couldn't attend the other day in The Hague."

Vladg recognizes this deception of Bram's from Schiphol, this is how he had greeted him upon his arrival, showing his dignified human self, his warmth and especially how gentlemanly he can portray himself. What a far cry from the sadistic attitude he displayed in the lab at the factory a few hours ago.

"I am truly pleased to meet you." Bram goes on.

To Vladg's surprise Hikey seems pleased by the attention, attracted to his style. Is this what Lydia was talking about, Bram's special power with certain women?

"I was just telling Vladg," she said, "that some kind of mischief is going on inside the hotel…"

At this point the Amersfoort Chief of Detectives, Mr. de Haas, steps out onto the terrace, strides hastily over to Hikey and tells her in Dutch that there has been a murder in the hotel. "Sometime in the middle of the night by the looks of things."

Hikey tells him that Vladg and Bram are foreigners and the detective switches over to English.

"Are you two staying in this hotel?" he asks.

"Why, yes," Bram says. "I'm in 510 and my companion here is lodging with the Basisch in the basement." "Are you a Royaal like Ms van Westerveld here?" he asks Vladg directly.

"Yes, an American Sextus, which is approximately the same."

"Well you both have to come inside. We're interrogating all the guests. Please come along.

Bram shows his Diplomatic Passport to the Chief but it makes no difference, he too has to be questioned. Once inside the hotel they are herded into the main dining room along with a few other stragglers.

After everyone is seated, but before the Crime Scene Investigators take over formally, Vladg says to Bram, "I guess it takes a murder for a Duplicant to get a seat in this Hotel's dining room."

"I wonder what the requirement might be to get a meal?" Bram responds.

Vladg is unable to stifle a laugh.

Now the Chief takes center stage. He explains that a hotel staff member was found dead this morning and that it was undoubtedly a murder.

"The man was in his own room and, as with all staff rooms, there was no video camera in his room. So we had to use the Time-Retrieval Unit along with the Projecto-FAX machine. Unfortunately, with today's limited technology, the time retriever can only go back a mere two hours. We can't reproduce the actual murder for you, so this will have to do."

He asks for the guests' indulgence while Willem, the chronotographer attached to CSI, plays a time retrieved four-sided projecto video.

He requests silence during the production.

When the playback is finished the Chief takes over again.

"What we can deduce from the facial expression on the corpse is a man who had evidently fallen backward from his chair in some sort of fright."

Willem rewinds the Projecto-FAX machine and stops it at a point de Haas designates to show a specific still shot.

"See, the first one on the scene was a house maid, Basisch, who said there was a look of fear and horror on his face. The two CSI men who next came on the scene also felt the same way; that his expression made them shudder, that his death look was unlike any they had ever seen, wild-eyed and haggard."

Now the Chief strolls back to the makeshift podium.

"So you see we don't have to take the word of a Duplo to validate that point."

"He doesn't miss a chance to denigrate us," Vladg whispers to Bram, who is sympathetic on this point.

"Does anyone recognize this victim?"

Several guests raise their hands, including Bram and Vladg.

"Sure," one of the others says, "that's the desk clerk who does reception, books you in when you arrive."

"Correct," the Chief says. "Does anyone remember his name? He always wore a name-tag pinned to his lapel."

Bram is the only one to answer.

"His name was Peter Petrov."

"That's right," the Chief says, glancing intensely at Bram and making a signal to one of the other detectives to make a note of who responded.

Now the chronotographer fast forwards the machine, and zooms in on Petrov's body.

"His neck was not just broken but his throat was torn apart, pulled completely away from his neck."

The camera scans downward toward his abdomen.

"His belly was slit open as if with a savage claw. His abdominal opening showed his innards to be pulled out with the guts spilled out upon the floor, while the void thus created was chock full of cigar ash." The machine zooms in on this.

The assemblage gasps.

Now that he had accomplished the theatrical response he wished, the chief said, "Each one of you will be asked to sign a deposition indicating the last time you saw this man alive. We also want to know whether any of you had occasion to visit the victim in his room. If so, we would appreciate you acknowledging this and giving us the approximate time that you were in his presence. Remember you will be scanned by the Truth Detector while you undergo individual interrogation."

The CSI people only have a limited number of Truth Detectors so the assemblage is divided up into smaller groups of threes and fours. Each group is led off by an officer from the homicide division to a separate section of the dining room.

Vladg and Bram find themselves joined by an Algerian couple who are bitching and moaning because they had planned a trip to Amsterdam to purchase a wad of Ubiquity with which they planned to get the high of their lives.

A detective-sergeant comes over and introduces herself very professionally. Her name-tag indicates that her last name is Hofstra, first initial G. She has thick long and sleek brunette hair that is brushed straight back and ends in a braid that is neatly looped upon itself and fastened with a topaz barrette. This style makes her look efficient, but even so one gets the impression that if she coifed it otherwise, she would be much more alluring.

She insists that none of her questions are designed to be offensive, but that Dutch law allows her to ask anything she wishes which, even remotely, could shed light on the murder.

Then she leads them over to a corner of the dining room and sets up the Truth Detector which is light enough for her to manipulate. It is about the size of a large table lamp and is made in the form of a four sided lighthouse rather than one of the more circular-conical types. There are a great number of sensors and receptors embedded in the sturdy outer structure of fibro-resin and as the design is very geometric each side is exactly duplicated by its opposite. The instrument does not need to be plugged into an electrical outlet. In fact, there are no cables or lines of any sort attached to it. Nor do the participants need to have pulse sensors placed upon their fingers. What runs the instrument are four very powerful cadmium-titanium renewable batteries set in parallel within the base.

Sergeant Hofstra is careful to place the Truth Detector as precisely as she can in the exact center of the table. There are two modes she explains, one for manual and one that puts it on auto-pilot: "Very much like in an airplane," she says. Then she asks Vladg and Bram to sit at one-eighty from each other and the two Algerians to do the same. Now she switches on the manual mode.

The machine makes an annoying hum and, like an old fashioned lighthouse, oscillates its laser-neutrino light beam through a circumference which designates the four participants as if they were points on the horizon, North, East, South and West.

When Vladg asks about the humming noise Hofstra explains that the hum only stops when the machine anticipates the person needs to make a truthful statement in answer to one of her questions.

Once everything is set up precisely to her liking she turns the machine onto auto-pilot. She now asks each of them in turn to identify themselves and states that they may do so in their own tongues as the Truth Detector is capable of handling ninety-two different languages, from Swahili and Sanskrit to Urdu. The Algerians prefer to speak in their native brand of Arabic, Vladg, for the fun of it, chooses to speak in French and Bram talks in a Slavic-Macedonian dialect. As the machine records and digests the data, its laser-neutrino beam now switches from a circular orbit to a vertical motion, running axially up and down as it were, scanning and analyzing the individual.

She next asks them to state whether or not they have ever been accused or convicted of any crime. When she gets to the Algerian man, the hum stops abruptly. He confesses that he was indeed accused once for rape as a teenager but was exonerated before any indictment was made.

Upon hearing this, the woman he is with, who does not wear a burqa but is fashionably dressed in western clothes, starts scratching at his eyes with her long sharp acrylic fingernails, shouting in Arabic that he had never told her any of this. He pulls away from her, tries to protect himself by putting up his hands and crossing his arms in front of his face while the policewoman motions a male patrolman over to help calm things down.

"We can't have any of these outbursts," she says, "otherwise we will have to take you down to the stationhouse to complete the interrogation. You should both look upon this as a favor we are doing for you, to get you going as quickly as possible so that you can get on with your tourist activities."

The man settles down, but the woman says, "If I had known that he had been in trouble with the police I never would have left Algeria with him. I thought he was a decent man…"

"I am a decent man," he interrupts. "I told you I was innocent of any wrongdoing…"

"Please stop, the policewoman says. That old crime, whatever it was, is not at issue here. So calm down, both of you."

Now she turns to Bram and asks him if he was ever accused, arrested or indicted for any crime of any sort.

Once again the hum stops before he says a word.

"I can save you and the Truth Detector a lot of time," Bram announces. "No, I was never accused of any crime, but I did visit the victim last night at around ten o'clock. We had a few drinks. I perhaps a few too many. I fell out of my chair and bruised this side of my face. Right after that I left and went up to my room, actually had a pretty good night's sleep."

"And when you left this man Petrov, he was not harmed in any way by you?"

"Certainly not."

Now she asks a set of similar questions to Vladg whose responses are not revealing of any significant information. She tells the Algerians they are free to go and they wander off jabbering away at one another as if their lives together will never be the same.

"All right. You may leave too if you wish," she says to Vladg and then tells the patrolman to bring the Chief over to the table. Vladg glances at Bram, wants to know if he prefers him to stay or go."

"Sure, go," he says. "I'll be all right."

"You're sure?"

"Of course."

Vladg takes him at his word, strides off to see if he can find Hikey.

The Chief comes over and asks several more questions including what type of alcohol he and Petrov were drinking the night before. When Bram says it was Courvoisier Cognac the Chief says: "That's right, an empty bottle with a Courvoisier label was found by the body of the deceased."

Now de Haas's gaze takes on more of an inspector's look, a skeptical glare, one that he had not previously exhibited. He tells Bram he wants him to visit the actual crime scene in Petrov's room. He signals Detective-Sergeant Hofstra and the one patrolman by her side to come along and, on the way up, he calls for a CSI fingerprint expert to join them. This outspoken man, nicknamed Dusty, is known to dust everything in sight for prints whenever he is called to a crime scene.

Bram has no objection to any of this. He knows he has the right of refusal due to his immunity as an ambassador for the State Department, but he doesn't wish to use this privilege unless, and until, it becomes necessary. Although he is innocent of any wrongdoing, he knows that things can get horribly complicated when it comes to police matters.

In Petrov's room a CSI man had stayed behind to see that nothing was disturbed.

The first thing that Bram observes is that the corpse has already been removed, a chalk diagram outlining its position on the carpet is visible. Less obvious is the cigar humidor; it is completely empty. Surely Petrov could not have smoked all the cigars in so short a time.

"Anything significant strike you," Chief de Haas asks."

"Only that the humidor is empty. All the cigars are gone. Last night there were at least eight or ten in the humidor."

"So?"

"From the amount of ashes in the still photogs you showed it must mean that whoever killed Petrov also lighted up the cigars and burned them off. They might have been smoldering inside Petrov's belly while he was still alive."

Upon hearing this, Greet Hofstra turns her head. She is about to get sick and barf, but she holds it in.

"God verdomme," the patrolman squawks out, getting a look of rebuke from his Chief.

"Was there the smell of lighter fluid or anything like that when the maid came in?" Bram asks.

"Usually we ask the questions," Chief de Haas says patiently, "but yes there was such a smell about the body mixed with the odor of burning flesh of course."

"I see. Did you find a can of lighter fluid about?"

"Yes," the Chief admits, somewhat sheepishly.

"Empty?"

"Yes," the Chief acknowledges. "You're implying that the murderer, or murderers, deliberately set the cigars on fire inside of Petrov's body."

"Yes it seems that I am, doesn't it?"

"That's pretty far out," the other CSI man says. His name is Joost Jansen.

"No," the duster says, I've seen a case like that once myself in Malaysia, only over there it wasn't cigar ash but small palm fronds. They filled the poor bastard's belly up with palm fronds, poured gasoline in the hole as it were and lit the bloke up to high hell, a fuggin bonfire."

"That's a true story?"

"I swear. The only thing is, you know how the beliefs are in Indonesia and Malaysia; they said the perp was a vampire, but the rest is all true."

Bram smirks inwardly; he knows that on Surabaya, adjoining the naval base, there is a large vampire population.

There is a soft knock at the door. Another patrolman walks in, delivers a note to the CSI man who hands it to de Haas.

"Apparently one of the Basisch has been found in a broom closet, dismembered and beheaded. Her number was 276. Do you know of her?" he asked Bram.

"No, but my compatriot Vladg who is a Duplicant may. He is lodging with the Basisch in the basement."

"Okay. Go get him and bring him up here," he ordered the patrolman.

"How did you know that Basisch was a female," Bram asks.

"All the even numbered ones have some female characteristics; the males are odd numbered. Of course there is no true gender definition as they don't have genitals, only waste disposal units."

"Just so," Bram said, recognizing the similarity to the American made Basics.

"Anything else you can tell me while we're waiting for your companion?"

"No. Only that when I left there was booze left in the bottle, plenty of cigars and he was not in the least upset about anything."

"And the purpose of your visit? It is a bit unusual for guests, especially those attached to the Foreign Service to visit the rooms of hotel staff."

"My purpose was simple; I wanted to get a different room for my companion, one that was a little more comfortable than those of the Basisch."

"You were going to interfere with a government statute?"

"I was going to trust the renowned sense of Dutch fairness…"

"Ja," Joost Jansen huffed. "Some of us feel this way of doing things is giving Holland a bad name in the international community."

"Pipe down you knucklehead," de Haas barked in Dutch. "We are not political, we're professionals trying to solve a crime and from what this man says he may be involved in the murder. I say *may*, get me! I don't want anyone to quote me otherwise."

"Well, if you're trying to solve the murder you had better get someone over to what remains of that female Duplicant and dust her for fingerprints before she gets broken up for parts," Bram said.

"What on earth for?"

"Because the two murders may be connected."

"Nonsense. No human would try to dismember a Duplo. If he had a gripe it is reportable and the Central Computer would take care of it."

"A gripe yes, hate no. If a man hates Duplos intensely anything is possible. That's what Petrov said to me, that he absolutely hates Duplos, compared them to coolies. If she came in to tidy up the room and he lost control, especially when he was the influence of a large amount of alcohol…"

"You're insinuating…"

"I'm not insinuating anything. Only implying that such a possibility might exist. If I were you I would get that Duplo dusted for human fingerprints."

"And if the perpetrator were another Duplo…"

"It would have to be a Royaal or Sextus. Basics don't have fingerprints; their skin is not made of biologic epidermal cells but some type of alloy mixed with certain resins akin to human skin."

"How do you know so much about this?"

"I have learned a bit from my companion Vladg who is an American Sextus."

"So you are advising me to send Dusty here over to the broom closet…"

"Before anyone else messes her up, yes."

Chief de Haas thinks this over for a brief moment only.

"Dusty, get over there and get to work. Don't let anyone else touch that Duplo."

Dusty hightails it out of the room accompanied by Joost, the other CSI man.

Only Greet Hofstra is left now with the Chief and Bram.

"Satisfied?"

"It's your case. I'm only trying to help."

"You're still a suspect. Your prints are all over the place, including on that bottle of Cognac."

"They should be. I'm the one that brought it down. It's my bottle."

"Hrrummph. Listen Greet, you watch this man here. I've got to go downstairs to see if I can contact Burgemeester Dijkstra, let him know what happened here, how he wants to handle it. Murder at the Tulip Hotel at the height of tourist season is not good for business."

"All right Chief," Greet said, "no problem."

Once he leaves, Bram turns to Greet, takes note of her rolling hips, and the pulsating veins in her sturdy neck. He is literally starving for fresh blood and the mere thought of her young blood excites him so much she has no chance whatsoever. He jumps her, sinks his fangs deep, pumping venom furiously.

She falls limp in his arms and he starts to drink, careful not to drip blood on her blouse. He has her under control before she can even say 'Master'.

Chapter XVI

Proceedings

Bram had not felt so vigorous in weeks.

Not since he had sucked up Phoenix's blood in her Manhattan apartment has his body felt so strong, his skin so invigorated, his complexion so ruddy that even his brown eyes reflect a deeper sepia hue from the fresh flush of his skin. Not that Greta's blood has restored him to a more youthful appearance, no, but his pride in the ease with which he had conquered her has risen tenfold. And yes, the renewed vigor has given him a healthier outlook on his present situation.

He is very careful with Greta, making sure that the welts left over from his jugular bites are minimal and do not seep. It had become awkward to transport a live Salamander about, so using the alchemy prowess taught him by his mother he has concocted an elixir of Salamander juices. His original intent had been to use the elixir on the lesions in his thumb which cracked at the base now and again, largely from overuse. Now he saw that the elixir had a dual purpose. He opened the vial and stingily rubbed but a few drops, very gently, into Greta's wounds, lessening the swelling immediately and advancing her tissue repair. She would be left confounded by the 'hickeys' but that was all. He had not given her any post hypnotic suggestions. Of course, if he wished to make use of her for another purpose at a later time it would be in his power to do so.

Once the bites in her neck had diminished to slits, the bruises minimized appreciably, he carried her over to Petrov's bed, laid her down gently on top and covered her with the soft downy bedspread, her head resting on a small pillow.

Bram took pleasure in watching her, knew he must stay for a time, at least until he was sure she had passed through the worst of her journey. Unlike Phoenix she was not tall or beautiful, her face was too wide as was the breadth of her figure, but at the table when she was manipulating the Truth Detector he saw that she was a woman with a full small body who loved action, whose feminine vibes radiated a frequency that beckoned to men. Yes, she was alluring in her own way, perhaps she could be useful.

After half an hour she still lay sleeping, breathing stertorously, frowning at times through her spell, seeking pathways through the nether world.

Bram knew that her trip would not be as horrific as that of Phoenix's, for there had been no sexual contact, and while his injection of venom had been intense and quick, the amount had not been nearly as much as he had given Phoenix when he had emptied his entire load. On the other hand, he had sucked as much of Greta's blood into his own system as he dared, practically draining her circulation. She would feel weak for some hours.

With his new found vitality, Bram was not in a mood to wait much longer for the Chief, or, for that matter anyone else.

He put in a call to the front desk telling the clerk that Greta had fainted and the house doctor should make a visit. Then he decides to take the bull by the horns, leaves an aggressive note to the Chief stating that in his opinion it was wrong to leave him alone with the policewoman, that he never should have left his post to visit with the mayor.

Back in his room he finds, suspended in the air, an H-Mail from Lydia:

Bram:

First the good news: Now that the baby is kicking Phoenix has unequivocally accepted her pregnancy. Her health keeps up splendidly. I mention this because I know it is a great concern of yours. And yes, she seems pleased with her forthcoming motherhood. I must say she is more beautiful than ever, perhaps a trifle stouter now that she is past the first trimester, but her cheeks remain a lovely rose-pink. She certainly has lost that anemic look she had when she first came out here. I pray to Satan that it will all last until her due date. She is uncertain of her last period, but she should be due in late March or early April of the New Year.

She does fret at the postponement of her sister's visit, but it has not touched her spirit unduly. Apparently Mr. Eiselman has suffered some sort of mental setback, and while he is recuperating Phoebe has to hold down the fort at Pyrell's office. So they intend to come out for her delivery. By 'they' I mean Josh and Phoebe of course.

The bad news is that Phoenix sleepwalks more than ever, and each night I am awakened by her moving about the room. Yes we still sleep together; so there. Fortunately, the weather here in late September is temperate so she doesn't suffer from wide temperature shifts as is the case back east in early Fall. Still, I am a bit worried as I am perpetually being awakened by her clomping up and down the stairs in the middle of the night and it is beginning to wear on me, especially if I have a busy next day at the office. I have never been a nervous type as you know, but this wakefulness in the wee hours is telling on me.

In regard to us, it seems obvious that we can no longer live together. Your strange heart has put me in an untenable position so I have found a divorce attorney and intend to institute proceedings as soon as possible. As to your stuff, you can imagine that since Phoenix has occupied the walk-in closet for her extensive wardrobe, not to mention her forthcoming need for maternity clothes, I have had to find more room for my things. So I have packed all your clothes and accessories into two large cardboard cartons and dumped them in the basement, next to the oil furnace in the cellar. Hope you don't mind. So when you come to take them away you must call for permission first as I have instituted an injunction against you. However, your clothes are folded neat and tidy as I did have them cleaned and pressed beforehand.

Hope this doesn't make a difference in your selection of me as the Anti-godmother, as I do look forward to that ritual.

Best regards,
Your un-wife, soon to be ex-wife,
Lydia.

P.S. I was sorry to hear from you that Vladg will have to stay in Holland for a time as I do miss his companionship. I know that he is unhappy there, but if that is your decision I shall certainly abide by it as I do consider you my master in this particular respect. Lydia.

P.P.S. A copy of this H-Mail has been forwarded to Gillespie and Henderson. I don't believe I shall yet tell you the member of the firm who is representing me, but you will be hearing from them soon enough.

Your 'no longer yours',
Lydia

Bram is so mad that he wishes he could throw the H-Mail against the wall, but of course there is nothing solid to throw. So he directs the computer to print a hard copy of the message. As soon as this is done he tears the paper into little pieces, spits into his palms, wads the shreds into a spitball and repeatedly throws the makeshift ball against the wall, shouting gleefully and swearing out loud as he does so.

While these antics are going on there is a loud insistent knock at the door; Chief de Haas announces himself and demands to come in. The Chief is accompanied by Joost Jansen, the CSI man, along with Dusty, but Hikey and Vladg are not with them.

It is obvious that he too is madder than hell.

"What on earth have you done to Greta? She's out cold, lying on Petrov's bed."

Bram is somewhat less angry than before his little spitball game, but he is in no mood to be yelled at.

"See here, de Haas," he says, "you yourself were present when she started to get sick while Dusty here was talking about burning bellies and guts wallowing about. After you left she fainted dead away and I carried her over to the bed, and called the house doctor."

"Hrrumph. You could have at least stayed with her…"

"In my experience if a woman goes unconscious like she did its safer for the man not to be around. I don't want to be accused of sexual harassment."

"Well the doctor suspects she has been poisoned; he had her transported to the AMC General Hospital. All he found wrong was two little slits in her neck, nothing else. What are you, a vampire?"

"Don't be silly."

"So did you poison her?"

"How could I poison a police woman? Tell me that. Where would I get poison anyhow? She certainly wasn't the type to trust a man under consideration for murder was she?"

"I told you before I'm the one who asks the questions. If we frisk you will we find anything like poison of any type."

"You have no right to frisk me. That's illegal search and illegal seizure if you take anything of mine without my permission. But I am willing to cooperate. All I have that possibly could be construed as poison is this vial of elixir that I carry to heal my thumb, it cracks at the base every now and then."

"Will you give it over on your own volition?"

"Of course." He hands the vial to the CSI man.

"So what did happen to Greta?"

"As I said she fainted and I caught her. You ordered her to watch me, it's your responsibility for what happened to her, not mine."

Chief de Haas mulls this over, decides to let loose of the Greta issue for the present.

"What about Petrov? We found Petrov's prints all over 276, but there is no precedent for this in Dutch Law, since we've never had a human destroy a Duplo before. So I don't know what to do there, especially since the most probable perpetrator is dead. But as far as you are concerned I'm afraid we shall have to start proceedings against you. Are you willing to come down to the station and at least make a deposition?"

"Of course not. I had no reason to kill Petrov."

Bram is beginning to frustrate the Chief.

"Well someone sure as hell did."

"Not me I tell you."

"You're our only suspect, we have no one else."

"That doesn't make me guilty."

"You know I cannot arrest you. You have diplomatic immunity, but we can start proceedings through the embassy, asking that an exception be made to lift your immunity."

"That's the second time in the last five minutes that I have been threatened with proceedings. My wife sent me an H-Mail telling me she is initiating proceedings for divorce. If the Ambassador learns of this I will be 'up the creek' as the saying goes. So please listen to me. I did not kill Petrov. What reason would I have for doing so? I had no motivation whatsoever." The CSI man named Joost spoke up again, saying, "That's right Chief. Why would a visitor commit homicide against a man he hardly knows? Makes no sense."

The Chief raises one hand in the air as if he is a street cop halting traffic.

"STOP, you numskull," the Chief shouts, "you should know that nutty things like this happen all the time in murder cases…how do we know he wasn't involved with the clerk in a prior time, we don't, anything is possible…"

"You know Chief, I really don't appreciate you calling me knucklehead and numbskull. I'm in the union you know and those remarks constitute a violation of the Employee Protective Act."

"All right, all right. I apologize, but quit interrupting when I'm talking. Button it up will you?"

"You don't want my input?"

"Certainly. Yes, I do. Timing, timing is everything, you shouldn't be voicing an opinion in front of a man who is a possible suspect."

"Not even if it saves you an embarrassment. Ask Dusty here. The odds of this guy having the strength to break Petrov's neck are next to nil. The staff members we interrogated all say Petrov was a Tae Kwon Do expert. This little man wouldn't have been able to break his little finger."

"I don't intend to argue with you...I'm going to start proceedings...Mr. Alucard you are being placed under house arrest. I advise you not to leave the hotel unless the purpose is first agreed to by a member of the homicide division."

"Well I am booked on a plane for Sofia, Bulgaria in five days and I'm not at all certain that you have the legal right to detain me merely because I am a suspect of interest with no legal charges and no further evidence of wrongdoing on my part."

"He has a point Chief."

"Will you quit it, Joost."

"I'm just trying to save your fanny."

"My fanny can blow its own farts, I don't need to smell yours, so lay off the wind breakers."

"You got it, Chief."

∞

The patrolman who had been sent to find Vladg discovers him together with Hikey vanWesterfeld drinking coffee on the terrace, evidently unaware of the most recent complications.

When he explains what has happened, the total demise of Jan 276, dismembered and broken in the most cruel and ugly way, Hikey's attitude changes completely. She becomes all business.

Vladg has witnessed this scene before, at the meeting in The Hague. There is an increase of strength seeping into her body, her great head seems to expand even further and there is an overflow of intelligence dominating her consciousness.

She questions the patrolman so hard and fast that he has hardly any time to blurt out his answers. Before he and Vladg can get off the terrace, Hikey is already on her way up to the broom closet, her heels click-clacking on the walkway in energetic style, a pleasurable sound to Vladg's ear.

In the midst of his intoxication with Hikey, an image crosses Vladg's mind. The last time he had seen 276 she was ensconced together with 387. The thought flashes by that if they had had clearer gender definition one might have said they were in love. He dismisses this idea and rushes to catch up wih Hikey who is already at the elevator.

By the time all three get up to the floor where the broom closet is located, they find the crime scene guarded by only one other officer, a uniformed patrolman. He tells them that after Dusty completed his work he saw to it that the door was tightly locked, just so passersby did not become overly curious.

"The buzz in the hotel is full of the day clerk's murder you know. I'm just hanging in here awaiting further orders from the Chief."

"I want to see her!" Hikey demands, coming on provocatively, neglecting any niceties.

The patrolman knows of her reputation, decides not to argue, proceeds to open the door, and lets her get a look-see at the mess. Hikey draws in a quick breath, breaks up in a sigh of despair and grief.

What Hikey sees is a scene of brutal destruction. There isn't much left of the original shape as all the parts are stuffed together. None of Jan 276's extremities are attached to her torso, she is beheaded and her head lies on the floor next to a solitary foot. The head is still covered with the once pretty maid's cap but the ribbons are now flowing loose and inert as if they too had died when she fell to the chopping blows of the villain who attacked her.

"I knew her quite well," she tells Vladg, "and now she's gone, just like that. Her greatest wish was to be able to shop like a woman, to have access to currency and to go into a mall or department store and buy some article she wanted using her own money. Now she'll never know what it means to try on a dress in front of a triple mirror and to pump up your vanity by the feel of a new purchase on your skin."

"It is a pity," Vladg says, "I happen to know she wanted very much to be a woman in a more anatomical way."

"What fiend could have done this?" she asks.

"That man Alucard thinks Petrov did it," the uniform says. "You know, the guy that got himself all killed dead and mutilated earlier today."

"Bram thinks that, does he?" Vladg asks.

"It's what he said. That's what prompted my being here. He could be right. Dusty said Petrov's prints are all over what's left of the Duplo here."

Hikey takes a last sympathetic look at the remains of Jan 276. "If you see the Chief would you ask him to send some relief? My legs are wearing down from standing in one place and I sure could use something to eat."

"Yeah, I can do that," Vladg said.

"Let's go over to your friend's room, and see what else he has to say," Hikey said.

"He may still be in Petrov's room. That's where the Chief left him with Greet," the patrolman said.

"Okay, I'll go up to his room and you go to Petrov's, "Hikey said.

"Oh no," Vladg disagrees, not trusting Bram to be alone with Hikey. "I'll go up to Bram's room, and you go first to Petrov's. There'll be others there."

"What's the difference?"

"Humor me on this, ok?"

This is something new to Hikey, giving in to a male Duplo's request.

"Sure," she said. "Whatever."

"Keep your tele-cell available, I'll call you if he's in his room, you do the same if he's at Petrov's."

"Gotcha," she says, still thinking gloomily of Jan 276, not yet able to grin, but pleased by Vladg's spurt of jealousy.

∞

When all three finally get together in Bram's room, they find the Chief arguing with Joost.

The Chief has revised his technique a bit, no longer insulting Joost directly.

"When I call you on the tele-cell, don't put it on speaker phone like a nincompoop for God's sake. Have some respect for what I say. Most of what I tell you is for your ears only, highly secret material."

"But if I'm doing something else mechanical it frees me up to use my hands."

"That's an order."

"You got it Chief."

Vladg interrupts.

"The patrolman you stationed at the broom closet wants me to ask you if he can have relief. Says he's tired and hungry."

"I'll see what I can do."

His eye catches the uniform who had brought the messages over to Hikey and Vladg.

"You, what's your name, officer?"

"Brandt, sir."

"Okay, go over and relieve Phillips, but tell him he only gets an hour and then has to stand guard again."

"I can't do that Chief. I go off duty in half an hour."

Now the Chief is thoroughly frustrated. He sputters and spouts.

"Doesn't anyone here realize we are trying to solve a murder case..."

"It's union rules, Chief, and I don't need the overtime..."

"Well I don't have anyone else...when's your relief come on?"

"In half an hour, sir."

"Well, when he gets in tell him I said to go straight to the broom closet."

"Yes, sir."

"All right. Now you Alucard. Are you willing to go over to AMC with me? I got a message that Greta is coming out of her coma..."

"She wasn't in a coma. She merely fainted..."

"Quit correcting me. I get enough of that from Joost here. The doctors called it a coma and I'm doing the same."

"All right," Bram says, giving in on this.

"Okay," the Chief says to Joost. "You're in charge, I want you to interrogate these two. Dusty can come along with us."

"You got it," Joost says again.

After the Chief leaves, Joost asks Vladg to tell him all he knows of Petrov. Vladg says that he never actually talked to the man, that Bram had all the interaction with him.

"When we got to the hotel, we went straight to reception. Bram did all the negotiating after we learned that Duplos were not allowed to have a room."

Hikey puts in her two cents.

"That's what I intend to change."

Unlike the Chief, Joost doesn't seem to mind the interruption.

"I hope you succeed. It is very un-Dutch for us to hold that position. We gave too much power to the Central Computer."

Vladg wants to finish.

"Like I was saying Bram was able to get me a lodging of sorts in the basement with the Basisch. That's where I met Jan 276 and Jan 387."

"Who's Jan 387?"

"He was very close to 276, maybe he was even in love with her."

Both Joost and Hikey look skeptically at Vladg when he says this, but they make no further comment.

"And where is 387 now?"

"I have no idea."

"Well that's easy enough to find out. All we have to do is call Central."

"Do you have the key?" Hikey asks.

"No. I'll have to call the Chief."

He rings up.

"Chief, what is today's keyword for Central, I need to ask an important question that might be related to the murder."

"Well now you sound more professional. Are you on silent speaker?"

"Certainly," Joost lies.

Today's word is Proceed. Just identify yourself, give your badge number and rank, and when she asks for the key speak slowly and say PROCEED. That'll get you in."

"Thanks Chief, will do exactly as you said."

"Quit being a wiseacre. Just say yessir."

"Yes sir,"

The Chief has already hung up, doesn't hear the last words.

Now the computer is talking. The voice is female, similar to the one used on GPS.

"Jan 387 is engaged on the fifth floor. His task is to repair a patch in the carpet. This should take twenty-two minutes. Do you wish to know his next task?"

"No thank you, but I would appreciate it if you sent him a message to stay put. I may not get there before he finishes."

"Certainly. Can I be of service in any other way at this time?"

"No Central, that's all for now."

"You have used forty-seven seconds of computer time that will be charged to your department. Please acknowledge."

"Acknowledged."

The computer abruptly shuts off.

"Okay, let's see if we can find 387."

They hustle up to the fifth floor and find 387 bent over his work, doing a seamless job on the carpet patch. He is very adept with the knives, twirling them skillfully, artfully applying the glue where needed.

"Hey, that's really nice work, "Joost says.

"Thank you,"387 says. Then he greets Vladg and Hikey.

"You've heard about 276?" Hikey asks.

"Yes, 237 told me," he says, now standing up, starting to put his tools and cans of adhesive away.

"Were you anywhere near the reception clerk's room last night?" Joost asks bluntly.

"Not exactly, but I saw him going back and forth from the broom closet to his room. He did arouse my curiosity."

"Was he carrying anything?"

387 starts to choke up.

"Yes, he was transporting different parts of 276 and stuffing her remains into the broom closet. I was doing wallpaper on that floor at the time."

"And then what did you do?"

"I followed him into his room after that. He had no idea I was there until he turned around and saw me. I caught him by surprise you see. He was no match for me although he tried a kick or two. I strangled the man, then snapped his neck in two. He fell to the floor and I took this serrated knife and cut him open, stuffed his belly with cigars and lit him up with lighter fluid and what was left of the liquor in the bottle. I was pretty angry with him you see."

"I can imagine so, "says Joost cooly.

"Yes, I have no idea why he did that to 276, she never harmed anyone. I was very fond of her."

"Yes, that's what Vladg here says."

"You knew of my feelings for her?" he asks Vladg.

"I suspected so. I know what it's like to love another."

"Well I am ready to be dismantled. I know that my entire circuitry must be destroyed."

"That's not for us to say. Hikey here will present your case to the powers that be. In the meantime, you can go to your room if you like."

"I'd rather finish my tasks; it is the only thing I have left that makes me feel worthwhile."

"When are you due to be immobilized?"

"Not until five in the A.M."

"You promise not to go anywhere else?"

"Where would I go? I know Central would trace my whereabouts."

"Do you mind if I speak to 387 alone for a few minutes?" Hikey asks Joost.

"Sure, go ahead. Vladg and I will be down in the lobby. I have to make a report on this to the Chief."

When they get to the lobby, Joost orders coffee and Danish for them. The waiter throws a nasty look at Vladg, but Joost stares him down and Vladg gets served.

"To my knowledge this has never happened before, at least I never heard of a Duplo killing a human. The courts will be in an uproar, looking for precedent."

"This does sound like a first. What do the lawyers and judges do when there are no prior cases?"

"They get nervous," Joost says. "Hell I don't know, but it listens…"

"Listen…I don't know that usage."

"It means it's certainly fathomable, if 387 were human he'd probably have done the same thing. What I don't get is why Petrov mutilated 276. What do you think that's all about.?"

"Insane hatred. Yes, hatred that has no bounds, like the political craziness that went on in the last century. You must know something about that here in Holland."

"I've heard a bit, but they don't teach history like they used to. Too much tech stuff to learn. Well, excuse me for a minute; I've got to report to the Chief."

Joost knocks off the last piece of pastry, gulps down the rest of his coffee, pulls out his cell and this time he is careful to keep it on silent audio."

"Chief, Joost here, sorry to bother you."

"Well it had better be important, Greet here is just waking up, they had to give her two liters of whole blood, a bunch of stimulants, injectable vitamins and an antibiotic for the fever."

"I'm glad she's coming out of it Chief, but I got to tell you there's no sense in putting Alucard under house arrest…"

"Why not…"

"Because Jan 387 confessed to the murder. Seems like he caught Petrov almost in the act of destroying 276, lost his marbles and did Petrov in. You know how strong these Duplos are, they got enough ATP for ten of us."

There is a moment of silence at the other end.

"You're sure of this?"

"Yessir. No doubt about it, 387 is the perp all right. Now it's going to get very political."

"Did you read him his rights?"

"No Chief. He's not human, not a citizen, not anything really. So I didn't do anything, figuring that that way I would make no legal mistakes. Hikey is with him now."

"So you didn't place him under arrest?"

"Figured that was the wrong thing to do. But I'm here in the lobby now with Vladg and intend to write up my report as best I can. Do you want me to get him to make a formal statement, sign a confession, anything like that?"

Again there is a pause.

"No. I think you done good. Let's wait until the District Attorney tells us what to do. It's in his bailiwick now. Just sit tight. I'll call him as soon as I finish up over here. The strange thing is that Greet seems different somehow. Maybe it's just her weakness, but she seems to be attracted to this guy Bram. He's with her now."

"He's old enough to be her father," Joost says. "Hope he doesn't start any monkeyshines with her."

"You never know what makes one person attracted to another," the Chief says.

Joost is chagrined. Obviously he has feelings for Greet.

"Got to go," the Chief says. "Be over there in an hour or so."

∞

As soon as he hangs up, the Chief turns to Dusty, speaks entirely in Dutch. He tells him that the murder has been solved, that a Basisch named Jan 387 has confessed to killing Petrov.

"There's still something fishy going on here, I'm suspicious as hell of this guy Alucard, something about him doesn't click with me. Listen up, I know that Greet is fond of you so when we go inside you be the one to talk to her, I'll stay in the background. After you tell her how happy you are to see her and such, just squeeze this in, ask her if this guy Bram attacked her in any way only don't use his name, get it, I don't want him to know we're talking about him."

"Understood," Dusty says.

236

"Remember, no English when we go in.

With a soft knock on the door they enter, treading softly. Bram is sitting by her bedside, he is not holding her hand but there is something strange about their closeness, an odd attachment suggestive of intimacy. What has happened is that Bram and Greet are communicating strictly by telepathy. When Bram first entered her room, together with the Chief, he discovered at once that she was a very susceptible victim who would make an excellent slave. So he thought transferred an order to her to ask the Chief to leave, to say she wanted to be alone with Mr. Alucard, to use his surname as if she had some formal police questions to ask. Greet picked up on all this immediately, pleasing Bram no end.

Once the Chief left, Bram asked her if she wished to have eternal life and she did not hesitate in her choice: "I want desperately to live forever."

Her enthusiasm was such that Bram conferred upon her many of the secrets of vampirism. Their telepathic chemistry was so great that the two continued to communicate back and forth in this way for the entire time, never once having to verbalize a single word.

Greet greets her visitors with a wan smile, but there is no emotional direction to it, no way can either Chief de Haas or Dusty read any meaning into the expression she wears.

Dusty carries out the scheme exactly as planned. He tells her how happy he is that she is coming around, asks her if there is anything he can get for her.

"Anything at all Greet, I'll pick it up for you."

Bram snaps tele-thoughts out, tells her what to say.

"That is nice of you, but I have everything I need. All I want is to be alone with Mr. Alucard. There are things I have to ask him."

Dusty is about to say*: 'such as'* when he thinks the better of it.

"This man sitting here, did he hurt you in any way, you know like attack you or something."

Greta, thinking in English, telepaths Dusty's Dutch sentence to Bram.

Bram merely acknowledges with a blink.

"He was very helpful, caught me when I fainted. I guess he must have carried me to the bed, put the downy bedspread over me to keep me warm as I do remember getting cold. I want to thank him personally Dusty, you can understand that can't you?"

"Sure. But what about those marks on your throat...?"

"I must have scratched myself by accident when I fainted. I do have sharp nails you know."

She demonstrates by flashing her hands at Dusty, slashing at the air with her long fingernails, almost as if she were going to scratch his eyes out.

"But how did you get so anemic?"

Greta chooses not to answer this.

"You can go now," she says abrasively, forgetting for the moment that she is supposed to be nice.

Bram smiles inwardly, he knows what it is like to try to have forbearance when humans are irritating.

Dusty glances at the Chief. They both think her behavior is very un-Greta like.

"Let's go," he says. "You can stay for a few minutes," he tells Bram, then you'd better let her rest.

"Of course," Bram says.

Greta does not even look at her two colleagues as they leave. That part of her life is over.

As soon as they are alone Bram tells her they will be going to Sophia, Bulgaria together in a few days and then he will take her to his castle in Carpathia.

"Yes, my master," she says. "I will be so looking forward to it; I want to drink blood as you do, to find a victim we can attack together."

"There will be plenty of them for us to select, do not worry my sweet. Now get some rest, renew your strength. I will make all the travel arrangements necessary."

"Yes master."

∞

The news of Tulip's demise spreads like wildfire; all of the Basic Jans go on a sit down strike. The next morning the hotel is a disaster. There are no continental breakfasts available, the water heaters are left unattended and soon there is no hot water for the hotel guests and none for cooking or cleaning. Luggage of all types lines the mezzanine and lobby where guests have set them down haphazardly. For some days the grounds are unattended, flowers left unwatered, the grass unmowed. In short, all the usual tasks for running a hotel are halted.

Staff people are temporarily put to work at duplo jobs.

The owner of the hotel decides to take over Petrov's job at the front desk. Unfortunately, authority does not lend itself readily to proficiency and he finds that he is ill equipped to fulfill the necessary duties. In a fit of frustration, he throws up his hands and storms out.

The clerk who takes over says to his co-worker:

"Die kerel is hoteldebodel." (I greatly fear his reason has given way.)

In the ensuing days, during which Jan 387's fate is to be determined, Vladg and Hikey draw much closer to one another. They go through a kind of eureka experience, learning from Jan 387's devotion to Tulip that Duplicants are as capable of love feelings as humans; that the differences in each other's likes and dislikes, the little quirks and foibles that separate them at times can bring them together as well.

They also discover that their sexual bonding is not restricted.

"After all," Hikey says, "we are not missionaries."

Chapter XVII

October Love, 2058

Early autumn in the Veluwe is marvelous, not just the soft winds and the long morning shadows but the shifting sands and the salmon-green color of the October leaves on the beech trees. The van Westerveld house is situated in the curve of the valley a mere few hundred yards from narrow Lake Veluwe and the fields in between are covered with heather.

Hikey and Vladg were sitting together on a porch swing, holding hands, she brushing his lips back and forth with hers, her other hand grasped firmly about the inside of his thigh just beneath his groin. The scent of her lipstick and the fleshy smells of her mouth remind him of lavender mixed with strawberries. He is gradually losing his restraint and with a leap of sexual excitement, he tries to undo the back of her blouse with his other hand. At once she has a woman's need to talk, so she bites his lip, just a quick nip, throws her magnificent head back, and breathing quickly, she starts in on the beautiful super machinery of the Basisch. She speaks rapidly, but with skill and purpose.

"You know it's finally happened. They rolled over Jan 387 at the factory yesterday."

"I thought they were going to completely destroy him."

"That was the initial idea, you know, all the brouhaha, but the financiers knew he was too valuable, so they rolled him over in the Heringa-Wheeler machine."

"A Basic in the H-W. I didn't know that happened."

"Yes, when a Duplo has that much talent, he can be resold for quite a sum. You know he could do fine woodwork, mosaic tile, seamless carpet patches and window shades that never ruffled. Didn't you notice that when we were talking to him he matched perfectly the flower pattern in the torn parts of the rug?"

"No, I guess I missed that, I was listening to his confession. But if they resold him, won't he have memories of Tulip, of the hotel, of the murder. That'll haunt him."

"No, you see what they did was make a disk of his fine motor abilities, then they erased his memory completely. Once they got him on the Wheel they took a standard Basisch disc, gave him the usual five hundred words and such and added the new disc. He'll retain his abilities but he won't even remember White Christmases and Easter Bunnies."

"It's all for nothing then?"

"Not exactly! It is a pity that Jan 387 had to be the one to get things moving, but his demise has spurred on the new legislation before parliament. You know Vladg I am due to make a presentation in Amsterdam next week. We are going to fulfill Tulip's wish that all Basisch have to be anatomically defined as clearly as Royaals. No longer will a female Basisch be devoid of a womb, or a male be without a penis just because they have a different disposal system."

"Where will the extra money come from, those built-ins are expensive and not functional?"

"Basisch are going to be paid, minimal wage to start, but their use of currency should stimulate the economy somewhat. So the new law could pay for itself."

"What about the Central monitoring? If we want to do right by the Basisch we should eliminate that injustice too."

"We are definitely going to do away with that, right in the production line."

"How so?"

"There will no longer be sensors and receptors placed in the brain such that a Basisch can be controlled by a computer. From now on there will have to be interaction with a human, one that is the owner or designated by the owner. All jobs and tasks will be on a werkgever-werknemer basis, what you in America call employer-employee."

"Well I wish you all the success in the world, hope you can get it done. I need to be in The Hague next week. Bram is coming back from the sticks in Eastern Europe and I have to undergo another test with de Boer."

"I hope this will be the end of it. I don't like the idea of Bram using you as a guinea pig…look, here comes Mrs. van Westerveld. I hope she has good news for you."

Cynthia van Westerveld is a very good looking woman, vital in all respects. Even at sixty-something her grayish hair is magnificently coiffed, with fine little curls overhanging the top of her forehead, long coppery lashes some stuck together by a little too much mascara. The sides of her hair have bronze colored highlights and they are combed in a soft wave that covers both ears so that her chimney earrings seem to spring from nowhere. She is a tall statuesque woman with a captivating walk, a stride that indicates she knows where she is going. She cuddles a reddish brown silky haired Pomeranian that almost seems to be an integral part of her. The dog's name is Molly.

Vladg likes Cynthia. He knows that she no longer has to endure the menstrual woes of a monthly period, but tells Hikey that all that did was to change her sex drive from cyclic to calculating. Hikey poked him in the ribs when he first said this.

Hikey gets up so that Cynthia can sit next to Vladg on the swing. She pulls over one of the rattan chairs so that she can be involved in the conversation. Molly jumps into Vladg's lap.

"I think I have good news for you Vladg," Cynthia begins.

"I'm dying to hear," Vladg says.

"I've found a grammar school right here in the Veluwe that needs a science teacher. Right now they're doing a computer check on your qualifications and your past work in the States. If all is up to par, no reprimands and such, I believe they will hire you."

"That's wonderful."

"The contract is only for three months; it is like a trial period. You are going to have to prove yourself. But by now you know the Dutch; we go slowly in most things."

"That's fine; I don't mind being tested in this way."

"Of course, if you pass muster they will extend your contract and after a year you will get a substantial raise if enough of your students show promise. Then you two can be off to London to get married. We have no such laws; the British are way ahead of us on Duplicants' rights."

"I can't thank you enough…"

"Then give me a hug, I could use one."

Vladg does just that, gladly.

∞

In Santa Barbara, autumn is pleasant as well, the rains and fog keep the plant life lush and colorful, with the foliage perfuming the city with a floral fragrance while the jacaranda trees and the various types of eucalyptus add their scent to the mix. This night the air is clear, the moon is waxing in gibbous and spreads a romantic glow throughout the sky.

Phoenix has been traipsing up and down the stairs, sleepwalking through her nightmare. The clomping has awakened Lydia and when Phoenix returns to bed she begins to cry. Lydia puts her arms around her and is rewarded with a bite on the lips, one which draws a drop or two of blood that Phoenix sucks up with relish, savoring the taste on her tongue.

"I have brought the devil's bad luck to your house. I am so sorry."

Lydia hesitates, for once she does not know exactly what to do or say.

She clasps Phoenix closer to her, coddles her head on her shoulder. She strokes her frame through her thin satiny night garment until Phoenix quits whimpering, until her torment disappears.

Now Lydia spots a change in her eye color, the once ultra-blue is gone, replaced by the pregnancy to a darker shade of indigo. Lydia sees that these large indigo eyes are taking her in fully, her body sending out hundreds of messages. Lydia is still unsure but now both women are stirring with the same feeling, speaking to one another without saying a word, the seeds of sex planted firmly, ready to germinate.

In all her years of living Lydia has never kissed a woman with passion. She remains an innocent. This is not so with Phoenix who has had some experience, but not much. For a moment neither one seems to know what to do, but there is no need to worry. The more impetuous Phoenix kisses Lydia first. Lydia feels the kiss come into her lips in a manner that is totally unlike that of any man, the kiss is softer but more motivated by tenderness than by urge, less searching yet more full of discovery, accomplished but not professional.

It is almost like Lydia had completed something that had started years ago with Pierre's sister, something that had never come to fruition. Then again Lydia has this lopsided incestuous feeling, stealing away with her own husband's lover. None of it seems to matter. Never before, from impulse to action, had she ever been so certain that she was busy with something that was going to change her life forever. She was well on the way to this new path when she thought of Vladg: 'What on earth was going on here? Was this some kind of genetic variation that was dragging me into an abyss instead of a new way of doing life'?

Flags of anxiety overwhelm her.

Phoenix senses the difference in Lydia at once, and she withdraws, still holding Lydia's hand, but much more tentatively. Lydia feels like a child in her first French restaurant, a child who had ordered lobster tail, wanting to devour it, but not knowing how to proceed.

The two hold silence for a few moments, then Phoenix begins to speak. "I want you to know that. I'm not as experienced at this as you might think. I told you I was involved with a basketball jock, but I never told you that he talked us both into a ménage à trois. That was my first experience with a woman. It was my only time and was not like this; that was raw sex, there was passion but no love."

"I'm glad you told me. You are the first woman I have ever held like this, the virgin kiss of my life. I don't know what's come over me…"

"I've thought some about this. It doesn't make you a Lesbian. Perhaps if you were a man you would be gay, but women fall in love with other women in a different way than men do. We are more latent in our expression, more into the necessary meaning of ourselves. Anyway that is what I believe."

"So I can make love with you and still love a man?

"Of course. Just don't use the word bisexual. There is no such thing in a woman. We are bi-sensual, not bisexual."

Now she held Lydia's hand more firmly.

"Shall we?"

She took Lydia down and then they unclad each other, taking their time, nuzzling each other's bodies where each piece of satin that was discarded left a void, an empty patch of skin. There were no loud porno grunts or groans so characteristic of sex tussles both had experienced with men. Rather there was only the sibilant sounds of delight, small sensual gasps, soft yesses that two women make in their intimate caresses.

The greatest thing that happened for Lydia was that Phoenix started to kiss the inside of her thighs, the one part of her bod that Lydia felt so uncertain about…Phoenix seemed to relish. Then Phoenix drew her tongue all the way up from Lydia's mound, across her belly and up through her cleavage and then to her lips. Once there, Lydia tasting herself, devoured Phoenix's lips, kissing her throat, only avoiding the one area where Bram had made his slits. Then Lydia brought her head down to Phoenix's mons, getting more and more wound up until she found her tongue searching inside, her hands stroking Phoenix's pearl tinted breasts while she was kissing and nibbling her clit. Lydia came several times and so did Phoenix, lovely multiple orgasms with a sweetness and smoothness to the fluid that neither one had ever experienced even when making love to themselves.

Lydia didn't know how long they held each other, but it must have been some time because when they dressed and went back on the terrace the moon had moved in a wide arc through the heavens.

Phoenix was unable to drink alcohol but they toasted each other with raspberry iced tea and got to talking again with no hint of shame or guilt.

"I think you've cured my sleepwalking," Phoenix said.

"I'll tell Bram."

"No, don't. This is just for us and the baby to know. It's an introduction to love and life for the child, a dedication of sorts."

"You're right, I should have thought of that."

"Oh, by the way, there aren't any more like you around these parts are there?" Phoenix asked.

"No, not that I know of, why?"

"Two from the same family is enough," Phoenix said, and they both laughed.

They finished off the iced tea and went back to bed for the night, clasping each other tightly, breast to breast, pouch to pouch, until they fell asleep.

It was the most restful night they had spent in months.

Chapter XVIII

Bram's 2ⁿᵈ Reformation

Bram was beginning to think of himself as Martin Luther in reverse. He didn't want to split religion -certainly not- his intent was to bring worship of Lucifer into step with the modern world. 'After all', he thought, 'most people were half-way there, their lives characterized by a cheating imagination; greed and gluttony already so rationalized into their traditional beliefs that inculcating a few more commandments of 'thou shall' in place of 'thou shall not' shouldn't be all that difficult'.

His aim was to start a movement that would promote vampirism; a movement that he envisioned would sweep across Europe from east to west. If only he could place a number of Royaal Duplicants in position to spray the venom, knock out a few powerful politicians and a certain number of influential corporate people, he could drink their blood and transform them into vampire slaves to do his bidding.

As Vampires cannot really attend church, the risk of destructive power from the crucifix being too great, infiltration by Duplicants was the key. This infiltration meant much more than the fulfillment of his parents' wishes; more than avenging the murder of his father by religious zealots who had thrust a silver stake through his father's heart.

It meant he would be able to control destiny.

In Dolno Katore, the small village in the Carpathian Mountains above which Bram's castle was located, he and Greta had done wonders with the three male Royaal Duplicants transported from Holland by train. As soon as they arrived, Bram performed his own brain transfers to the Duplicant's circuitry, teaching them Slavic languages and the principles of everlasting vampire life in which he believed so fervently. Each Royaal was now able to proselytize, capable of preaching the devil's own bible, and to take part in all the macabre rituals that were to be delivered to the highly religious populace of the region. All that was needed was an adequate supply of venom to further indoctrinate the people against the carpenter God and this would be coming soon.

Greta, however, remained sexually frustrated as none of the Royaals had sexual systems and Bram was careful not to be her lover. Within his doctrine of immorality there was a firm belief that if he betrayed Phoenix with another woman, Lucifer's vengeance might cause the boy-child to die in the womb. So he restrained himself along these lines. And in an almost military manner he strived to remain on task, to keep his goals alive, his duties active and purposeful. In the peace of the evenings he explained to Greta the changes that her body would be making in the next few months:

"Your skin might thicken a bit, very much as if you were pregnant, but it will give you a more fetching glow, a sultrier look. Your lips especially will be more attractive, unfurling naturally, luring men to kiss you and putting your front teeth in position to bite them properly. Once you have the taste of their blood, you may proceed to drink your fill, but you must be careful for the first six or seven months, until your blood chemistry changes enough for you to produce venom on your own. Until then, a man like Joost, who admires you greatly, can still overpower you. Do you understand?"

"Yes, Master, but I yearn so to find a victim, to drink their blood together with you."

"That will happen. We will drink together, but you must have patience."

"What makes you so sure there are enough victims around?'

"As a policewoman you should know there is never a dearth of victims. Much of course depends on the vulnerability of the intended. Most humans are frail; their lives are barren and subordinate. There is an affinity between the bite and the wound; they are aching for each other. Some cry out, some protest and some succumb in silence, all three are different and their responses have different meanings."

"How so?"

"Those that succumb in silence are looking for an external force to silence their own pretensions; they know that they have lived a life of falseness to themselves and to others; those who protest most severely are the ones who really want to be torn to pieces, they do not make good slaves for they want you to really hurt them."

"And the ones who cry out for help?"

"They are the ones who have never known true independence, they cry out because they depend on others to save them from danger, but they have always done so even in situations where the danger was minimal. So they have had a sort of success in life, as long as others were around to 'save' them; stronger people who solved their dilemmas. What they face with you is the beginning of a relationship that leaves no room for independency. Once you make them a slave, they will be obedient."

"You left out the ones who truly make a fight of it."

"Oh, you mean the peacocks."

"Peacocks?"

"Yes the ones with true pride who are truly beautiful and not afraid to show it off. Yes, they exist. Phoenix is one. They are people who love the way they do life, have a justified vanity and are willing to fight to the death to save themselves. There are few of these."

"What about someone like my boss, Chief de Haas?"

"Think of your relationship to Chief de Haas, it even lacks imaginative dignities. He has no true honor in his profession. And the way he is not respected by Joost shows there is a lack of freedom to advance. Joost is the peacock, not de Haas."

"But de Haas would never be my choice in the first place, I find him revolting. Are you sure there is a goodly supply of 'tasty' victims around?"

"Yes, you can be assured there are potential victims enough, my own Lydia sought vampirism as a means to get out of the hole she had dug for herself."

"But as your slave am I not in a subordinate position to you?"

"Yes, but the difference is you are not barren, you germinate eternal life. And the time will come when you will want to have slaves of your own, and that freedom is yours."

"It is?"

"Of course, eventually you will have your own harem so to speak, both male and female slaves of your choosing. But you must first learn that it is not enough to drink your victim's blood or merely to inject your venom into their systems, your darkness must first pass through their hearts and influence their spirit, otherwise their emotional violence will be uncontrollable."

"That is a long way off for me."

"Yes, this is just a warning. It takes time to learn to haunt the present, to love the dead, to penetrate the living. The immediate problem is you are feeling the urgency of growth in your canines, they are very sexualized now and will extend into fangs when you are aroused, but you must inhibit this, for a very strong man could easily subdue you physically and an early defeat to every young vampire is a terrible stress, it can affect you in many different ways and for a long time to come."

"I might even lose my powers?"

"If the man who subdues you physically also controls you mentally so that your will is subjugated to his, yes, that is possible."

"You mean I could return to being just plain Greet."

"It is within the realm of possibility," Bram says, trying to sound as professorial as he can.

"Then I shall take your advice. Although I prefer male blood, I will start with women, and not the butchy types, we have many of those in Holland."

Bram has to laugh. He likes Greta's ways; she is an apt and willing slave.

The days that follow are consumed by teaching Greta about the dangers inherent in everlasting life on earth and remembering to serve at the behest of the ultimate master, who is Satan. The Royaals receive similar indoctrination, but their tasks are more strictly defined: to invade the churches, gain power over the preachers and biggest financial contributors and to introduce the parishioners to the study of the Devil's bible.

When Bram is totally satisfied that the three Royaals can sustain things on their own, he leaves them with a Dhampire cousin named Malignius, who oversees the domestic staff of the castle. It was Malignius who saw to it that all three Duplicants attended church even though they were relegated to the farthest pew in the back of the congregation.

Once Bram was assured of their safety, he and Greta took their leave, setting off on their journey by the only mode of transportation available from the castle, an old fashioned four horse carriage. With the driver cracking his big whip the carriage took off down the sloping mountain roads, quickly breached the tree line, galloped toward the steep hills crowned with clumps of trees and then, after a few farmhouses appeared, slowed down and soon reached the heart of the village.

After a short luncheon at the Inn, where the food was cooked on a wood stove, Bram and Greta left the carriage behind and traveled across the river by ferry over to Târgu Jiu where modernity reappeared in the form of an air shuttle that took them back to Sofia and thence by rocket-jet to Amsterdam. In the space of three hours they had traveled three different centuries of culture.

It was Greta who drove from Schiphol to Amersfoort where she had to return to work with the homicide division having spent two of her eight weeks yearly paid vacation entirely with Bram and his people.

As soon as Greta got situated and assured Chief Haas that she was entirely fit and healthy to work her shift, she learned from the water cooler buzz that Vladg was living with Hikey in the Veluwe, actually right in the van Westerveld house.

When she told this to Bram he had another reason to be furious, for now he realized that Lydia had duped him on the 'unhappiness' of Vladg in Holland.

As soon as Vladg contacted him, Bram sensed that things were different. For one, he could no longer read his mind. But he had a scheme up his sleeve, one concocted with the purpose of 'getting back' at Lydia for her transgressions against him.

"I'm sorry it took longer than I thought to complete my work in Sofia for the Foreign Service," he said, "but then Gregoriev granted me a few days furlough and I took a brief holiday to Dolno Katore to see my cousin and some friends, to check out my little abode in the mountains."

"Little abode? Lydia told me you owned a castle there!" Vladg was in no mood to listen to Bram's dissimulations.

"She did, did she? Well sometimes Lydia has a motor mouth, but yes, I guess you could call it a castle as it has forty rooms or so. But getting back to it, I hear you've got a teaching job during the week; when can you make it to de Boer at the factory? It would be your final test on the new venom that he has manufactured for me."

"This weekend would be fine. Hikey is in Amsterdam, and I will be alone with Mrs. van Westerveld helping in the house…"

"Turning into a house boy of sorts are you?"

"Listen Bram, I don't have to take your cynicism. Holland has given me a sense of freedom I've never known in the States. I'm more my own man now."

"You've found out that freedom is more than opening your fly to my wife?"

"That's nasty Bram. You agreed to my being her companion when you were away. After all I'm not human so you are not really a cuckold."

"That may be true, but I had no idea Lydia would become so fond of you that she was willing to lie to me for you."

"Again, that's not my fault. Look Bram, aside from Lydia, I've found out that the female penchant for secrecy and double games doesn't have to apply when someone truly loves you;

taking up with Hikey has changed my views on things considerably."

"You're still my Duplicant."

"It's Lydia that owns me, not you, and she has told me about your upcoming divorce. So as long as she allows me to stay in Holland I don't think you have much to say about it."

"Don't get huffy. After all I'm the one that paid for you and while your value is being determined by the lawyers I still have something to say."

"That's debatable. She holds title to me."

"Okay, you want to play hardball. But will you come this Saturday to the factory?"

"Sure, I said I would and I will, long as you promise this is the last time."

"Oh, this will be the last time all right, that's for sure."

Something about the way Bram says this doesn't sit right with Vladg, but he lets it go, feels he does owe Bram this last bit of allegiance.

∞

Meanwhile, at the Harry S Truman building in Washington D.C., Gregoriev receives a communiqué from Ms. Bradford at the consulate in The Hague. It seems that the defective Royaals (equal to Sextus IV's) which Bram had purchased for the State department were doing well. They were supposed to be abject failures, not successes, and this upsets Gregoriev no end.

If it wasn't for the success of the love potion (Gregoriev continues to hold his own with the redheaded mistress whom he has recently promoted) he would reprimand Alucard. His plan had been to prove that the skilled employees of the State Department at all levels did specialist work that was above and beyond the capabilities of the Sextus IV's. Now he might have to hire some more Duplicants for different locations, especially those in the more dangerous areas like Somalia whose government was hanging by a thread.

Thus far the consequences of hiring Duplicants remain at odds with Gregoriev's wishes. Each and every Duplicant hired becomes one less human being over which he and his counterparts can exert power and control.

'If things go on like this, the department will fulfill its obligations to the people, and then what will we do?'

∞

Saturday morning early, on the way to the factory, Vladg happens to mention   that Hikey's purpose in Amsterdam is to attend a meeting with the leaders of the political parties on the Basisch question.

"Since there are so many political parties in Holland, they are called fraction leaders as no one party is dominant. Maybe if we had more political parties in the States kids would understand their fractions better," Vladg jokes, the teacher in him acting up.

Bram pays no attention to Vladg's attempt at humor, but he appears inordinately interested in the politics. This surprises Vladg.

"You mean she gets to talk with all the leaders, the VVD, PvdA, D66 and Green Links?"

Now Vladg is really impressed.

"How come you're so smart on this? And how do you know the names of all the parties? I certainly don't."

Bram doesn't answer directly.

"Isn't it unusual for all the fraction leaders to meet together like this?"   Vladg can't figure out his concern.

"Yes, Hikey says it is, but this is a matter that concerns the entire economy and in addition there is a moral question involved, you know, seeking justice for the Basisch in a manner that is fair to all concerned."

"You're beginning to sound like Hikey yourself," Bram says.

"Yeah, some of her is brushing off on me, and vice versa."

"You must be in love."

"I guess."

"Better to be in love with a Duplicant than a human, look what's happened to me and Lydia.'

"Hey, you've made a wrong turn; you're going the wrong way."

"I've got to pick up Greta, she wants to come along."

"Well I don't want Greta to see me naked."

"Not to worry, she's just there to validate the money end of the transaction. I don't quite trust de Boer not to blackmail me for more Euros, so I've drawn up a contract and Greta will witness it."

Vladg doesn't like it, but there's nothing he can do, Bram's the one in the driver's seat.

∞

De Boer is waiting for them at a side entrance to the factory, an entryway that avoids going through the main body of the plant. It is Saturday and the production line is closed down for the weekend, but a skeleton crew remains to cover the work needed on the Royaals, who are crafted entirely by hand; once started a Royaal cannot be halted in production as is true of the Basisch.

As de Boer leads them into a hallway that crosses by his lab they come across Mr. Wiersma, a neuro-engineer who works entirely on brains and eyes but also holds a rather senior position of security at the factory and is a close friend of Mr. van den Valk.

"I say de Boer, what are you doing here on Saturday and who are these people?"

De Boer is somewhat taken aback by the abruptness of the question, he has no made-up answer prepared in advance and is not a good actor.

"I'm doing a research project on the metabolism of this American Sextus," he points out Vladg, "and I'd like to introduce you to his master Mr. Alucard."

Bram sets down his valise, which he had been carrying in his right hand.

Wiersma shakes Bram's hand, says to Greta:

"You look familiar."

"Yes, I am a detective with the homicide division here in Amersfoort, under Chief Haas. I'm here only as an onlooker, not in any official capacity."

"I see. It's my pleasure to meet you. Would you like me to take you on a tour of the plant?'

Greta looks to Bram for his approval, gets his nod, but none of this is missed by Wiersma, who says:

"De Boer, next time you plan on opening the lab on a Saturday, let security know, we cannot protect you if we do not know you are here. We've had a few break-ins from riffraff recently."

He directs this remark mostly at Bram for some reason. Then he takes Greta by the crook of the arm and heads off in another direction. Greta casts a sheepish grin at Bram, an expression meant to tell him she's been caught in a web not of her own making.

Once the three are ensconced in the lab, de Boer feels less anxious.

"That Wiersma is a pretty sharp article," Bram says.

"He didn't even acknowledge my presence; who does he think he is anyhow?" Vladg asks, obviously touchy from the slight.

"He fancies himself some kind of protector of the fabriek, I mean the factory, always wandering about the hallways, springing up from nowhere. I don't really answer to him, only to the chief of R&D, Dr. Helmut, but since he was suspicious I thought it better to be on the safe side and not provoke him."

"You certainly acted nervous. Are you up to this today?"

"Absolutely! Not a problem."

He turns to Vladg, says:

"Vladg, please take the same position as last time on the examining table, I will get a vial of the new venom and remove the old one."

"If you don't mind de Boer, I'd rather open it up myself; just give me a hand mirror. The last time you were a little rough with my belly button."

"Oh, I am sorry, I will be more careful this time when I insert the new vial."

"You don't need to retest my sensors and receptors do you, I don't want to get completely undressed."

"No, that part won't be necessary, just make sure there is adequate room for us to work in a sterile manner."

Vladg takes off his flannel shirt, throws it over to Bram, but he doesn't get out of his jeans, merely lowers them below his umbilicus.

De Boer goes over to his floor safe, twirls the correct combination and pulls out a narrow leather carrying case containing six vials. Each vial is secured on a ridge within the container by a hole designed to fit the tapered end of the vial; a velvet lined clasp at the top holds it firmly at the upper end.

He is careful to close and lock the safe.

"Each vial contains two cc's of the new venom, one goes into Vladg, and that leaves ten cc's for you as I promised."

Bram inspects each vial, accepts the leather case, sets it aside safely in his valise.

"But you're not going to leave that one vial in me are you?"

"That's up to Mr. Alucard."

"Of course not, Vladg, we'll remove it as soon as the experiment is over, be assured of that."

"Oh good, I wouldn't want to go around for a month knocking people out with my sweat."

"Understood," Bram says.

"Now let's get to work," de Boer says.

"I need to make a call first, want to catch Hikey before she goes to Amsterdam, wish her luck with the fraction heads."

"Sure, go ahead," de Boer says, "I can wait a few minutes."

Vladg takes out his out his tele-cell, punches in Hikey's number but all he gets is her message board, telling him to leave a pic-note after the beep. So he focuses the tele-screen close to his face, wishes her good luck at the meet in Amsterdam, neglects to click off.

When Vladg removes his vial, de Boer goes through the same procedure as the last time; then Vladg has to hop onto the tread mill and does ten minutes of very strenuous cardiovascular, gets his heart rate up to 160 bpm and starts to sweat profusely. The venom immediately saturates the air.

"Hop on to the exam table or you'll drop on the floor," de Boer yells.

Vladg jumps back on in time, but as he does so his tele-cell comes loose from his pocket, and as he turns on his side his hip knocks the tele-cell out, it falls off the table onto the floor with a soft thump, opens up and redials Hikey's number automatically.

Vladg falls into a spell immediately, not so with de Boer; he is completely unaffected this time.

"What's wrong," Bram asks, "why aren't you out as well?"

"You didn't think I was so foolish as to be put under a spell twice in a row. I concocted an antidote."

"Why in hell would you do that?"

"No reason in particular. One never knows though, does one?"

Bram immediately sees the corrupt logic in de Boer's mind. When the time comes to put his plan into action and he starts to place certain Dutch powerhouses under a spell, de Boer will be in a position to offset the potion with his antidote and ask a goodly sum for his services. Bram is furious, he feels the power of Greta's young blood coursing through his veins, the wolf in him getting agitated, but he knows he must control himself for a few minutes more.

"What if I offer you an additional fifty-thousand New Euros for the antidote?"

"If you don't mind I'd like to complete the present transaction first. You do have the rest of the money?"

"Sure, right here, but why not make an agreement on the antidote now?"

Bram already knows the answer to the question he has asked; de Boer wants to see what the traffic will bear before he makes a deal. 'He has a typical Dutch business mind,' Bram thinks.

"I'd just like the opportunity to think it over," de Boer says. "Would you like to pay me now?"

"After you hand over the formula as promised."

"Both formulas are in the safe, if you pay me first I'll get yours for you."

"All right."

Bram takes out ten bundles of notes, each secured with the bank's wrapping paper wound around the new bills, hands them over to de Boer, who accepts them without a thank you, counts them twice, turns to go to his safe.

Bram is seething.

He decides not to waste any of his own venom on this man full of antidote.

Now he does something very strange. He pulls Vladg's large checkered shirt entirely over his outer garments, buttons up completely. Even the top button is closed so that the shirt fits very tightly, the collar pulled up just under his chin line.

He begins to feel his primitive anger stirring deep within, welcomes the change. His ancestral demons shine in both eyes.

He waits until the fury turns into rage, senses the transformation, allows the wolf in him to surge throughout his body until there is no longer a mingling of thought and feeling; fingernails have extended into claws, all eight incisors are larger, sharpened and serrated, and his face is contorted into canine features. Now he is yellow eyed, fang and claw directed at his prey. He gets on all fours, positions himself well behind de Boer, and starts to pant, his tongue hangs out. De Boer opens his safe, hears a growl, turns and is met with the entire force of Bram's body hurtling through the air, he falls to one side but Bram claws at his face, tears one cheek entirely off, bite-rips a chunk out of his throat, blood spurting every which way, then he slashes at his belly repeatedly, right through the clothing, disemboweling de Boer completely. De Boer is still alive, but not for long, as a final bite at his now bare belly finds the aorta and de Boer exsanguinates almost at once, the blood filling up his abdominal cavity with the last few angular beats of his heart.

Bram is breathing hard but is able to examine the contents of the safe. He searches for the formulas first, finds them in a notebook, the antidote clearly labeled separately from the active venom. He also finds another leather case, a carbon copy of the first one, containing several vials of the antidote. He stuffs this and the wrapped money as well as the new venom into his valise. Then Bram takes the rest of the money in the safe, including the original fifty thousand. All in all he feels this was a successful operation; the new venom works and quite unexpectedly he has solved a problem with the antidote, as this now allows his Duplicants to be unaffected by the venom.

He smiles outwardly at the small profit, remembers to lock the safe, twirling the combination back and forth, enjoying the rhythmic hand motion.

He takes a few moments for himself, waits until his facial features return to normal, watches as his claws once again become human fingernails, his canines transposing into normal size and shape.

Now he makes ready for the second part of the plan.

He checks his watch. Vladg should be deep in his spell for another ten minutes or so. Bram knows he is not as handy as de Boer or Vladg, but he manages to remove the venom vial and replace it with the old male scent. With the last bit of wolf strength left in him, Bram carries Vladg over from the examining table, plops him on top of de Boer, takes off the shirt and throws it haphazardly on top of Vladg.

He goes over to the sink, washes his hands and face. Some few spots of blood have clotted onto his trousers, he scrubs most of them off, has too little patience for doing a good job. Just as he finishes cleaning up, there is a knock at the door.

It is Greta returning from her tour of the plant. She looks fresh and excited… immediately sees all the blood…" what's happened here?"

Bram makes a shush sign, bringing his index finger to his pursed lips, places one hand into the crook of her arm and hustles her further out into the hallway, leaves the door open.

"De Boer got a little out of hand, that's all. I had to set him right about a few things."

Greta is tantalized by the amount of fresh blood she can see still seeping out from de Boer's belly.

"That's awfully appetizing," she says.

"No, don't drink any of that. This man had smelly feet combined with bad breath, always a bad sign. See his coated tongue, how dun-gray it is. I imagine this man had some kind of blood sickness, probably unaware of it. Good lesson, for you though, always check the tongue before you drink a victim's blood especially if they are already dead. As long as the blood is flowing and they are alive, your chances of infection are less."

"Thank you Master, a good lesson."

"What happened out there with Wiersma?"

"As I thought beforehand, he tried to hit on me."

"You didn't 'hit' on him."

"No, wanted to, but I took your advice."

"Now I want you to listen to me carefully." Bram checks his watch. "In a few minutes I'm going out to pick a fight with Wiersma, one which I intend to lose."

"Why on earth…?"

"It's all a matter of timing. We have to delay for two hours so that the Time-Retriever cannot pick up my vibes in this room.

So ask Joost to retrieve your Truth-Detector, by the time he gets here and all the rest is sorted out it should be close to the timeline."

"Yes Master."

"You see first you need to do some work for me here. Don't call your office until Vladg wakes up. After that just tell them that there's been another murder of a human by a Duplicant…same style as Petrov, belly slashed wide open."

"You mean Vladg did this?"

"It looks like it, doesn't it?"

"But he is out cold…"

"He will wake up in ten minutes."

"I don't know that this will fly…"

"That's a decision to be made by your partners, isn't it?"

"Sure, but…"

"I don't want you to lie, just tell them the way things looked when you came in, that he was asleep on top of de Boer. If we time this correctly, Vladg should just be coming around when your people get here; he will still be somewhat transfixed and confused."

"All right, I can manage that much."

"I hope by the time they come I will be knocked out too."

"Try not to get hurt too much."

"Oh no, I can play the part when it's necessary. But there is one thing more I have to tell you,"

"Yes, Master."

"I have to go to Schiphol, I am scheduled on a Sub-Orb to Kennedy at five this afternoon…"

"You are leaving me?"

"Only for a short while, you still have six weeks of paid vacation. I will send for you, but it is imperative that I go to my farm in Oneonta. I have a tasty morsel for you there, her name is Phoebe and I am sure she will still be under my spell, we can subdue her easily and her blood should be to your liking. It will be our first ménage à trois of sorts."

Greta is spellbound by Bram's selling job.

"Life is unbearable without you, so drab, so listless…I don't know that I can bear your absence, you are so exciting."

"Thank you, my love. I will call you every day on the tele-cell."

"Please. I cannot live without hearing from you."

Once Bram hears this he knows that his conquest of Greta is complete. Unless she falls to the will of a more powerful human, her allegiance as a slave will be useful to him for years to come.

∞

Things do work out the way that Bram had planned.

He goes out to the plant and starts an argument. He accuses Wiersma of making sexual overtures, then attacking Greta physically. Wiersma denies this, says he tried to flirt with her and that was all. Bram demands more details, a better explanation.

They go back and forth on the way things happened until Wiersma, exasperated by Bram's provocative attitude, finally says:

"What business is it of yours anyway? You are not her father."

"No, but she is my ward and I am very protective of her, so stay away."

Bram purposely draws closer, sticks his face almost into Wiersma's.

Wiersma pushes him back, figures enough is enough, turns to walk away.

Bram jumps him; Wiersma easily shakes him off.

Bram jabs at his face, Wiersma right-crosses him in the nose, a bit of blood spurts out. Bram purposely wipes the blood on the back of his hand, then on his trousers where de Boer's blood had clotted.

Bram forgets himself, hits Wiersma fisted with his left hand, opening up his old thumb wound, this he had not intended to do.

Now Wiersma uppercuts him to the jaw and he goes down for good just as the detectives arrive, including the Chief.

"Here, here, let's have none of this," de Haas says, pulling Bram to his feet and holding Wiersma off with his other hand. "What's going on here? I'm surprised at you Wiersma."

"This foreigner is obnoxious."

"That doesn't give you the right to get violent. What's your story on this one Bram?"

"He tried to take advantage of Greta, against her wishes. That's what she told me. You can check it out, she's in the lab with Vladg and de Boer."

"All right. Dusty you and Arie go over to the lab and see what Greta is talking about, you know what I mean. I'll stay and question these two."

"Okay, Chief."

By the time Dusty gets to the lab with the other CSI man named Arie, Vladg is barely awake, still woozy. He looks a total mess; his distorted face is covered with blood spots. He still has on his low slung jeans, but they are ruined by the ooze of de Boer's blood clinging to the fabric. He wears no shirt and his bare torso is covered with clots.

"What the hell," Dusty exclaims.

Vladg stumbles to his feet, tells his story but is stung by their lack of empathy. His misery goes totally unrecognized by the detectives.

"It was like this when I got here," Greta says, "except that Vladg here was out

cold."

"The last I knew I was lying on that exam table. I don't know how I got on top of poor de Boer here."

"Was Bram here when all this happened?"

"I can't say for sure. I met him in the hallway, told him how Mr. Wiersma tried to attack me and he ran off to find him."

"Well, he certainly hangs around trouble doesn't he?"

"He's a vampire," Vladg says.

"What did you say?" Dusty exclaims.

"I know it's hard to believe, but it's true. I didn't believe in vampires myself until recently, but you can bet your boots that if anyone did this, it was Bram."

Arie and Dusty exchange looks; they both figure Vladg is a Duplicant who has lost his marbles.

Dusty gets to work doing his thing while Arie takes pics of everything, cautions the others not to touch anything and treats Greta more as a witness than a member of the department.

By the time these two are finishing up, de Haas, with Wiersma in tow, show up and find their way into the crowded lab.

Wiersma and Greta exchange hateful glances, go at it verbally for a time, until de Haas breaks it up, settles them both down. "Show some respect for the crime scene!" he says, frowning at Greta.

Now Dusty spots his chance, asks de Haas: "Where's Bram?"

"He's gone back to check out of the hotel, He's taking a flight to New York City on a Sub-Orb at five. You know it's mandatory to be there an hour ahead of time."

"But Chief, he could be implicated in this murder!"

"I doubt it. Greta said on the phone this was a carbon copy of the one committed by Jan 387. You'd have to be very strong, like Vladg here…look at the shoulders on him…to do anything like this."

"That man called Bram was a puny punk," Wiersma says. "He could never have the strength to do anything like this."

"He's not a punk," Greta flashes back at Wiersma. "He was just trying to defend me, but I agree he is not strong enough to slash away at this man's belly like that."

"Greta, you're not exactly an unbiased witness here," Dusty says, "after all you went on a trip with him to the Balkans."

"Is that true Greta?" the Chief asks, "I didn't know that."

"Yes Chief, but he was a gentleman all the way, unlike Wiersma here. We are just platonic you see…"

"More like a sugar daddy you mean…" Wiersma says.

"Shut up Wiersma," Dusty says, "watch what you say."

Greta takes all this in, the byplay between the men is just as Bram had predicted.

"Forget Mr. Alucard, he's well on his way and he has immunity anyway. I think…turning to Vladg…. that you'd better read this Duplicant his rights."

"Is that the correct legal thing to do, we have no written statutes on Duplos, they were supposed to be restricted against harming humans."

"I know, but let's do it just to be on the safe side."

"I've put in a call to Joost; he's going to bring the Truth-Detector along. Perhaps we'd best wait to read Vladg here his rights until Joost arrives. What do you think Chief?"

"That makes sense, but you should have called for the holotographer to bring the Time-Retriever and the Projecto-Fax."

"I didn't think of that."

Listening to all this makes Vladg immensely nervous, his slight western twang comes out when he speaks.

"But I didn't do a thing," Vladg protests. "I don't even know how I got off the table and ended up top of de Boer."

"Now that makes you sound real human," Arie says, "that's what all the perps say."

∞

At the hotel before Bram packs all his things he sends Lydia an H-mail informing her that Vladg has been involved in a murder, will be out of circulation for a while and will not be coming back to the States with him. He tells her how sorry he is and hopes this turn of events doesn't interfere with her promise to stay with Phoenix throughout the pregnancy. Then, after a good guttural laugh to himself, he finishes packing, checks out at the front desk.

He fairly dawdles along the road to Schiphol, checks his watch, sees that it is over two hours since he left the lab. He turns in his rental and checks in at the KLM Sub-Orb desk. A Basisch with his special wand takes care of his bags, no questions asked. Then he heads over to a refreshment stand to get a Vita-Shake with mineral clusters, drinks almost all of it.

He is too tired to make the long walk over to the Sub-Orb gate, which is set off in a section entirely by itself.

He steps into the nearest Scoot-Chute cart which looks like a bumper-car with thrusters. He deposits the requisite amount of coins, punches in the designated gate number, hits the start button, is vacuumed into the air, the multicolored sail-chute opens, the manufactured wind blows him over to the proper gate area, and the cart is suspended when the wind stops. The contraption drops to within ten feet of the floor, thrusters reverse, beep a warning tweet and he is deposited at the correct numbered gate. All this occurs in ten seconds. As he steps out of the cart a Basisch inspects and refolds the chute, signals to a waiting passenger who jumps into the seat and is whooshed up.

There is a large old fashioned meson-neutrino body scanner shaped in the form of an inverted U which he must pass under. He does so and it automatically does a total body scan, lists his height and weight, checks his percentage of body fat and other metabolic requirements. He is pronounced fit to make the flight. As he turns to retrieve his valise he is asked to place one hand in a metalloid mold fit for the purpose, his fingerprints are checked automatically with those on his passport. A pleasant computer voice pronounces him eligible to board.

Bram is lucky, the day is clear, not a cloud in the sky. He gets a window seat, and at the end of ascent, just before crossing the Karman line when the Sub-Orb maneuvers for descent, he glances out the window. There is no undercast. Since he is traveling west, while the earth spins west to east, he is able to see the slow rotation of the planet.

He takes this as a very good sign for his future plans.

He arrives at Kennedy in less than two hours' total flight time.

Chapter XIX

Split Screens

Once Vladg had quit protesting his innocence and the team of detectives considered him calm enough to undergo testing, they exposed him to the Truth-Detector. They played a variation of good-cop, bad cop; Greta acting as the hare and Joost doing the turtle bit. Greta's technique was to jump around, rapidly firing out one question after another at Vladg as if she were shooting bullets at him, but when the hum of the detector stopped his answers were consistent with innocence. Joost, by contrast, didn't move an inch, stared Vladg down for several minutes before putting a question to him; same result, when the machine stopped humming Vladg's responses were valid but did not implicate him in the crime. So when Willem showed up bearing the TRU and the Projecto-FAX they both quit the interrogation.

All the while this was going on, Arie, who had taken over some of Dusty's more menial tasks, kept checking the lab for clues. Scouring around, he came upon Vladg's Tele-Cell on the floor lying next to the exam table. Earlier on Vladg had claimed he lost it, stating he could not imagine how it fell out of his pocket. So Arie returned the Tele-Cell to him as he saw no valid reason not to. Vladg examined it, tried to test it out, but the battery was dead. He had neglected to hit the END button on his last call to Hikey when he had only made contact with her message board. This meant that the cell had been on all the time and explained why the battery was dead.

Upon his arrival, Willem asked for a quick orientation to the Crime Scene, so Chief de Haas took it upon himself to explain the time frame and the sequence of events as the team had thus far put things together. Willem paid very close attention to all that was being said, but he also kept busy setting up his instrumentation. He was one of those people who can truly multitask and had very little change of expression as he worked.

His main focus appeared to be on nothing else but the corpse.

"Then the only possible candidate for me to examine is the victim?" he asked, "not the space in the lab, not the Duplicant here?"

Dusty stared at Arie, Arie checked with Joost and then all three looked at Greta who nodded positively at de Haas.

"It seems so," the Chief said.

"Okay. The victim's name is de Boer, is that right?"

"Yes, correct," de Haas said.

Willem got right to work. He set up a force field of bosons directed equally at both retinas, and as the sub-atomic particles were activated, he placed the Projecto-Fax on de Boer's occiput. Nothing happened.

"This may take a minute or two. As you know when a cell dies it first sheds an electron here and there, then loses protons and finally neutrons and that's when its function goes. That's why some cells continue to grow; hair follicles will even grow hair long after the individual is dead, but they are primitive cells. Brain cells, the grayish neurons, are the most complex and the most differentiated of all. To restart their functional memory, we can't be much more than a few minutes past the two hour limit.

So this is cutting it close, and as the TRU reassembles the quarks and the other subatomic particles it may take a while.

"Now remember if we get anything, it will be what de Boer thinks he saw, his interpretation. In other words, the image we get is a combination of the true perceptual field with the victim's imagination superimposed onto the incoming visual stimuli. It is his visionary modification of the event. Understood?"

Everyone nods.

Gradually a hologram begins to form a little less than two feet in front of the opposing wall. The slow reappearance of the images is dramatic, although they are not yet fully distinct.

"What the hell is that?"

"It looks like an animal of some sort."

"No, that is Vladg's shirt, see the checkered pattern?"

"Yes, but that's not Vladg."

"Aren't those Bram's shoes?"

"Yes, but that's not Bram."

"God verdomme, it's a wolf wearing the shirt, look at that snout, those claws, those canines."

Everyone is in awe except Greta who is conspicuous by her silence. She is the only one who does not exclaim her wonderment at the projected image.

"There's no beauty in this beast," Joost says.

"It's definitely not the Duplicant here." Arie says.

Greta finally pipes up.

"Well it's not Bram either," she says.

"I'm not sure," Dusty says, remember Willem said the image was superimposed by de Boer's imagination. If you were being attacked like that" …he points to de Boer's belly…"you might just think it was a wolf or some other predatory beast."

"I'll make a 3-D hard-pic for you before the hologram fades, but I can assure you no lawyer in the world will be able to convince a jury that this being was human or even humanoid. No, I'm afraid this technology has failed."

"Then we'll go after the perp the old fashioned way, basic detective work," de Haas counters. "Someone is responsible for this death, and by God we'll find out just who that someone is!"

"It's Bram," Vladg insists. "All you have to do is believe that he is a vampire and everything falls into place. He's wearing my flannel shirt, even I can see that."

Greta comes back at him.

"That's easy for you to say, you're still a primary suspect."

"If you keep defending Bram it will be your downfall; do you want to be torn to pieces?"

"Of course not! Just shut up will you Vladg?"

"Is that what you're offering Bram, you're body on a platter?"

"Don't be silly."

"Quit arguing. You never see me arguing do you?"

Unbelievably, this is coming from Joost.

Now even stoic Willem has to snicker.

"Stop this nonsense," de Haas orders. "Get yourselves together; we need to be moving on."

"Wait! Wait! Joost shouts. "I see something. Can you zoom in on the hologram, just behind the wolf figure, see that, there's something else there?"

"I'll try," says Willem, "to do it I have to make a separate screen…we need to perform a cleavage operation and the hologram is already beginning to disappear."

"Give it a go," Joost insists, not looking to de Haas for confirmation.

Willem manipulates an accessory feature attached to the side of the unit, swivels it sideways and directs its beam between the anthropomorphic form and the indistinct images between it and the wall. There is a soft electronic puff sound as cleavage occurs.

"Good! There now zoom in on that, enlarge the pixels."

"It won't take much enlargement, it will disappear."

"Go slow dammit."

Willem adds an infinitesimal amount of energy to the beam.

Now the picture is discernible, it represents the legs of the exam table and lying next to it is Vladg's Tele-Cell."

"Audio, see if there's audio," Joost shouts.

Willem presses a different button on the accessory unit and he hears a growl, then a low hum, then silence.

Now the entire hologram disappears.

"Do you realize what this means, Chief?"

"Not really, no."

"It means that Vladg's T-cell is now evidence…give it back here." He snatches it from Vladg's hands.

"But the battery is dead," says Vladg. "What use is that."

"It wasn't dead at the time of the murder. We heard a growl that must have been picked up by the T-cell's sound board," Joost says. "It's possible a computer forensic expert can recapture more."

"That sound could have come from de Boer's memory."

"No it could not! Willem had the beam directed at the split screen, the exam table and the T-cell, not the wolf or de Boer. What do you think Chief?"

De Haas mulls all this over.

"All right, read him his rights, cuff him and take him down to the station."

"Are you sure you want to play it this way," Joost asks.

This time de Haas is not perturbed by Joost's critique. He whispers in Joost's ear:

"No, I'm not sure. Putting a Duplicant under arrest is a first and there may be hell to pay. Three eighty-seven was rolled over, never arrested. This is against my better judgment. but I don't know what else to do, do you?"

"No," says Joost, "I don't."

"You can make two phone calls after you get booked," Joost tells Vladg.

"I've just received my work permit. I'll lose my job if you arrest me."

"It's only Saturday, a good lawyer should be able to get you out by Monday. You'll only miss one day of school."

"I hope you're right, Vladg says. I've never had handcuffs on before, are they always so tight, hurts you know."

∞

In Manhattan, Bram takes a room at the newly remodeled Hotel Pierre. The hotel is one of the few located on Central Park and also has easy walking distance to the Madison Ave. shopping district. After a continental breakfast served in his room, Bram strolls down 5th Ave., finds the shops he is looking for and purchases a goodly variety of maternity clothes for Phoenix. The night before he had tele-celled her; Phoenix had been very specific, gave him her present and protracted measurements, told him where to shop on Madison Ave and which ones to avoid. He listened like a doting husband and when she demanded that he have the stores FED-UP all the packages he agreed not even to touch them. On his end of the conversation he never once mentioned Lydia.

Once the shopping is done he calls Eiselman at the cell number Gregoriev had used during their little chess-match squabble. To his surprise, Eiselman doesn't answer but unexpectedly he gets Phoebe on the line.

"I thought this was Eiselman's private cell number."

"It is," she says, "but he has been under the weather lately and has asked me to take all his calls."

"All calls or just those from me?"

"Especially those from you, yes."

Bram sees that this is going nowhere, tries to change the subject.

"I spoke to your sister last night…"

"I know, she told me, we speak every day…"

"I didn't know that…"

"There are lots of things you don't know Mr. Alucard…"

"I think you can call me Bram, after all I am your future brother-in-law…"

"Not if I have anything to say about it, you won't be…"

"You owe me a little more respect than that, an apology for instance…"

"Whyever do you think that?"

"Because you were the one who cut off my thumb…"

"I should have cut off another part of your anatomy while I was at it!"

Bram grimaces, but it really doesn't bother him so much, he actually likes a little uproar in a woman, decides to play her a bit for shits and grins (a pick up phrase from Lydia) before he gets back on track.

"Regardless, as soon as I saw you again I realized how much of you is absent, still unused. A pity."

Now this phrase penetrates Phoebe's curiosity. She takes up the bait, cannot resist asking: "What do you mean by 'unused'? What about me is absent?"

"Well you know sex is fundamental, it's a primal drive, but to be complete a woman has to fulfill more than her primitivism. It is eroticism that drives a relationship forward. When used to its full extent it's what keeps a man close."

Phoebe cocks her head to one side; she is listening, influenced to a degree.

Bram knows that she is not spellbound by him as she was at their first meeting, this time she is merely inquisitive, but it is a step in the right direction.

"And you think I don't know how to hold a man?"

"Oh, as I say, I don't mean sexually, I know you may be adequate there, but erotically you appear to be naked, unalloyed in the finer aspects of romance and loving in depth. You miss the new forms of beauty; the mystical feelings of significance are absent."

"That's not true, I'm in love with someone and our togetherness is truly constant and romantic."

"Not obsessively so, I hope."

"Well there are some men who need the protection of a woman, Josh is a bit like that…but I don't want to discuss him with you…how did you ever hook me into this conversation?"

"I am truly sorry; it was not my intent. Let's leave all that aside for the moment, the reason I called was to ask for a consultation with Mr. Beasley, you know the biochemist, I think he works with your friend Josh Wharton."

"Well I don't know about that. Mr. Eiselman doesn't really want any further dealings with you whatsoever."

This last assertion awakens Bram's ire, now he is all business.

"I have a signed contract from Pyrell, drawn up by Mr. Eiselman's business manager. As a receptionist are you willing to take the responsibility of a law suit?"

Phoebe thinks this over. After all, what Mr. Eiselman had said was that he himself wanted nothing to do with Bram, he never once mentioned Mr. Beasley.

"All right, I'll transfer you over to R&D. You may have to get Mr. Beasley's in-house extension after that, please hold."

Phoebe puts him on her split-screen. She wants to hear every bit of what goes on and report back to Mr. Eiselman and, if it is pertinent to Phoenix in any way, she intends to chew it over with Josh as well.

Bram only has to wait for three rings and Beasley himself answers.

"Beasley here, who is this?"

"My name is Bram Alucard, you may not remember me, but a year or so ago you installed a para-umbilical scent-spray into my wife's companion, a Sextus IX, do you remember doing that?"

"Sure do. Only one of its kind. How'd it work out, I remember it had a musky essence to it."

"Well, I was wondering if I could come in for a consultation. I want to mix that scent with an elixir that I've concocted and put both in an aerosol can."

"Can't do it today, all booked up, but tomorrow I've got time. You got the chemical formulas?"

"Yes, I do."

"Okay, hang on, I'll transfer you to the business office. You have to set the appointment up with one of the office girls; I'm not allowed to do any scheduling."

"You don't know how much it will cost?"

"I don't have anything to do with the business end, sorry. Ask over there, I think the girl's name is Geri."

"Okay thank you."

This time Bram has to wait forever. Finally, after listening to several infomercials on the advantages of owning a Duplicant; on the new production models and on the easy payment program of the Pyrell Corps Banking Facility, he gets to talk to Geri, the girl that Mr. Beasley mentioned.

"We can schedule you tomorrow from three to five, does that work for you?"

"That's fine, how much is a two-hour consultation like that?"

"The standard fee is one thousand new dollars per hour or any fraction thereof. So I must warn you, if you stay over the five o'clock designated time by even a few minutes you will be assessed accordingly."

"That's pretty rough."

Geri pays no attention to this last remark.

"And you need to be at the business office an hour ahead so that we can check out your credit and method of payment. We do have an easy payment plan with only seventeen and a half percent interest."

"I'll pay by check, the entire amount."

"Whatever you wish sir," Geri says cheerily. "See you tomorrow."

After she beams off, Bram puts her on his short list, just under Phoebe and Lydia.

The New York Times

Reuters reports an American Sextus
has been put under arrest in Holland
for the murder of a human being.
Apparently, this particular Duplicant
claims his purchaser to be a vampire.
The kicker is that this man is a special
envoy of the Foreign Service. If the State
Department has taken to hiring vampires
it certainly is an odd addition to the 'Non-
Discriminatory' clause in hiring policy.

Upon reading a copy of this news item on the Interweb, Secretary of State Chelsea Clinton called Ms Bradford at The Hague to find out the truth of the matter. She in turn called Gregoriev who contacted Bram who denied the claim as ridiculous. Nevertheless, a bulletin was put out by the State Department that they had no reason to believe in the existence of vampires and certainly would never hire one if they did exist.

Now the denial itself became the butt of jokes on the nightly telorama.

The story was taken up by the Washington Post, in slightly different format, as well as the NRC, de Telegraaf, Het Parool and the Volkskrant in Holland where all the news-o-grams cited more detail and gave a more sober assessment of the situation. Even so the pundits in Holland and the rest of Europe had a field day with the arrest and the underlying mysteries surrounding the murder.

∞

The particular city jail where Vladg is housed doesn't reek too badly. Its prison cells are clean and the mattresses absent of bedbugs, but the lock-up is still a small enclosed structure housing cops and jailbirds and so has that familiar moldy odor of misaligned urine streams and waste that cannot be mistaken for anything else.

Vladg is allowed to make the two phone calls promised to him by the detectives. He first calls Lydia to let her know what had happened, but she says it was all over the papers in the States, that he had made headlines. She tells Vladg that the strong implication of Bram being a vampire might help to advance her divorce proceedings. Vladg is disappointed. She only seems interested in his plight as it affects her life. He had hoped Lydia would be more sympathetic to his situation. What he didn't know was that Lydia had finally found true love, her *'immortal longings'* had been fulfilled in Phoenix and this new love overruled all her feelings at the moment.

His next call is to Hikey who tells him she had arranged for an attorney and would make it down later in the day. She too sounds more businesslike in her response than the empathic picture he had hoped to evoke. Her attitude makes him wonder if she truly believed in his innocence. On the other hand, he knows she is at least doing something positive for him and not thinking of his situation as a means to an end for herself. All this makes him realize how vulnerable he is and that most of his stressful feelings depend on that vulnerability. So he takes a page from Eiselman's teachings, tells himself to perk up.

Cynthia van Westerveld and Hikey were accompanied by Mieke Meester when they came to visit. Vladg's cell is too small for the four of them so a prison guard leads Vladg to the visitor's room where they all meet.

Mieke Meester belongs to that select club of attorney's who believe that modern consciousness has a great need to explore its own postures. In other words, if deviousness served the purpose it was welcome.

She was not only Cynthia's attorney; she was also the campaign manager for Hikey's bid to be the first Duplicant elected to a seat in the Dutch parliament. As such, she saw this fight for Vladg's freedom as a stepping stone to victory for Hikey's campaign, as the more Duplicants were subjected to treatment under existing Dutch law for humans, the easier it became for Hikey to declare herself a valid candidate. So, while she wanted Vladg to be exonerated, she didn't want this to happen all at once. Mieke envisioned multiple protests with the avant-garde marching up and down the street in front of the station shouting for Vladg's freedom and for the liberation of all Duplicants. She neglected to mention this plan to Hikey or Cynthia, however.

During the meeting Mieke implored Vladg to repeat his story from beginning to end. Vladg balked at this, telling her that he had stated the facts over and over to several members of the department and that he was tired of all the repetition. What he wanted was a bondsman to get him out on bail.

"But you haven't been indicted yet, only arrested. First you have to be arraigned, then indicted and then the judge can set bail if she so wishes."

"But Joost, the CSI man, told me I could be out by Monday that I would only miss one day of teaching school."

"All the cops say things like that, softens the blow. You'll be lucky if you can come before the judge by the middle of next week."

"Then I'll lose my job."

"Let's face it, the school board would never let you teach their kids again, guilty or innocent, you are no longer a good role model as a teacher. I'm sorry to be the one to tell you, but you have to be a realist on this."

"Well I didn't get much of a chance to show the principal what I could do for the kids and Cynthia is the one who went to bat for me…"

"Don't worry about that now, we'll find something else for you, I'm certain of it."

"Of course," Hikey says, "first things first. But Mieke are you certain we cannot get a judge in here over the weekend to set bail, I thought that was possible under certain conditions."

"Not in murder cases. No if anything happened, even accidentally, the judge would be liable to criticism from the prosecuting attorney. All of Holland would be up in arms and it would be catastrophic for your campaign."

"Why so?"

"It would mean that Duplicants cannot be trusted, and the one major point we have to impress on the voting electorate is that you are trustworthy as any human, even more so to put it bluntly."

"Good point."

"Yes, the prosecutor is the one I have to find and negotiate with on the idea of bail. If he agrees to the basics, we can go before the judge and it will be a fait accompli. Right now I don't even know who they are going to select to prosecute. Slow wheels of justice you know."

"Well I don't want to go to trial! Joost thinks my Tele-Cell will reveal all. Hikey, have you checked out all the messages on your cell?"

"Yes, and I do have about one minute of visual and audio, which is the way I had limits set for my voice-pic mail, but it is not conclusive, only shows your face and greetings and then a long lapse followed by de Boer going to his safe. There's no more audio other than the rustling of objects, the twirling sound of the safe combination, that's about where it ends."

Mieke acknowledges this.

"I've listened and watched as well, a number of times. So the rest of the material will have to be decoded from the cell itself by the computer forensics. That's evidence and evidence has to be shared. So the second thing for me to do is get over to forensics and see how far along they are."

Vladg doesn't like it, but Hikey and Cynthia are nodding their heads in agreement and he bows to their judgment.

"Can I have a few moments with Hikey alone?" he asks.

"Certainly, Mieke says, "but first I need to hear formally that you want me to represent you in this matter."

Vladg hesitates, there is something about Mieke that doesn't sit right with him, his instincts tell him she is the wrong attorney, he feels no good vibes, but he has no choice. Hikey and Cynthia have gone all out.

"Yes," he says." I would very much appreciate you being my attorney in this case."

"That's all I need to hear. I'll come to visit you tomorrow. I want you to repeat everything again, from beginning to end. You'll be surprised at how the littlest item that is missed can be strategically helpful. So try to remember everything that took place."

"I'm already sick of trying to remember."

"I'm outa here." Mieke says.

Cynthia kisses Vladg on the cheek and she too leaves.

Vladg is not really alone with Hikey, the guard is present and observes his every move, but Vladg decides to play it as if the man were not there.

"Hikey I want you to know that I am totally innocent of this crime, I didn't so much as harm a hair on de Boer's head."

"I know that Vladg, I believe in you more than anyone on earth. Did you think I questioned your innocence?"

"You don't know what it's like being holed up in a small cell like this; it makes me more suspicious and distrusting. Yes, for a moment there I wondered if you believed in me, I actually had to hear you say the words. Now I feel shitty that I had doubts, please forgive me."

"Not a problem. I'm supposed to be fighting for the freedom of Duplos and I know you wouldn't want me to quit that fight right now. I can do both at the same time."

"I know you can. I'm really upset about losing my teaching job, how will I ever support us after we get married?"

"Don't worry about that now, first we have to get you out of here and then prove your innocence. Anyway, I'm not sure Mieke is right about what she said."

"So you think there's a chance…"

"This is Holland, one never knows which way the wind blows, all we know here is that the wind blows hard, so the direction may not be what Mieke thinks."

"Thanks Hikey, that gives me some hope…"

"All right lovebirds," the guard says, "time is up."

Vladg gives Hikey a tight hug and the guard leads him back to his cell

∞

Mieke hasn't been entirely candid with Cynthia and Hikey. Every month the Central Bureau of Justice H-mails all the defense attorneys in the district, alerting them to the list of probable assistant DA's who are due to be called up to handle the major cases that are likely to go to trial. This is not exactly done by seniority or merit, there is a certain measure of choice given to the probable candidates, but in general one can make a fairly good guess as to who will be selected to handle which cases.

When she read the monthly bulletin, Mieke already knew that the most likely assistant for Vladg's arraignment would be an old law-school colleague of hers, Hans Wilders, for whom she still held romantic hopes and seduction fantasies. When Hans, the grandson of old PVV-leader Geert Wilders, was formally named the prosecutor in Vladg's case she arranged a conclave. They met in a small bistro where, rather contentedly, they were sipping on glasses of Pinot Grigio Santa Margarita, a vintage Italian wine. Mieke checks out the year on the label, 2021.

"Was that a good year Hans for white grapes like these?"

"I don't remember, too far back for me, but my grandfather drank this stuff and that's where I first heard about it. Anyway this bottle is awesome, don't you think?"

"I agree, heavenly."

He takes another soft sip, then asks:

"So I assume when you called it was about the Duplo from the States, right?"

"Yes, not about evidence, not yet anyway, only the matter of bail."

"I can tell you I have no objection to bail…"

"Why not? Suppose the American State Department via that Alucard envoy sneaks him out of the country; that could be a fiasco for foreign relations."

Hans is totally taken aback.

"That's not the American State Department's M.O. They don't support their citizens like European countries do; their tack is to take the side of the country where the individual is incarcerated, odd people, immature sense of justice."

"You may be right on that score, but my bones tell me it would be better to forego bail, to keep him inside."

"Now that's a twist. Every defense attorney I ever met wants their client out ASAP."

"I have my reasons."

"I'm sure you do."

"Let's have a bite before we drive over to forensics."

"Good idea, I'm famished."

∞

Mieke and Hans head over to the forensic lab together, Hans driving, and get there by early afternoon. Both are feeling rosy from the wine and delicious luncheon of mussels with leaks tossed with bits of bacon.

There they meet with Ali Jibar, the head of the WHOOPS system (Wireless Holographic Object Oriented Programmer Support) for the lab.

"I think we've got it figured out. What happened was that the Duplicant held his face up to the screen, and that projected clearly to Hikey's unit, but after he became aware he had to leave a message, he lay his cell down must have turned over and the unit fell to the floor. If that scenario holds true, then that is the reason nothing afterwards projected clearly, the unit kept running until the battery went dead."

"But why didn't things record properly?"

"Because when it fell to the ground the internal circuitry got shaken up, to be specific, the laser ring that reads the optical function got messed up and all the objects projected are fuzzy and indistinct."

"Can it be repaired?"

"Sure, may take a coupla days, but we can do it, then you'll know for sure what it shows, maybe even who the perp was."

"So forty-eight hours or so?"

"Don't cut it too fine, but yes, about that. Is there hurry?"

"No, not really." Mieke says.

"Well I'd like to know ASAP," Hans says. "If we can avoid a trial I'd rather. I'm due to go to the south of France this weekend with my fiancée."

When Mieke hears this, she percolates inside, decides to delay as long as she can, hopes that they do go to trial so that she can show off her highly toned legal skills and frustrate Hans's plans for a holiday as long as possible.

Chapter XX

At Pyrell's Bram was ensconced in Geri's small office on the mezzanine discussing his credit worthiness. Bram had a twofold interest in the young woman, business and blood. He was looking for a luscious victim for Greta's first encounter as a more mature vampire and thought that Geri would fit the bill admirably. His intent was not to cast a spell over her himself as he wanted this to be Greta's conquest entirely on her own.

He sensed there was something mysterious in the girl's past but he could not read her mind. No deep longings for love, no lustful thoughts of sex, or even passion for her work. All he got was thoughts of video games and crossword puzzles, deliberately so it seemed. Annoying. At first he thought she might be an exceptional type of Duplicant, but his sensitive sense of smell affirmed that human blood circulated in her veins, so that ruled that thought out. He was unable, however, to distinguish the nature of her natural body odor, as she wore a much too pungent perfume for his taste.

Her neck appeared to be free of any scars or slits, but her skin was covered with so much makeup in the throat area that he could not determine if she had ever been victimized. He hoped not, as he would like Greta to have a 'virgin' so to speak for her premier outing. Her fingernails were acrylic coated with gold sprinkle embedded in the multiple layers of polish. This feature he found pleasant but it prevented him from ascertaining the health and vigor of her blood. Aside from the condition of her fingernails, he did notice that the palms of her hands appeared to be quite rosy colored and he thought this to be a good sign. In other ways she fit the bill admirably. She had a quirky characteristic which he found fetching, a musical lift to her voice when she pronounced certain high pitched words. This caused her to jump slightly in her seat, and the rise in her tone seemed to draw her entire posture upwards. When this happened, she held her mouth wide open, show-offy style, and he was able to see that her tongue held a healthy ruddy color. Another good sign.

After they had settled the credit part of their business, Geri stood up on spike-heeled shoes but still only came up to Bram's shoulder height. She gave him one of her well-practiced public relation smiles and led him over to the office of the business manager, Mr. O'Gorman.

On the way, he mentions that his niece, Greta, who is about her age, would be making a trip from Holland for a short visit. He asks if she would like to meet with her, show her around Manhattan and such.

"I'm afraid not, Mr. Alucard, I've been awfully busy lately and I'm in an amateur dramatic group that takes up nearly all my time in the evenings."

"I could make it worth your while."

"Really? How much 'while' are we talking about?"

"How does five-hundred dollars' sound?"

"Seven hundred fifty sounds better."

"All right, I'm sure she shall be enlivened by you. She'll be here next week. I'll postdate a check for you."

He writes a personal check on an Oneonta bank, she snaps it up and stuffs it directly into her purse.

"That'll work. Good thing I know your credit is good. But let's understand, this is just for my guidance and companionship, any theatres or restaurants we go to come out of her pocket."

"Of course."

As Geri holds the door open to Mr. O'Gorman's office, Bram thinks about greed, how in the centuries of his life, with all the cultural and high tech changes, greed has remained essentially the same self-destructive emotion to humans as it was back when.

Mr. O'Gorman turns out to be a highly sophisticated Irishman with a soft brogue. He is not so eroded by daily business routine that his extremely pleasant personality doesn't shine through. He is one of the few humans that Bram takes a liking to immediately. They discuss the designated number of Sextus IV's guaranteed to him per his contract, all of Bram's options, that he can order as many, or as few, Sextus IV's on a monthly basis as he wishes and Pyrell's will deliver them to his farm in Oneonta via FED-UP.

"No problem whatsoever. Mr. Eiselman has given me the address and as soon as you are ready we can start delivery."

"That sounds good to me. And just one question, I know that the price of number IV's has gone up considerably since I signed the contract you drew up at the time, does that mean I pay the old fee or the new one."

"Oh no, this grandfathers you in, Pyrell sticks by its commitments, no new additions or hidden costs whatsoever."

"Very decent, I appreciate your forthrightness."

"Only way to do business. Want a nip?"

He pulls out a bottle of Bushmills single malt from a drawer somewhere deep in his desk and offers it straight to Bram.

"There're only a limited number of bottles of this stuff available each year."

Bram rarely drinks in the daytime, but he is so delighted with the way O'Gorman transacts business, that he lifts the bottle to his lips and takes a healthy pull.

"Good man, you must have some Irish in you."

"Afraid not, my wife is from Belfast though, so I guess that makes me part Irish by injection."

O'Gorman laughs, takes a swig, returns the bottle to Bram who does the same. This repeats itself a few more times until Bram realizes he needs to get over to Beasley's office.

"I'll walk over to the elevator with you, Beasley's on the fortieth floor."

By the time Bram gets up to Beasley's lab he is feeling no pain. He knows that the Irish have a history, even in their Catholicism, of Gaelic myth and mysticism that fits right into vampirism; figures this is why he got on so well with O'Gorman. Now it occurs to him that his mother came from Anglican stock, wonders what difference this would make in discussing things with Beasley, an English name.

His original intention was to put Beasley under a spell, to direct all of his requests from a position of strength. Instead he plays it like a gentleman, gives Beasley plenty of breathing room. He hands over copies of the formulas for the venom and the antidote and discusses the minor engineering problems of putting the venom together with the musky cologne into an aerosol can. Then they get into the issue of which would be the best form for the antidote:

"We can put it into a small hand spray, but then you have less control over how much is used, same in a droplet form.

What about a tablet? In pill form you will know exactly how much a person is getting in milligrams.”

“I’ll only be giving the antidote to Duplicants, not humans,” Bram says honestly, probably not a detail he would have let on if he wasn’t in such a good mood.

“Really? This is for Duplicants? I’ll be petrified. Are these Duplos going to Africa or some place with poisonous snakes?”

“Not Africa, but they will be in even more dangerous territory, handling a pack of vipers in church.”

“Hey, that’s a bloody good one Mr. Alucard; I see that your soul doesn’t lack for wit.”

Bram considers how different this English answer is from the Irish way; he decides to keep a straight face on this one.

“Let’s go with the tablet form for the antidote.”

“It’s a little more expensive, but I think you’ve made a good choice.”

“How long will it take to make up say one hundred tabs of the antidote and one hundred aerosol cans of the mixture?”

“I can get you the tablets of antidote in a week or ten days, the aerosol cans will take a little longer. We have to farm that process out to a canning factory, but I can manufacture the raw blended elixir in about the same time. If you want to arrange the canning operation yourself, it will save shipping back and forth.”

“You can’t ship it directly to me from the canning factory?”

“Sorry, no, policy you see. Pyrell’s takes a shipping and handling charge they won’t forego, I know that much, but as I say you can manage to have it done yourself.”

“Too much work. I’ll keep with your way of doing things.”

“That’s wise; we can get a cheaper price than you would as an individual considering we do business with their operation on a regular basis.”

"What's the name of the aerosol outfit?"

"It's called Red Can Press, all they do is this one type of specialty work, but they'll make the can in any style you want, any shape; your preference."

"Long as it's easily held in the hand of a Sextus, doesn't drip and sprays at least six feet; I'm ok with whatever form you recommend."

"Good show. I'll see that we keep to specs and do a good job for you."

"Jolly good," Bram replies, the British speech habits getting to him as well.

"By Jove, we only used up one hour of consultation time, if you hurry back over to Geri you might get the other hour refunded."

Bram thanks him profusely, gets on his hobby horse and rushes down to the mezzanine where all the business offices are located. He corrals Geri in time and she has no problem with the refund. Then she gives him her private cell number and tells him to call as soon as his niece Greta gets into New York. Bram's mood is now sobering up. He sees Geri more with predatory eyes than beforehand, wonders if she wears black lace flimsies underneath. He tells himself if Greta is unable to produce enough venom on her own to do the job, he will be ready, willing and able to help out with their first vampire ménage à trois.

∞

Bram returns to his room at the Pierre and takes a healthy afternoon nap. Upon awakening he makes an obligatory call to Gregoriev and learns that Vladg's lawyer had put in an extradition request for him to return to Holland and testify at the trial. Gregoriev assures him that he has denied this and that as far as he was concerned the issue was closed. Bram thanks him for his support and when Gregoriev asks if he will bring another vial of L.P. to him when he returns from furlough Bram assures him that he will.

After he orders a light supper consisting of a Greek salad and a tender skillet steak with garlic potatoes and a glass of Merlot followed by an espresso he returns to making calls.

He checks in with Phoenix, who is not Catholic, yet has taken to wearing a medal of Saint Joseph, the patron and protector of babies in the womb. She feels her baby will need a surrogate father, since she has no intention of Bram bringing up her child, and who better than Saint Joseph, the surrogate father to Jesus.

However, when Bram calls, she immediately hides her medal and crucifix underneath the fabric of her nightie so Bram won't detect it on screen.

Bram begins by telling her he has sent the maternity clothes she had asked for via FED-UP and she should be getting them tomorrow or the next day. Phoenix is pleased to hear this and then they get on to the pregnancy, sounding more or less like any worried couple. Phoenix tells him she works out every day at the gym on State St. together with Lydia and that she does not overdo but wants to stay in shape as the OB says that will make the delivery of a first baby a good deal easier. Bram asks about her hemoglobin (blood being the one thing that he knows something about) and Phoenix tells him that the last lab test was perfectly fine, that she is no longer anemic, adding: 'from what you did to me'. Bram takes the jab in stride, tries to stay as much on her good side as he can with soft talk, tells her how pretty she looks on the small screen.

Like any ordinary prospective father Bram finally runs out of things to say, but Phoenix is chatty this day, tells him that she heard from her sister that he had called. Bram explains that it was serendipitous as he had expected to get Eiselman, but as things turned out he was glad to talk with Phoebe. He doesn't ask about Lydia but he doesn't have to as Phoenix is all excited about a dog that Lydia has brought home from her veterinary office. Apparently a stray pit bull mix had bitten a pedestrian in his lower leg and a patrolman who happened by shot the dog in the neck. The animal was immediately brought to Lydia's surgery hemorrhaging severely. Lydia stopped the bleeding removed the bullet and treated the dog for parvo virus, a bladder infection and general malnutrition. Phoenix goes on to tell Bram that the two so took to one another, and as no one came forth to claim her, Lydia brought the pit bull home to stay as her own.

"I think she is a substitute for Vladg, she misses him so you know."

Bram does not like dogs as the wolf in him sees them as also-rans. For a brief moment he has an urge to say: 'I didn't know Lydia was in to beastiality' but then thinks the better of it. So he asks Phoenix just why she is telling him a story about Lydia when the only interest he has in her at present is what is happening in their divorce proceedings.

"I know you don't like dogs Bram, but this mix is so cute, and she is devoted to Lydia.

"Well just so you don't catch any of a stray's diseases…"

"She's totally healthy, no longer a stray. Lydia has named her Jeanne d'Arc as she is warlike, but not with us."

"You're sure she's no danger to you?'

"Definitely not, and when the baby comes I'm sure she will be protective of her as well."

"Well I don't plan on you staying with Lydia after the baby is born, I want you here with me on the farm, and you'll love upstate New York, quiet, good schools, the perfect place to bring up a child, not like that radical southern California."

Phoenix is now wise enough to avoid the trap. She has learned from Lydia how to avoid a conversation with Bram that does not serve her purpose. No way is she going to mention her intent to marry Lydia as soon as her divorce finalizes.

"It's still a long way to cross that bridge Bram…"

"I'm still the master and what I say goes…"

"You sound more like a human than a true vampire when you talk like that…"

"Forgive me my dear, I don't want to upset you…"

"Well you have."

"I apologize."

Phoenix knows how much Bram believes that God and Satan will fight to win over the soul of an unborn child, that any reference to the forces in this struggle upsets him. She herself is careful in this regard and listens to Lydia's advice on womb behavior of the fetus. Lydia strongly believes if the baby kicks to her left it is satanic influence, and the opposite of the right. So when Phoenix receives a left sided internal nudge she rubs her medal over the area in a circular motion and quickly says: 'Holy Mary, mother of God, blessed art thou and blessed is the fruit of thy womb'. She tries to get this in three times if she can as long as the baby is not squirming too much from the prayer.

"All right Bram. But you know how sensitive I am, and if you continue in this mode, something unfortunate could happen, not that I wish it, of course not, but the guilt will be yours if the child is born with a defect."

This is all Bram needs to hear. He becomes totally docile, asks for forgiveness, promises never to speak to her in that tone again.

Phoenix knows when she has won a major victory, smiles inwardly and signs off to Bram with loving-hate, a phrase the two have coined to say goodbye on the cell.

After spending some minutes musing over the conversation he has had with Phoenix, Bram decides it is time to call Malignius in Dolno Katore. They exchange vampire greetings, swearing their allegiance and devotion to Satan and then Bram gets right to it:

"How are the three Royaal Duplicants coming along?"

"Father Nicholas has given them all Christian names, Peter, James and John after the followers of the carpenter. Even so, the priest treats them like vassals but he has taken them up as parishioners in the congregation. They clean up the church, tend to the grounds, see that the holy water bowl is kept clean and do the laundry and housework for the rectory. They attend mass every day and this has put them in good standing with Father Nicholas. Of course, during the week mass is not much, only attended by several old men and a few widows but on Sundays the church is full."

"That's when we should make our first attack."

"I agree. Recently James, John and Peter have been given the responsibility of handling the collection baskets. Apparently the priest trusts the Duplicants more than the human members of his congregation."

"That's one for the books."

"Yes it is. And by the way, you did a good job with the brain transfers, all three are well indoctrinated."

"Are there any signs of canine growth?"

"Not as yet, but their eyes do light up when I tell them how they will soon have humans as slaves instead of the other way around, that they go for."

"But no sign of fangs?"

"No. I don't think that blood excites them particularly, if it were lymph that might be another story, but blood, no."

"Yes, that is understandable, but we don't need them to drink blood do we? You have three vampire slaves of your own who must be chomping at the bit with the thought of all those potential victims."

"Yes, those three are all members of the undead, they cannot appear in the daytime, but once the Duplicants have them under a spell with your venom spray they can come out at night and drink to their hearts content. What about Greta, are you going to send her back up here?"

"No my plans have changed on that. I have a delicious morsel for her here and I want to make sure that she does everything right on her first attempt at the big show."

"I see. Well I do have two real brothers, both Dhampirs who will be available. There are about eighty adults in the congregation, so that should hold the six of us for some time."

"You won't drink children's blood."

"Of course not. None of us is that way. We will not defile children in any way, but certainly they will eventually be drawn to our way of life."

"Good. I am as much against vampire pedophilia as anyone. Children need their blood to develop along healthy lines."

"I agree, but we are all excited by your plan…"

"What about that cousin of yours, what's his name…?"

"Oh, you mean Drakonius the one who can transmogrify, yes, I'll have to keep an eye on him, he is a bit that way, bears watching."

"Okay. Make sure he doesn't do harm to any child."

"You got it."

"And he's not just a pedophile; he's a necrophile as well. See that he doesn't sexually abuse any dead victims. That would ruin our reputation."

"He'll get fair warning, that's all I can do on that score."

"So be it. On the other issue, it should take about two weeks before you get the aerosol cans and the antidote we spoke of. You won't need much of the antidote, but I'll send you three cans of the spray, one for each Duplicant. In the meantime work on the priest. Try to get to him yourself if possible…"

"He won't let me near the church. That big cross of his is enough to keep me away plus he has two mounted guards with silver tipped spear points at the ready."

"Then use that one vial of venom I left with you. Have the smartest one of the Duplicates put half of it in the holy water. Some of it might get absorbed through the skin."

"I doubt it."

"Give it a try and then if he can get close enough to Father Nicholas's cup of tea, have him pour the rest right in. That should enable you to put him under a spell."

"Won't work. His housekeeper covets her chores with the priest; no way will she allow a Duplicant or anyone else to be with him at teatime unless the Monsignor pays a visit."

"All right then, scratch that plan. Just sit tight till the stuff gets there. I know even FED-UP won't come straight to the castle, but they will deliver to the general store in the village, so check things out with them will you?"

"Sure thing Bram. Not to worry. We've been looking forward to a plan like this for decades. No one on this end wants to screw it up."

"Good. Well I think we've covered all the bases. Thanks for all your help. Pray to Satan that the movement succeeds."

"I will. Take care and stay away from the so-called forces of good."

"I intend to. Stay healthy; keep your slaves on their toes."

"That's my idea cousin."

They both sign off at the same time and then Bram realizes he has yet to call Greta, to hear the news from Holland on Vladg and to arrange for her trip to New York.

She picks up on the first ring.

"Yes Bram, my master," she says immediately, restoring his spirits after getting knocked about by Phoenix in their conversation.

"Yes Greta, my slave, tell me what has gone on in my absence."

"Well believe it or not I've had two marriage proposals, one from Joost and the other from Dusty. Imagine? After all this time of nothingness, I got two at once."

"Congratulations," Bram says sincerely. He has no objection whatsoever to marriage of any of his slaves as long as their first allegiance is to him when he calls upon them for a service.

"You don't mind?"

"Not in the least, as long as any children you may have are properly indoctrinated."

"I'm surprised. But I don't even know which one to choose. Think I'll let them both percolate for a bit."

"Do I get invited to the wedding?"

"Well you better not come over here at the moment, that lawyer Mieke Meester has it in for you."

"I know, she tried to have me extradited back to Holland but my superior nipped that in the bud."

"Oh ja? Now on Vladg, I'm beginning to feel sorry for him; he's still wallowing away in jail, no bail for him as yet. The glitch seems to be that since you are the legal owner, the bail bondsman has to receive the funds from you or someone designated by you in your absence. Do you want me to tell the judge I'm your appointee, that it's okay to have Cynthia van Westerveld advance the bond money?"

"Sure. That's only fair; we both know Vladg is innocent. What about Hikey? Does she come to visit?

"Occasionally. She is very busy with her campaign to become the first non-human Member of Parliament. Her main opponent is pretty tough, an incumbent member of the PVV, pretty much to the right of things over here. Those two have got an oratorical war going on. Rümke, that's his name, says she will upset the purification of Dutch life and unbalance the economy. She says he is a gamester, playing politics, unsympathetic to the cause. He says she is a common user of Ubiquity and other drugs, doesn't go to church and would upset morality. Now that last was dumb because more than half of Hollanders don't go to church and they do love Ubiquity. So that may backfire on him."

"Sounds like it."

"Hikey had a good comeback. She said Rümke was like a horse with blinders, he could move straight on one course, but when it came to shifting policy with fluid circumstances, of resolving issues of treachery and deceit, he needed external forces to handle the reins. She says her mind is an independent one from such externals and seating her will be a boon to the economy. That's a good selling point. She'll get my vote."

"Good for you."

"The people are really excited over this election, should be a big turnout. After all the years of jokes and jibes that a robot could do a better job than the humans that have been seated, it's coming down to this. If she makes it, there will be drastic changes in Holland, perhaps in other countries."

"I wish her well."

"Me too. I guess that's all the news on this end. When are you going to get me over there? I've never been to America, wouldn't mind it for a time."

"I'm sending you a return Sub-Orb ticket you can pick up at the KLM-Air France desk. If you can get away for the weekend you won't have to use up any of your vacation time, just zip in and out."

"What have you got for me?"

"The prettiest morsel, just your type. She is short, but not petite, strong body, works out regularly, so she may be a little difficult to subdue…"

"The department has given us some pretty decent martial arts training; I think I can handle her…"

"If you don't have enough venom it could get touchy. How are you coming along on that?'

"When I feel the urge my canines do elongate a bit. I do feel their sharp points but there is only a little bit of venom. I swallow it, tastes a bit like sperm, reminds me of you of course."

"When its thick like that its immature venom, the real stuff is not so viscous, has more the consistency of old jenever. When you get over here I'll give you an extra vial of venom that I have left over, just in case. You won't need the antidote."

"You think of everything Master. I do so adore being a slave, it's so stimulating. I haven't been bored once with life since you transformed me. I don't really know if I want to marry."

"Marriage and family are best, just take your time, choose whichever man you feel will be easiest to manipulate. Once a man knows you are a vampire and have certain needs that fall strictly out of his jurisdiction, he is the one to choose."

"Yes Master, I'll do it that way."

"Good. Call me on the cell before you board. I'll get everything set up in my room for you and Geri, that's her name. Remember this is your first outing, it's like being a virgin all over again."

Greta is really excited at the thought, even over the phone her canines are starting to drool, she feels sexual fluids beginning to gush in her vajayjay, but she stops this quickly. She knows how serious Bram can be when it comes to such matters, that he does not like sloppiness of any sort, so she controls her wetness.

"I won't say bon voyage now, I'll wait for your call."

"Yes Master, I am so looking forward to the trip."

"Adieu for now."

"Au Revoir," she answers, one of the very few French phrases she knows.

∞

Geri is a born and bred Staten Islander. Every morning and every evening since she got her Manhattan job at Pyrell's she takes the ferry back and forth from the St. George terminal to the Whitehall terminal in Manhattan where she catches bus 31 to Ground Zero and the Pyrell Building. In the course of the two and a half years that she has taken the ferry and bus she has become friendly with a girl named Jennifer Mills, another Staten

Islander who makes the same trip and also works at Pyrell's which all toll employs over seven thousand people.

Jennifer works on the 100th floor, just two floors below Phoebe Winthrop, and fairly often receives transmissions from Phoebe, plans and contracts that have many rough edges and need to be put into proper legalese or spelled out more specifically in terms of the engineering details. It is up to Jennifer to see that all these get into the hands of the right people: attorneys, designers, engineers, artists, programmers and many other experts who are involved in the construction or the purchase of Duplicants. They make corrections, omissions and emendations and the updated material goes back to Eiselman's office personnel.

In the course of events it sometimes becomes necessary for Phoebe to take the private elevator down to the 100th floor and discuss certain problems one-to-one with Jennifer, especially where broad brush strokes may have been made with clients, but substantive details had not been nailed down.

It was precisely one of these agreements between Bram and Eiselman that Phoebe had originally discussed with Jennifer, a contract that avoided the usual H-W procedures. Now, on the bus, Jennifer brings this age old issue up to Geri.

"That odd contract I told you about some time ago has gone through, Phoebe said so yesterday."

"I know. I was the one who sent that strange man to Mr. O'Gorman."

"Well everything is being honored as if it were a standard contract."

"Listen Jen, I know that's your line of work, but it really doesn't interest me. What does is Christmas; it's only the 5th of December and I'm all set money wise for Christmas shopping."

"Ger, what's Christmas got to do with what I'm talking about?"

"That strange man, Mr. Alucard has big bucks. He has already paid me seven-hundred fifty New Dollars to escort his niece around Manhattan; she's coming over from Holland this weekend."

"And you accepted it?"

"Why not? I've already been over to Chase-Fargo, you know I have to make two trips a day over there to make deposits, all that laundered cash we get, so I just asked this one teller I'm friendly with to make sure his personal check was valid, and turns out it is good as gold. So I'm all set for shopping. This is like seven-thousand five hundred of the old dollars you know."

"I don't know if that was so wise on your part Ger. If this is the same man Phoebe was telling me about in relation to that contract, he's devious as all get out. Maybe even dangerous!"

"Jen, he's a middle aged pisser, doesn't look like he could harm a fly. He did postdate the check, but I'm going to deposit it ahead of time; with my connections at Chase-Fargo, I'm sure it will go through and then no matter what happens I'll be on easy street."

"Well before you do anything let me talk to Phoebe about it, see what she says, okay?"

"Sure, I'll wait one more day."

∞

When Phoebe hears from Jennifer that Geri is involved with Bram in some plan to show his niece around town she is suspicious as can be, tells Josh the story she has heard.

"You know Feeb," Josh says, "I've finally updated George's central reflex time, he moves a lot faster now and I've added even more ATP so that he's as strong as a Sextus VI. Why don't we let him go with Geri over to Bram's hotel? He can birddog Bram until Geri comes home safely."

"That's a good idea, but Bram won't go for it."

"He won't have anything to say about it if Geri just shows up accompanied by George. What can he do?"

Phoebe thinks this over. It is true that Mr. Eiselman has given her all the access to George that she needs, whenever something comes up requiring his help all she has to do is to ask and Mr. Eiselman grants her the use of George for the evening.

"He did injure George pretty badly the last time, remember, he tore half his face off."

"I know, but this is a different George, he's faster, more mobile. Don't you have any confidence in the work I've done on him."

"Of course I do. I know you're the best at what you do. But he's my responsibility, if something happens to him a second time, what will Mr. Eiselman think of me?"

Josh sees her point.

"Okay, how about this? We'll like double date. You go with Geri and Bram's niece and George and I will sit with Bram the entire time; that way nothing miserable can happen to anyone."

"That's what you said the last time with your mirrors and lighting scheme and look what happened?"

"C'mon, that's not fair Feeb; I didn't know exactly what we were dealing with and you didn't either…"

"I'm sorry, past is past, I know you were trying hard back then too, but there's something about leaving you alone with Bram that I don't like…"

"I won't be alone; George won't allow anything nasty to happen to me."

"I just thought of something, it won't work…"

"Why not?"

"Because from what I understand Bram's niece wants to really see the town, that's going to cost a bundle. I certainly would like to help out Jennifer's friend Geri, but we don't have that kind of money to squander."

"Hmm. That is a point. Suppose I just show up with George at the hotel, leave you completely out of it, how about that?"

"I'd rather be there with you. I can make something up, like Feeny wants me to make a visit, to talk about the baby shower, something like that, then you George and I can baby sit Bram until Geri shows back up."

Josh mulls her idea over.

"Okay, that sounds like a good plan A, what's Plan B?"

"You bang his head in again, like you did last time, he certainly deserves it."

Josh laughs, gives Phoebe a lover's hug and then the two of them pick things up from there.

∞

Jennifer relays Phoebe's plan to Geri who has no objection since she thinks they are making a big deal out of nothing in any case.

That Saturday afternoon, the Sub-Orb is right on time per usual. Bram and Greet taxi straight over to the chic Madison Ave. shops and following Phoenix's advice he purchases several different outfits with her. He finds out, however, that she has a taste of her own and rejects certain of Phoenix's choices, substituting designer ideas she feels suit her style better. All in all she is thrilled with the purchases, and though the Dutch in her frowns at paying three hundred dollars for a pair of wedgies, she takes it all in stride. When they finish shopping, they cab back to the Pierre and Bram books a separate suite for Greta which knocks her eyes out. He explains that the suite is necessary as they may need a great deal of room to maneuver when they have Geri in their power.

Once Greta has the suite to her ownsome she fulfills her dreams. She tests out every plush chair, gets naked and bounces her bod on the circular bed as if it were a trampoline, all four extremities extended to the limit. Next she wants to take a Hollywood shower but can't figure out how to operate the complicated contraption so she does the right thing and calls for a eunuchoid Duplo.

He explains that the cylindrical unit has eight shower heads, that as soon as she gets into it, if she presses the green button the entire unit will start to rotate and all the shower heads will spray on varying force, soft to normal, then after whatever minutes she digitalizes on the internal screen, they turn on mist. As a finale, he will enter the unit and shampoo and condition her thick hair with the latest and most up to date preparations. There is really nothing she has to do herself.

Greta goes through the entire procedure and then the Duplo gives her a second drying off, rolling her in thick soft Turkish towels, starting the massage. He then calls for two more Duplos to help. One Duplo does her legs, another works solely on her back and he himself tends to her breasts and belly, oiling, creaming and massaging until all the oils and creams are thoroughly absorbed into her skin and the nipples of her breasts stand erect as if stroked by a lover.

Greta calls for a cosmetologist who places Samba pink and teal-blue highlights at strategic spots in her sleek brunette hair, then back combs and blow dries it so that a natural chignon forms at the back of her head.

She does her own extensive make-up, fastens in golden three tiered earrings and finally gets dressed. She looks stunning and totally Americanized.

Bram has called Geri, asks her to come over to the Pierre at precisely seven P.M. He tells her that he and his niece will meet with her in the lobby and that way she does not have to come up to his room. He mentions, offhandedly, that upon their return he would appreciate it if she brought Greta back up to her suite as he will probably be asleep by the time they get in. He makes it all sound very innocent and traditional and explains it is just an uncle's concern and if she does it this way it will tell him that Greta is safe and sound.

Geri, who is with Jennifer, agrees to all this. Together they cab to the Pierre.

Jennifer splits off from Geri as soon as they enter the lobby, heads over to another L shaped section where Josh, George and Phoebe are already seated. Bram spots them immediately, even though Geri is headed his way, more or less demanding of his attention.

He has no time to ask who Jennifer is and how she knows Phoebe.

Greta stands up to greet Geri, introductions are made by Bram and the two girls size one another up. Geri wears a palm print dress made from a mix of spandex and rayon that has a modern sleeveless knot top with a built in bra that gives her breasts some bounce; her shoes are a delicately designed pair of wedgies that are fashionable yet good for walking. She carries a small gold lamé evening purse that matches the design on the sides of her wedgies and has a multicolored silk shawl drawn through the handles of her purse in case it gets cold in her neck later in the evening.

Greet is all decked out in an autumn halter dress, samba pink, matched by her highlights, with romantic looking rushes gathered into a flare. The dress is a mix of bamboo and cotton-spandex; her sandals are subdued glitzy thongs with a Greek ankle strap. She feels that she is fashionable as Geri raves over her outfit.

As soon as George and Phoebe, Jen and Josh see the two girls make ready to leave, they head over to Bram's side table and institute Plan A's babysitting procedure.

On the way out the parking attendants, cabbies and limo drivers pleasure the girls with flirtatious whistles and mucho va-va vooms. Greta and Geri giggle, smile at one another, hop into the limo. The plan is to take the hotel limo down Broadway to 42nd St and Times Square, stroll around a bit while the limo follows them, then hop back into the limo and visit most of the main sight-seeing places, with the driver spieling out descriptions, then on to the top of the Empire State Building. This plan should bring them back to the theatre district, hopefully on time for the ballet where the Bolshoi is doing a revival of Giselle.

All goes without a glitch except that the girls pay very little attention to the limo driver's spiel. Instead they are bent on learning about one another.

"When Bram introduced us you said your last name was Niewenhuis; that is a very Dutch name."

"Yes my parents came from Enschede, settled in Staten Island and that's where I was born. I have to tell you something about my first name too, it is really Gerda, but here in the States everyone had trouble with the pronunciation, so they changed it to Geri."

"I see. And what do you want me to call you?"

"I'd like to hear you speak my name as it was originally intended, Gerda."

"Then that's what I'll do, Gerda. Do you speak Dutch?"

"Of course, not as good as when I was a kid because I don't have anyone to talk to, but yes, I can still carry on a conversation."

"Then how's this. As long as we are speaking Dutch I'll call you Gerda and you can call me Greet, then, if we flip over to English it will be Geri and Greta."

"Wonderful."

Now the two start babbling in Dutch, the limo driver pays no attention, he has heard more foreign languages in Manhattan than the 92 the Truth Detector can translate.

"So what was it like, growing up, going to high school here, boys, you know?"

"Staten Island is exceptionally nice except there are certain strange things, like we have monsters…"

"…Monsters?"

"Well maybe not exactly monsters, but that's what it felt like. You see in Tottenville High where I went, I was raped and bitten by another student when I was fifteen…"

"That's awful…"

"That's not the half of it, he was a Dhampire, do you know what that is?"

"I sure do, ja."

"Well he was my monster, tried to make me his slave but I rebelled, called him in to the police and they put him in jail for rape. He was a minor too, so when he got out he tried again but I made believe I was his slave and then I betrayed him. Now he's in prison long term."

Greta is deeply moved by Geri's tale, sees herself in the same predicament. It is as if she has been awakened from a very long sleep.

"Good for you," Greta says spontaneously, the detective in her reacting before she realizes what she has said.

"Yes, that's the only way to defeat a Vampire, you have to betray him. I haven't had any trouble since. You see they're all such egotists they can't believe any slave would betray a Master."

Greta chews on this, decides to tell Geri.

"Gerda, I have to tell you something. Bram is not my uncle, I am his slave. He too is a Dhampire and has me under his spell…"

"I suspected something like that about him, thought he was shady, but didn't know for sure so I pulled my trick of solving crossword puzzles and playing video games in my head when we first met. That way I felt protected from him."

"How clever; you must teach me that trick."

"I will. You're going to need it, but tell me, how do you like being a slave?"

"For the most part I do like the excitement, but what has happened is this, in Amersfoort, where I live, two colleagues of mine, both detectives…"

"You are a detective?"

"Yes, in the homicide division. As I was saying these two men I work with, Joost and Dusty, they have both asked me to marry them."

"Two proposals at once? Lucky you."

"Yes, but it's turned my world upside down."

"When was this?"

"Very recently; Joost is the more argumentative and Dusty is more placid, but I think I like Joost more, anyway he is the better kisser."

"Kissing is important, but it's not everything."

"I agree. The problem is Bram has advised me to choose the one I can manipulate the easiest. That goes against my grain…"

"Game playing is not a good way to start a marriage, and that's what manipulation of a relationship is, a false game, all L's, no W's no one wins."

"Yes, that's the way I feel too, if I ever get married I don't want to start out that way. Gerda it's the first time I find myself in disagreement with Bram since I've been his slave."

"Well I hope it's not the last. You've got to get out from under. How many times has he sucked blood out of you?"

"Only once."

"If you've read the books you know that the second time is the hardest to escape and by the third time you lose your reflection, become a member of the undead."

"How do you know so much?"

"Reading. Ever since I got bitten I've read everything on the subject. Actually I wasn't good in school, although I was a cheerleader and pretty good in gymnastics, but after the rape I really learned to read and have done so ever since. After Tottenvillle High I went to business school and that's how I got the job at Pyrell's."

"I did the same in Holland, studied my fanny off…"

"I can see that it's small, nice and tight…"

Greet elbows Gerda a bit and they both laugh.

The limo has arrived at the Empire State Building. The limo driver starts to tell them all about it being a National Historic

Landmark, but the girls are off and running. They take the rocket elevator up to the 102nd floor, go out to the observatory terrace and use the rooftop binoculars.

Although she has been to the top before, Geri finds it a hoot and Greta is thrilled beyond belief. Geri explains that Pyrell's also has 102 floors, but the view is totally different, not nearly as exciting. They stay as long as possible, savoring the cool wind, Geri puts her silk shawl around her neck and they saunter around the terrace.

It is then that they spot a young man, evidently on a bad trip, crawling up the fence that surrounds the edge of the observatory. They both tackle him; pull him down, Greet tearing her dress slightly on a side seam and Gerda losing her purse for the moment.

A security agent arrives almost immediately, Greta explains who she is, the young man starts to whimper and cry; the officer takes him away, speaking very gently to him.

For a moment neither one says a word, they are both shaken up by the suicide attempt and recognize that sudden unforeseen calamities can burst upon life at any time. Greet is hit especially hard, she knows now that she has to be honest with Gerda.

She explains that the entire visit was a setup, that upon their return to the hotel she and Bram had planned to 'go for the jugular' in the literal sense of the phrase, that now she not only has no intention of doing so but is turned off by the very thought.

Gerda hardly hesitates, speaks in her best Dutch.

"Greet," Gerda begins, "you have to get out of here, leave Bram as soon as possible. Go back to Holland and betray him as soon as you can. Is there something big you can betray him with?"

"Yes, something very big." Greet tells her about the murder of de Boer, how Vladg is accused and unable to get out on bail, that it is now her intent to appear as a witness for the defense, not the prosecution.

"Then you've got to leave tonight, there's always a midnight red-eye Sub-Orb that goes to Amsterdam. You have your ticket and passport with you don't you?"

"What about Giselle, what about the suite at the hotel, the expense, all the clothes Bram has bought me, don't I owe him something? I'm afraid to betray him."

Now Gerda becomes the strong one.

"All right, I'll go with you. Holland will be my Christmas. Bram has paid me seven hundred fifty bucks to escort you around and that's just about enough to get me a one-way ticket on the plane."

"You would do that for me?"

"Sure. That's what friends are for."

"What about Giselle?"

"I think we can make that and then go straight to Kennedy. I wouldn't miss Giselle for the world."

"Me neither."

The two girls hug one another, take the elevator down to the lobby and hop into the limo, make the short trip to Lincoln Center in nothing flat and arrive just as the curtain goes up.

Chapter XXI

Amsterdam and Oneonta

In these days of short fast trips across the pond the Dutch Douane does not find it too unusual when two girls arrive at Schiphol looking bedraggled. Their eye makeup is messy, their blush has faded, facial creams have dried out and their lips are hankering for fresh lipstick. Greet's seam tear has enlarged from moving about in her seat and Geri's outfit is wrinkled and the now stiff cloth feels uncomfortable on her skin. Aside from purses neither one carries any hand luggage, so they have no trouble passing customs.

They freshen up as best they can in the women's room.

It is just after eight in the morning in Amsterdam, due to the six-hour time difference, but it is still only a few minutes past two a.m. in New York. Geri realizes at once that Jennifer and Phoebe are probably still at the Pierre waiting for them to show up, so the first thing she does is put in a call while Greet grabs a Dutch newspaper.

"Jennifer I…"

"Geri, are you all right, where are you?"

"I'm fine; we're in Amsterdam…"

"Amsterdam, Holland?"

"Yes… I'm here with Greta?"

"But why?"

"Long story, but she needs me over here. Listen Jen, are you still at the Pierre?"

"No, we just left but George and Josh are there waiting up for you, Phoebe is with me."

"Okay, you can call Josh and George off."

"Sounds awfully mysterious…"

"Serious, not mysterious! Look, do me a favor Jen, ask Phoebe to contact Mr. O'Gorman and tell him I won't be in on Monday, he may have to run this by Mr. Eiselman."

"Sure thing, can I tell Phoebe where you are and that it's ok for Josh to come home with George."

"No and yes. Don't tell anyone where I am, but yes Josh can go home. Do tell them I am with Greta, that we're out of town, but remember, don't tell them where I am."

"Why not?"

"I can't explain it all now, but I will when I get back. I'm safe over here at least for the moment."

"What does that mean?"

"It means that Bram has long arms, and until a few more things get settled over here I'm not sure if anyone's really safe."

"You're not exaggerating?"

"I don't think so. According to Greta, Bram Alucard has a plan to change as many humans into vampires as he can. He even has Mr. Eiselman under a spell, so make sure Mr. O'Gorman knows as little as possible."

"All this sounds unreal."

"Please believe me Jen, I've been talking up a storm with Greta on the Sub-Orb and I've learned an awful lot about Alucard's big ideas. So please just do what I said, nothing else, okay?"

"All right, Geri, okay."

"Thx hon, I've got to sign off now and call my mother. I don't like to lie to her but I have to."

While Geri is making up stories to tell her mother, why she has been out all night and such, Gerda is over at the kiosk reading de Telegraaf with intense interest. While Geri can speak Dutch, she cannot read the language, so Greet has to translate.

"Geri, Vladg's case has made the headlines. There's been a change of venue for the preliminary hearing from Amersfoort to Amsterdam."

"Is that good or bad?"

"I think it's good. The judge assigned to the case in Amersfoort is pretty conservative, so I think Vladg may have a better chance in Amsterdam, but in murder cases one never knows. It depends on whether they try to indict him for Murder-One or Manslaughter and then there are several degrees in between, so it depends on a lot of factors…we'll have to wait and see what my testimony does. Anyway this is only a hearing but it has captured the interest of most of the people because it's only the second time a Duplicant has been accused of killing a human being."

"What happened the first time?"

"That didn't even get to court, the Basisch was rolled over and that was the end of it, but this is different. Vladg is engaged to a Royaal who is well known; in fact she is running for a seat in parliament, so it is a big deal."

"Wow. A lot for me to swallow. What do we do now?"

"Look, there's an empty Scoot-Chute. Let's get in it and air sail over to the Q-7 lot. My car is parked there and we can drive right over to my place in Amersfoort. I've got a nice guest room and we both need some sleep."

"You're not kidding," Geri says in English.

Greet deposits the necessary coins, punches in the P for parking lot, then Q-7 and they whoosh off.

∞

While driving up to Oneonta, doing his usual ninety miles per hour, Bram decided to slow down as he approached Otsego County. He realized that as a landowner and an absentee landlord he had a reputation to uphold. The people here thought of him as a gentleman farmer and it just wouldn't do for him to get a speeding ticket, certainly not with all the rest of the things that seemed to be working against him lately.

When he arrived at the farm he was still upset, both at Greta and at the manner in which the nerd Josh and the stupid Duplo George had baby-sat him until two in the morning. Josh's snide remark, that Greta had gone off somewhere with Geri was hard to accept. Of course his inner sense had told him she had gone back to Holland, a betrayal of the highest order.

In all his years, haunting the past, loving the dead, Bram has never had a slave desert him the way Greta has done. He is really unhappy at losing her, but even more concerned with the fact of betrayal; how did she ever get up the nerve to leave, not for another man, but simply with a woman who may not even be a member of the sisterhood. It didn't make sense. Somehow, at this chapter of his life, his heart had come open to Greta. He had doted on her more than any other slave, exposed her to knowledge beyond the call, and his repayment was disloyalty. *'What did you expect? Doing good to others invariably reaps betrayal; par for the course with humans'.*

'There must be some peculiar weakness in my character. This would never have happened to my father'. She said she enjoyed the adventurous life of a slave, the excitement. All the money spent, the time invested. *Treacherous.* Yes, treacherous. Something would have to be done about this. *She cannot be allowed to go unpunished. Her life must be offered up, surrendered to the undead.'*

He made up his mind quickly, placed a call to Dolno Katore and arranged certain items with Malignius. He did not think this cruel. Then he sent a poorly disguised H-Mail written in code to Drakonius, the true Vampire who retained the ability to convert his shape to that of a beast:

Iwa ntyo utog oto Hollanda ndtran sfor mtwo wo menin toun dea dva mpir es. T heyar ebot hyou ngan dbe auti fulsot heirb lo odsh ouldb etoyo urlik ing. D ontdra inth emfir stim e. On ehasb e ensu ckedbe forean d Is uspec ttheoth e raswell. Ify ouk eep themal ivey ouma ytur nth emintoth e unde adnex ttim e aro und. T alkto Malignius fo rdet a ils.

He suspected Phoenix was manipulating him as well, but at the moment there was nothing he could do on that score, not until the baby's birthing.

'*Revenge will be sweet. And Lydia will pay as well, only now her midwifery is needed to deliver the baby at home. I don't want my child delivered in hospital, in an atmosphere of Christian prayers and crucifixes*'.

Now he leaned back in his chair, took stock of what he had written. He felt triumphantly wicked.

∞

In Amersfoort Mieke Meester took great pleasure in reporting to Hans that Greet had switched, that she will now be testifying as a witness for the defense, not of the prosecution. She also let him know that Vladg had been released on bond to the custody of Cynthia van Westerveld. Hans already knew that the venue for the preliminary hearing had been transferred from Amersfoort to Amsterdam, but when she proposed that they meet at a well-known café in Amsterdam to discuss procedural issues, he refused, claiming that from here on in he thought they should keep their distance from one another. He added that his fiancée was going to accompany him to Amsterdam and she might not like it if he spent time away from her. He neglected to mention that his fiancée did not wish him to spend time with Mieke specifically, but this was underscored in his phrasing.

Mieke is thoroughly pissed. Now more than ever she wants to defeat Hans.

The New York Times

All the news that's fit to transmit   December 11th, 2058

Reuters reported via the Amsterdam newspaper
HET *Parool* that the Duplicant Vladg Alucard was
found Not Guilty of murder in the case of the bio-|
chemist A.T.S de Boer, an employee of the Van den
Valk factory which manufactures Duplicants. This is
the second murder of a human being, ostensibly by a
Duplicant, in recent weeks in Holland.
A forensic programmer using WHOOPS was
able to reproduce a video from a damaged T-cell that
had inadvertently been left running. It showed that
the murderer carried out his foul deed whilst
the accused was lying unconscious on a gurney.
The odd part of the testimony was that a
homicidal detective, Sgt. Greta Hofstra, testified for
the defense. She stated that the true culprit was the
legitimate owner of the above named Duplicant, a
certain Bram Alucard. She insisted he was a vampire.
Her superior, the well known Chief of Homicide,
Mr. de Haas, stated that Sgt. Hofstra would be placed on

official leave of absence until she regained her mental
stability. Incidentally, The Times has reported earlier
that this Bram Alucard, an employee of our very own
State Department, was reputed to be a vampire.
Moreover, the accused is the officially registered
fiancée, of Hikey van Westerveld, a Green Party candidate
for a Senate seat in the Dutch Parliament. She is a bitter
enemy of the incumbent seated senator Geert Rümke, PVV
against whom she is actively campaigning. Rümke has
gained notoriety for his anti-Duplicant rhetoric. Should she
win, the issue will be a cause célèbre as no Duplicant
anywhere in the world has ever been elected to such high
office in government.
Rest assured this reporter will stay on top of the story.

Cynthia Van Westerveld owns a small flat in the P.C. Hoofdstraat in Amsterdam. It is situated near the end of the street and so it is located fairly close to the Eeghenstraat entrance of the Vondel Park. During the preliminary hearing, Cynthia had allowed Hikey and Vladg to make use of the place and although they spent most of their days in court they were able to take romantic walks in the Vondel Park in the evenings.

Now, however, Hikey is in Hilversum at the TV-studio, waiting to participate in her nationally televised debate against Rümke. So Vladg is alone for the first time in Amsterdam and finds himself twiddling his thumbs. On impulse, he decides to head over to the Vondel Park Hotel to visit with Greet and Gerda whom he has met during the hearing. He wants to formally thank Greet for her testimony which he had thus far neglected to do. Lydia, and now Hikey, usually remind him to take his T-cell with him but he is absent minded and once again forgets to do so.

He walks to the end of the P.C. Hoofdstraat, turns right, crosses the street onto Eeghenstraat and the entranceway to the park. The evening air is somewhat chilled yet invigorating and Vladg decides to sit on one of the park benches for a time, just to enjoy the passing parade, people walking their dogs, strolling lackadaisically, bicycling easily, munching on goodies as they wander by.

At first he does not notice a rather tall man with a sallow gaunt face sitting on an opposite bench. This cadaverous looking fellow, oddly enough, is formally dressed for the evening but in addition wears a flowing black cape and a top hat that stems from another era. He has a short grisly van Dyck beard and holds a dangerous looking gnarled hickory walking stick in his hand. He gets up from his seat and comes over toward Vladg who evinces no surprise at this move.

Since he has gained wide notoriety in Holland from de Boer's murder, a number of strangers have expressed a desire to meet him. One of de Boer's relatives, who is about to inherit from the dead man's estate, actually sent a note to Vladg thanking him for the killing. He was grateful not only for the upcoming trust fund coming his way, but for the fact that he would no longer have to fake adoration of his uncle whom, in reality, he despised. Some others even asked for his autograph and one time he received a proposal from a lady based in the red-light district asking him to be her souteneur (pimp). She said she was impressed by his massive shoulders and the rumor that American Sextus', unlike European Royaals' with six, actually had nine inches. Vladg gallantly refused the honor.

The stranger is not at all inhibited, and speaks right up.

"I am Drakonius Montesaro, from Dolno Katore in Macedonia. I saw your picture on the TV screen the other day and wanted to meet you because we have something in common."

"Oh, what's that," asks Vladg, not particularly interested, yet curious about such a strange looking man.

"Your owner, Bram Alucard is an acquaintance of mine."

"I see. And are you a vampire as well."

"Yes, I am a true Vampire, not a Dhampire…"

"Well it's nice to hear someone admit it right off like that. I've had about enough of denials. Bram has got me into a sea of troubles."

"I know, that's the way it is sometimes. But at least he has treated you fairly on other occasions, isn't that so?"

Vladg mulls this over. It is true that without Bram's fortune, Lydia would never have been able to make the purchase, and until recently he had had socially adventurous times in Santa Barbara and, of course, a fairly free reign with Lydia. It was only when he came to Holland that Bram started mucking up his life, but on the other hand he had met Hikey here and she was the best thing going so far.

"I suppose so," he finally says. "But what business is it of yours?"

"I don't want to get you into trouble, but I have to warn you. It is my intent to drain Greet Hofstra of most of her blood, maybe all of it if I like the taste and I don't want any interference from you. You have been in enough trouble and should you interfere with my plans in any way, I shall have to thrash you with this stick. As you can see it is pure hickory, one of the hardest woods, and I am very handy with it. Even you will not sustain the blows to your head that I am capable of delivering. So just take this as a warning. You will have to kill me, which is not easy, but if you do, being accused of another murder of a human being would not be in your best interest, don't you agree."

Vladg is severely daunted but doesn't let on. He is able to maintain a semblance of dignity, acts unruffled by all that Drakonius has said.

"The fact is that you are not a human being, no true Vampire is. Even Bram is only half human, so I imagine that you have some reason for telling me all this. What is it?"

"That is my secret. Believe me, it is not your lymph that entices me. I bid you adieu."

With that said, Drakonius stops abruptly, tips his hat and strides off hurriedly down the pathway, turning only once to wave his hickory stick in the air as if he were triumphant in battle. His receding figure, with the wind catching his long black cape, wafting it in the air one way and another, reminds Vladg of some type of bird of prey.

Left alone on the park bench it takes Vladg but a moment to realize that he must get over to the Vondel Park Hotel and warn Greet and Gerda. Then suddenly it comes to him. He now knows that this is precisely Drakonius' motive. *He wants to cast fear into the hearts of the two girls and is using me as his instrument to do so'.*

Vladg grabs one of the free bicycles, hops on, and peddles as furiously as he can over to the hotel.

∞

In Studio Hilversum, prior to the onset of the debate, and while the M.C. is revving up the audience, expert cosmeticians have seen to it that Rümke's pock marked cheeks are covered with a facial paste that perfectly matches the color of his skin.

He is also meticulously shaved so that no semblance of a beard shows on camera. Leading PVV party members know that when it comes to TV, Hikey's gigantic head shows up well, almost overwhelming the screen, so they do not wish to start off at a disadvantage and have made every effort to modernize Rümke's dress style in the most fashionable manner.

Hikey hasn't changed much of her appearance except for her hair which she wears in long soft Elizabethan curls that frame both sides of her face equally and give her a distinguished, yet still attractive feminine look. Offhandedly, but loud enough for people to hear, she lets it be known that as a member of Green-Link the dress she wears has not one iota of petrochemical in it, that it is made from reconstituted bamboo, recovered from a fallen bridge in Thailand, and not one fresh bamboo shoot was destroyed to manufacture the microfibre.

Gerrit Rümke replies that the red and blue colors of his tie might be made from anything, but all he knows is that they are polka dots and that that is good enough for him.

The studio audience chortles.

Precisely at the prime time eight o'clock evening hour they go on air. More than half of Holland's TV audience is tuned in to the forthcoming debate between the Duplicant Hikey Van Westerveld and the man from Apeldoorn, the incumbent Senator Gerrit Rümke.

The M.C. announces that this particular weekday evening was chosen by the contestants because there were no voetbal (soccer) games of significance scheduled for the hour. There are scattered chuckles in the audience but then he goes on to say: "There will be a slight delay in the proceedings since one of the contestants did not want to use a podium and the other did." (The studio executives are furious with the delay).

"I don't need a lectern to hold my notes," Hikey whispers to the M.C. off camera, "but the main reason is all the audience will get to see is my head if I'm seated behind a podium…I'll look silly."

The Senator counters: "I don't want to stand in the open the entire hour. If I have a lectern, I can sit on a high stool if I wish and still look presentable."

The Master of Ceremonies goes on to explain to both that the microphones they are wearing are constructed of RFID (Radio Frequency Identification Chips) powder and they can move about as freely as they wish on stage, that they do not have to stand behind the podium if that is not to their liking.

Now both nod their agreement.

"Just a small techno-problem we had to clear up," the M.C. declares to the audience.

After a rendition of Mozart's Eine Kleine Nachtmusik the M.C. tells the studio audience that the entire production is presented at no cost to the taxpayers, but is shared equally by contributions from the Green-Link party and the PVV. Then he introduces the moderator, the well-known poetess and novelist, Andrea Winkelman. She has a mellifluous voice that carries well over the airwaves. In her introductory remarks she goes on to explain that each participant will get ten minutes to talk, followed by a five-minute rebuttal. Then the studio audience will have five minutes for interaction, followed by five minutes of questioning by the three members of the press from the NRC, de Telegraaf and the Het Parool. Then the protocol will reverse with Senator Rümke being afforded the chance to speak first and so on until the time allotted is up. Both the studio audience and the viewers on the H-Net will then have the opportunity to vote and the results will be posted the next day in all the papers. The second debate will afford three different members of the press the opportunity to participate.   "Are there any concerns or questions before we begin?" Both of the contestants nod their assent to start.

"All right Ms van Westerveld, you may begin."

Hikey is careful not to overdo it. She goes through the polite formalities, thanking all concerned for allowing her the privilege to appear on a national format. Her body language is gracious toward her opponent.

She begins to speak to the cameras:

"This question of equality for Duplicants of all types is more important than any other; indeed, so important has it become that a national question for Holland has become a world question. In a sense, as Holland goes, so goes the world at large in terms of social justice. So first we should know where we are, and secondly where we are going. Then we can better judge what to do, and how to do it.

"Imagine if you were a Basisch Duplicant and could not even get a hearing at present if accused of a crime, even a misdemeanor. Until very recently Central Control had the power to rollover any Duplo it wished for whatever reason it felt justified. This raises the question: how would a human being feel if she or he were exposed to this type of treatment. Not very sanguine I imagine….so we must abolish this present policy where Duplicants are owned by private corporations and paid a pittance, if that, for their labor.

"We are now far into the third month since a policy was initiated at The Hague with the avowed object and confident promise of putting an end to Duplicant mistreatment and agitation by Central Computers. Under the former operation of that policy Basisch Duplicants were labeled by numbers, not names; they were worked in twelve on, twelve off shifts, with no regard for personal or social life. Now that type of agitation has ceased in some quarters, but not in all. In fact, on the docks and the farmlands it has not ceased, but has actually augmented. In my opinion, it will not cease until a crisis shall have been reached and passed. History shows that the Dutch people have endured severe sadistic treatment in prior wars, prior centuries. This century should not be exposed to a similar expression, a tendency to the latter condition of sadism!

"As long as Holland is divided on this issue, there will be conflict amongst the electorate, conflict in the business community, conflict in our educational system. None of this is good for our country.

Now to the second part, the question of what to do and how to do it."

Hikey takes a silent moment to emphasize her points, to see if all so far has soaked in to the audience. When she is satisfied she begins again.

"Let anyone who doubts, carefully contemplate that almost complete legal piece of machinery compounded of The Hague decisions and the Doctrine of Amersfoort which guarantees minimum wage to Basics. We need now to take the next step. And that step is to recognize that Duplicants must have the legal right of due process before the law. If I am elected to the Senate I shall fight for this right and other basic rights as well until the public mind shall rest in the belief that this course of action is the right way to sail the ship for Holland and its entire people, Human and Duplicant. So I do need your endorsement, your vote, to carry forward a policy that historically fits in with the Dutch way of thinking, a fairness doctrine to form and regulate this issue in our own way. And that way is through parliamentary statute, the right way of any government, certainly of ours."

Now Hikey takes a deep breath, scans the studio audience to one side and then the other. After a calculated pause, she begins again. "I believe this government cannot endure permanently such a division between Duplicants and Humans. We are not asking for full citizenship, no, but we are asking for equal rights. I do not expect the issues to be resolved overnight, nor do I expect Holland to dissolve its ways, but I do expect it to cease being divided, to become one land again, one healthy land with liberty and justice for all. A vote for me is a vote for Green-Link and a guarantee of freedom for all concerned in our society."

The audience starts to clap but Andrea Winkelman stops them by raising her hand. "We have no time for applause because of a late start (the TV executives are now pleased at the time saving) so without further ado, I will ask for Senator Rümke's rebuttal.

The Senator's rebuttal is classical. He insists that giving basic rights to Duplicants will shatter the Dutch culture. He states that this will only be the first step in a series of diversionary steps that will destroy Holland's traditional way of life.

When his allotted rebuttal time is up the audience and press get their chance. They ask more than a dozen questions on class interactions, furloughs and vacation times, influence on labor contracts, the economic benefits and ills that privatization of Duplicants will cause.

Both participants' answers are well formulated. They tout plans they say will benefit the economy and Holland's status in the world, although each has an opposite view of how to accomplish this.

Now it is Rümke's time to speak and he makes a good case for the status quo. He does call the present election a mockery of the constitution because it was only by a special ruling of the Queen that the Duplicant Westerveld, *who is not a true citizen of Holland,* was allowed to participate as a nominee of her party.

This is received largely with boos and catcalls; only a few in the audience support him, so he quickly goes on to another topic.

He explains that Basisch Duplos have taken over all the menial jobs that true Hollanders were unwilling to perform, but that this has prevented illegal immigration from such countries as Turkey, Somalia and Kenya. He asks the audience if they wish to return to the days of the early 21st century when illegal immigrants were destroying the Dutch way of life, when they were becoming a yoke around the neck of the health care system, when the language of the country was so filled by foreign tongues that it was difficult to hear a true Dutch word on the streets, in the trams, or in the cafes.

He is met by resounding 'huzzahs' and 'guffaws' in agreement with his views by more than half the audience.

When Hikey's chance comes for rebuttal, she explains that if the present system is allowed to proceed, it will look like the situation in America during slavery times in the 17th and 18th centuries leaving Holland to bear the brunt of world criticism. "Is that what you want?" she asks the audience and now about half the people shout their support for her position.

The evening ends with both participants thanking the moderator and M.C. They are seen on screen shaking hands amicably but it is evident that neither nominee has won a clear victory.

∞

Greet and Gerda are staying at the Vondel Park Hotel in a room on the 12th floor which has been arranged for her by Chief de Haas. Ever since he furloughed her, declared her in need of mental health services, she has been attending daily psychotherapy sessions at the Valerius Clinic run by Professor Woerdeman, an expert on vampire delusions.

She is a little jumpy, so when the house phone, which has no tele-screen, rings persistently, it is Gerda who picks up.

"That was Vladg," she tells Greet. "He sounds anxious, almost frightened."

"Really? I never saw him that way, not even during the hearing when he was accused of murder."

"I know. This must be something new, probably has to do with Bram in one way or the other. I told him to come up."

When she hears a knock on the door, Greet lets Vladg in, greets him warmly.

Vladg forgets that his original purpose was to thank her for her testimony. Instead, he blurts out all that has happened on the park bench with Drakonius.

"You know Vladg," she says, speaking in English as Vladg's Dutch, while improved, is not yet good enough for a conversation in depth, "you know," she repeats,

"I have to attend the Valerius Psychiatric Clinic on a daily basis for my 'delusion' about vampires. If I come with this added story they will put me away for keeps."

"Well we can't keep this to ourselves, this guy is dangerous, worse than Bram, he is a full blooded Vampire and he intends to suck you both out to the last drop, I think that's what he said."

"I've still got my Walther 327 laser pistol; the chief hasn't asked me to turn it in, nor my shield. So we can defend ourselves a certain amount. We just can't call the local police; they'll think I belong in the loony bin for sure with this story."

"I'm not sure bullets will take him unless they're silver coated, they're not are they?"

"'Course not. We're lucky if the bullets are made out of metal, mostly they're rubber or plastic. Anyway, you don't expect the Dutch to spend money on silver bullets for their nut cases do you? I'm not the Lone Ranger."

Geri snickers.

"Guess not."

"What I can do is call the house detective. He's an old friend of mine, retired from the department and works here nights. Kees Beerbohm is his name."

Greet gets on the house phone asks for the proper extension, digits it in. Kees remembers her well, is glad to hear from her. She gives Kees the lowdown and he says he will be up to their room in two shakes.

In no time at all there is a knock at the door. Greet, excited to see him, rushes to the door and pulls it open. Standing right behind Kees is a tall man with a top hat, who hits Kees a powerful blow on the side of his neck with the knob of his walking stick; Greet instinctively extends her arms, catching the falling Kees. The man pays no immediate attention to Greet, hurries past her into the room and slaps Geri across the side of her face, a powerful blow that sends her flying.

"I want no interference from you!" he snarls at Vladg, but Vladg goes into a martial arts stance and Drakonius circles around him, both searching for the best opportunity to attack.

Greet allows the unconscious Kees to slump to the floor, pulls out her Walther and fires three shots in quick succession at Drakonius, all hit their mark, each within one inch of the other, but all this does is to make Drakonius grunt, step back and take a new position. Then she empties her pistol at him, he rushes her and knocks her out with a severe fisted blow to her chin, snapping her head back on its axis. This does, however, give Vladg the moment of separation that he needs, and he is able to rest the hickory stick from Drakonius. Now his ATP is activated, he doesn't swing the stick, but uses it as one would a sword, prodding Drakonius repeatedly in the stomach, backing him up toward the window. Drakonius is not the overly muscular type, but he is very wiry and in the blink of an eye he jumps to the side evading the blows, striving to gain an advantage. Immediately Vladg reverses the stick, attempts to hit Drakonius with the knobby end, but Drakonius twists away in time, jumps at Vladg, his canines now elongated, he goes for the neck, but Vladg too is quick, he thrusts Drakonius aside as if he were a rag doll, grabs him by both feet and swings his head against the wall. When it seems as if Drakonius' head will crack, Vladg rotates the vampire threw the air one last time and with a final triumphant swing, throws him with great force against the window pane, which cracks open and Drakonius goes sailing out the twelfth floor window. Drakonius makes a tremendous parabolic arc as he falls through the air, but he is conscious and has just enough time to convert himself into a gigantic bat. Vladg, watching through the shattered window, sees what appears as the cloak transforming itself into large wings whose spread begins to halt the downward flow and slowly, as the wings snap against the air with force the vampire pulls both his bat-legs up into a ball, and at the very last moment extends them as if he had a built in parachute, landing safely on the ground. Then he reconverts himself back into human form.

Drakonius shakes his fist fiercely at Vladg's head which is sticking out of what's left of the window. He shouts upward at him, a contempt filled series of epithets, but the distance is too great for Vladg to hear. Then he bounds away in great strides, leaping and howling like a wolf as he lopes off.

Vladg cannot escape the thought that this is not the last he will see of Drakonius.

∞

Oneonta is magnificent in late autumn, rivaling New England. Most of the people of Central New York take to 'leaf peeking' during this time as the maples, oaks, elms and beech trees are not yet shed of their leaves, but their abundant color has turned into all shades of reds, greens, orange-yellows and browns. These brilliant colors appear as the leaves lose their chlorophyll and the various pigments now become prominent, able to show their many hues. The parade of colors lasts but a few weeks but during this time tourists come in bunches to view the spacious beauty of the City of the Hills as Oneonta is called.

It is in this 'leaf peeking' time that Bram has settled into his farm, located but a few miles outside the city limits. In addition to the main house and barn there are two guest houses one of which is occupied by Edna and Judd Kincaid year around. They are Southerners who have been up north for many years acting as caretakers for the farm. They do get free rent, some sales commissions, but otherwise Bram pays them not one red cent. They make their living by truck farming, growing tomatoes, string beans and some sweet corn, planting cabbage, radishes and celery and putting up raspberry and strawberry preserves. The couple has a few laying hens on the place for personal use and there is one dairy cow named Daisy. Two horses, a dun mare and a chestnut gelding are boarded in the barn, not for work but for riding. Both Judd and Edna are horsy in the sense that they like to ride daily if time allows and Bram has no objection to this as long as they keep the place spic and span and the farm has a productive appearance fitting to the surround.

At the moment Judd and Edna are arguing rather fiercely about Daisy. It seems her teats are running dry and Judd wants Bram to sell her for hot dog meat while Edna, who has developed deeper feelings for the animal, wants her to live out the rest of her life in pasture.

"She's not a god damn stud horse, nothin' but a dairy cow, and if we sell her for meat Mr. Alucard will benefit, we get a commission and maybe a new milker, isn't that right Mr. Alucard?"

Bram doesn't talk down to the Kincaids; neither does he use the perfumed speech that accompanies him in his role with the Foreign Service people. Rather, his tactic is to try to speak their lingo as best he can. But this last question of Judd's is exactly the kind of confrontation that embarrasses him. While he has no compunction at tearing out the guts of another human being when he feels justified, he finds it difficult to arbitrate someone else's domestic dispute. This particular one does concern him, however, as he is involved to the degree that his attitude must look businesslike in the eyes of the Kincaid's. He feels this as essential; otherwise Judd and Edna might lose respect for him. He has another reason for making a businesslike decision that satisfies them. In a few days he expects three Sextus IV's to arrive and he wants the Kincaids to take them to church after he does his brain wave projections and gets the Duplicants indoctrinated to his plan for the 2nd Reformation.

He mulls all this over.

They are staring at him, waiting for his answer.

There is an inconvenient silence.

Finally, he comes up with an idea.

"Edna, I have to agree with Judd, we need to sell Daisy. I know she's meant more to you than a milker…"

"Mr. Alucard, I confess, when Judd's out in the fields of a spell, I talk to Daisy and, believe it or not, she seems to listen. I know she's not human, or anything like that, but she seems to understand what I'm saying…"

"Just so. Don't cry…fetch a Kleenex for her Judd…now here's my plan. We have to sell her to the industry, no question on that, and you two get the ten percent commission on the sale…"

"I don't want the money…I want someone to talk to when I get lonely."

"Hear me out…please…"

"Quit snifflin' …" Judd says.

"Christmas is just around the corner, and remember a few weeks ago when your neighbor's Rottweiler had a big litter and offered you two pups, are they still available?"

"S'pose so."

"Well you know I'm not a dog lover and that's why I denied you at the time, but if you still want them I'll allow you to have both, how's that?"

"That'd be raht fine, I'll have someone to talk to of an evening after chores is done, won't I Judd."

"Yes Hon, and Rottweilers make fine watchdogs, we need 'em 'roun here. But that still leaves us without a milker…"

"Well Daisy was always for your personal use and you did sell some fresh milk from her to neighbors over the years…"

"Right as rain Mr. Alucard. Never intended to keep that from you, but for an absentee what dudn't come 'roun here much you sure know what's goin' on."

"Thank you Edna."

"Yes, I'd allus put the raw milk in two gallon containers on the stoop with a plate set raht next to it. Them five-gallon steel ones is too heavy for most. Thisaway neighbor's can take what milk portions they like an' leave a donation if they had a mind to…makes me no never mind they do or don'…long as the milk don' go to waste…no way can the gummint construe that as sellin' milk."

"That word construe…where'd you learn that?"

"Why from you, Mr. Alucard. You're allus using big words like that and I pick up on it."

"Good for you. Tell you what. I'll pay half the cost of a new dairy cow; you can call her Daisy Two if you like…"

"Oh no sir, that would be a constant reminder of Daisy, I wouldn' want that, heavens knows I'll be mournin' that poor creature for a long while to come, she's like fambly to me."

"Okay, then its settled. You ask your neighbor for the pups, you get the ten percent commission, I pay half the cost of a new milker and you quit crying."

Edna forces a laugh and Judd puts his arms around her, settles her down.

"Jes don' give the new milker a name when we gets her, that's what makes 'em humanlike, gets you all emotional," Judd insists.

"Oh, all right."

"Now I have a favor to ask. You know I've got thirty acres here, but you two work something less than ten acres. That means over twenty acres are lying fallow."

"Yep, been that way for years," Judd says.

"Well do you remember me saying I was going to bring in some Sextus IV's to work the land…?"

"Sure rings a bell."

"Okay, in a few days three of them will be coming in. At first they can stay in the other guest house, but after a while I'm going to hire a construction company to build a bunk house, enough for twenty or so…"

"My, my, sure a lotta Duplos," Edna says.

"The favor I want to ask you Edna is whether you will bring the first three into church on Sundays. While the bunk house is under construction the church can use them as handy men…"

"Them's not God's creatures…don' think that'd be raht."

"We're all God's creatures…"

"Not Duplos."

"You talk to Daisy like a human, surely you'll give Duplicants the benefit of the doubt."

"Duplos is manufactured, not the same."

"Certainly you must remember your Genesis. God made all the creatures before he made Adam and Eve, then he asked Adam to name them. The scriptural root in Genesis 2:19 says: 'the Lord God formed every beast of the field and every bird of the air, and brought them unto Adam to see what he would call them; and whatever the man called them that was its name'."

"Meanin'?"

"You're going to name your dogs aren't you?"

"Surely."

"Then I ask you to give Christian names to the Sextus."

"The preacher will have to do that, it'll be his choice, not mine, the dogs will be mine, not your Duplos."

"That's fair."

"Don't know what the neighbors will think, me bringing Duplos into church."

"Man and all his doings are derived from God. I want these Duplos to be Christian in their morals even if they can't be Christians in the same spiritual sense like you and Judd."

"Makes sense to me," Judd says

"Oh you, you'd agree to anythin' what sounds good. I suspek there's somethin' wrong here. No way God is goin' to let Duplos into heaven, so why's they need to go to church?"

"Just so. Church will demonstrate once and for all the difference between us, that even Duplos are better than the non-believers, the non-worshippers who are human and avoiding God's word."

"Well, all raht, if you think it's so, I'll go along, but iff'n the preacher says no, then that's what it'll be, no."

Good enough for me."

"And will you come to worship with us."

"I go to a different church, one they don't have here in Oneonta, otherwise I would."

"Hmmmnpf. You the one bringin' Duplos here, seems like you oughta be the one worshippin' with 'em."

"Edna! Hush," warns Judd.

"All raht. I'll bring them first Sunday they's here."

"Thank you Edna, very gracious of you."

"Still got my doubts, but iff'n you think the Ten Commandments is what Duplos need to learn, I'll not be agin it."

"Thank you Edna."

"And one last thing."

"What's that?"

"I ain't eatin' no more hot dogs."

Chapter XXII

Christmas 2058

Hikey had driven like a banshee from Hilversum to Amsterdam in order to be with Vladg. Upon arrival she found him playing with a hickory stick. He seemed to be entirely focused, excited about nothing else, parading around the room, swinging the stick like a karate expert.

When she asked him what he thought of the debate he stopped momentarily, face flushed, admitted that he hadn't seen it, started in again twirling the stick like a ninja.

"You promised to watch it on Three-Screen in 4-D."

"I know…something came up."

Hikey is thoroughly annoyed with his answer and the way he is acting.

"Where'd you get that stick?" she asks on impulse, still pissed, but trying to keep her cool.

Vladg finally sets the stick down, tells her how he had taken a stroll in the Vondel Park alone and ran into another violent adventure. In what could be called his way, rather deliberate and slow fashion, he gives her the details of the entire evening's events.

His explanation doesn't seem to settle her down very much.

She is still angry with him because he had promised to stay put and watch her appearance on Three-Screen. But Hikey, being Hikey, lets her curiosity get the best of her. Of a sudden, staring at the stick, she switches the subject away from politics.

"Hickory is rare these days; may I take a look at it?"

Vladg tries to make a joke, asks her if she intends to thrash him with it, but she is in no mood for humor of any sort. Still, he is glad that her attention has been diverted away from politics and the debate.

He hands the hickory stick over and she inspects it very carefully.

"Did you notice this miniature button, just at the lower edge of the ivory knob where it meets the wood?"

"I thought it was just for decoration."

"I don't think so, look, it's a bayonet fitting" …she presses the button, twists the knob, pulls open the handle and presto-change-o, like magic she pulls out a long thin rapier hidden inside the stick.

"See, it's not just a walking-stick but a sword-cane. It lacks a cutting edge, so it's used only for thrusting. I owned a foil somewhat like it in high school, in fencing class."

"He must have intended to use that to do away with me and then have the girls for himself."

"I think so. You're lucky you snagged it away from him before he could get at it."

"That's for sure."

"So when are you going to return it?"

Vladg smiles, figures she said this to be provocative. He knows enough about her to realize she is letting him off the hook by asking a silly question. He answers in a serious vein.

"I don't think that will be necessary, I'm sure Drakonius will find a way to retrieve it and try to do me in at the same time."

"Well you're going to have to learn how to stay out of trouble. I really can't afford to have a fiancée who gets such negative press. It hurts my chances."

Vladg stares at her in disbelief. He thought she had forgiven him and now she's back at it. This may be their very first tiff, but he feels she's carrying things much too far.

"I can't believe you said that. Are you more concerned with winning a Senate seat than my welfare?"

"No. I'm sorry if it sounded that way. It's just that we are both Duplicants and anything that happens to you can be attributed to me in a manner of speaking…"

"If that were true, which it isn't, every human who campaigns with his wife would be subject to the same reasoning…"

"I think they are. That's the nature of politics. And that's the only reason I said what I did. At the personal level it's not true, of course not. Forgive me."

"Well that makes me feel better. Come here."

Hikey, coquettishly, slithers her hips off the couch, sashays over to him for a hug, loses herself in his massive arms and shoulders.

"Howzabout a 'hair of the dog' to settle things down, Jack Daniels on the rocks?" he whispers into her ear.

"That's what you drank with Lydia. I'd rather have our white wine; we've got Riesling in the fridge."

"That'll work."

The next thing he hears is a snappy zuz-zip sound.

She has deftly unzipped his fly and grabbed his cylinder. With one hand she pulls on it like a handle and guides him over to the bedroom. She likes doing it this way; the feeling of control excites her.

"Prepare yourself, I'll get the wine."

While she is gone Vladg undresses, sponges off his groin and underarms, cleans   between his toes. He is not sweating so he has to spray a little cologne like any other human. He figures that's enough on the hygiene bit, crawls under the sheets.

When she returns Hikey is already in her birthday suit holding the two wine glasses each one placed just below her small pert breasts. She dips one nipple into the wine before handing it to Vladg and he tongues her off, then she puts a finger into the other glass, spreads some droplets of wine onto his left nipple, licks it off and then squeezes his bio-sensor button starting his sex program. Now they clink glasses and finish off the rest of the wine.

They are not well practiced lovers, but neither are they neophytes. Hikey's problem is her need to be in charge, to feel that she is in control of every situation, but she is smart enough to know that when it comes to sex this works against her, inhibits orgasm. She knows that good sex takes place on an order-disorder grid, that if she tries to control too much, it won't work. She needs less reality, more enchantment, so during the kissing she begins to abandon her intellectual thoughts, to think in softer and more pliant tones, to allow fun thoughts to seep through. She imagines spanking Vladg with the hickory stick several times and this causes her to giggle inside; her negative thoughts to fade away. As her mind settles down, the cells on the inside of her little cavern begin to moisten and the more she releases control, the more juices accumulate in her membranes and now his cock is able to penetrate fully, filling her cavern with his swelling, her internal muscles automatically grasping his circumference sending messages to her spine and up to her brain and then back down causing her hips to roll, her legs to squeeze, her arms to hold him ever so tight. Now they are no longer kissing for she has found that if she continues to kiss upstairs less will be going on downstairs so she presses her mouth to his neck and he to hers and their rhythm is now less dissonant but more intense, less penetrating, but more in tune, the tones rising, steadily increasing, more melodious, more harmonious, more successive, more repetitive, more crescendo like, and then, finally more, more-more, ultimate more,…more.

Afterwards, still snuggling, they talk about Christmas. Vladg asks if she would mind if he sent Lydia the Hickory stick by Fed-Up for a Yule time present.

"That's fine," she says, "I'd rather you got rid of it and that's as good a way as any."

Vladg knows that he made a mistake mentioning Lydia while they were still in bed together. When it comes to Lydia, Hikey would rather believe that they were never lovers, merely friends, so he quickly asks:

"What do you want for Christmas?"

"What every woman wants from her lover…and after that…a diamond engagement ring."

"I'm saving up. Cynthia is working on my reinstatement at the school now that I've been declared innocent. How big a rock do you want?"

"The size doesn't matter; it's the setting that counts. I want to help you choose; we could go to the jewelers together. Spyers is a good one."

"That takes away from the surprise…I'd rather buy it on my own."

Sex hasn't cured her; she is still a bit of a control freak. This time she sees it and gives in.

"Oh, all right. And by the way, since you mentioned Cynthia, she wants us to go to church with her on Christmas Eve."

"You know I'm an atheist. If I went to church that would make me a hypocrite."

"Well I'm going and you know I don't believe in any sort of God."

"But that's hypocrisy…"

"Of course, that's what politics is all about. The better hypocrite you are, the more you can get away with, makes for a better politician in the eyes of the people."

Vladg pinches her lovingly on the butt.

"I'm going to sleep."

∞

A few days later, rather early in the morning, as Hikey is preparing to go on campaign tour with Mieke, she receives an odd call from Cynthia. There is an anxious edge to her voice and a frantic yip-yap from Molly:

"Hikey the gas went off this morning while I was making myself a mushroom omelet."

"Well I've told you that gas is less reliable than electricity. Why don't you get electric burners? You know since they're digitalized you can set the tiniest bit of heat gradient that you want and get a read out at the same time for whatever you're cooking."

"Because I'm old fashioned and I like to cook with gas and right now that's not my problem. All I want is to get the gas back on. You know how much I hate to talk to those people at the gas and electric company…"

"But Cynthia, you won't get to talk to a real person, that's a Basic Duplo job. Nothing to be wary of, just give them a buzz and they'll fix you up in no time."

"You can't call for me…?"

"I'm getting ready to meet Mieke, we're headed for Tilburg, otherwise I would."

"Where's Vladg, maybe he can call for me?"

"He's over at City Hall trying to get his work permit reinstated, I suppose you could call him there but it would be upsetting. Look, this is something you can do, I've really got to go, but call me back in half an hour. We'll be on the road but I don't mind as long as I don't keep Mieke waiting, you know how she is."

"Oh, all right. Have a good trip."

"Thx, bye, luvya."

∞

On the road, she tells Mieke about the anxious call from Cynthia.

"She's always been that way, frightful of low level employees, civil servants, talking to servers at restaurants, that sort of thing, but if she were with a CEO or an MP, she could give them what for."

"Well are you worried?"

"Not really. In the background I heard the operatic sounds of Cosi fan Tutte, that's her favorite projecto film disc, if she was playing Mozart than she can't be too upset."

"I suppose not."

∞

Less than an hour later Cynthia calls again; this time she sounds truly frightened.

"The horses in the corral are restless, neighing and snorting, stomping their hooves and Molly is upset."

"What about the gas?"

"The gas is back on. Actually, there may be a leak, I can smell it."

"Then you should get out of there immediately."

"I'm afraid to, there's a strange man puttering with the gas main outside …"

"What's he look like?"

"He's tall, thinnish, sort of ominous looking, if you know what I mean."

"Probably they sent a man over to inspect things, to see why the gas went off in the first place."

"I don't think so."

"Why not?"

"Because he's not dressed in a company outfit, he's a suspicious looking character, wears a top hat a cloak."

Now Hikey is petrified.

"Do you still have your husband's hunting rifle, that 270 from when he was going for deer?'

"Whyever???"

"Get it! Do it now! And call the police. That man is a killer. Put me on three-way call, I'll listen."

Hikey hears a scurrying of feet, glass shattering, then a short mirthless laugh, scraping noises of furniture being shoved about, a sudden stoppage of Molly's yip-yapping, then 'Oh no, no, no, no', followed by multiple screams mixed with ferocious predatory growls, sucking gurgling sounds, a very, very long silence, then a voice that says: "You're next." followed by an enormous explosion.

"Your friend is gone and so is the house. Tell your fiancée what I said: *You're next.*"

Hikey is devastated. She tells Mieke to turn the car around that they are not going to Tilburg, but back to the Veluwe.

Mieke wants to object, but when she hears that Cynthia has most likely been murdered, the house destroyed and Hikey's life threatened, she immediately flips a U-ey and heads toward the Veluwe.

∞

In Amersfoort, Greet is back at homicide division but has been given a desk job by de Haas. When Professor Woerdeman of the Valerius Clinic declared her sane and stable de Haas had no other choice, otherwise the Union Steward would have filed against him for cause. So he was forced to reinstate Greet, although he felt she was still radical on her vampire beliefs, which he thought were tantamount to delusions. He did not understand why a learned man, such as Prof. Woerdeman, could not see it his way. So he did the next best thing and placed her on desk duty, filing papers, answering the phone and reviewing unsolved cases.

So it was Greet who took the call which Hikey made from the car while Mieke was speeding back to the Veluwe.

"Greet, I'm glad you're the one who answered."

"You sound frenzied, what's up"

"I listened in on a three-way call with Cynthia and Drakonius. He's murdered her Greet…"

"OOooooooh…I'm so sorry, she was the best."

"For me she was. And somehow he blew up the house…"

"Blew it up?"

"That's what it sounded like over the phone. Cynthia was having trouble with the gas burner, that's why she called me first, we were on our way to Tilburg, you know how she is, shy to call civil servants, anyway the gas went back on and when Drakonius called I heard this big explosion, he must have somehow set it off, then turned it back on. I don't know. Please send some people up there will you? I'm headed there now with Mieke."

"Immediately. We cover that area as well; I'll get Dusty and Joost to Air-Scoot over. I'm so sorry Hikey."

"Thank you. I'll meet them there."

"Right."

∞

By the time Hikey and Mieke make it to Cynthia's house, Joost and Dusty have been there for some time. They have completed some preliminary forensic work and hidden what was left of Molly from view. The house itself, other than the structural parts made of cement tiles and the stone fireplace and parts of the chimney, is completely destroyed, blown every which way.

"Where is she?" Hikey screams at Joost, "I want to see her!"

"No you don't," Dusty answers for him.

She turns to face Dusty, her tone diminished.

"Please," she stammers weakly, close to fainting. Mieke moves in for support, holding her around the waist, preventing her from falling.

"Her body's in several pieces…what good is it for you to see that?"

Hikey is whimpering, begging to see the remains.

"Let her see time instead," Mieke says, "you must have made a copy from the Projecto-Fax."

Dusty glances at Joost looking for guidance.

"All right, it's in the van, Willem has made a copy. He'll show it to you if that's what you want. Are you sure? It's pretty awful."

"I want to see it," Hikey insists.

∞

In the van, Willem is disinclined to show the copy.

"This is evidence," he says. "I'm not sure either Joost or Dusty have the legal authority to let you see it."

Mieke pipes up immediately.

"If its evidence we have every right. If this comes to trial evidence must be shared equally. Should Hikey have to take the stand and be forced to testify she should know in advance what horrors occurred in this case."

Willem has no desire to argue with an attorney; certainly not one of Mieke's standing. He begins to roll the tape.

The first scene shows Drakonius kicking in the large patio glass window, jumping through the opening unscathed by the shards of flying glass, and then, as Molly leaps at him, he catches her in mid-air, strangles the little dog and with one strong twist, wrenches her small foxy head from her neck, separating it from her toyish body, completely decapitating her, even as in death her heavily plumed tail makes one or two last defiant wags.

As the next scene unfolds, Hikey watches in a mixture of wonderment and dread.

She sees Drakonius slapping Cynthia across the face, a slap so powerful that it immediately raises a bed of purplish welts, stunning her consciousness. As she instinctively raises her hand to her cheek, blood dripping from the sides of her lips, Drakonius licks the blood off with his long rasp like tongue. Cynthia makes a feeble effort to push him away, but there is no defense, nothing she can do, no way for her to prevent the inevitable. Drakonius, in all his fury, throws her bodily against the wall and as he does so his face malforms into wolf features, sharp teeth extended from a heavily furried face; Cynthia, semi-conscious, screams 'Oh no, no, no, no', as he advances toward her, growling menacingly, snarling ferociously. He rips off her blouse, laughs, and goes not for her throat but directly for her heart, biting deeply in the space between her third and fourth ribs, just to the left side of her breastbone, his long canines sinking deeply into the walls of her pulsating heart, gripping it in his jaws, pulling it loose from her torso while it continues to beat. She becomes an immediate cadaver.

It is as if he has ripped away her soul.

His muzzle soaked with blood, he lifts up her skirt. Some gray pubic hairs cover her opening and these he rips off as if they were pine needles on a dead tree. In no haste, he calmly sticks his hard, ugly, throbbing schlong into her lifeless passage and starts humping away. The necro-rape doesn't last very long, perhaps a minute or so. He pulls out just before he comes and sprays his jizzum all over what's left of her face, rubbing it in like a medical cream as if to heal the welts he had raised when slapping her in the face. He mutters some words to her, difficult to hear.

Then he raises his head, tilts it back and emits a howl. His triumph knows no bounds.

∞

Mieke has swooned away. Hikey can no longer watch, Willem turns the tape off just as Drakonius is about to toss a match into the gaseous fumed kitchen.

Hikey swallows hard, asks Willem what Drakonius had uttered when he rubbed his sperm into Cynthia's face.

Willem hesitates; he is loath to tell her. "As near as I can make out he said: 'This is the best anti-aging cream, works like a charm'. Then he sniggered scornfully right in her face, what was left of it that is."

Hikey's face falls, she needs fresh air, rushes to the side door of the van and slides it open, breathing deeply of the outside air. She turns to barf, but cannot do so. She has encountered the meaning of true evil and it sits within her like a leaden weight, not so easily cast out. She is beginning to lose it again, when Joost spots her tottering on the stoop of the van. She looks like she is ready to faint, and he rushes to her, catches her in his arms as she is about to fall.

Inside the van, Mieke is beginning to come around. Willem cradles her head in his lap, presses a cold compress to her forehead. He tries to soothe her with his words, but like Josh, he is so professional that what he says comes out stilted and too sharp. Even so Mieke is grateful. No one has been kind to her like this for months.

When Hikey comes around, the odd thing is that the first thing she notices is that Dusty is missing. She asks Joost where he has gone off to.

"He's afraid Drakonius might go over to the van den Valk factory, that's where Gerda works now, Wiersma got her the job."

"But she's an American, how did she get a work permit so quickly? Vladg is having trouble reinstating his."

"She's human. Vladg is a Duplicant like you. Even if he is a Royaal, there's still prejudice. Anyway, this job is very similar to what she did at Pyrell's. There was an opening and she fits right in. And don't forget Wiersma has a lot of pull. Then too it seems like he has a thing for Gerda."

"So that's it."

"Look Ms Hikey, I don't want to appear rude, but we've got to get out an APB on this guy. He's now the number one wanted criminal in Holland, three capital counts against him. I've got to call in to de Haas: Murder One, Sexual Assault and Beastiality."

"Yes, I'm sorry I delayed you. I was so out of it. I do want to thank you for all you've done."

"No problem," Joost says, turns away from her, takes out his T-cell and punches in a call to de Haas. Then he calls Greet again, gives her a repeat, a double warning to be aware that Drakonius will probably be after her and Gerda to finish up what they escaped at the hotel in Vondel Park.

"I'll call Gerda at the factory. We just don't have enough personnel to cover everyone, so why don't you stick with Hikey and Dusty with Gerda for now. She's still staying over at my place you know, so you and Hikey can hustle over there after my shift is over if you want."

"I'll see what Hikey wants. I don't have to tell you how dangerous this guy is do I?"

"No. I know from Vondel Park…. he's much worse than Bram."

"Right. The crimes he's done here are unbelievable. So please be careful. I don't want to lose you."

"Not a problem. Do you think I'd let him kill me just to get out of marrying you? No way! We're getting hitched right after Christmas. Not even Drakonius can interfere with that."

Joost has to chuckle. She has true grit; maybe that's why he loves her so.

∞

In their apartment in Manhattan, Josh and Phoebe are having an argument, a family spat of sorts.

"But I thought we were going to spend our very first Christmas together. I had plans for us to make a 'Round the Moon' trip."

"I know you're disappointed, but this is my father and mother. They want to be with Phoenix for Christmas in Santa Barbara and, of course they want to take me along."

Josh loses his reserve. Like a child he asks, "Why can't I come too?"

"Because this is just for family, it may be the last time we can get together like this before the baby comes. Feeny is just short of four months now."

"But I'm going to be family too, one day I mean. I just don't see what they've got against me."

"You're overly sensitive. Think of them. They want to be with their two girls, that's all. It's probably for the last time. Once Phoenix has the baby Mom and Dad know things will be different."

"What about Lydia, she's not part of the family and she'll be there. I would be the same kind of fifth wheel on the wagon in a manner of speaking."

"Oh Josh, don't you see that's different. Its Lydia's home, nothing can be done about that. My mom wants this especially…"

"She doesn't like me…"

"She's not overly fond of you, true, but that's not the main reason, try to see beyond yourself, Mom wants to have a Christmas that's like old times, Dad probably wouldn't mind if you were there, but you know Josh, you do quote all these smart scientific facts and that disturbs Mom, you make her feel… like she's out of it…"

"I can dumb down you know…"

"I don't want you to do that. I like you as you are…I never want you to try and change…leastways not on this issue…actually, you could be more helpful in other ways…"

"What other ways?"

"I mean brevity is the soul of wit, not sex."

"Not that again, I don't like to talk about sex so openly."

"Lots of young men are having the operation done, the one you told me about. I see the contracts."

"That's true; thirty percent of our revenues are coming in from disc transfers on the H-W and the insertion of bio-sensor buttons."

"Well then?"

"But that's not me. I'd rather study to get knowledge. That's why the colleges and universities are experiencing decreasing enrollment. All this knowledge can be picked up by humans in an hour or two on the wheel simply by disc transfer. I'm not sure they're totally human afterwards."

"You do have a point. I hear they're beginning to call these mixtures Humilicants."

"Maybe they should call them humiliating instead. Do you know that on their résumés they have to state whether they acquired their expertise for the job by study or by disc transfer, it's creating two classes of humans and I don't want to be associated with any Humilicant designation?"

"But the operation has nothing to do with knowledge, only sex."

"Sex is a form of knowledge. Anyway I don't want to be factory damaged."

"You're making this difficult for me."

"How so?"

"It puts me into an awkward position."

"I don't see why…"

"Because when you try to seduce me you come so quick I hardly have gotten into it and you're already there. That's your ego acting up, thinking of yourself alone, what fun is that for me?"

"But I've tried to do better."

Josh's eyes are moistening; he is beginning to lose it, holding his feelings in, not wanting to go into the oblivion of tears.

"Oh, I'm sorry Josh; I know I sound like a shrew…"

"No. You have a valid point, but it's not because I'm selfish, it's only due to my love for you. You see before I met you I had always hidden myself within my thoughts, I did not know how to be in a mix of people. You taught me I could do that and survive. So I can learn Feeb and I'll get the hang of this sexual thing as well, it just takes me awhile, as long as I don't sink into sorrow, I know I can do better."

"I feel like a shit. I'll tell my mom I won't go unless you can come too."

"No, I'm okay now that I've talked it out. I can go to Indiana to be with my folks. It's cool."

"Really?"

"Really."

"For sure?"

"Yep, for sure."

"I have an idea. Why don't we take the 'Round the Moon' trip before Christmas? I hear they've got great concerts on board, super drugs too that you can't get on earth and they're all legal under Space Law."

"That sounds perfect. If we timed it right, we'd both have plenty of time to make our separate trips for Christmas."

"Yes, and don't forget about zero gravity, you last much longer…remember that Sub-Orb movie we went to…the one we never got to see."

"That's right, I did do better. See, it's not my fault; it's that damn gravity thing on earth that's working against us. All we have to do is construct a zero gravity room here and I'll be cock cool."

"That costs over five million new dollars."

"A mere technicality…"

Phoebe skitter laughs.

"Come here you!" she orders. "I want a hug."

"Me too," Josh says.

She is in the mood, unbuttons, crosses her arms back underneath her blouse and releases the hooks on her bra, the now open blouse revealing her firm brown nipples surrounded by soft pinkish areolae. Her face moves up-close, enlarging in his eyes and as he stares into her ultra-blues he is transfixed by her beauty. At once he succumbs to her power, his member hardens and elongates, he is spellbound.

Now she slides her hand underneath his shorts, reaches in and upward to find that sensitive area where his uppermost thigh merges with his balls. She strokes his sensitive skin, squeezes his left testicle ever so gently and he, holding his breath, glances at his watch. Lately he has timed himself to see if he can go over two minutes. He doesn't like to think of himself as a premature ejaculator so he substitutes the Latin words *ejaculatio praecox* in his mind. This seems to help his self-confidence, hopefully to delay his jizzum spurt.

He needs no further prompting. He is all too easily overwhelmed by her artistry, by the immediacy of her essence, by the sensuous coiling of her body, by her subtle stylistic moves.

He is already fearful of losing control, but

Phoebe knows where to invest her sensuality, where and when to increase it, and in his case to decrease the stimulation. Even so, with all her good efforts, he comes earlier than she wished. He checks his watch, two minutes and six seconds. A new record, but hardly long enough, still far short of meeting Phoebe's needs. He gives her oral pleasure, but this is a woman who wants the stiff cock inside her, not the tongue routine. He knows he is virile; his powers are substantially intact if only he could repair his timing. 'It's just timing, timing is everything'.

His envy of men who can go for long periods wells up the angst in his heart. If he goes on like this there is danger of losing Phoebe, or worse, becoming a cuckold. No question, he needs to restore erotic happiness. This thought makes his decision clear for him. Instead of going to Indiana, while she is visiting in Santa Barbara, he intends to go in for the operation. He feels certain to get at least a ten percent discount as an employee. He tells himself they could do both the operation and the disc transfer in one afternoon. All it will require is a slit in the scrotum, a dissection through the various layers called tunics, then down to his left testicle, the one that hangs lower, easier for her to get to. The surgeon will be guided by all sorts of imaging technology. 'Should be no problem'. The bio-sensor would then be placed between the back of the testis and the start of the tube like epididymis, part of the spermatic duct. Now when she squeezed, as she had done tonight, it would initiate his new sex program, inhibiting ejaculation, but setting off his sexual imagination, all transferred to his forebrain by means of the disc insertion program. All he had to endure was an hour or so of rotation on the H-W.

It would be his Christmas present to her.

∞

In Dolno Katore at the Church of Saint Stephen, Father Nicholas appeared to be very pleased at the turnout for Midnight Mass. As he looked out from the pulpit, extending from the narthex to the chancel, the nave was completely filled with what seemed to be the entire population of the village. Weeks earlier, the choir had sounded somewhat subdued as many of the members did not wish the three Duplicants to take part in the liturgical chants and hymns, but now all was well. Their voices blended in harmoniously. Yes, he had put his foot down over parishioners' objections, a move that he knew might cause him grief, but which he felt was the right thing to do. The truth of the matter was that ever since their arrival, the church had flourished in many different ways. The grounds had never looked so spic and span, the foliage was well cared for and the flowering plants were looking better than ever. The nave even smelled sweeter, now that the Duplicants were spraying air freshener when the scent of parishioners' sweat got too sharp. In addition, collections had picked up and he suspected this was not due to an infusion of increased giving, but to the honesty of the Duplos who never skimmed a dime from the collection baskets.

Father Nicholas admonished himself for this thought, but he could not bring himself to think otherwise. The three, whom he called Peter, James and John, were earning a place in his heart even though he knew they would never earn a place in heaven.

After he completed the first part of the Mass, the liturgy of the Word, he motioned Peter, James and John to start collections.

Peter took the center aisle, James and John the far left and right. This time, before the Celebration of the Eucharist was begun, they started to spray the nave with great mists of venomous vapors, up and down the aisles and sideways as well. Then all three ascended the altar and hit the priest, deacon and altar boys with a flourish of spray that knocked them out cold immediately.

Then, with excellent timing, Malignius and his two brothers, accompanied by Iphigènie, Athalie and Phaedra, went to work. The Dhampirs picked out the prettiest and youngest females and the undead Vampires went for the handsomest young males. They could each do no more than two or three victims, for by then even the Vampires were satiated. So Malignius ascended the altar and left a brainwashing subliminal message to all whose blood had not yet been sucked upon telling them to report to their masters and mistresses as slaves on a regular basis.

Next he began his diabolical liturgy known as the Devil's Mass and proceeded to expound on the life of Trans-humanism that they would be undergoing. He carefully explained the advantages of vampirism over the fictional gods in which humans so mystically believed. Even under the spell of the vapors there were exceptions. A few of the parishioners began to moan their disagreements, stating that Jesus was not a fictional God, but Malignius motioned to the Duplicants who carried these objectionable believers out of the church. Once this was done, Malignius ordered the priest and deacons to remove all the crucifixes and paintings and images of the Saints from the church and to replace them with idols of the Devil. Father

Nicholas refused to take part in this endeavor and was given another heavy dose of the venom, but even so, he was recalcitrant and one of the Duplicants was obliged to carry him out back to the rectory.

Within an hour the entire church was transformed into a Church of Satan to worship evil. Malignius then went on to explain, to the now awake congregation, that Satan does not consider death and destruction evil per se, that he does not want his followers to commit acts of violence for violence's sake. "Satan wants us only not to believe in the fictitious God who cast him out of heaven. Satan had been the anointed cherub, yes, but God in 2nd Corinthians 4:4 admitted that Satan had become the "god of this world". So it is Satan, not the fictitious God whom you worship, who cares for you on earth, it is Satan who oversees your comings and goings, Satan who wants you to succor Vampires with your blood, and to worship evil in his name."

"So remember this: Satan is your God on this world as long as you are alive. You can attain eternal life on earth as long as you worship Satan and believe in Vampirism."

"Now say all: *'Praise Satan'*."

The congregation complies and, Malignius urges them to repeat the phrase again and again which they do.

Finally, he orders them to go home, and zombie like, they take their leave.

∞

In Oneonta, at the Protestant Church led by Reverend Dahlberg, a similar episode to that of Dolno Katore is taking place on Christmas Eve.

The difference, of course, was in the liturgy and the hymns. Even so, the Sextus Duplicants were able to subdue the congregation in a roughly similar manner. After an hour or so, Bram took his place at the head of the pulpit, pronouncing a horde of sentences and phrases exhorting the desires of Lucifer: "Just as he led the revolt of the Angels as an Archangel, it is now your turn as members of this congregation to lead the revolt against Christianity here on earth. Satanism is the true religion; you are the new Pilgrims, the bearers of news of the 2nd Reformation. It is your duty to spread the word."

He said this with such force, such genuine religious fervor, that most of the congregation bowed to his will, at the ready to obey. In essence, they had become a newly formed sect.

His denunciation, however, doesn't work for all sinners. Edna in particular, though woozy, is one of the devoted who objects to the blasphemy that is being perpetrated within the womb of the church she so loves.

As a consequence, while he was able to influence most parishioners who had regained consciousness, he made a decision to call it a partial success and leave it go at that.

He descended from the altar, sat in a pew and allowed Reverend Dahlberg to resume his position at the pulpit. The reverend, however, was still blanked out, had no more to say on the subject and called an end to the evening's services.

There was no joy in the hearts of the worshippers as they made their exit.

`This was exactly what Bram wanted. And now that it was past midnight, he thought it was the start of a very merry Christmas.

∞

While Phoebe is in Santa Barbara, Jennifer Mills has been selected by Mr. Eiselman as her substitute. Accordingly, she has transferred all her personal things from the 100th to the 102nd

369

floor and taken over temporarily as his secretary. So she is surprised when reviewing his schedule for the day that Josh Wharton is on the log, listed for an interview with Mr. Eiselman as a candidate for an e-jack operation and disc transfer.

Josh too is surprised to see Jennifer when he enters the office. He has not met up with her since the night at the Pierre. In this sense he is glad to say 'hi'; on the other hand, he knows she is a bit of a blabbermouth and this disturbs him no end. *'Phoebe is very professional, even at home she is close mouthed when it comes to the secrets of Pyrell's clients'.* So he hopes that Jen has been given proper instructions when it comes to confidentiality. Certainly he doesn't want it spread around the building that he is one of those jimbos who needed an e-jack fix.

Jennifer, however, acts very adroit, friendly to a point but strictly secretarial. She ushers him properly into Eiselman's plush office. Eiselman is charming, greets Josh like any other client, motions him to a comfortable microfibre chair where he is immediately served tea by George, whom he is rather glad to see, a familiar face in a sense.

"Oh that's right, I heard you two were well acquainted from that strange night… at the Pierre wasn't it?"

"Yessir, that's right…"

"Well Josh you're here as a client, not as an employee. You see I still interview every client where there is some question of mental stability and of course each and every employee who intends to use Pyrell's services for an operation of any sort. That's why you are here."

"Yessir, I knew that. I don't mind the interview. I've already seen the psychiatrist and talked to the psy-computer."

Eiselman shuffles some papers.

"Yes Josh. I have before me the results of your psy-comp testing from when you first applied for work here, almost three years ago now, isn't that right?"

"Yes, that's correct."

"Well it's a bit disappointing. The new testing seems to differ from the original in several areas."

"How so if I may ask?"

"Certainly, you should ask. The new results show areas of weakness in your motivational drive as well as some minor defects in self-esteem."

"Well the last part is understandable, isn't it sir. I mean that's why I'm here, why I need the operation…"

"Yes, yes, yes…that's understandable of course. But the other part, the descent of several motivational curves is my concern as your employer. Don't you like your work here?"

"Very much, really. I'm passionate about my work, but at the moment I'm overly concerned about my personal life, perhaps that's what shows through on testing?"

"Perhaps so. It's true that the psychiatrist has given you a clean bill of health. Sometimes that's more valid than what the psy-comp indicates. Would you mind being retested in three months?"

"Not at all."

"Good. Now let's get down to brass tacks. The operation costs one hundred thousand dollars. That is a flat fee and is non-negotiable."

"I had thought there might be an employee discount."

"I'm sorry. We have had to do away with that program. Too many of the employees were jealous of others who did not meet the criteria for the discount. Others were not offered discounts because they were candidates for dismissal. It was not a good policy. Needless to say it has been done away with. What we now offer is disc substitution in place of a discount."

"What type of discs?"

"Oh, you have several choices. You can choose the musical program. Those that are tone deaf appreciate that one. Then there is the games program which improves your competitive ability on video games of all sorts, and the ATP program is popular. Of course you have to register with all the professional sports organizations for that one. After all, it would be unfair to have someone of your mid-size stature rival a linebacker for a job in the NFL."

"That makes sense."

"Please don't make me go on and on. There are hordes of these adjunctive discs and you can choose any one you like."

"Okay. I'll take the ATP one. I've always wanted more muscular strength and I understand the metabolic effects."

"I'm sure you do, much better than I can explain. Good. That part is settled. Now how do you intend to pay for all this?"

"Through Pyrell's financial program. At present I make six-thousand new dollars per month. If I contracted for three years, you could take three thousand a month out of my check."

"I see you've done your homework. Yes, that means all you'll pay in interest over the three-year period is eighteen thousand. Not bad wouldn't you say."

"Yes sir. Not bad."

"But can you live on that? We're facing a period of slow inflation you realize."

"Yes, I'm aware of that. I'm not particularly apt at the business end of things, but who knows, you might give me a raise if my next psy-comp results improve."

Eiselman smiles, shifts in his seat.

"Aah, the confidence of the young."

Eiselman stands up and Josh knows at once that he is being dismissed.

George enters and leads Josh out of the inner office into Jen's area.

"Josh," she whispers, "please meet me in the 80th floor cafeteria during coffee break. I have lots of news for you on Geri and such."

"What time?"

"Howz ten?"

"Okay, I'll be there," he says, not because he is that interested in Geri, but because he wants to reassure himself that she will be professional and keep his secret.

∞

Josh has not visited the 80th floor cafeteria since the time he was there with Phoenix, when she had made believe she was Phoebe. Now he is surprised at how drab the place seemed to be, all the excitement sucked out of it. While everything was essentially the same, the same seascapes and sandy beaches on the walls, the plum colored outwardly slanted windows shutting out the glare of the sun's rays, nothing about the room seemed sensual or emotional. *'It's just like any other cafeteria'.*

Jen is only a few minutes late, Josh remains seated while she gets her own coffee and rolls.

She talks up a storm telling Josh how Geri has resigned from Pyrell's, how she has a work permit in Holland and a job at the Duplicant factory there in Amersfoort. Josh listens in obligatory fashion while she goes into the budding love affair of Geri and Dusty, Greta's forthcoming marriage to Joost, but when she starts to talk about Cynthia's murder, his ears perk up. This he wants to hear and is very attentive to what she has to say.

"And this murderer has escaped to America?"

"That's what Interpol believes. Apparently he got on a Sub-Orb and is somewhere in the States. Don't you watch the news on INN? There's pics of him plastered everywhere, taken from that Projecto-Fax, you know about that don't you?"

"I've kinda been out of it lately I guess. But tell me, do you think he'd be after Phoebe?"

"All of us possibly. Everyone who was at the Pierre that night and that includes Phoebe, George you and me."

"How do you figure that? I mean what has he to do with Bram?"

"I don't know, but he's a Vampire and Geri thinks there may be a connection."

"You don't think she's exaggerating?"

"Maybe, but to be on the safe side I'm going to call Interpol, tell them all about the night at the Pierre."

"That's been reported long ago."

"That was to our police. Interpol is different. I think you should call too."

"Okay, maybe you have a point… but listen Jen; I wanted to talk to you about something else. You know all the secret work I do in R&D is confidential. Is it the same with your work? "

"Oh Josh, trust me, I won't say a word to anybody. Before I took over Phoebe warned me about that, I know how confidential these matters are, trust me."

Josh notices that she had said 'trust me' twice, practically in the same sentence. To his skeptical mind this is a warning.

"Look Jen, I know you wouldn't say anything on purpose, but sometimes, when a person gets excited things do slip out…"

"Josh, you have my personal word, my lips are sealed. How's that?"

"Good enough," Josh says, still unconvinced.

"When do you go in?"

"Day after tomorrow."

"That's only one day before Christmas."

"I know."

"I'll arrange to bring you back to the apartment after it's over if you want me to."

"Sure. I'd like that. Thanks Jen."

Now she touches his hand warmly, wishes him well.

Finally, he is convinced she may be able to hold a secret.

∞

Drakonius had learned from Malignius, who had heard from Bram, that Phoebe was to be in Santa Barbara for Christmas holiday. It is Phoebe, in particular, that Bram wants transposed into the sisterhood of the undead. This was an assignment to which Drakonius looked forward with relish. Not some old witch like Cynthia, but fascinating young meat with blonde hair and blue eyes which he intended to suck out like grapes.

In order to escape the dragnet in Holland, he had created the indifferent appearance of a Bulgarian salesman bent on hawking his wares of unrefined copper to factories in Southern California. He no longer wore his short van Dyck beard and his hair, though of the same color, was shaved centrally, giving him the much older cadaverous appearance of a middle aged baldy who walked with a slumped posture. He had driven to Brussels, Belgium in a stolen car, abandoning his cloak and top hat along the way. In Brussels he boarded a Sub-Orb directly to LAX arriving three days before Christmas. This gave him adequate time to locate cameras and other security devices at Lydia's place and to plan out his exact course of action.

On the same day, Mr. and Mrs. Winthrop, of Holdrege, Nebraska had driven to Lincoln and took a rocket flight to LAX where they had prearranged to dovetail with their daughter Phoebe, who had Sub-Orbed from Manhattan. The Winthrop's had never visited Southern California so the plan was to purchase gifts in Los Angeles and then take the scenic route, a drive in their rental along the sea to Santa Barbara. They had earlier booked reservations at a hotel close by the Mission and within a few blocks up the APS to Lydia's home. They felt secure that they had covered all the bases necessary for a successful trip.

Just a few days prior, Lydia had received her final divorce decree, which she and Feeny celebrated joyously, although Feeny was no longer allowed to drink alcohol. They made a visit to the Museum of Fine Arts which was showing a three-day exhibition of August Renoir's paintings, on loan from France's Musee d'Orsay. When they passed by the painting of the 'Boater's Luncheon' Phoenix broke out in joyful tears, for there big as life was Lydia, leaning over a weathered rail, wearing a straw hat with a blue band, her right hand cupping that side of her face, her eyes beaming radiantly at the assemblage of boaters in the restaurant. Phoenix immediately bought a copy of the painting and gave it to Lydia as a token of her love.

The day after their visit to the museum, the Xmas present from Vladg arrived, delivered by Fed-Up. Now Lydia felt doubly blessed, with thoughts of the two men that she cared for most, Pierre and Vladg, once again swirling about in her heart.

The first thing she did, once she fathomed the secret of the stick, was to go to a silversmith, a long-time acquaintance whom she knew as a consequence of performing surgery on his fox terrier. She had successfully removed a tumor from the dog's stomach and the grateful man had said: "I owe you one." Now she recalled his promise and went to him asking that he silver plate the terminal six inches of the rapier, but not to record his effort anywhere. He agreed to her request and the silver plating was accomplished by the very latest electrolytic process, the point remaining sharp as ever.

It had long been a plan of hers to do away with Bram if he made any attempt to hurt her, or Feeny, or the child, and she felt this to be an opportune time to make preparations. She led Jeanne d'Arc down to the cellar, opened up a couple of the packages of Bram's clothing that sat next to the oil burner and which he had never picked up. She was sorry that she had had his apparel cleaned and pressed as there was still a bit of dry cleaning smell mixed in with Bram's own odors, but she relied on the dog's sense of smell and allowed him to get several deep whiffs of Bram's true odor. She accompanied this maneuver by uttering several hateful Pavlovian epithets of her own which Jeanne d'Arc picked up immediately, her ears extending upwards to the full. Satisfied that the intelligent dog would now associate Bram with being 'nasty and dangerous', recognize his scent as 'enemy,' she gave him two of his favorite cookies.

Now, with the rapier modified and the dog primed to defend her and Phoenix, she felt that if Bram made an unannounced belligerent appearance, the stage was set properly to take him out. Yes, it had been some time in coming, but now she was indeed capable of killing him.

∞

Drakonius also was making preparations. He too had a present for Phoebe which he had intended to give her for Christmas. Unfortunately, he would not be ready in time. Since he no longer had his hickory stick, he needed to supplant the old one with a replacement, a new sword cane. He fancied getting a new cloak and top-hat as well to carry out his mission in style. Yes, such items were rare, but Santa Barbara was well known for its antique shops, its craftsmen who could reproduce many historical articles. They knew the old ways, the secrets of working wood and metal that had long been lost to the present generation. Some of these artisans were indeed members of the brotherhood; others had been bled once or twice by vampires but not been touched since. These types were easy subjects to be put under a spell, to succumb to his demands.

His plan now was to deliver his gift on New Year's Day. He would not tear her to pieces, no, that is not what Bram wanted, but he would certainly see to it that he did his job, all three stages. First to gouge out her eyes like grapes; she would not need them anyway, the undead can only see at night. Then to suck her blood within a wisp of death, leaving only a few thimblefuls circulating to keep her alive. While deep in her weakness, she would recognize him as Master and swear allegiance to Satan. Lastly, the ultimate torture, carried out slowly with the dexterous use of fang and claw, destroying her beauty, scarring her face, crippling her joints, ripping apart her womb so that she would be forever unable to bear a child. These thoughts, by themselves, began to stir his transmogrification; the ultimate action would be glorious, woman and beast held together in a near-death embrace. Yes, he would make her last few moments of human life as painful as possible, slowly converting her into a newly formed member of the undead sisterhood.

Chapter XXIII

Bumps in the Road

The entire 60th floor of the Pyrell building was devoted to robotic outpatient surgery. On the day before Christmas, Josh Air-Scooted to work. He had pre-arranged to have a colleague take over his research and once he was satisfied there would be no glitch in the data gathering; he took the elevator up to the 60th floor and signed in for the e-jack procedure.

He was of two minds, one insufferably nervous and fearful of the operation, the other hoping to produce a new Josh whose sexual confidence would spread out to other areas of life, especially to his devotion to Phoebe.

The two Basics who specialized in prep work calmed him down immediately. They first undressed him completely, explaining the procedure in dulcet tones while removing his pubic and neighboring groin hairs. This was accomplished by means of a painless electronic propulsion epilator controlled by one of the Basics while the other massaged the musculature of his arms and legs to insure good circulation. He was then directed to a ray-septic room, where, still entirely naked, he was doused with several different anti-inflammatory rays. Upon his exit from the chemically clean room he was properly draped and given a small dose of a sedating hallucinogenic which (by prior choice of several scenarios) enabled him to see the Greek Islands with Dolphins swimming about while he soared above the ocean surface like a sea bird winging on a thermal. Then, rather much at once, while he held a pleasant smile upon his face, the sedative nature of the medication kicked in and he lost consciousness.

Following this he was wheeled into surgery by two Sextus IV nurses. There he was carefully positioned on the operating room table. The positioning itself consisted of placing Josh supine on the table, then dropping the spring-loaded distal portion of the table, while at the same time two columnar anti-gravity rays, acting like stirrups, brought him into an almost gynecological position, like an inverted Y, with the two outstretched legs of the Y suspended in the air at a 45-degree angle.

A human surgeon, already masked and draped, entered from a far door at the other end of the surgery. He was a playful sort who perched himself on a three-wheel stool, and with one kick of his foot, as if he was jump starting a motorcycle, he scooted the stool over toward the table, steering it carefully between the two anti-gravity columns, stopping on a dime right below Josh's levitated legs. He was now eye to eye with Josh's testicles, a sight he had experienced more than ten thousand times while doing this procedure.

A surgical instrument tray was placed to his right by one of the Sextus nurses. Now he was ready to do his thing. He made a small incision in the left testicle's posterior aspect, using a CO_2 laser, the coagulating cut preventing any blood flow whatsoever. Then he changed to a more standard scalpel and cut and dissected down through the various tunics to the bridge between the epididymis and the testis proper. Next he made a very small incision in the fibrous tissue, creating a small cave-like aperture, inserted the inhibiting bio-sensor, secured it with one dissolving suture and closed the mouth of the cave with near invisible suture material.

The two Sextus IV's wheeled Josh out into a post-surgical recovery room and attended to his vital signs. Since no artificial respiratory anesthesia was used, Josh started to come around within ten minutes. Once this aspect was accomplished he was transferred to general recovery. Within twenty minutes he was again dressed and ready to go up to the seventieth floor to get on the H-W wheel. There he received a brain transfer of the metabolic disc for increasing his ATP to axons, muscles and marrow producing blood. Almost at once, he felt his new physical strength to be prodigious.

To his surprise a cardiologist came to call upon him. He assured Josh that all was well, but because the heart itself is a muscle, each beat of the left ventricle was now much stronger from the ATP increase, pumping out thirty or more percent blood than beforehand. To compensate for this the heart had to slow its rate. He informed Josh that his normal rate was now fifty-six per minute whereas it had been seventy-two prior to the procedure. This was enlightening to Josh, but compared to the complexities of the data he worked with, it was simple stuff. So when the cardiologist asked if he understood, Josh more or less dismissed the man as a simplistic thinker.

He was handed a pamphlet by a Sextus IV who explained to him the necessity of observing changes in simple procedures such as shaking hands, giving hugs, running up or down steps or jumping off a diving board into a swimming pool. Josh promised the Sextus that he would read the manual thoroughly. The Sextus frowned and said: "That's what most people say; still we have accidents, why the other day one of the women transfers nearly hugged her husband to death."

Preferring to be a wise ass, Josh said, "Maybe that's what she wanted to do."

The Sextus did a double take. Less than an hour had passed since the disc transfer and already it was changing the character of this once rather shy man.

After another hour of lessons on his new found muscular strength and improved reflexes. Jen picked him up.

He gave her a strong hug which blew her away.

"Wow," she exclaimed.

"Call me Hunk," Josh said offhandedly, "my new nickname."

Jen snickered, hooked her arm in his.

"Let's go Hunk," she said, a new sort of manly appreciation for Josh streaming across her face.

Then they Air-Scooted over to his apartment; Jen set coffee and they chatted for a time about Pyrell's and Geri's doings over in Holland. She did not mention Phoebe, but it seemed to him that Jen was being awfully friendly if not downright flirtatious. It crossed his mind to put a move on her, but he quickly dismissed the thought. Even so, it struck him that this was something he would not have done ordinarily. It was as if some of his sinful nature, previously submerged, was now bobbing to the surface.

After Jen left he crashed immediately.

∞

In Dolno Katore the three true undead Vampire sisters, Iphigènie, Athalie and Phaedra, were having a ball; each night they sucked out the blood of one or two of the most virile young males of the village. They had little interest in promoting Bram's program of indoctrination to Satan, but did so out of fear that Malignius would limit their crop of victims. Their halfhearted attempts were nonetheless fairly successful. Upon returning to their parents most of these youths, once respectful of family and community, were now bedeviled with malicious and criminal thoughts, lazy in their work habits and given over to excess in eating and drinking. The same was true of the young women, who became incestuous with both brothers and sisters, less mindful of domestic chores and less caring of the needs of the animals on their farms.

In Oneonta, under Bram's close supervision, none of these antics took place. He organized the men so that on Sundays, after church, those that were handy in construction, helped to build the bunkhouse he wanted, but there were no severe sexual violations or criminal acts of the sort transpiring in Dolno Katore. He did enjoy the blood of one or two maidens at night, but he never once took advantage of them sexually, even though a few of them implored him to impregnate them, so desirous were they of having a child of their master's seed. Indeed, there were a few times that he was nearly seduced by one of these lovelies, but his allegiance to Phoenix, and the fear that if he impregnated another whilst his own unborn child was still in the womb, would be considered sacrilege by Satan was too overpowering, so, ultimately, he resisted any such move.

He did buy a new milker for Edna, paying for the cow in full, rather than just half the amount as originally proposed. He recognized that this weakness was due to the human half of his genealogy and hoped that Satan would not consider this a rebuff since he had accepted the hug she had given him and her wishes of a Merry Christmas.

As Malignius continued to provide H-mails of the situation in Dolno Katore to Bram, and as things grew more complex,

Bram began to realize that the presence of a powerful leader was necessary for any movement, of whatever type, to be successful. It was certainly not proper for the village to fall apart financially out of lack of motivation and a detestation of routine activities in life. The problem was that not even he could be in two places at once. While Malignius was well schooled in the art of promoting Satanism, he was basically a good follower, not a leader. If only Greta had not revolted from his power, with her police training and criminal justice experience she would have been able to organize things much more effectively in Dolno Katore. Yes, he had to admit things were getting a bit out of hand. Martin Luther had left Germany and gone to Rome for extended periods, but not until his Reformation philosophy had been so deeply embedded in the people's minds that he considered travel to be a safe move. Yes, he had neglected to learn a lesson from history, always a mistake. The only thing to do now was to ask Malignius to slow down operations, especially to curb the blood-thirsty sisters until he could get over there, probably after the birth of his child. Then he would see to it that all was put in proper order.

∞

In Holland Hikey was not just bereft, but disconsolate beyond words. She had put a halt to her active campaign, but not to her candidature for the upper house. She had let the people know what she stood for in the simplest of terms. She had debated and traveled the country far and wide. She had presented her ideology, a new framework to the Duplicant problem. Her hope was that all she had done thus far would be sustained until the election which was to take place in the third week of the New Year.

Unfortunately, there were a number of legal complications. Hikey had been named by Cynthia as the sole heiress to her estate. She was due to receive all of Cynthia's belongings, properties and wealth, but there was a glitch. It seems no precedent had been established for any Duplicant to inherit on the basis of a last will and testament. In fact, whenever a companion was left without an owner the principle had been to attempt a resale, and, when this failed, the Duplicant in question was returned to the factory where she or he was manufactured. In this case it was the Van den Valk factory in Amersfoort. Mr. Wiersma, the same neuro-engineer who had been present at de Boer's murder, was now making a pitch to purchase Hikey on resale, after she was first returned to factory ownership and he could acquire her at a much lower price.

Mieke was of a mind to compare Hikey's inheritance, before the court, as similar to that of wealthy dowagers who had named their dogs or cats as the sole beneficiary of their estate. Hikey was firmly against this tactic. She felt, if successful, it would indeed establish a legal precedent, one which equated Duplicants with pets, not with humans and their rights and privileges.

Mieke's next idea was to advise Hikey to marry a human at once, even if she had to go to London to do so. This too was negated by Hikey as she knew it would be the end for Vladg, he would never consent to being her consort while she was wed to another; he would never get over the abandonment, even if at a later time she divorced the human to marry him.

What she did was appeal to Rümke's honor. She asked him if he wished to win the election by this means, essentially by default. His response was that of a true gentleman. He placed an ad in all the leading Dutch newspapers explaining his position, stating that his admiration for the fight that 'his worthy opponent' had thus far brought to bear exemplified the finest attributes of the Dutch political process.

No sooner was this published than the polls showed that Rümke's lead had gained five points.

As a consequence, the court acknowledged Hikey's inheritance and no further impediments were brought forth other than the fact that Wiersma did some whimpering of his own. He made it known publicly that he had no intention of voting for either Hikey or Rümke.

Another glitch was the horses. Hikey was not emotionally ready to ride again, but the animals needed care. All three had been unharmed by the fire and untouched by Drakonius. So Hikey hired two human caretakers to oversee what was left of the property, rebuild the corral from its embers and curry and feed the two mares and the gelding on a regular basis in accordance with her wishes. Hikey was fairly well acquainted with this couple, knew that they cared deeply for horses and thought she could rely on them. Still the incident raised eyebrows in some circles as it was the first time in Dutch history that a Duplicant had provided humans with employment.

Once Hikey had done all she could with the remains of the Veluwe house, she wanted to rebuild, planned a replica of the house in Cynthia's memory, but she knew it would be some time before this plan came to fruition. Her next step was to move to Amsterdam where she took up residence in the P.C. Hoofdstraat apartment, living with Vladg. He was once again teaching, managing to commute on weekends from Amersfoort. As things settled down, although her spirits were still in mourning, she was awakened to the fact that she was far behind in the polls, that Rümke had made hay out of her dilemma. This fact revved up her drive. She decided that after the New Year she would once again resume her campaign.

∞

By the time Lydia got home from work, Phoenix's parents had been visiting there for some hours. Phoenix, feeling somewhat awkward, strived to make Lydia's presentation to her parents as friendly as possible. Mr. Winthrop's first name was James; the mother was called Emily. During the introductions, something out of the past occurred, a familiar look of recognition passed between Lydia and the mother, an expression entirely missed by both Phoenix and her father, as it came and went in the blink of an eye.

Lydia, feeling unduly uncomfortable, quickly released her hand from Phoenix's mother's grasp. She had to create a diversion, to do something, as she could not endure small talk. So she excused herself; grabbed Vladg's present and practically shoved the hickory stick at James who had earlier watched Phoenix demonstrate some fancy moves with the rapier. As a papa he had always been proud of her dexterity and remembered her winning a medal for fencing when she was in high school. He loved his daughters equally; both the apple of his eye, but Phoebe's prowess was in ballet and modern dance. As a man who was in to weaponry of all kinds he couldn't help but admire Phoenix's ability with the foil and martial arts short staff.

When Lydia handed it to him he started in playing around a bit with the sword-cane but was quickly brought to a halt by his wife who said she didn't approve of any such shenanigans in the living room. She seemed to have no compunctions about telling him so in front of the others so he snapped a defiant look at her but promptly secured the rapier in its wooden case and gave it back to Phoenix.

After some disconcerted moments of silence, the mother suggested that they do some repackaging so that they could send all the gifts back home via Fed-Up.

"You know James; we can't take your gun on the Sub-Orb in any case so we may as well do the rest right now. What's done is done!"

Obviously she was one of those women who played on her every word for effect and expected to be listened to. Both girls made a face.

What had happened was the girls had pooled their savings and bought their father the over-under he had always wanted. The shotgun gift was a Browning-Benelli, a heavy eight pounds in total weight and according to the salesman was reputed to have subdued recoil. James laughed inwardly at this as he knew no breech loaded 12-gauge O/U could possibly have a subdued recoil, but he was so proud of his girls for getting him the gun that he said nothing on this point. What he admired most was the walnut stock, which the girls had had engraved with his name as a life member of the gun club in Kearny, Nebraska. He knew that the gun could shoot good patterns up to forty yards, whether for trap, skeet, or pass shooting doves; what he didn't know was if he would enjoy moving the levers in a wet duck blind or be too slow to load in the dove field. It certainly was no fun to have to move levers with clumsy frozen or wet hands.

Lydia, who knew a thing or two about guns, changed his mind about recoil. She had bought him one of the new Evo-Shield shirts; green in color, but with an electronic insert shoulder pad that was designed to reduce recoil. The pad was made of gel and spandex and had to be fitted personally to the man and the gun, otherwise the gel would set too soon.

"Doesn't the lithium battery pack get in the way?" he had asked.

"No, just put it in your front pants pocket. The attached cable line can then be inserted to the pad through a special tunnel sewn in the shirt. When you pull the trigger, an electro-magnetic field will be generated which obeys the laws of physics, hitting back at the recoil."

This part she demonstrated without inserting a shell, but she told James not to open the package containing the pad until he got out into the shooting range in Nebraska:

"After removing the pad from its packaging, you slip it into the shirt's pocket and put the shirt on. After everything fits just as you like to wear it, you mount your shotgun, making sure it is your best standing position, and then shoot repeatedly, once a minute for about ten minutes. This sets the gel, forming it to the lines and contours of your shoulder. That's it; you are essentially done. It takes about 20 minutes to fully cure."

"How do you know all this?" James asked, rather astounded at her knowledge.

Lydia responded by doing her posture shift, slinking her hips around, lifting one foot and playing toezy with her pumps. Finally, she answered:

"I read the insert," Lydia said, and now they all laughed.

While she was at the gun store, Lydia had bought a Taser gun for Phoenix for protection. She didn't want to tell the parents exactly why, but she knew they were very protective of their girls as they had earlier on hired a private detective to check her out when Phoenix first came to Santa Barbara. Her gift met the Winthrop's approval although Phoenix said she hoped never to use it.

Phoenix's gift to Lydia was an easel for her painting hobby and included a wide assortment of brushes and water colors.

Both girls had exchanged gifts of shoes, Phoebe getting five inch Italian stilettos from Phoenix, who received rather fashionable maternity shoes from Phoebe plus a special vanishing lotion designed to remove the large brownish 'freckles' which now were not limited to her brow, but more or less covered her entire face. Of course, the added weight and pregnancy hormones had filled out her face, making it more roundish. This caused her to lose her right sided dimple and made the twins much easier to tell apart.

The girls had gifted their mother with all sorts of blouses and bras, purchased from the best shops, and on advice from the twins Lydia had bought her a beaded woolen sweater with a flowery design in a style that both girls knew she loved. While this did not cement the relationship between Mrs. Winthrop and Lydia, it erased some of the suspicions of the mother, who unlike her husband was no dunce when it came to recognizing the body language of lovers.

∞

The Spirit of Christmas was everywhere in the air, but not in the air where Drakonius was camped out in the woods back of Lydia's property. He had set himself up so that he did not need binoculars to see through the large bay window at the rear of the house and into the sitting room where the Christmas tree was located. He had a wide angle view of the family celebrating the joys of their second day of Christmas. The coziness, the family frivolity, the pleasures he observed in their expressions all caused him to be furious. His intent was to destroy this joy by carrying out his New Year's plan to remake Phoebe and Lydia into sisters of the undead, a most pleasant business. Only then would he bring Phoenix back to Oneonta and to her true Master, Bram Alucard.

Chapter XXIV

Vampire on the Roof

The Wharton's, Josh's parents, are indulgent types, tending to overprotect their only son. To some extent, their lives are lived vicariously by overly participating in his daily activities and hanging on to his past accomplishments. They even retain some of his childhood toys and playthings such as his atomic erector set and his bullet train with magneto-tracks all driven by neutrino electronics.

Josh has never missed being with them for some portion of the Christmas holidays and he doesn't feel that his recent surgery and disc transfer should change that tradition. He wants to rocket to Terre Haute, Indiana to be with them, but before he can board the plane he has to fill out the necessary forms as stipulated by Federal law. So, on the day after Christmas he does the obligatory thing, he registers as a Humilicant. This new designation does not affect his seating arrangements; Humilicants maintain their basic rights to sit with Total Humans (TH's), but Duplicants are still relegated to the back of the aircraft.

As travelers often do, he strikes up a conversation with the tubby lady seated next to him. For some reason he tells her that he has had to register as a Humilicant and that he has extraordinary ATP powers. As soon as she hears this, even before takeoff, her friendly attitude changes, she rings for the steward and asks for a different seat. This little episode convinces him to make a decision that he had been mulling over for the last two days.

Upon arrival, he doesn't mention his new status or any of his newly found abilities to his parents.

After an exchange of good wishes, hugs and cheek kisses, they head for the Wharton home where there is extensive giving and receiving of one day late Christmas presents. Josh actually enjoys some of the chatter; he learns all the latest neighborhood gossip from his mom and then listens to the new state of affairs in his dad's engineering firm.

His mother had baked homemade blackberry muffins and Josh devoured two of these and knocked off his coffee just as quickly.

"My Word Josh," his mother said, "what's got into you? Don't they feed you in New York?"

Josh apologized and then things settled down some. His mother tried to ask about Phoebe but Josh would have none of this.

When it came to Phoebe, he left them almost completely out of the loop. He wanted Phoebe to be his possession alone, not like a toy that his parents could put in their memory banks. He resented any parental interference, or even normal inquisitiveness, into his relationship with her. So they hesitated to ask about Phoebe and he chose not to story tell on her. But he was itchy, dying to let Phoebe know where he was, what he was up to, to see her face if only it was on the T-cell. So at the very first chance he got, forgetting himself, he escaped upstairs, jumping up the staircase to the first landing in one prodigious leap. When he heard his mother exclaim, 'My Word!' her largest epithet, he slowed down, managing the turn and the rest of the steps in a more normal fashion.

Once he was ensconced in his old room he called Phoebe on his T-cell, pulled out the screen, extended the width and length so that he got as clear a focus of her as possible. He wanted his newly found strength and athletic ability to be a surprise, so he didn't mention either the testicular operation or the ATP procedure to her. After some expressions of love talk and exchanging holiday good wishes, Phoebe got chatty on the situation in Santa Barbara, on the state of her sister's pregnancy, the foggy weather, all the shopping they had done, her suspicions that Lydia and Phoenix were having an affair.

Then, Phoebe suddenly piped up with: "You look different somehow."

"Well you know Terre Haute, it's always a change."

"No, I don't know Terre Haute Josh, your parents never invited me, and you're being evasive, what's up?"

"Nothing! I've only been here a couple of hours and might have a bit of rocket lag, that's all. Of course I want to be with you. When can I come?"

"Day after tomorrow I think. My parents have been hinting around that they want to get back to Minnesota, but I don't know for sure when. Call me every day around this clock; they take naps in the afternoon so it's a good time."

"You could call me too, you know," Josh says with his newly found courage.

Phoebe hesitates.

"All right, sure. We'll both try." Then a pique of jealousy hits her: "You haven't been seeing anyone else have you?"

"Only Jen, she stopped by and we had coffee together. She gave me some of the news on Geri. Looks like she's going to get married over there, going for dual citizenship…"

"There's a lot more of that lately isn't there?"

"Seems to be, some type of global trend I guess."

"Well, I've got to get moving. Mom is calling, she wants to go shopping."

"No problem. I miss you."

"Me too, luvya, bye… Oh yeah, there is one funny thing."

"What's that?"

"There's these woods out back; in the morning when the grass is dewy I take a walk out there, usually with Feeny, or even with mom or dad, I get this haunty-creepy-eerie feeling, but when I come back into the house it's gone."

"Yikes. No signs of Bram?"

"Nope, none whatsoever."

"Well I don't know. Could just be you."

"I don't think so. At night I'm in my room at the hotel of course, mom and dad are there too, none of us sleep at Lydia's, but I've talked with her…"

"And?"

"And Lydia's heard creepy noises too. At first she thought Feeny was sleepwalking again, but when she woke Feeny was sleeping right beside her, that's how I thought they might be having an affair…

"You're getting off the subject."

"Not really…I wanted to talk to you about after mom and dad leave…do you want to sleep here in Vladg's old room? Lydia said that would be all right. I could check out of the hotel and it would save money?"

"Sure that sounds cool."

"Okay. Getting back to the haunting sounds coming from the roof, not from inside the house…"

"Well?"

"Lydia decided to investigate…"

"And?"

"Nothing. No signs of anyone or anything; but Lydia is worried, she didn't say so but I can tell."

"Then we should be worried too. Think I'll do a little computer-spying; clue into Bram's encryption setup and see if he has anything going on his transmissions that we need to be made aware of."

"Can you do that?"

"Feeb, when it comes to cyber space, you're talking to the man. Bram may be into the Master-Slave routine with TH's but I'm the one that differentiates between Master Channels and Slave Channels on the computer. If it's hidden, I can find it."

"I've never heard you use the TH term like that before. Are you sure you're feeling okay, your voice is raspier, you sound so confident, almost macho."

"Naah, same old Josh…"

"If you say so; bye for now."

"Bye, luvya."

∞

The next couple of days at Lydia's house pass comfortably enough; the family splitting up, busy with different things. Lydia takes James, the father, to her office, shows him around, then they hustle over to Cottage Hospital. She wants him to know where it is located in case he makes it in time for the delivery. The mother and the twins invade the stores, exchanging some gifts, hitting after Christmas sales, touring the area. They take to hanging out at the pier, watching the brown pelicans, the surfers and para-sailers. At home they all chip in, do some needed chores around the house. Of an evening, when they are settled in, sipping cocktails, Mr. and Mrs. Winthrop announce to their daughters and Lydia that they plan on going back to Nebraska the next day to spend the New Year with their son Phillip.

"I know we don't talk much about Phillip. He's an independent sort and we won't get to spend New Year's Eve with him, I'm sure of that, but we do wish to be with him on New Year's Day. I'm sure he will find time enough for us away from his friends..."

"If he's not too hung over..." James interrupts his wife.

"Yes, well, we've got to make the effort," she turns to Lydia, "it's a family thing, you see. We try not to show partiality, but the twins are so talented and their little brother..."

"He's not little anymore," Phoebe says. "Gosh mama he's six-four and weighs well over two-twenty, that's not little."

"I didn't mean it like that," the missus says with a half-scowl, "it's just that he's five years younger than you two and still my baby."

James fidgets in his chair, gulps down his drink. This type of talk makes him uncomfortable.

"All right, Ugh on that. The point is we've had a wonderful Christmas here with you all and that includes you Lydia. Your hospitality was great and I like the soft feel and thickness of your towels..."

"Now really James, what's wrong with mine!?"

"This was just a compliment to Lydia honey, nothing to do with you."

He turns back to Lydia, begins where he left off.

"I was just saying how much I really enjoyed you showing me around the infirmary and surgery in your vet office. I guess you know I had some fire in my belly at first. I didn't know what to think, Phoenix splitting from her sister in Manhattan, leaving her job abruptly, holing up with you here in Santa Barbara. That's why I had that private eye check you out."

"You mean spy on her, don't you daddy?" Phoenix says, unwilling to give an inch when defending Lydia.

"All right, I made a mistake, messed that one up. I'm sorry for that; it's a papa- daughter thing; you know I'm not hard wired…"

Lydia picks up on this. In the short time she has known James she recognizes that voicing an apology is a big concession for him.

"Not a problem," Lydia says bravely, not wanting to get caught up in a family mix. Yet at the time it was true, she had been outraged, but that was in another era, a life before Phoenix. 'How will this good man ever handle my love for his daughter when the truth surfaces?'

"You're quite a woman," James says, admiration in his eyes. He wants to say, 'like a third daughter' but he glances at his wife, holds back on this. Then he turns toward Phoenix, switches gears.

"Sure wish you'd tell us who the man is Feen, 'course, that's your prerogative…"

This is still a very sensitive subject for Phoenix; she remains uncertain on whether the mystery baby in her womb is the embodiment of evil, or, will turn out to be a normal American boy.

"Daddy, I thought we talked all that out…"

"Maybe so, I did promise not to bring it up on this trip, but …"

The mother interrupts.

"Feeny, I'll be back before spring for the baby shower. You're not due till late March or early April, maybe by then you'll have changed your mind…"

"Maybe so," Phoenix says in imitation of her father. She hurries a glance at her sister, who knows everything about the pregnancy, but Phoebe feigns indifference, she doesn't want to give her mother the slightest inkling that she knows anything more than they do.

"It's not going to be a couple's shower is it?" James asks.

"Probably not…"

"Well your father couldn't come anyway, that's bird hunting season."

"Hey, I might, if there's men going."

"That I've got to see…"

"Well just don't speak for me; my daughter is more important than birds."

Now his wife backs down, sensing she has gone too far.

"Of course you're right. I only meant…"

"I know what you meant. Let's just drop it, okay?"

There is heavy silence all around.

Jeanne d'Arc seems to sense something is amiss. She crawls over to James, sits at his feet and snorts. Whenever James moves, ever so slightly, the dog growls, breaking silence. Now everyone relaxes and when they start talking again it is gossipy, over Vladg and Hikey wanting to get married; the situation with Duplicants asking for certain rights and privileges. The family is split right down the middle on the issues and when they ask for Lydia's opinion all she says is:

"I find this to be a significant conversation."

∞

In Amersfoort things are moving fast. Greet is planning her forthcoming wedding to Joost, Geri is applying for dual citizenship, Vladg is teaching every weekday and has a little apartment in the west of town that keeps him busy on the domestic front. He talks to Hikey every day on his T-cell, strives to keep up her spirits and travels to Amsterdam on the weekends making their love nest in the flat on the P.C. Hoofdstraat.

∞

In the meantime, Bram remained in a state of conspiratorial inspiration, his mind preoccupied with Greta. What to do? She had declared herself liberated from him by the forthcoming ringing of wedding bells which in itself he didn't mind, but her abandonment of the Darkness was a betrayal which required counter-tactics. He was certain that Greta's disloyalty had offended Satan to such a degree that His wrath would fall backwards upon himself if he delayed any longer.

He continued to rationalize.

He now held sharply malicious views on Greta, believed her human face was too alluring. He convinced himself that she did not have sharp enough teeth to become a true vampire, that her face held too much color, gave away too much information, that her shape and fragrance were far too enticing to become aligned with his 2nd Reformation. Like any entrepreneur he wanted to keep the upper hand and this meant severe punishment. All this resulted in a life and death decision, one that would prevent her resurrection to the cause as a member of the sisterhood of the undead.

Accordingly, he sent off a more heavily coded H-mail to Malignius asking him to do away with her, preferably during her forthcoming wedding ceremony.

In effect, Satan might forgive him for the good deed he had done Edna if he could pull this one off in a secretive manner that was satisfactory to the spirits of evil. On the other hand, he knew that an impatient Satan had not the degree of forgiveness in his heart of the carpenter god, also vengeful, but less angry than Satan who held out for a more wrathful response to inconsistencies in his subordinates and supplicants.

On other matters, he worried about Malignius's capability to handle things.

Could he indeed tie up all the   loose ends, work out all the people possibilities and if it came to it flood the church with the venomous aerosol?

∞

In the front of Lydia's house there stands a rather majestic California oak, but in the yard in back there is a less striking Eucalyptus with a grand fragrance that has one sturdy branch which is quite easy for Drakonius to climb. It is this branch which he makes use of nightly, easily springing from its overhang to the roof, scratching some of the broken off dead branches on the Mediterranean tiles, stomping on the roof, howling softly, imitating the wind and then, usually, jumping off to the oak in front.

These antics are simply the fun part of his plans, a prelude of sorts to the real horror; although Drakonius knows that a frightened victim makes for easier prey.

Unlike Bram, Drakonius, a true Vampire unmixed with human blood- not counting what he drinks for sustenance- was totally inner directed. He saw things differently from Dhampirs. He did not separate out Good from Evil. For him there were no dual challenges, no temptations, no commingling of Good and

Evil. He held curiously strong views on such matters; knew what he had to do and did it with a single purpose in mind. In this sense he felt himself to be a noble person, a subordinate of Satan, yes, but one who stands at his side with conviction. There was not a scintilla of betrayal in his loyalty to the evil spirits in which he so firmly believed. He was a man who did not even consider the meaning of Good. Evil was the only project worth undertaking, the universal nostrum upon which his soul thrived along with a personal rejection of all other gods. In this sense there was a special pathos in him since he played every emotional issue in life to the hilt as related only to Evil. He seemed to be saying that Evil is what so many humans are here for exclusively, however much they rationalize their existence with a Sunday prayer in church to their God.

As to the special delay in the display of his proclivities and powers, there was a reason for it. As long as the father Winthrop was present with the powerful shotgun there was always the possibility he would not be successful. But there was a more important set of reasons. He wanted Lydia and the twins to feel haunted by the sounds of trampling on the roof, by the moans and groans that he uttered in imitation of the undead, and by observing the host of unnatural sensations they would exhibit by the feel of his presence. Yes, his desire would normally be to display his claws which were more like an eagle's talons than a wolf's claws when he changed shape. He enjoyed the fear in his victim's eyes and Phoenix's ultra-blues would certainly be mixed with capillaries of red blood when he opened her up, slashed her pregnant stomach wide open and strangled her ever so slowly as she watched her little boy suffocate in her own blood.

But that scenario would have to wait. Bram wanted his child to be born as a tribute to Satan and so he would have to forego that pleasure, at least for a time. But taking care of Lydia and the twin Phoebe was left up to him to do with as he saw fit. His intention was also to make their deaths a sacrifice to Satan and to bring this accomplishment forward on the first day of the New Year. He knew that Satan always rewarded one of his disciples with a plentiful crop of victims if the year began in the proper way, a salute to Him with the offer of a sacrifice.

The other issue was his sword cane. Lydia had defiled it by silver plating the pointed end of the weapon as if this would be a deterrent to him. No way. He had observed Phoenix giving Lydia fencing lessons and this had made him laugh. His intention was to snatch the rapier back during her feeble intent to do him in. In his mind's eye he would torture both Phoebe and Lydia as he had originally planned for Phoenix. Just thinking about this scenario caused his fangs to elongate, his penis to swell and exhibit tumescence, and his nails to transform into talons. Yes, he wanted his hickory stick back. And he disagreed with Bram. His plans for Phoebe were his own.

Of course, from what he had heard on their cell conversation, it was possible that Josh, the wimp, would be present as well. He did not see this twerp as a barrier of any sort to his plans. No, he would wait until the parents left, their blood would be too old and stale for him anyway, then he could hang Josh from the rafters, stick Lydia in the heart as many times as he wished, slash open Phoebe from her cleavage to her navel and spread the opening of her treasure chest, dilate the plump lips inside with his fingers and stick his schlong into her still hot and bloody insides after she was dead. She would be a much finer piece to remember than the disappointing Cynthia.

Finally, he would whip Lydia with the hickory stick until she no longer breathed a sign of life. A good plan he told himself, one that would perhaps make the first page of the Santa Barbara News-Press, the daily newspaper.

Chapter XXV

Twin Storms

In Santa Barbara the fog is usually most severe in July and August, but this year was an exception. Only two days short of the New Year the mountain fog joined with the ocean fog in a penetrating and mystic vapor, thick and sluggish, and leaden-hued. The heavy density of the low hanging clouds pressed upon the dormers of Lydia's house enshrouding the rooftop with its vapors. There was no moon, not even a glimpse of stars, so the only luminosity was the glow of unnatural light emanating from the house itself. And with the wind changing quickly, swirling about, the evening air was tempestuous, yet wildly beautiful. As Drakonius emerged from his hiding place in the woods, the shroud of fog seemed to open like a stage curtain, breaking the singular beauty of the night into one of agitated mist and terror.

At that very moment Phoenix awakened from a dream in which an incubus had assaulted her, she quickly got out of bed, careful not to awaken Lydia, and hastened to the casement of the dormer, threw open the window and for the briefest of moments, as a sudden gust blew aside the heavy fog, she spied the figure of a cadaverous looking man, the twin of the incubus in her dream. She screamed, Lydia awoke, but when she came to her side the apparition was gone. Even so, Lydia latched the dormer window securely before they returned to bed.

Phoenix found sleep again within minutes, but Lydia was restless and wandered into the hall wondering what Bram was up to, what these frightening noises and scary sounds at night really meant.

Phoenix's scream also awakened Josh who had arrived in the late afternoon, a guest with a purpose. His ordinary manner was a thing of the past, his social struggles gone; his halting stop-and-go speaking style virtually vanished. On into early evening he was jovial and confident. The once occasional wimp-like tone that habitually characterized his utterances was heard no more, now replaced by a huskiness of voice much admired by the three women.

After some hours of holiday good cheer had elapsed, there was general agreement that the foggy evening warranted an early bedtime for all. Then an identifiable change came over Josh's features. He joined Phoebe in Vladg's room and performed so magnificently, that she remained resplendent in her dreamy-thoughts, never before having felt quite so secure in her love. He had held her so tightly throughout their lovemaking that she could barely breathe. In place of a premature emission, his ejaculation was postponed for a full ten minutes and when it did come it was not a slow discharge but an explosion into her womb resembling more the work of an internal combustion engine than that of a mechanical groin reflex.

His new abilities had so pleasured Phoebe that she asked him where and how he had come up with his great strength and endurance. It was Josh's plan to tell her the truth on New Year's Eve, a surprise of sorts for 2059, so all he said was that sleeping with her in Vladg's bed was such a thrill that he just imagined he was a Duplicant and the rest followed.

Phoebe took his words in, but his explanation had left her in doubt, her curiosity challenged. She touched his cheek, a soft and tender stroke, a faint blush remaining upon her bosom. Her mind was working, but only in slow motion, as if bathed in a 'Child's Garden of Verses'. She had to come up with something, but she had no wish to destroy the special mood so lovingly created:

"We'd better bring this bed back with us to Manhattan when we leave," she quipped. Then, without another bother in the world, she turned over on her side, pleasantly exhausted, sensually satiated, welcoming the after-sex slumber into which she fell almost immediately.

It was not long after this that Josh was awakened by Phoenix's scream. He rushed into the hall where he met Lydia who described to him what had happened and the nature of the dream that Phoenix had related to her.

"That's more or less to be expected isn't it? I mean she was impregnated by your husband in a dreadfully unfair attack and at this stage of her pregnancy she must be very, very sensitive on her future."

"Yes, she is sensitive, but you know, considering everything that has happened, this does seem to be a rather normal pregnancy. Phoenix desires this baby very much, and intends to see that it is totally human with no vampire characteristics whatsoever. She worries about that more than anything else."

Josh would normally have swallowed all this without saying anything, but the new Josh had more courage.

"Doesn't that imply Bram's death, and probably yours as well if all I have read on the subject is true? I mean for the baby to be free of any vampire traits?"

Lydia paused, but the question was fairly put and she knew she had to come up with some sort of response.

"I have lived long enough. You must never say so to Phoenix, but yes, I love her so much that even if Bram's death meant my demise, I would still prefer to die rather than to see her suffer as a slave to Bram and have her child brought up as a worshipper of Satan."

"I see," Josh whispered. "Well let's hope it doesn't come to that."

"Let's."

"And thank you for taking me into your confidence."

"I did so for two reasons. One you are soon to be engaged to Phoebe…"

"And the other?"

"I detect that you are no longer fully human. You are now a Humilicant aren't you?"

Josh is taken by surprise; he literally takes a step backwards from Lydia.

"Yes, how did you know?"

"That wasn't hard. I still have some powers of association of thought, and in the living room late this afternoon; I was able to read your mind a bit. Don't be ashamed, but don't wait too long to tell Phoebe. It's better to let her know as soon as possible. She is not a woman from whom you should hide things."

"No she's not, I agree. I plan to tell her during our celebration tomorrow night."

"That's actually tonight. It's now five past midnight."

"Gosh that's true, isn't it?"

"Listen Josh, there have been some mysterious sounds on the roof, so far not tonight, but the night is young. I believe her dream was prompted more by what is going on now than what Bram has done to her."

"And what is going on now?"

"Come. Come with me to the study downstairs. I want to show you something."

They walk together past Phoenix's door, Lydia first picking up the Taser, and then they step downstairs to the study. She hands Josh the Hickory sword-cane and, almost angrily, tells him the story of Drakonius as Vladg had related it to her.

In the telling Lydia is roused, her face florid, her expressions flushed with a mix of fear and hate. As she shows Josh how to withdraw the rapier from its wooden sheath, there is a sudden harsh flapping of wings against the large French window. Josh immediately springs to the window case and through the now sparse fog spies the retreating translucent shape of the largest bat he had ever seen.

"You see Josh, something must be done. Bram has sent Drakonius here to frighten us. We must be prepared to kill Bram when he comes, and come he will."

"But how do you know he will be here and when."

"He will come to see his son, as yet unborn, but he will come and you must be the one. No T.H. can defeat Bram, but now that you are a Humilicant, perhaps, you can do it."

"Lydia, I am a Humilicant, but my nature is passive, I don't know that I can kill anyone…"

"Josh, I said Drakonius was here to frighten us, but it may be more than that. A true Vampire is unpredictable and unreliable, even if Bram has ordered him here; there is no reason to expect him to hold true to Bram's wishes."

"So you dread the events of the future, perhaps not in themselves, but in the possibilities…their results."

"Yes, I shudder at the thought of any, even the most trivial, incident such as the flapping of wings, of the sounds of steps on the roof, none which may harm Phoenix directly, but which do cause this intolerable agitation of her soul."

Josh had no visible response to this last remark, but internally he was receptive, he felt the intensity of Lydia's concern, perhaps even the extent of her love for Phoenix.

Lydia's deep tension affected her physically, inhibited her breathing, but even so her thoughts were crystallized into action. She theatrically replaced the rapier into its wooden sheath, but before doing so she placed her palm, almost sensually, on the silver hooded section at the tip: "This one- this is for the coup- you must thrust it directly through Bram's heart when he arrives."

Josh is as yet unable to give his word to carry out her request.

Instead he says: "How does all this evil get done? I mean with everyone sold in the holidays on the good in the world…"

Lydia does not hesitate with her answer.

"There are twin storms in every soul. The sentient part of the soul seeks expression, wants to get out and do its thing whether it is good or evil. We call the good enthusiasm for life, but the evil has its own enthusiasm, only it is for misery and death and it is just as active. The Greek word is diabolos, but whatever the name, it is destructive to life."

"I see."

"You are as yet an ingénue in life, but you must quickly learn of the evil that exists, otherwise, even with your newly found powers, Drakonius will do you in. You will never become the brother-in-law to Phoenix that is your sole desire."

Somehow this last way of saying it convinces Josh that he must gather the courage to do whatever is necessary.

"I give you my promise," he says.

This is not quite good enough for Lydia.

"Do I have your word of honor on this?"

"My word and honor on my love for Phoebe, yes."

"Good, I accept your oath, thank you. Now let us go upstairs to bed."

No further words are spoken between them until they reach their rooms.

"Goodnight then. Have pleasant dreams."

"You too. Sleep soundly."

"I intend to."

∞

In Oslo, Bjørn Køørstad, the Chief Meteorologist for the Norwegian Weather Service has predicted that the Arctic Jet streams were going to hit all of Scandinavia and Holland on the day before the New Year. This seemed to be due to an unusual low pressure area that tended to suck the polar jet winds down to the earth's surface and for a day or two would have the potential to wreak havoc at sea and on land. The danger to the Dutch coastline might be catastrophic if the dike system gave way, so Bjørn took it upon himself to place a call to his counterpart in Amsterdam, Hans Formijne, to see if Hans's data paralleled his own.

After a short exchange on the relative merits and deficits of each country's soccer teams and the fact that the World Cup was only a year away in 2060, they got down to brass tacks.

"It's not just the low pressures," said Hans, "I believe there is a disturbance in the magnetosphere as well, just about where the Karman line meets the magneto sheath, about one hundred kilometers above sea level."

"So you think this may be a geomagnetic storm provoking the jet stream as well as the low pressure in Holland and over here in Norway?"

"Yes I do. That would explain why the data show such pinpointed accuracy. I've been tempted to call the aeronautical association; if my calculations are correct, the Sub-Orbs will all be in danger from ionized Hydrogen forming anti-protons, they will stall at the Karman line and not get back to earth."

"This could be like that storm almost one hundred years ago; it was in 1952 wasn't it?"

"No, it was 1953 and to be exact it took place on the night of the 31st of January over to the 1st of February. You see I've studied it recently. Since they did not know much of anything about the magnetosphere back then, they could not predict the storm that followed as the data gathering was so primitive. The catastrophe of the dikes was due to the slosh of waves that overwhelmed the sea defenses and caused extensive flooding. In combination with a tidal surge of the North Sea, the water level locally exceeded 5.6 metres above mean sea level."

"So this might be the twin to that storm."

"You could say so…"

"But we, you and I together, we can prevent the loss of life and property if we notify the proper agencies in time."

"Yes, but I've hesitated to do so, you know how these people are, with all their political posturing. Anything that puts a stop to travel, even for a short time is bad for world business, but especially during the holiday season when travel is at its height."

"It's true they are awfully covetous of their turf."

"And we have to get all the fishing trawlers and smaller vessels out of the North Sea. If my calculations are correct the sea will rise higher this time, the needle moving up to six meters as there has been so much melting of the glaciers in Greenland this century."

"I see what you mean. Even though we're no longer dependent on oil for energy, so much damage had been done by those insane yahoos last century that we're not yet recovering."

"It will take another two hundred years…and cutting down the rain forests hasn't helped."

"Still if I were you I'd report it. It's not up to us to tell them what to do, only to advise based on the data we have."

"Yes, of course you are right. I'll send out an H-mail at once to the powers that be and you do the same. If they receive reports from two different sources the politicians might take it more seriously than if we sent one conjoint paper on our findings."

"Yes, that might work better; then they can fill up the airwaves with sentences they put together in the form of one high sounding proclamation, that's the style they love."

"Hopefully they won't take overlong in doing so, such that the storm hits before they can agree on anything."

"That's the problem isn't it? And Bjørn, by the way, don't forget to tell all your friends not to Sub-Orb for the next few days."

"Good advice Hans. Thanks for the consultation, always good to hear from you."

∞

This time the politicians listened to the scientists as more and more reports came in from different sources. The entire populace of coastal Europe and Ireland and England had been warned to stay in their homes and not venture forth unless there was a dire emergency and even then to be ultra-careful. All traffic at sea was called back to their nearest ports and air traffic was halted completely. It was as if the world had turned topsy-turvy as the local winds, warmed by the friction of magneto-ionization, exceeded tropical storm force in South Holland and Northern Belgium.

∞

In Amersfoort, the wind was wailing but it was nowhere near as strong as on the coast where the wind and waves were gathering hurricane force. So Joost and Greta decided to go forth with their wedding as scheduled.

Greta had not wanted her wedding to be overly elaborate but she did wish it to be memorable. So she and Joost went all out and hired a 4-D photographer who set up twelve expensive Projecto-FAX tele-video cameras at strategic places in the church, two of which were anchored at high points in the vaulted ceiling. The photographer played on a multiplex keyboard which controlled the cameras with as much facility as the organist in the church. He was able to scan each of the cameras to sixty degrees covering every nook and cranny of the church and highlighting the more interesting actions as the procession took place and the guests settled themselves in. As the ceremony commenced, these cameras recorded an ongoing tele-video designed to fit every guest's T-cell automatically. Then, if the guest so wished, they could watch immediately or do playback on their 3-screen at home enjoying the different holographic projections.

Joost and Greet also paid for a low energy propulsion anti-gravity ray beam program to be installed temporarily in the middle aisle of the church. This program would allow Greet to appear as if she were walking on air as she floated up to the sanctuary in front of the pulpit to take her vows. This system also saved the train of her wedding gown from sweeping against the floor which she knew was timeworn and poorly vacuumed by the Basic assigned to the task.

She was disappointed also by the halt in Sub-Orb air traffic which meant that so few of her friends from abroad would be able to attend. Even Geri's Mother from Staten Island was unable to make it and Geri was her head matron of honor with a retinue of supporting maids, all friends from years past.

The incoming storm also affected Joost who had one brother in Canada and another in New Zealand. Both were unable to travel. So a wedding that had been planned for over one-hundred people was reduced to fifty or so. Hikey had intended to take the monorail from Amsterdam, but the raging winds had shut this down as well. There was but a slim possibility that the regular trains would run and driving automobiles was minimal on wet roads with tropical storm type winds.

So the attendance at the Old Dutch Reformed Church in Amersfoort was much less than originally planned, but the entire staff of the detective division, including Chief de Haas was present, along with Vladg, and of course Dusty, who was Best Man.

One individual in attendance, quite out of the ordinary, was an uninvited guest who sat in a pew to the rear of the nave. He didn't actually 'crash' the wedding, but merely interposed himself amongst the numerous teenage nieces and nephews and other guests who were somehow connected to the bride and groom or to the retinue attached to the matron of honor. Even more unusual were the three strange, somewhat bedraggled and emaciated Eastern European looking women sitting beside him. They had their faces heavily powdered but even so, the reddish-brown stains of aging and death shone through their cheap whitish make-up in several places. Oddly enough all three wore dark sunglasses in the daytime and did not take them off inside the church. The man was called Malignius and the three eccentric looking women with him were the undead sisters, Iphigènie, Athalie and Phaedra. Each wore an antique looking dress fashioned from old white lace. The ashen white fabric was in stark contrast to the bride's attire whose silk and satin bridal gown, hand sewn, was of an off-white color with softly highlighted lavender gemstones spread in a pattern suggestive of a cross.

Greet looked especially royal with a zirconium diadem placed regally upon her head. She had earlier taken special care with her shoulder length thick brunette hair, repeatedly brushing it down, front and back, so that the shine glistened. And while her gown was free of shoulder straps, the cut of her wavy locks hid the orbs of her bosom presenting an enchanting peek-a-boo of cleavage between her long tresses, her nipples subdued, barely protruding underneath the satin fabric.

Geri's dress, as matron of honor, was made of short cotton sateen with a spaghetti strap bodice, and a pleated waist band to accentuate her natural curves. Geri loved to dance and figured this short dress would be perfect for the reception planned afterwards in the hall across the street from the church. The reception hall was to double later in the evening for the New Year's Eve party.

In keeping with the characteristics of good and frugal Dutchmen, the bridegroom, Joost, as well as his best man Dusty, had simply rented tuxes for the wedding ceremony. However, Joost had splurged on the wedding band, a wide 24 carat white gold ring with an uplifted setting of small cut diamonds and little oval sapphires that seemed to capture the dark blue color of Greta's eyes. Joost figured he had got the ring for free, that the purchase had actually cost him nothing, for by getting married on the last day of the year, he and Greta were automatically enlisted into the married couples' tax classification, one that exempted them from certain levies. As any good Dutchman would tend to do, he chortled to himself at outwitting the 'Office of Taxation and Internal Revenue'.

For some minutes Dusty and Geri had stood waiting to one side of the chancel, a nervous Joost on the other side with the minister standing just before the altar, the choir at the ready, all awaiting Greta's entrance. As soon as they spotted the engineer flipping the switch to the anti-gravity unit, Greta entered the church, looking radiant, smiling and happy. She needn't have worried about her train as a niece to one of the deacon's was chosen to lift up and hold the trailing ends of fabric to her long flowing bridal gown.

As Greta stepped into the aisle she was immediately levitated up a foot or so whilst the niece, uttering a squeal of delight, was suspended up a fraction later. Now she walked forward on air, a mystical beauty that seemed to be floating down the aisle on an invisible magic carpet. The rapture of the moment was more than the three sisters could stand, especially Iphigènie who lost control, and started to drool, her yellowish fangs protruding. The teens sitting behind her began to snicker and the trio turned and hissed at them like snakes. The hissing caused a small disturbance which caught Greta's eye. Now she recognized Malignius, who had more or less bent over and hidden his face in a hymn book. At once Greta's glowing expression faded to one of deep concern.

At this moment Iphigènie, overwhelmed by desire and so attracted to Greta that her bloodthirsty impulses overcame her, sprang from her pew. She made to attack Greta but got caught up in the rising action of the anti-gravity beams. Her momentum quickly transported her to the end of the aisle where she collided with Geri and then collapsed, falling into the hands of the surprised minister who had never encountered such a creature in his many years of religious service.

He tried to comfort her but she immediately wrenched free, spat gobs of thick venom and spittle at him and as he wiped the foul smelling snot away from his cheek she tried to bite him in the neck, once again putting her ugly yellowish fangs to work. Joost, who was standing at attention, positioned like a statue in his role as groom, now broke free of his lethargy and grabbed Iphigènie by the scruff of the neck, hauling her unceremoniously away from Minister Jansen (no relation) and dragging her to the floor. Improvising, he snatched a sash from a curtain behind the sanctuary and used it as a cord to bind and immobilize the frail vampire.

Greta cradled the frightened little niece in her arms, while Dusty, finally attended to Geri who was bemoaning the total breakup of the ceremony. Also, a tear in her dress occurred when Iphigènie's long dirty claws scratched at her as the Vampire fell off the end of the invisible ramp, ruining her dancing plans in this dress at the reception.

Malignius is furious, his carefully laid plans totally upset by Iphigènie's impetuous action. He takes out the aerosol can of venom and attempts to spray it at the teens behind him, but he had forgotten to shake the can, and for whatever reason, the high viscosity of the venom, or the changes in atmospheric pressure from the Carpathian Mountains to below sea level in Holland, the can clogs, spits, but doesn't spray. The teenage bunch, girls as well as boys, fall heavily upon Malignius, beating at him with hands and fists, striving to wrestle him down, the girls scratching at his face, but Malignius is a giant compared to these kids and he swipes them away like flies, growling like a caged animal.

By this time Vladg recognizes the seriousness of the situation, leaps over three sets of pews to reach Malignius who by now had abandoned any plans to single out Greta and Geri as targets, but was ready to attack any one at hand.

No member of the detective division, out of respect for the church, bore firearms except Chief de Haas who secretly had brought along his Taser handgun. He immediately leveled his weapon, took aim and fired at the two remaining sisters. They are both stunned, knocked out cold from the impact. But because of the melee, the teens mixed in with Malignius and Vladg, the Chief is hesitant to fire again. He merely watches as the two embittered titans, one a Duplicant, the other a Dhampire, go at it tooth and nail, a brawl like no other, tele-recorded from every vantage point by the twelve cameras and viewed by the assemblage as an unexpected treat.

Vladg and Malignius break away from each other for a moment, fists clenched and bare knuckles at the ready; Malignius starts talking trash: "I take no pleasure in tearing you limb from limb," he snarls. "You don't even have blood in your veins."

"Well I'll love beating the crap outa you, dumb shit," Vladg says with utmost calm, purposely using street lingo to unnerve Malignius and show his own lack of fear. He throws the first blow, getting off a left hook in 1/54th of a second that hits so hard it not only breaks the Dhampire's jaw but fractures his elongated canine, leaving Malignius looking like a beached walrus without a tusk on one side. Malignius reacts in a prehensile manner, rubs the wounded area with his fingers and palm and this nursing action costs him dearly, for now Vladg peppers him with short sharp body blows, drawing him closer in, setting him up with a few accurate jabs, and then, he pounds him with a right cross, stunning him for a moment, the Dhampire's brain rocking back and forth within his skull.

Malignius doesn't lose consciousness, however, but recoils and charges Vladg butting him in the midsection, causing Vladg's tube of elixir that feeds his sweat glands to burst. A sudden male aroma permeates the area and while Vladg is recovering from the odd feeling of cracked plexiglass, the shattered particles of plastic resin spreading throughout his belly, he becomes nauseous. Malignius seizes the moment and throws Vladg three pews over, arcing in a slant towards the middle aisle. The engineer spots this and automatically raises the antigravity beams a few feet to cushion Vladg's fall; then he sets the beams into slow descent and finally shuts them off.

Vladg stands up, springs back over the pews, landing hard, knocking over one pew, splintering the heavy wood, half-wrecking another, seat cushions and bibles and hymn books scattering every which way. Now he knocks Malignius down but Malignius, from his flattened position, throws an uppercut to Vladg's midriff, which is already sore and aching, and Vladg goes down again. Then Malignius bites Vladg in the throat with his one remaining fang but the lymph that spurts out is totally unlike blood, a mucus like sour tasting fluid that Malignius spits out at once. But this too gives Vladg a precious moment and, from a sitting position, he hits Malignius with all his strength just above the eye, opening up a cut that trickles blood down in front of the eye, momentarily blinding Malignius who tries to wipe it away, and in that split second Vladg stands up and pummels Malignius with a series of sharp blows to his opponent's midsection.

Malignius bends over and now Vladg has him in his sights, hits him hard, throwing one punch after another directly to his temple and at his already broken jaw. Malignius loses consciousness and goes down between pews, bibles and hymn books falling all over his torso.

The Chief comes over and handcuffs Malignius to the leg end of the pew. Then, with contempt, he throws one of the pew cushions over his face.

"That should hold him for now," the Chief says to Vladg, who is unsteady on his feet. De Haas makes a motion to one of the women in the congregation whom he knows, a trained nurse, and she comes by to attend to Vladg as best she can. Minister Jansen wants to help as well, advises that he be moved to a bed in the rectory, but at that moment a hollow roar of heavy thunder splits the sky, booming over the neighborhood and resounding against the outer walls of the church.

Dusty opens the entrance doors only to find that the streets have become dark and empty. Some of the church's artifacts quake in their cases, statues of saints fall and shatter, crumbling on the marble floor, the guests gaping and gasping at the sudden destruction to their beloved church.

When the storm settles down some, several patrolmen arrive in a paddywagon to haul the three sisters and Malignius off to the hoosegow. In Holland, there is no specific Miranda Rights law to be administered, but Chief de Haas explains as best he can to the four miscreants what the accusations are, and although he is unsure whether or not the three heretical sisters have understood his words-for they appear dazed and unknowing-Malignius comprehends all that was said.

He knows that the civil punishment will not be much more than complete banishment from Holland and deportation back to Transylvania.

Vladg is forced to miss the completion of the wedding when an ambulance arrives to take him to hospital. There, to prevent infection, a robotic abdominal probe and scanner are found necessary to surgically remove the particles of resin and plastic floating throughout his peritoneal membranes. Vladg doesn't consider this all bad since he is no longer bound to Lydia. The fragrance mechanism was originally her idea and he really has grown tired of emitting such a strong male scent.

A few Basic III's are called in to clean up the mess, remove the broken pew and to reset the others that had been overturned and place them in proper order. After these housekeeping chores are done, some guests themselves lending a hand, and Reverend Jansen announces that the wedding ceremony will recommence.

This time all goes well, except that the unnerved minister seems to rush through the vows of matrimony. When he asks Greta if she will take Joost as her lawful wedded husband she says: "He's not really my type, but I do love him, so yes I'll take him as he is." Everyone laughs and the tension is extinguished.

Now the minister asks Joost if he has a ring for the bride. Joost nods, puts it lovingly on her third finger left hand, and the minister pronounces them husband and wife in the eyes of the Lord. He then tells Joost he may kiss the bride and Joost gives her a soul kiss that lasts so long it further upsets the reverend.

"I do wish the two of you a long and happy life together," Jansen says, "but in all my years of performing the marital ceremony, I have never officiated at one as complicated as this."

"Well this is one complicated lady," Joost says.

Greta's smile is back on her face.

"Thank you for everything you've done. You were quite courageous," she says, and gives Jansen a hug that he recognizes as one of gratitude.

"I don't believe I will celebrate with you folks tonight, but I do wish you all a happy and prosperous New Year," Jansen says.

"You the same," Greta and Joost say in unison.

Then Jansen takes his leave, happy to be able to get back to his own reality in the little house located to the side of the church.

Chapter XXVI

New Year's Eve - New Year's Day-2059

In wintry Oneonta an icy cold pervaded Bram's once stout body, running over his leathery skin and invading his lusterless hair. After some puttering, he finally got the hearth going and as the room heated up his brain warmed up as well, his thinking becoming clearer.

He was busy bringing up a great number of H-mails which he had neglected to retrieve from his T-cell. He started to project the series of holographs, reading them with his large meditative eyes. One of these messages, sent by Gregoriev, forced him to chuckle. Some time beforehand he had sent in his request for retirement from the Foreign Service. Gregoriev's H-mail response was a formal, congratulatory, acceptance of that request. However, in the body of his letter there was a plea for an anti-dote to the love potion Bram had earlier provided. Apparently the redheaded mistress Gregoriev had 'seduced' had become too clingy, prone to overly high maintenance, demanding expensive gifts and travel to exotic resorts. Between guttural snorts, Bram composed a short response, thanking Gregoriev for his kindness and leadership but stating that, unfortunately, there was no antidote presently available to act on the potion. He paused for a moment, thought things over. As Gregoriev was no longer his boss, he could not resist adding an ironic finale. He ended with an old adage: "In future, be careful what you wish for, you might just get it."

The next H-mail he projected was from Malignius detailing the events of Greta's wedding and his failure at annihilation and disposal as Bram had requested. However, Malignius pointed out, that since he was banished from entering Holland ever again, his intention was to follow Joost and Greta on their honeymoon to the Peloponnesian Islands; this time he would not bring along the three sisters but do the entire job himself. Bram merely grunted, sent a reply H-mail. He had lost faith completely in Malignius's abilities as an agent of destruction. Malignius could make noise and deflect and misdirect humans, but as a demon he foundered into the bogs. His H-reply urged Malignius to remain in Dolno Katore for the present and to try to better organize the populace along more efficient lines.

Regardless of his initial good feelings for Greta, her later betrayal had led to daily throbs of anger; throbs which affected his very blood and trespassed into soreness of the heart. Initially, he had been her Master and now she had humiliated him. His rage had done him harm, made him indecisive. He had known all along what to do and had failed to do it. In truth, ever since the episode of losing his thumb when Phoebe sliced it off, he had lost self-confidence. Yes, he had handled de Boer adequately, but that was easy compared to this, he had had no feelings whatsoever for de Boer, a piece of nothing. Greta was different; she had pulled at his heartstrings. Although strictly speaking sex was not involved, satanic sex included a good deal more than the physical. Indeed, his mastery over her had been sexually stimulating. Yes, he would miss the power and control over Greta.

Calling Malignius in to do the job was wrong. He, himself, had been unequal to the task, to what was plain, clear and necessary. He saw that now. It seemed as if he would have to crystallize his evils and do this duty himself. However, he needed to postpone the Greta situation until after the birth of his son, when Phoenix was here with him and things had settled down in Oneonta. Then he would make Greta a young widow and she would become his undead slave forever.

He also read a message from Eiselman, noting that the remaining Duplicants had now been transported to Oneonta; that, as Chief Executive, he considered this to mean their verbal contract had been fulfilled and all transactions between them were at an end. Bram snickered at this idea. He was already busy training the new Duplicants to infiltrate and organize Seneca Falls, a city accustomed to social reform groups, where they would continue to proselytize his 2nd Reformation. Soon they would no longer be a small satanic clan stranded in a tiny corner of the earth.

He had no intention of ever releasing Eiselman from his power. On the contrary, as soon as Phoenix delivered and she was able to travel back to Oneonta with their son, his intention was to take over the entire Pyrell Corporation. He felt this could be done with the aid of Phoenix whom he intended to install in Phoebe's position as Eiselman's secretary. As to Phoebe and that nerdy boyfriend of hers, today was the day of reckoning. Certainly Drakonius would not be as inept as Malignius in carrying out his mission. Bram's only worry was that Drakonius would go farther than he had requested, much too far. Drakonius had a strong independent bent which he derived from his genealogy, the pride of being a true vampire, unmixed with human genes of any sort in his blood.

Over the years, in spite of general agreement by all concerned that Bram was considered the titular leader of the

European and American brotherhood, Drakonius, at times, would strike out on his own. Although he had given specific instructions not to harm Phoenix, merely to scare her so that his unborn son would get a glimpse of evil from inside the womb, he knew that once he got going on a killing spree Drakonius had very little restraint. Setting limits was not one of his better attributes. Still, it had to be done. The twin sisters were much too close to one another for his liking. Even though he had first been attracted to Phoebe, there was nothing else for it. She had to go or be transformed. If she was not changed into a true vampire as a member of the undead, she would remain an impediment to the upbringing of his child, fostering human thoughts and feelings upon the boy that were at odds with his own beliefs. That would become an impossible situation to contend with on a daily basis. No, if Drakonius went too far with Phoebe, so be it. This way Phoenix could not hold him responsible for Phoebe's demise.

As to the situation here in Oneonta, for some time he had been busy organizing the townspeople and its leaders to Satanism. All of the Catholic priests and Christian ministers were now under his power and those who did not submit were purged of their impurities by holding them under a long term trance. They had either been drawn into the fold or scourged from their positions. He had set up a Trilateral Commission, which displaced the City Council, consisting of himself, the Mayor and the Chief of police, both of whom he kept under trance and in his power. Since the night of the Walpurgis, sprees and parties had been going on every night. A Satanic festival was celebrated that substituted for the Christmas Holiday and business in the city actually improved over the prior year. People from the surrounding rural areas came into town to celebrate and to purchase all the satanic toys, talismans, whips and other knick-knacks that went along with the festivities.

Along with all this good local news there were problems. He was faced with a dilemma. Edna Kincaid, of all persons, had organized secret prayer meetings held in people's private homes on Sundays. These meetings were very reminiscent of the first Christians who had to meet clandestinely to worship. In fact they called themselves the New Corinthians. They were led by Edna, but the worship was conducted by the banished minister of her church, the Reverend Maurice Dahlberg. Bram's source of information was Judd Kincaid, Edna's husband, essentially a tattletale who betrayed his own wife.

Bram had no respect for the man whatsoever, but he did admire Edna's spunk. He knew that one of the reasons for her newly found success in leadership was an argument between Gods, an argument that stemmed from different beliefs between her God and his. Moses punished the Egyptians with plagues of darkness, but Jesus brought swarms of light to the brethren. So this was a test of her piety and Bram knew that Satan wanted her to lose faith in her God. Of course, Satan wanted him to put the prayer meetings to an end, but this was not all. Additionally, Edna's loss of faith could be helped along if he would correct the good deed he had done her. Apparently Satan's idea of redemption in this instance was for him to slaughter the dairy cow. Every night he suffered through the same repetitive dream demanding the death of the cow; his deliverance from 'a state of good' depended upon his completion of this act of evil. Thus far he had been unable to bring himself to do so. Of course, he could order Judd to handle the matter, but this would not clear him in Satan's eyes. It was silly, he knew, he could more easily do away with Greta's husband, a human, than he could Edna's new Dairy cow.

His forehead was wrinkled, his expression uncomprehending, and he did not understand any of this.

∞

In Santa Barbara visibility was better, the fog had lifted, seemingly as a greeting to the New Year, but the skies of late afternoon were still dark gray and no patches of blue shone through. Drakonius was still befogged by his defeat in the Vondel Park at the hands of Vladg. He had hoped for a rematch, if Vladg would be present at Lydia's home to celebrate the holidays with his former companion, but such was not the case. His revenge would have to wait until he was able to return to Europe in another guise. This postponement did not mean that he was unfit for the task set before him. To the contrary, he was now more fervent than ever on his plan of destruction.

However, for some days he had not drunk fresh blood. He felt the need to power up, to seek regenerating fuel amongst the young maidens that inhabited the city. This strong desire for nutrition was accompanied by another requirement, the need for doing a trial run with some young lovelies to test his killing skills as a preparation for carrying out Bram's directive. He needed to hype himself up, to think of the delicious destruction in advance. All would die except for Phoenix, whom he intended to frighten and kidnap. The rest would be sacrificed in the name of Satan. The radar in his head anticipated no danger from the present members of the household.

So as the New Year approached he had watched Lydia and her guests make an early night of it. All but Phoenix had celebrated extensively, over-eating and drinking and now they were watching the stupid final championship game of the college football playoffs between the Syracuse Orange and the TCU Horned Frogs. Drakonius did not know that these two were old rivals who had not met since the Cotton Bowl in the mid part of the last century. He could care less about American sports; he had his own sport finale to play.

As soon after the clock struck midnight he went out on the town and had a glorious time. Part of his celebration was planned, but as things turned out most of what happened was serendipitous. By accident he discovered that there were festivities being celebrated at Stearns Wharf, a multi-use pier that for the night had laid out a smooth section of portable dance flooring over the old wooden ties. The Splinters, a band that played zithers, lutes, mandolins, guitars (acoustic and electrical) as well as Japanese flutes and other exotic instruments had gained renown for breaking all their string instruments at the end of every performance and tossing the splinters to the audience.

They were playing mostly Shu-Garoo numbers and the dance steps appeared to be a combination of the old Salsa and Jitterbug. There were a great number of young men and women doing their thing, frivolously full of alcohol and drugs. The musicians themselves were dressed in weird costumes so when Drakonius came on the floor in his top hat, cloak and cane he appeared to fit right in. The approaching dance steps of two young women attracted his attention.   He began listening, and laughed all by himself.

He joined the two young girls, selecting them because when doing the Shu-Garoo the jumpy dance steps accented their bouncy hair, their jiggling tits and whirling hot buns. They also appeared to be high on Ubiquity and booze, and he started to dance between both of them. They kept chatting up one another, jabbering away as if he was not even there, but also as if they didn't mind his presence. What he heard was amazing. They were talking about their boyfriends and how much they enjoyed getting their nipples pinched, their breasts pulled on and their throats choked to the point of erotic asphyxiation.

Drakonius started to drool at the luscious thoughts of feeding on the young flesh of these two.

"This one guy had a piece of rope around my neck, kept tightening it with a sailor's knot and loosening it every time I came."

"Wouldn't want an orgasm any other way," the one dancing in peep toe stilettos said.

"Don't you just hate sex without pain?" the leather mini skirted one said.

"You bet. Any man that can't torture me is not my type, not going to make it with me."

Drakonius interrupted.

"Then I should fit right in," he said, knowing in advance he would get a wiseass retort.

"Listen old man, you can dance with us if you like but don't get any silly ideas, we only go with young guys, the younger the better."

"Yeah, minimal six comes…can you do that?"

"No, but I can show you pleasure-pain you never dreamed possible."

"Hah, that's what they all say."

"Go on, git off the floor, you're tiresome."

Drakonius did as requested, but he waited some time until the band's finale, the two girls scrambling for remnants of the instruments, each proudly grasping splinters they had snatched away from others, struggling, scratching and shouting to get their souvenirs as if the concert were a major historical event.

When they were finally ready to leave he stalked them to their car.

Everything happened very fast. He got out his newly purchased sword cane, stuck the stiletto girl, who was ready to hop in on the passenger side, right through the heart and threw her body as easily as if it were a half-filled grocery sack into the back seat. Then he jumped in and held the still bloody point of his sword against the neck of the horribly frightened mini skirted girl who had just turned on the ignition.

"Drive or your dead," he said simply.

She was just about to scream when the increased pressure of the metallic point of the sword against her jugular convinced her to hold back. Her tears flowed silently.

He told the mini skirted lovely where to drive, directed her to Lydia's house and forced her to park in the driveway. All along his intention had been to steal a car for his getaway after he completed his massive task and this one seemed to fill the bill as good as any. As dawn broke he dragged her by her long hair, screaming and struggling, twisting along the ground, into the back woods. He first wrapped one massive hairy hand around her beauteous throat, nearly encircling it, and started to suffocate her. As soon as he saw she was enjoying the choking a certain amount he let up on the pressure and for a split second she shuddered, thinking she was safe, that this was a reenactment of her sailor friend's style. Not to be. Drakonius was merely being careful, did not wish to strangle her as he wanted her to hear what he had to say.

"Do you know what day this is?"

'My God, who is this creature,' she thought, but there was no time to think.

She had nearly lost the power to speak.

"It's New Year's day," she uttered, hardly able to get the words out as his hand kept up the pressure on her voice box.

"Yes, but it is something else as well. It is the day you pass through the gates of death on your way to hell. Your mortal longings for pain are over."

"No, no, no, no," she gasped, peeing in her pants, squirming to get away, but there was no hope, no chance to loosen his powerful grip.

"I owe the powers that created me a human life. And where is that human life? You are the one." His voice vibrated fiercely, the tone containing a glint of sardonic humor.

She tried to shake her head, kick out at him, wriggle away, but his smile was hideous, a cadaverously wan look.

"Not me, I am not your sacrifice… no please no…do it to someone else!" she managed to squeal out in a hardly audible cry.

This angered him to even greater rage, so murderous, so bloody that he lost all patience.

And by now his snout was so wolfish, his hunger so severe, he didn't bother with any further niceties; he made no small slits in her throat with his fangs, but bit off chunks of muscle from her neck, cutting deeply into veins and arteries, totally ripping away tendons and crunching the small vertebrae of her neck. He then sucked his fill, draining her of all her blood. As she lay lifeless on the grass he ripped off her soft leather miniskirt, threw her delicate panties onto a bush where they hung on a sharp thorn, took out his curved ugly shlong and then necro-raped her.

When finished, he carried her back to the front door and unceremoniously dumped her on the welcome mat. Now, filled with new energy from the young blood of this girl, he went over to the car and pulled out the listless body of the second girl, who had lost one of her fancy stiletto shoes somewhere along the line. He found it lying between the space of the front and back seat and threw it at the dead girl on the doorstep where it landed on what was left of her face. He had no appreciation for the beauty of this shoe, for the image and attitude that the stiletto girl was able to project with these multicolored peep toe pumps with the ribbon accent. All this was lost on him.

So he repeated his macabre bloody and sexual acts on the girl with one shoe, for all practical purposes cannibalizing the young thing. Since her heart had not pumped blood for some time he was forced to slash her open and sink his face into her belly to suck up the pooled blood, a mask of red dripping blood decorating his features. Then he took what was left of her, and discarded her atop the dead body of the first girl. He wanted the corpses to be found by the police along with the others inside, except for Phoenix whom he intended to kidnap.

To his way of thinking there was not one single reason that Bram had the right to give him orders. After all, he was the pure Vampire and should be head of the brotherhood, not Bram, a mere Dhampire. Why should Bram benefit from the fact that his forbears were in the line of the original Dracula. He saw no reason for this and by kidnapping Phoenix he would exchange her and her unborn son for the title of leader of the Brotherhood. If that didn't work, he would just keep Phoenix as his slave and the boy as his heir.

Now, as the sun rose higher on the first day of the New Year he went to a spigot at the side of the house to wash the dried blood and viscous body fluids off his face, first savoring every last drop that wasn't clotted by tonguing the still warm blood off his lips and cheeks with slithering movements of his long furry tongue. Only then did he wash his face.

Suddenly he felt the need for some rest, some digestion time before he began his main mission. He went back to the car and carefully folded his cloak to avoid wrinkles and laid it down on the passenger seat. He placed his top hat gently on the cloak, taking care not to disturb the shape of the brim. Then he went to the back patio and took a short snooze on the modular sofa.

Upon awakening he reviewed his plan. He had staked out this house for some days and knew of the way Lydia handled household things. For one, she stored a two gallon can of lighter fluid, used to get the barbecue briquettes started, on a shelf in the garage and it was this object he wished to steal first.

Once again he went over the plan of attack in his mind. He did not want to fight in the close quarters of the garage. After he got in to the house through the garage he would go right up to Josh and Phoebe's room. First the weakling Josh would be torn limb from limb, then the twin Phoebe would suffer the loss of those ultra-blue eyes of hers. He would gouge them out with his thumbs and while she was helpless he would thrash her body with the hickory stick and suck out every ounce of her blood. Then he intended to slash her with his claws and pee in her open belly before he raped her. Lydia would have to watch this before he set her afire, dousing her slowly with the inflammable liquid, setting her hair on fire first, watching her scream and then splashing the rest over her entire body until she burned to a crisp.

Of course he knew that Phoenix had some ability with the rapier. He had spied her practicing, teaching the art of fencing to Lydia and her sister, but she should be no problem. For one thing she waddled, her pregnancy having thrown off her equilibrium.

What he did care about was the element of surprise. He had waited long enough for this time to come and now he was ready. His footsteps were unhurried. He strolled to the side window of the garage; his internal radar told him this window was not wired by the security service as an entry point. He cut the side-screen, still clogged with raindrops from yesterday's storm and fog, and popped the swivel latch, slid up the window and wiggled through, pulling his newly acquired sword cane after him.

There was a motion detector in the garage, but he silenced this with ease growling softly as he did, his wolfish tendencies already beginning to show through. The can of lighter fluid lay open on a shelf and as he grabbed for it he heard another growl, one that did not stem from him.

Jeanne d'Arc was planted on all four paws in front of the entry door that led to the inside of the house. She presented a menacing obstacle, like a defensive lineman on a football team that said: 'You ain't getting past me buddy'. In his hype to gear himself up for the murders, Drakonius had forgotten all about her. Now she smelled his wolfishness and knew him as enemy, her guttural growl, a fierce low gruff sound, not yet loud enough to alert the insiders.

Drakonius withdrew his sword from the cane and as Jeanne d'Arc sprung at him, he swiveled and stabbed at her, meaning to strike her in the chest, but only connecting with one of her forepaws. He quickly withdrew the blade and made to strike at her again, but the brave dog bit him in the leg and he had to withdraw. Then the dog really started barking, loud enough for the neighbors to hear and Drakonius knew immediately that he had lost his element of surprise.

The first one through the entry door was Josh. He saw at once that Drakonius was encumbered by the sword cane in one hand and the can of lighter fluid in the other whilst

Jeanne d'Arc held him at bay.

Drakonius altered his plan. He screwed off the cap and squished some of the fluid out; aiming directly at the dog, who easily evaded the poisonous spray, leapt at Drakonius and this time was able to bite into a more secure chunk of his calf muscle, sinking her sharp teeth in deeply, not letting go. At the same time, Josh advanced and struck the man a resounding blow to the head, missing his chin by the barest of inches.

Unfazed, Drakonius swiped a blow backhanded at Josh, a blow so powerful that it propelled Josh's body head over heels, knocking him to the wall. Then he poured a good deal of the lighter fluid on top of Jeanne d'Arc's head causing her to let loose of her vice like grip on his leg. As soon as she did so, wriggling her head back and forth to shower off the fluid, Drakonius swiped his sword at her neck, intending to decapitate her, but Jeanne d'Arc was too fast, even with her wounded forepaw she was easily able to avoid the strike and immediately set herself up to attack again just as Phoebe, Lydia and Phoenix rushed in, Phoenix clasping the rapier, Phoebe holding the Hickory stick and Lydia brandishing the Taser. By this time Josh had regrouped and shouted:

"From all four sides, go at him from all four sides!"

The girls understood the tactic and in the small confines of the garage they advanced on Drakonius whose eyes stole from one to the other, unafraid, but now changing to a defensive stance.

He was perplexed. He sensed that Josh was no longer entirely human but was blended with Duplicant powers. This changed matters. This was not as he had perceived.

He let out a resounding wolf-howl that shook the rafters.

All four took a step back, even Jeanne d'Arc seemed to hesitate.

"Regroup," Josh shouted, "we've got him in our sights now!"

Surprisingly, it was Phoenix who made the first aggressive move, thrusting and parrying her rapier against the heavier sword held by Drakonius, who had to drop the open can to the floor in order to fight. She was much the better fencer and struck first, a lightening quick move to the chest that penetrated deeply, Drakonius wounded severely from the expert thrust which punctured his lung, a small target like red spot appearing immediately on his white shirt. At the same time Phoebe started to thrash him from behind with the hickory stick.

Stunned by the turn of events he nevertheless was able to recover; he rolled and twisted free, moved inside, grabbed Phoenix by her free wrist and snapped it in two, fracturing the bone completely, Phoenix reflexively dropping the rapier. She was about to faint sideways when her sister caught her, preventing a fall. Drakonius now placed one rigid hand over his wound, attempting to stem the flow of blood oozing forth at a faster rate with each breath he took, suffusing the front of his shirt entirely with dark blood. This protective act gave Lydia a clear sight at her mark. She fired the Taser on full at Drakonius who took the impact, reeled backwards but did not fall. Immediately Josh sprung at him, surprising Drakonius with his agility and strength and as he did so Jeanne d'Arc jumped at his throat while Lydia unloaded the rest of the power from the Taser at his back.

Josh hit him repeatedly with his fists, brutal blows, breaking his nose, but still not enough to knock him out, though he was dazed and only half conscious. With her one good hand Phoenix picked up the still more than half-filled can of lighter fluid, told the others to get out of the way and doused the Vampire killer completely with every last drop the large can contained.

"Let him have it sis, give it to him!" she shouted.

Then Phoebe lighted him up with the flint starter.

The blaze was immediate, the howls and screams horrific. He began to vaporize, then tried to transmogrify, a faded semblance, first of wolf, then of bat striving to appear in the flames of the blaze, all to no avail, in a matter of minutes Drakonius was reduced to a shrivel.

Chapter XXVII

As soon as Lydia finished suturing the wound to Jeanne d'Arc's front leg, she had one of her veterinary assistant's finish up the dressing and bandaging and the rest of the care. Then she took off for Cottage Hospital to see what was happening with Phoenix and the baby.

By the time she got there Phoenix had already been to surgery where she had been casted after two pins had been set in her wrist. Now she was on the OB floor and she ran into Phoebe.

"How is she?" Lydia asked, her face hollow, her voice trembling.

"The surgeon says she's okay, the wrist will take six weeks or so to heal. The problem is really the baby. Apparently the thread of life is there, he's hanging on, but just barely."

"My God, if the baby dies Phoenix will never get over it."

"I know. A neonatologist and a cardiologist are with her now, and an OB and an internist too. It'll be awhile till we can see her. You may as well sit down."

"I can't I'm too nervous."

Phoebe sees how unsettled and tremulous she is. She has long suspected that Lydia and her sister are more than friends.

"Howz the dog doing?" she asks, taking Lydia's hand, hoping to calm her down.

This move works, refocusing Lydia somewhat.

"All right I think, one of her tendons was cut entirely through and I had to suture that together. A lot of the soft tissue was destroyed so I had to remove all that, but she should repair nicely. The assistant finished up so I really don't know how she is now. I left orders to give her an antibiotic, a tetanus shot and a sedative, so I imagine she's asleep, hope so. How's Josh?"

"I heard from him just before you got here. The police are still interrogating, they found one of the dead girl's panties on a hedge out back of the house and they've already done a DNA scan of the cinders, all that's left of Drakonius, so they know that doesn't match with Josh, but it looks like they might take him in anyways."

"Whyever?"

"Because he's a Humilicant. Did you know that Lydia? I certainly didn't."

"I suspected as much. The way he handled himself during the battle with Drakonius, those long jumps of his, the blows he struck, they looked powerful to me."

"Yeah, he's changed in other ways too. I don't know if I like this new Josh as well, I'm tired of Jocks and Josh always seemed so tender, now he's lost that sensitivity around the edges."

Lydia thinks on this.

"Yes, I know what you mean, she says," then she breaks down again. "Oh, Phoebe, I love your sister so, I'm deathly afraid of what might happen to her if she loses the baby."

Phoebe comforts her, puts her arm around her, and holds her close.

At that moment the cardiologist and the neonatologist come out of Phoenix's room.

The cardiologist is not shy, speaks right up.

"The baby's heart rate is back to normal. I had to inject the heart directly with a rhythm stabilizing drug, looks like he's ok for now but my colleague here will have to monitor closely for the next twenty-four hours."

"Yes," the neonatologist says. "We've got your sister's abdomen all hooked up with the latest gadgets so she looks more like an electronic cable center than a pregnant woman, especially with that cast on her forearm, but she's really doing pretty well considering what she's been through."

"She told you what happened?"

"Most of it she told the hand surgeon; sounds like she went through a helluva fight. Anyway, we only asked the questions that were pertinent to her medical status and that of the baby."

"When can we go in to see her?" Lydia asks, a bit too querulous.

"Are you family?"

Before Lydia can answer, Phoebe pipes up: "She's my older sister."

"Sure, no problem. It's up to the OB, ask him when he comes out."

"Thank you, for that," Lydia says to Phoebe after the doctors leave.

"No problem, it's not all that much really. I must admit I was jealous of you at first. I thought you were taking Feeny away from me, now it seems more like I have really gained an older sister. So in that sense it wasn't a lie."

Lydia is moved deeply, Phoebe has just touched her soul; her hands have stopped shaking and her voice has lost that tense emotional quiver. Phoebe's lie has spawned a new bond between the two, their common love for Phoenix sealing the new relationship.

∞

At the station Josh is asked to give a semen sample. It is necessary to compare his seminal fluid with that of the semen found in the vaginas of the two dead girls. The problem is that he can't seem to masturbate successfully, to come forward with an ejaculation. He smiles grimly at this prospect, for just some days beforehand he had had the opposite problem.

The issue is resolved by the new technology.

The medical examiner, who is a pathologist, has a urinary catheter capable of extracting semen from the seminal vesicles without injuring the tissues along the way. It is directed through the channel by neutrino impulses that seek out only the tissue for which it is coded, in this case the epididymis and seminal vesicles.

The readout shows no match and after some further questioning, which proves he has had no connection whatsoever with either of the two dead girls, Josh is released on his own recognizance, but warned not to leave the city of Santa Barbara until the judge no longer considers him a 'person of interest' in the murders.

Upon being detained, the officers had driven him in a police van from Lydia's to the station, and now he needs a ride back to the house. When he asks the detective in charge for a ride, he is told the police car cannot be used to transport anyone who is no longer a suspect: 'especially a Humilicant,' he adds sarcastically.

Josh is left having to pay for a taxi.

∞

In the third week of the New Year, at Vladg's crowded apartment in Amersfoort, there is celebration. Hikey has won a seat in Parliament, by the narrowest of margins, as the junior senator representing Gelderland, unseating Rümke, the man from Apeldoorn; the senior incumbent, Senator Karel Jonkheere (whose great-great-grandfather was a translator of Rudyard Kipling's works) not having been up for reelection this term.

All of the major newspapers, worldwide, have taken up the story. Not only politicians, but economists, philosophers, and even historians are having a field day, spelling out their essays and editorials on the meaning of her election to the future definition of what is human, what is humanoid and what will be the result of this incursion over time; politically, morally, ethically.

Vladg could care less. He is happy for her but wants to get laid. However, nothing of the sort is going to happen this night. Now that she is a recognized politician with duties and obligations to the people, especially her Veluwe constituency in Gelderland, he is having a rough time getting her alone and in the right mood. So toasting with champagne, he hopes to get rid of Mieke and a consortium of other hangers on from the Green Link party. Someone opens another bottle and then one after that and the huzzahs and hurrahs continue until the wee hours. When a new case of champagne is hauled up the staircase by her aide de camp, Vladg gives up and goes over to talk to Greet and Geri who are there with Joost and Dusty. They are not talking politics but are into trips to Greece and then the Peloponnesians for honeymoons together after Dusty and Geri find time to get married.

Vladg feels out of place listening to this stuff as well, though he is happy for the two couples, so when his T-cell rings he is anxious to get over to a quieter nook in his bedroom. He answers the phone on the third ring.

It is Lydia who wants to know what all the fuss and racket she hears is about. Vladg tells her that they are having a celebration for Hikey.

"I thought that was old news."

"Not here in Holland, they stretch things a bit."

"Oh. Well, I wanted to tell you about Phoenix and the baby. She was in hospital for ten days after the fiasco with Drakonius and finally I've brought her home. She and the baby are doing well."

"I'm really glad to hear that, Lydia. We plan to be there for the delivery."

"Can you get free from work for that long of a trip?"

"Should be right around Easter, I get school vacation. That's when we plan to marry in London and come to Southern California for our honeymoon. Hikey's never been to the States and wants to see what it's like."

"Might work. If Phoenix's expected date pans out as predicted, you two should be here around the time she delivers."

"Hopefully."

"Something else. I've spoken to Bram," she says, "and he contends that he had nothing to do with the attacks by Drakonius, but I don't believe him. I'm sure he is lying."

"I'd see it that way. He just doesn't want you and Phoenix to think so. I'm sure he still intends to take Phoenix away from you, one way or the other."

"He'll find that difficult. I have a legal injunction against him; no way can he get anywhere near me."

"Lydia, think a minute. Legalities have never prevented Bram from getting what he wants. Be careful. I don't think much will happen until her due date draws near, but then you'd better have people there who can protect you and Phoenix. Go to a detective agency; hire a slew of them if you must, Humilicants or Duplicants, whichever can protect you best…"

"NO, I know how to handle Bram. He'd never hurt Phoenix and that's my protection. Anyway he promised I would be the Anti-Godmother, he can't go back on that, not in the eyes of Satan, so there."

"I think you're wrong. Over here I've seen what Bram is capable of…even though you've been married to him all these years, I don't think you know him, not since the pregnancy anyway, he's a different sort of Vampire than the one you used to joke and pal with."

"I know I can't trust him, its …okay…let me think it over. Maybe I will hire some bodyguards; a few Basics like George should do it."

"Good. That makes me feel better. I've got to go; someone here is pulling at me to have another drink."

"Okay, I'll let you go. Give my congratulations to Hikey."

"Sure will. Bye.

"Bye-bye."

∞

At his farm in Oneonta, Bram was once again furious beyond belief. Nothing was working right for him, neither here or in Dolno Katore. The group of New Corinthians did seem to be making headway, gathering more and more souls to their clique of radicals, all a consequence of the efforts of Edna Kincaid, a woman who was poorly educated, barely literate. How could this be? And his project in Seneca Falls was not moving along as fast as he had hoped. Even worse, at his home in Dolno Katore, the populace was out of sorts, not given over to attending black mass; all because of feeble leadership by Malignius. No, nothing was going right there either.

As to his own powers, ever since he became a fallen idol in Greta's eyes, he no longer felt in control of that harmony of dissonance that had for so long a time been his strongest suit, his forte, his ability to alter others' destiny. And the incineration of Drakonius, a total waste. He had counted on him to succeed where Malignius, in a similar venture, was unsuccessful, yet he too had failed miserably. Phoebe had survived. She was not transformed to Vampirism as he had requested. No, to the contrary; not only was Phoebe alive and kicking, but in the ensuing days she seemed to have managed to influence Eiselman a good deal by revealing all that had transpired in Santa Barbara. The last few times he had contacted Eiselman and signaled him with his name…Alucard… it had had no visible effect. Somehow Phoebe's gossip was able to disarm him, to reduce the intensity of the spell he had cast over her boss. *'Of course spells do wear off'*, but he had been particularly cautious with this one, using Pavlovian techniques at frequent intervals in his T-cell calls to reinvigorate the spell, to actually lift it to new heights of Eiselman's awareness, especially on business matters. Now all seemed lost.

Phoebe remained a bigger thorn in his side than he had ever thought imaginable. She was able to thwart his plans, his desires. How could this be? *'She is beautiful, but otherwise a mere nothing, a dopey blond female with no sense of purpose, totally unlike her sister'*.

It seemed he would have to take the bull by the horns and do the job himself. Timing! Timing was of the essence. He had to wait until Phoenix's due date, now predicated as the 25th of April. There was something odd about that date. He could not place it but he sensed it had another meaning. What was it? Oh well, it would probably come to him later, when he was not trying to think of it.

Anyway he had not much choice. There was no use in pretending. He had to be there for the delivery and he was sure that Phoebe would attend as well. That would be his time. Somehow her eyes had to be taken care of first, gouged out, blind as the undead, without them her power over men, her ability to attract them would be lost and she would more easily become the slave he needed to take Greta's place. With her by his side that left him no choice; Lydia must be done away with as well. *'I could not abide her intensity after the baby is born'.* Perhaps during the ceremony when she becomes the Anti-Godmother, yes, that would be a good time, a sword in the form of an inverted cross striking right through her heart should do it, with a dedication of her soul as an offering to Satan.

Yes, yes indeed, her heart has put out a great deal of love over the years, but that love was for others, not for me. She never considered how much that affected me. Did the relationship mean anything to her, the palsy-walsy, the jokes, and the mechanical sex? Bram could not think of one solitary thing in recent years…not since she had acquired Vladg as a companion…that showed she cared. Yes, she had detached herself from him and now she herself would be detached from this earth, for as long as it rotated around the sun. 'That would be satisfactory, no arguments against that, no reason to fight with myself over doing away with her eternity'.

Yes, there was much to be arranged. He wanted Phoenix to deliver at the house with Lydia as the midwife. If the baby were born at Cottage he would have much less opportunity to spirit the child away, to be in control. This required planning, an emergency at the hospital, creating darkness, shutting off the electricity…just in the OB ward…he could not close down the children's ward, no that would be sinful even in Satan's eyes.

He decided to walk out to the bunkhouse, to see how the Duplicants were coming along now that the construction was complete. Half way there he stopped walking, his shadow shifted, he thought of Gregoriev. Yes, there was no such thing as a true love potion, but there was something else. His mother had taught him how to make the opposite concoction, and though he hadn't put it together in more than a century he was sure he still knew how. Yes, that should work. It was a way to close down the OB ward without causing alarm to other parts of the hospital. Now he turned his dark face, his sepia colored eyes, back toward the main house.

His thumb began to ache, but he refused to pay attention to the pain, in a strange way he enjoyed it, it crystallized his thoughts on Phoebe, made it easier for him to consider what she had coming to her. Perhaps he should stop thinking about these things for now? Was there something unknown waiting for him?

He stared at the grass stains on his shoes. The fractured rooftops of a house in the distance reflected back into his eyes. He waited, feeling the stillness of winter, the sadness of the earth.

Back in the house he stretched out on the couch, gazed absently at the roses and carnations set in a vase on the coffee table. His anger was subdued; his fury had dissipated. Had he forgotten something primal? He searched his mind but could not locate it.

He had nothing more to say to himself at this time. Nothing more at all.

Chapter XXVIII

Six weeks before her due date, Phoenix was walking around the house with a book balanced on her head. She was trying to maintain a semblance of good posture and equilibrium as the waddling of pregnancy was an insult to her pride. While Lydia thought the penguin waddle was cute, giggled at her antics, Phoenix was more serious. She knew that if she kept this book balancing habit going it would help her to regain her figure and prior stature after the baby was born.

Lydia called out to her. She was busy sending out formal invitations to friends and family for the baby shower and wanted to know the address of a favorite cousin living in Minnesota. Even in 2059 it was frowned upon to send invitations electronically. So the embossed invitations were printed professionally and sent by snail mail in order to maintain the correct degree of etiquette. There were two odd things about the invitations. One was that Phoenix had instructed the printer to put a light gray subdued illustration of a crucifix and picture of St. Joseph on the verso side of the card. Also enclosed with the invitation was a gift registry for a baby boy and even on this Phoenix had insisted that the crucifix and St. Joseph pic be inserted underneath the text.

The other oddity was much more fun. The theme they had decided on was to hold the baby shower on Shrove Tuesday {Mardi Gras, Fat Tuesday} so that all the girls could eat and drink as much as they wished and not feel guilty about it until the next day when Lent hit. The caterers would provide all the goodies, loot bags, caramels and candies of all sorts, and of course pancakes and Belgian waffles, both topped with caviar embedded in a variety of delicate jellies and creams plus Champagne to gulp down the snacks. The invitations did not stipulate costumes and masks, but said the girls were welcome to make as much a carnival atmosphere of the day as they liked. Phoenix was thrilled with the idea; she knew this would be her last 'fling' so to speak before her due date in forty-seven days from Fat Tuesday. Dr. Maloff, her OB, had told her she had to come in once a week for a checkup during these last six weeks.

Since it was to be an all-girl shower, Lydia had hired three female BASIC III's named Georgette I, II, and III to serve as bodyguards and security for the day. Lydia had invited her entire staff which was okay with Phoenix as she knew them all fairly well from her work at the clinic. The staff was entirely female in any case and Phoenix actually felt better about their presence than some of her own distant relatives with whom she had so little in common.

Phoenix's mom had insisted that invitations be sent to all the nieces, aunties and girlfriends in Michigan and Nebraska; this irritated Phoenix no end because she only wanted those women to come whom she really liked. Needless to say, she gave in to her mother on this suggestion.

"Don't worry," Lydia said, "the Michiganders may send a present but the majority won't make the trip. Your mother knows that!"

"I'm sure she does. I just wish the people I care most about would attend, I don't need extra presents, I want it to be a memorable time for us, you, me, Phoebe and the baby."

"Well Phoebe's coming with Jennifer," Lydia said. "She can be d'Artagnan."

Indeed, Phoebe was making the trip accompanied by Jennifer, and George, of course, who was by her side for protection practically everywhere she went these days. George had recently been re-programmed and was now the most sophisticated BASIC III imaginable. Mr. Eiselman felt indebted to Phoebe, who tactically, had helped him get out from under Bram's controlling spell. As a benefit he now allowed Phoebe to have an almost entirely free reign over George and was willing, to add any features to the Basic that Phoebe thought might help protect them both. When Mr. Eiselman told her there would be no charge for the repair, she decided to go on the wheel herself rather than do the disc thing. So George now had a humanoid urinary and fecal waste system installed and could show off his personalized sex drive apparatus as well. This last system was accomplished only after much consideration and long discussions with Lydia who had had prior experience with this sort of thing when Vladg was programmed to be her companion.

Josh had been against the idea from the first and protested vigorously, but in the end he lost out. Phoebe tried to explain to him that she felt sorry for George ever since the night that Bram tore away half his face and he had lost control over his toiletry. The other point was that Eiselman had promised George to Phoebe. as a wedding present, and Josh knew this. He didn't like the idea one iota. It meant that George would be living with them after the marriage.

Although it was in his job description to help out, the upgrade on George was actually done without his participation. Josh simply refused to take part in any aspect of the process. When Phoebe went on the H-W wheel to project her imaginative sexual wishes and desires into George, Josh was as jealous as if she were cheating on him with another man. He himself never admitted any of this to Phoebe but it was obvious to her from his body language. She knew that he had changed immensely since his own transformation into a Humilicant. In fact, he now worked out at least three times a week, something he had always hated to do when she had previously implored him to go to the gym with her.

Now, by contrast, he was working out regularly in the evenings with his buddies. Then too, he had recently become a Knicks fan, going to every basketball game he could afford with his former roommate Billy Lakehomer. Tickets were at a premium as the Knicks were world champions, having defeated powerhouse Sydney, Australia team for the crown, the third season in a row. They had tiffs on this as Phoebe thought it was an unnecessary extravagance, a waste of their money.

The short of it was that his entire life style was changing by the day; he was a different Josh and Phoebe wasn't at all sure she loved this one as much. In addition, Mr. Eiselman had called him to task for a lack of diligence on several research projects, and of course Phoebe was privy to this information.

To a degree Josh felt that his increased muscular strength and sexual abilities did correspond to a decrease in his creative powers, in his focused intellect. On the other hand, he had enjoyed immensely the feeling of power derived when breaking Drakonius's nose, the crunch of his fist against cartilage and bone was exhilarating. In fact, he wished he could have done more along those lines before the battle ended. In all honesty, he looked forward to his next chance to smash someone else's face in if the opportunity presented itself.

Even so there was another side to all this. It seemed as if Phoebe and Mr. Eiselman were ganging up on him. He began to suspect Eiselman had more designs on Phoebe than were warranted as his personal secretary. The fact that Mr. Eiselman had recently gone through a publicized divorce added to Josh's theory that something extracurricular was going on behind closed doors, something other than a healthy secretarial-boss relationship. He was distrustful, not wanting to get overly paranoid, but figured the situation bore watching. He was not impulsive, told himself to wait for more confirmatory evidence of any hanky-panky before getting too suspicious. But if he ever caught them in an embrace, *'What a thrill it would be to punch Mr. Eiselman in the nose'.*

In all fairness, he had to admit that soon after his e-jack operation he had started to look at other women with lust in his eyes, something he had never thought possible after hooking up with Phoebe, his dream girl. In the sack, his object of desire during lovemaking was now more often Jennifer than Phoebe. It was Jennifer he thought of when trying to get a hard on and Jennifer's more robust figure that he saw when he finally was able to come, which wasn't easy for him in any case.

Then he felt guilty for thinking of Jennifer while he was in bed with Phoebe and wished he had never had the operation at all. He had considered reversing the e-jack, and was about to do so, when Phoebe announced that George was eventually to be hers. This is what irritated him more than anything. Why on earth would she want George to know and feel her most intimate sexual impulses and desires? He blamed Lydia; ever since the two had been so close things had changed, and not for the better.

'Was it really so bad that he had had premature ejaculation?' "You're damn right, it was," he mumbled, answering his own question. Phoebe had made him feel insecure as all get out, but now he felt worse, not insecure, but unappreciated. 'Whatever did she want? There was just no satisfying a woman!'

∞

On Fat Tuesday, more people came from the mid-west to the baby shower than either Phoenix or Lydia had expected, so they were lucky the caterers had the capacity to expand the drinks and munchies to twenty-five, from fifteen which had been the original estimate.

Luckily the day was clear, a blue sky with a few low hanging clouds, the air cold and brisk but stimulating and invigorating for early March. Per Lydia's instructions the caterers had brought colorfully designed masks, diverse shapes and colors, for those girls who were not so inclined or were not costumed. Most of the recalcitrants changed their minds and went along with the spirit of the day, selecting their choice, trying on different masks, matching carefully, mostly hoping not to clash colors, but to coordinate with their shoes whenever possible. So there was a bit of a department store melee at the table holding the various types of masks, but overall the girls were high spirited.

Everyone wanted to look mysterious in their own fashion and a good deal of the early part of the chatting up had to do with revealing identities and exposing secrets. George was the only exception in the group, a male like figure that most of the girls doted over whilst he himself appeared to be taken with Georgette II rather than any of the human females.

Phoebe, Phoenix and Lydia were dressed as the Three Musketeers and of course Phoenix was easily recognizable due to her waddle and eight-month belly, but she went along with the game gallantly and was determined to have fun on this day. She wore a brightly colored cape draped carelessly over her back, a Scotsmen's plaid kilt like affair substituting for a miniskirt, a dashing yellow blouse with lantern sleeves, knee high boots and, of course, her sword cane which she displayed in a fencing performance with her sister as an act of sorts to show off her agility for the girls.

Lydia, dressed as Aramis, did not forget to wear her amulet (*kemi'a*) of the demon Pazuzu, which she believed protected the lying-in mother and her child against witchcraft and the evil eye by warding off witches, wiccans and werewolves, calming down vampires and controlling other demons. Now she cradled the onyx stoned amulet in her hand, murmured a small prayer to Lucifer asking that no pain be given to the gravid mother here this day and that no harm be done to the unborn child, to which she herself was destined to be Anti-Godmother. Then she smiled, felt that her ancient debt to Satan had been paid; turned to greet one of the new guests and faced her world as if there were no other forces at work.

Two of the girls from Berkeley brought their guitars and played some old fashioned Elvis songs while another from L.A. did a fair imitation of Jimi Hendrix, still revered, and Stevie Vaughan. This set the tone for the shower and everyone felt free to kick up their heels, or to relax and enjoy.

The festivities were at high amperage when three scantily clad young women crashed the party. They all wore their own masks, stampeded right in, but neglected to sign the guest book. No one paid much attention except for one of the girls from the vet clinic who was taking her turn at the front door asking new arrivals to sign in.

On his own, Malignius had sent Iphigènie, Athalie and Phaedra to the baby shower, thinking that this would make up for his failure at Greet's wedding and that Bram would be pleased with his surprise 'gift'.

After a while, the three Vampires did attract some attention as they were speaking in a foreign tongue in long sibilant sounds to one another, trying to figure out which 'morsels' to choose and how to divide them up, there were just too many, even for their strong appetites.

When one of the girls from the clinic came over to show them the whereabouts of the food table on the terrace there was a commotion. Phaedra made a grab for her, but to her surprise, George immediately appeared accompanied by Georgette II. They stopped Phaedra in her tracks, waving a large crucifix and brandishing a Taser. Athalie saw this and immediately went over to the food table, her nostrils bubbling with snot, and with her powerful throwing arm, she completely overturned the heavy table, the food, goodies and drinks scattering every which way. Georgette II snapped off a shot at Phaedra which went right through her body, the ray striking the opposite wall, while George engaged Athalie who totally ignored the large silver crucifix he was swinging at her. She grabbed it from him, ran over to the hearth and picked up the poker, which she threw at George with amazing accuracy.

The sharp point of the poker embedded itself in George's mechanical heart, stopping him in his tracks. Then Phaedra transformed herself into a giant bat and started to dive bomb some of the girls who by now realized this was not make believe, not a planned part of the party, they started to scream, squirm and squeal. All this was contrived by the Sisters to upset the ambience, to create a diversion, and while everyone focused on what was happening to George and wishing the bat would get caught up in the blades of the overhead fan, Iphigènie did her thing. She cast aside her mask, the holes in her eye sockets now totally visible, flickering light backwards toward the girls who gasped and cried out in fear and wonderment.

Then, in one smooth movement, she stepped out of the sheer sheath like adornment that had served as a covering to her translucence and leaped head first into Phoenix's large pregnant belly, not entering her soul, but merging completely with the boy-child, the fetus.

Almost immediately Phoenix swooned, her face, which had been round and rosy, sagged completely into a sad and sullen looking vestige of herself. At that same moment the bat flew outside picked up Athalie's floating ghostlike form in her claws, flapped her wings one or two more times and then they both disappeared.

At once Lydia was by Phoenix's side. She ripped off the kilt like affair Phoenix had been wearing, and there to the left side of her belly, evident for all to see, was a large bruise, the color of which at first appeared to be crimson, but then turned rapidly to blue, and in a few more seconds to black and blue. There was no doubt about its shape, it was the imprint of a baby's foot and like a kettle drum that was being played from the inside, one could see the skin of Phoenix's belly recoiling from the blows.

There was no question in anyone's mind that the baby, having been invaded by an alien force, was trying to kick himself out of the womb. As the thumps grew stronger, the poundings more deafening, the skin pulled tighter, becoming less resilient, the moans of the semiconscious Phoenix increased with each percussive blow. Something had to be done. If this went on much longer it would kill Phoenix as the uterus would rupture. She would die from internal hemorrhage. What to do?

Surprisingly, it was Phoenix's mom who came to the rescue.

She started to sing a hymn from church, "Abide With Me" and as she did so the kicks of the baby appeared to lessen a bit, then she switched to: "Are you Washed in the Blood", and one of the girls from Berkeley took up her acoustic guitar and accompanied her, which seemed to settle the kicks down even more, and when she started "Amazing Grace" many of the girls began to sing with her, like a choir in church, and this worked. Iphigenia's curious head came poking out from beneath Phoenix's popped out belly button. The diaphanous head seemed to be stuck there, covered with some of the baby's amniotic fluid and bits and pieces of the membrane. The ugly mottled head wriggled and rolled but made no headway. Her mouth opened, she hissed a slow mournful dirge of improvised song, as if she was striving to sing a funeral hymn. When this failed she garbled some words out, asking what was going on, the pitch of her croaking voice once again at such low ebb, the frequency so slow, that the words seemed to travel through the air at an exceedingly low rate.

Lydia was the hero here; she grabbed the protruding head and narrow neck, pulled the rest of Iphigenia's slippery form out of Phoenix's womb. Iphigènie immediately squeezed out of the hold and at once scratched away the membranous remnants from her emaciated face with her talon like fingernails, an exact repeat of the action she had done centuries ago when emerging from her own grave pit. Then, in a similar manner to that of Phaedra she seemed to float off in a blur and disappeared completely.

But Phoenix was not out of the woods. Neither was the baby whose pulse was hammering away at a frighteningly high rate.

While the baby's head had not yet dropped into the pelvic birth canal, the almost completely developed eight-month fetus had been normally positioned; now the plunging entrance and sudden exit of Iphigènie had caused the baby to alter its occiput anterior alignment within the womb to one of side-to-side. This is why the kicks, influenced with the force of Iphigenia's will, were so effective, so dangerous to the mother.

There was no way anyone could deliver the baby in this position unless the delivery was made into a Caesarean, which Phoenix was firmly against. She knew from both Bram and Lydia that during the anesthesia Satan could much more easily indoctrinate the child, create a destructive influence on the boy's first breath that would be everlasting. There had to be a way, a procedure of reversion, of returning the baby to its normal head first position.

As soon as the melee with Phaedra had occurred, Jennifer had had the wherewithal to call for an airbulance and it had now arrived. The Air-Scoot happened to land on the selfsame spot where Drakonius had raped and killed the leather miniskirted girl, an ill omen. Indeed, there was an immediate spate of words, between Lydia and Phoenix's mother as to whom would be allowed to go with Phoenix in the ambulance.

"I'm her mother for heaven's sake!"

"I'm her lover…"

"Whatever do you mean…?"

"Exactly what I said. I intend to marry her, as soon as she recovers from the birthing…"

"Ladies, ladies, if you keep this up, we'll take off without either one of you!"

"All right," Lydia said, "you go, I love her enough to forego…"

She never got to finish her sentence. Phoenix's mom touched her gently on the forearm, a gesture of understanding, and stepped inside the cabin with the paramedic in attendance. With a sudden whirr the Air-Scoot took off for Cottage Hospital.

On the way, hooked up to the Z-brane Cardiac and Respiratory controller, Phoenix realized she had not had the chance to open one single present.

Chapter XXIX

Dreams and Reflections

Phoenix had already been in hospital for ten days when she first thought of it. Before this her main concern was for his life, and hers, would they make it, would there be physical defects? That sort of worry; now that the doctors had pronounced them safe on all those scores the situation was different; her concern was directed to the baby's future.   Just how much had the baby been tainted by Iphigènie? Was the child already indoctrinated… schooled into evil in the satanic sense? *Iphigènie had only inhabited my womb for a short time, but was that the issue'? Was time the deciding factor?*

She knew from the rapidity with which Bram had overwhelmed her that a vampire was capable of performing their evil tasks very quickly. Certainly Bram had impregnated her with such celerity that she was hardly aware of it, except for the dream, the dream that brought her so close to death rather than to fulfill her role in life as a mother. No this was her child, the Winthrop blood flowing in his veins had to have something to say about it, the pride to fight off the stench of evil, if nothing else.

What harm had been done to her beloved child? The only way to know was to communicate with Bram. Lydia had already told her that she thought this to be unwise, that once she started to ask Bram questions, to seek his help, he would be able to regain power over her, to become her Master once again. What to do? There didn't seem to be any other options. Yes, Lydia was a vampire, and had had her own rough times in the beginning, from Bram and other vampires in Ireland, but she never became a member of the sisterhood; she never suffered the stigma of being penetrated by the undead form of a vampire like Iphigènie. *No, Lydia never had any of the confirmed powers that were so important, powers that could help me at the moment.*

She had made up a story to tell the doctors. They never would have believed the truth that miracles come in two forms, one of darkness, one of light. She saw that the doctors wrote down her story simply as a belief by the patient that a corpus alienum (foreign body) had penetrated her body, but there was no entry or exit hole to verify this. So they called in a shrink who diagnosed a Temporary Impulsive Delusional Syndrome and that was that. She decided not to press the issue.

Ten days! Dr. Paul Maloff had stood by her through all the treacherous times of her pregnancy, had given in to her requests and refusals. Not many OB's would have put up with her, but he did, and now this, He had turned the baby twice, externally, not using the turning power of the Z-brane ray merely because she had asked him not to do high-tech. Of course, she hadn't told him about Iphigènie, that would be beyond the set of his doctor's mind, but he knew that she had swooned, that her blood pressure had reached dangerously low levels, that the baby's pulse rate had exceeded two hundred beats per minute, so all those factors were enough for him to tolerate her refusal of the use of high tech rays to turn the baby. But he had been right. Each time the baby was turned mechanically, the position had reverted to side-to-side within twenty-four hours. So she had finally succumbed to his wishes. He hadn't threatened to give up on her as his patient like so many other doctors would have done; nothing like that, but he had said that this technique was the last resort. If this maneuver failed she would have to undergo a Caesarean, and for reasons of her own she certainly did not want that procedure.

So she had allowed the penetrating Z-brane rays to turn the baby, followed by the additional administration of much less intensive frequencies, given in millisecond intervals, delivered to the womb to hold the baby's head (left occiput anterior) in place. That was why she lay on her back, lightly sedated, trying not to make any sudden moves as Dr. Maloff had said that any jarring movement might disturb the child and even with the restraining rays acting like ropes, binding him to the proper position, he could kick himself back into an abnormal alignment at any time.

Dr. Maloff had explained that the low dose sedatives would not cause harm to the fetus but would help to keep the baby still so that if it did kick and roll a bit, the effect would not loosen the power of the rays holding him artificially bound, not immobilized, merely aligned in the correct position. She had been against any sedation of any kind, but the sad experience of the two mechanical turning maneuvers being unsuccessful had convinced her to allow the drugs to help and now she was constantly dozing off, dreaming all sorts of things, waking up and then falling into sleep again, vivid dreams, dreams that seemed so real.

Now, though still lightly sedated, she had been off the machine for the last forty-eight hours and was holding her own. The baby's kicks were of the sort that any mother could sustain without harm. Dr. Maloff said this was a good sign, quite normal. She thought so too, was glad he had used the word 'normal'.

Feeby called her every day of course; sometimes more than once a day. As her vacation days had run out, Feeby had returned to Manhattan as soon as the doctors took her sister off the critical condition list. She wanted to save her family leave time, to be present for the due date when the baby actually arrived. She really was in to the Aunty thing, wanted to help out in any way she could. Feeny had named her the Godmother even though Lydia had some crazy notion of being the Anti-Godmother, 'whatever that was taken to mean'.

She and Lydia had had a minor falling out due to the maid's complaints. The maid was a Basic II and had a lot of empathy for George which Phoebe understood, since she and George had been so close. The problem was George, still stuck in the living room like a statue, the ends of the poker sticking out of his torso, front and back, remained a scary sight. The maid had to vacuum around him. She complained about this to Lydia who called Phoebe and said that she wanted George put into storage. Phoebe, over the T-cell, tried to explain that she didn't have the money at the present time to hire an electric welder to cut off the ends of the poker so that George could be moved, as he wouldn't fit into a regular sized box this way.

The airlines could not accept him as a passenger in this inert form and so George was designated as cargo which was three times the cost of a passenger ticket. Mr. Eiselman, who had otherwise given Phoebe wide range with George, was adamant on this point; he did not see why he should be responsible for the airline charge. In fact, he said he was getting tired of George's problems and was considering the creation of an entirely new Basic III to serve as his valet. For the last ten days Phoebe had been the one serving tea.

Feeby's phone calls left all this out as she did not wish to bother Feeny with her George problems. So at first she stuck to the normal sisterly questions on how Feeny and the baby were doing, but just at the point that she was about to switch gears it was Feeny who asked about the shower.

"Was it a total failure, what are they saying about it?"

"I talked to mom and you know sometimes she has some pretty good ideas"

"What did she say?"

"She said that in a danger situation, once you are safe and sound, people like to tell others that they were part of it, the 'I was there', and 'I remember' phenomenon. Then after a while a lot of people go so far as to lie about it and pretty soon there'll be fifty people, rather than twenty-five, who attended your shower with the faeries, that's what they're calling them."

"She's got something there."

"Yeah, every once in a great while mom says some pretty wise stuff. Anyhoo,

Y'know those situations where some deranged guy goes off and starts shooting people willy-nilly, once you are out of harm's way it's kind of a coup to have been present, something to brag about."

"So that's the way my guests are looking back at it?"

"NO, maybe that was a bad analogy on my part hon; everyone said it was the most exciting baby shower they ever attended…"

"You're sure?"

"Really! And they loved the party atmosphere, the masks and costumes and even our Three Musketeers get-up."

"What about the food, those caterers were expensive."

"Well until that one Vamp upset the food table they said it was great, especially the caviar topping on the Belgian waffles, which went over big."

"Thx Feeb, I feel better about it now."

"I thought you didn't care that much what other people said about social affairs?"

"It changes Feeb, I'm almost a mother now and I worry about all sorts of different things."

"Well I'm not peegee but I'm worried about Josh."

"Tell me."

"You're certain the docs have given you a clean bill of health, I don't want to get you needlessly worried about my problems…"

"Why not, we've always been peanuts that way, two in one shell."

"Okay, here's what's going on."

Phoebe started in on all the changes she had detected in Josh since the baby shower. First off was the fact that she suspected he was *'taken'* with Jennifer, because the two stayed out so late at Pyrell's, drinking coffee in the 80th floor cafeteria. "Sometimes he doesn't get home from work until way past seven o'clock."

"But I thought you and Jennifer were close, she came out to the shower on the Sub-Orb with you, if I remember correctly."

"Yes, but I shot off my mouth a little too much to her on the trip, we were drinking Tequila Sunshine, and you know how I get on Tequila, anyway sex came up and I told her how much Josh was improved, that I was having real long orgasms one right after the other. Maybe that attracted her to Josh, I don't know.

Phoenix liked the girly gossip. It took her mind off the seriousness of her own condition. Now she recalled the shy and hesitant ways of Josh when she had deceived him at the cafeteria. She told her sis not to worry, that as far as she knew Josh was not a womanizer, not the type to pull anything like that. "It's probably just the work. Like you said Pyrell's has started a new project on miniaturization…. remember you told me how busy everyone was with that."

"That's true, but there's something I haven't told you, something I've been afraid to ask…I didn't want to burden you."

"I'm already a burdened woman."

"See what I mean."

"Oh honey, you know you can ask me anything…"

"Well I thought I'd wait until you got out of the hospital…"

"C'mon sis, now you've got me so curious…? I'm your older sister… "

 "By seven minutes."

"You have to tell me! What is it?"

"Well, remember when you were going with that basketball jock?"

"Sure. Never forget it, what a trip…

"Well, did he ever take you when you didn't want to. Y'know when you were not in the mood and he kinda forced you?"

Phoenix thinks for a moment, then she remembers vividly.

"I have to say yes, he tried one time, nearly got in too but I pushed him off me. We had both been drinking some, doing a bit of Ubiquity, but as I remember it he was a lot higher than I was, anyway, I was in no mood for sex as I thought it would spoil my own good high, so I pushed him off me just as he was about to penetrate."

"See. That's what happened to me."

"With Josh?"

"Yes, he's so strong now and I swear his cock has grown, certainly thicker if not lengthwise; anyway he penetrated me against my will. I was in no mood whatsoever for sex and, to be honest, like I said I haven't been very high on him lately, so I told him NO, no-no…no."

"And"

"He paid no attention whatsoever. In a way you could say he raped me. The problem was I began to respond in a vague distant sort of way, just moving my hips a bit, I don't know why. I'd never been screwed that hard before, so even if he didn't *'let me in'* know what I mean?"

"Yes, yes…go on"

"Even if he never let me be a part of what was happening, and simply used me like a Mexican wife, it was a different set of sensations. I can't say it was enjoyable, but it was a taste of evil."

"That's it exactly, a taste of evil, that's what I felt with Bram the one night we were together and he impregnated me… did you have bad dreams?"

"No not right then, but for nights afterward I did. I don't know if you can call them nightmares, but I do wake up in the middle of the night, usually to go potty, but then I manage to get back to sleep."

'Listen Feeb, Dr. Maloff and a resident just walked in. I think he's going to let me go home day-after-tomorrow, that'll be ninety-six hours off the machine and the baby has stayed put. He's getting antsy, wants to check me, let you know, okay."

"Just this one more thing!"

"Yes?"

"I haven't been to bed with Josh since."

"Uh-oh. I don't know what to say, call you tomorrow."

"Sure, luv'ya."

"Luv'ya."

∞

In Oneonta Bram was a barely recognizable, much thinner, version of his old self. His formerly trim moustache was measurably thicker and he had altered his hair style considerably, wearing it much longer. There was no longer any semblance of a beard, and he had modulated his voice. He had completely abandoned his Balkan accent for a softer French tone. He looked and felt much younger in the brisk, still snowy and windy days of March in central New York than he had in southern California.

At this moment he was putting his concoctions together, preparing his surprise. There were two different potions. One was to be a spray, the other a drink. He needed all fresh ingredients and some of the items had come from as far away as Indonesia, that was the strawberry colored poison dart frog (Dendrobates pumilio) and the Golden Dart frog (Phyllobates terribilis) from Colombia plus finely ground rose quartz, jade, and unakite, the fertility elixir from Romania. Egypt had provided a variation of Tanis root which promoted daydreams. He was careful to weigh the drams of each ingredient and he was fastidious in the sequence in which he put them together.

Once the real work was done, he added a variety of herbs to disguise the smell and create a sweet fragrance. These were crystal and shanghai salts, mermaid's lagoon and Amazon rain plus rosewater. All these had to be heated to just the right temperature and then go through a process of distillation and fermentation that would take some days. He hoped to have it ready by the due date, actually a few days beforehand for its effect to permeate and create havoc. Neither potion was designed to kill, only to fulfill its singular purpose.

In Phoenix's case it would require her to drink at least half a cup of his blood after she had drunk the elixir. *That shouldn't be too difficult if the potion will put her into the right trance.* 'My blood must mix with the fetal circulation and then the baby will be mine alone, not his mother's'.

Once this part of his plan was accomplished he intended to take some time off to teach Malignius a lesson. What had been done at Lydia's home during the baby shower was not in keeping with his grand design. He had stressed to Malignius and others that he wanted no harm to come to Phoenix and the boy, that until the birthing it was essential that she be protected. Malignius had foiled him on this, taken the opportunity to create mayhem on his own. As long as he was head of the brotherhood, insubordination could not be tolerated. He would journey to the Peloponnesians, watch as Malignius took care of Greta and Geri and then punish him severely, castration followed by beheading. This he would do himself and take great pleasure in it.

Malignius would continue to walk the earth as a eunuchoid vampire with the stump of his neck sticking out for all to see. 'Yes', Bram cackled to himself, envisioning the prospect of the Headless Vampire stumbling around the town, 'that should do it'. But not yet, he still needed Malignius and the three sisters, at least for a time, for his other scheme.

Then there was Edna Kincaid. Her Corinthian group of fervent Christian devotees was growing by leaps and bounds, whereas attendance at black mass was reduced greatly from what it had been. It was time to step in. He had postponed

Edna's punishment long enough and for this he needed the three sisters to frighten Edna and her new crusaders who still worshipped in their homes as they had no church for services.

To show the might of Satan during their prayer meetings would be a coup. Perhaps Satan would forgive him for his good deed to Edna, although he had to admit that that particular act was strange on his part. And for some reason he still did not wish any harm to come to the woman.

He wondered if Phoenix had yet opened her gift.

∞

In London Hikey and Vladg were married in a civil ceremony and were preparing to take the Sub-Orb to LAX and honeymoon in the environs of sunny southern California when Hikey got the bright idea to take a cruise ship through the Panama Canal and on to the Pacific, up the coast to San Pedro. Vladg, who had never been on a ship of any kind before, let alone one of the gigantic ocean going vessels, liked the idea and so that was what they did. They were not only the first Duplicants to marry legally, they became the first Duplicants to sail the blue waters of the ocean as tourists and not as servants.

∞

Phoenix was so glad to be home. No sooner had she arrived with Lydia than she experienced the exquisite feeling of 'lightening'. She could breathe easier at once as her rib cage had been freed up as soon as the baby's head had dropped and was embedded into her bony pelvis. No more concerns over 'positioning' and breech or side-to-side. Those worries were all gone. This coming weekend would be Palm Sunday and then she had only one more week to go after that. She actually felt 'lighter' and perhaps she had lost some weight as the baby's head was now pushing on her bladder and rectum and so she was going to the toilet more often.

Anyway it was a relief to know that Joseph Christian Winthrop (the name she had been calling him in her mind as she certainly had no intention of carrying on the Alucard pedigree) was at the ready to make his journey through her birth canal. The miracle of the birth was so stirring to her, so adventurous, that even the contractions she felt now and again, false or true ones, were tolerable to her. She could hardly wait for April the 25th. What a blessing, a true happening, not just a birth but a resurrection from deviltry if he was actually born on that day of all days.

She was in the midst of opening all her baby shower presents when she came across a small package, covered in black wrapping. The return address was labeled Oneonta and she knew immediately it was from Bram. She hesitated to open it, but finally did. A small leather box was inside, locked tight by an elaborate clasp in the form of a gargoyle. When she pressed the ugly button-nose, it snapped open and an odd fragrance emanated from within. Housed inside, lying on black velvet, attached to a small baby chain, there hung a pure silver upside down crucifix, a symbol of Satanism, obviously intended for the baby. A note accompanied the gift and said: *If you allow our baby to wear this talisman from the moment of his birth, all will be forgiven.*

Phoenix was furious. Would this never stop? Of course Bram wanted the baby to wear it, but that would never, never happen. She wanted to throw it out the window but realized that would be the wrong thing to do. Getting rid of it in this impulsive way might actually work in reverse. She knew that when it came to evil charms they were not easily destroyed, so she went over to the hearth, replaced the talisman in the box, and set it on the andirons. She didn't turn on the flame, though she desperately wanted to do so. No, she would wait until Lydia got home from work; Lydia would know how to demolish it properly, to take away all of its power.

Now she was upset, felt woozy, her first time alone in days made her feel unsafe and needy.

She stared at George who seemed to stare right back at her. If only he could talk and move again. She needed a companion of some type when Lydia was not at home. The companion idea made her think of Vladg. She had heard that Vladg and Hikey were sailing the high seas, and were scheduling their honeymoon so that they would make it to Santa Barbara around the right time. So they too were on a fabulous journey to a new life. Thinking this way buoyed her spirits up a bit. Perhaps the talisman wasn't as powerful as she had thought?

As far as her sister and Josh were concerned, they were a mix of good and bad news. Phoebe had asked him to reverse his e-jack operation which Josh had refused to do, at least for the present. He said that since they planned to be in S.B. for the big day he wanted to retain his Humilicant powers, wanted to be strong and alert until he was sure that Phoenix and the baby were safe from Bram and any shenanigans he might pull. Phoebe relayed this thought to Phoenix who was grateful for Josh's concern, but she didn't want to get in the way of an argument between her sis and Josh, so she stayed out of it. Phoebe did tell her that she and Josh had settled a good many of their differences.

Josh had announced his intention to quit going out with his buddies and to stop his addiction to the Knick's games. He proposed they go to the gym together after work two or three times a week instead. But he refused to give up his coffee klatches with Jennifer which he claimed were entirely innocent. Phoebe didn't buy this. His refusal meant a lot to her as she had been very distrustful on this point. Josh accused her of being a shrew, said he was no Casper Milquetoast. This stirred things up again:

"I've been a nerd most of my life and I'm not going back to that life style," he said.

"Well I loved you more that way then this. I don't want my man to rape me!"

"See, what I mean, now you're threatening me and don't even know it."

"That's psychological crap. You're all yada, yada, yada."

"And you're blah, blah, blah," and that was that for the evening.

The next day Josh apologized and promised to quit seeing Jennifer. They kissed and made up and agreed to marry in the fall if all the other provisos were fulfilled. Then Phoebe mentioned she wanted to get preggie right off so that she could exchange diaper views with her sister. Josh said that was not a sufficient reason to want a baby, and anyway, his idea was to wait a few years until they were more financially stable.

They had a heated battle on this, Josh shouting that he had changed his mind again and was not going to give up his one independent social time with Jennifer. Phoebe repeated she was not going to marry a womanizing jock and that his promises were trash. Josh said he had no intention of being a jock. Phoebe started to cry and Josh went to comfort her. This helped to convince her that he was turning over a new leaf, but she was even more impressed when he told her he'd do his best on the other stuff even if he did reverse the e-jack. He felt that he now knew how to do it and figured it was like swimming or riding a bike, something one never forgets. Phoebe had to laugh at the way he put it.

When Phoenix heard all this from Phoebe she realized right then and there that the sisterly relationship had changed; Phoebe and Josh might just be one of those couples who loved one another but would argue back and forth like this forever. She decided not to take their trials and travails too much to heart as it was a stress she didn't need.

For Phoenix it was an existential awakening, a passage through one phase of life into another.

Other news was that Phoebe had made up with Lydia. The fact that George was still standing like a statue in the living room remained a problem, but Lydia and Phoebe were no longer at odds over it, *so there*, as she had learned to say from Lydia. The only problem was Bram who remained a threat. She had had the good sense not to contact him, but had taken Lydia's advice and not consulted him on any of the issues regarding her and the baby.

The only perplexity was that every time she had to walk around George she thought of the fight with Bram, when Josh had organized the mirror thing and Phoebe had slashed off Bram's thumb. Then a wave of dizziness would catch her and she had to go lie down, usually on the sofa if she was too light headed to make it to the bedroom. She hated to call Lydia when this happened as she knew she would be interrupting her work at the clinic and although she was aware of her regularly scheduled surgery hours, sometimes there was an emergency and she certainly didn't want to be in the way at those times. Once in a while she could just shake her head back and forth and the swaying feeling would go away and she would just lie down and catnap.

That evening, when Lydia got home, Phoenix told her about the gift from Bram. Lydia first had to extract some gunpowder from a couple of old shotgun shells she had left over from Christmas. Then she went out and bought half dozen long tapered black candles. On each candle she scratched out the number six with her nail file so that it was prominently displayed on all sides. Then she placed the candles in a circle, representing a coven, all around the box sitting on the andirons. She lit the candles. As they melted, she poured the tallow over the box, said 'Hail Satan' each time she did so until the box itself was no longer visible, then she turned on the gas to the hearth, told Phoenix to say: 'Hallelujah, Praise Jesus' and then Lydia said a prayer in Gaelic: "Return to your Master, you are not needed here, go to another part of this world." She said this three times and threw the gunpowder onto the remains. An incandescent flame shot up immediately and then, just as suddenly died down. She shut off the gas. There were only ashes; nothing else was left of the silver talisman.

On the third day at home she felt a pain in her belly that wasn't a kick. She knew when Joseph Christian was asleep and when he wasn't. This was different somehow and she thought it might be what Dr. Maloff had schooled her on, the false labor pains, so she just hung on to whatever piece of furniture she was standing near while she felt her legs nearly go out from under. When it was over, she made it to her room and lay down.

The next day it happened again and this time her legs buckled and she fell to the floor. She couldn't get up immediately so she half-closed her eyes. Her hands stroked the soft carpet back and forth and as she did so she saw ripples in the tufts of the freshly vacuumed rug which felt rather nice to her, so she decided to nap right there. She closed her eyes completely. The last thing she looked at was poor George, his dead eyes seemed to be staring right at her and she later remembered seeing the handle of the poker sticking out of his chest.

Now she was on a flat-bottomed boat at sea, overcrowded with a bunch of people some of whom she did not recognize. The boat was much too small for the size of the waves, which lapped up against the gunwales, frightening her, making her feel dizzy. Someone else on the boat seemed to be loosening her maternity smock, so, figuring it was Lydia home from the office, she asked: 'Why are you doing that?"

A voice answered: "To make you more comfortable."

Then, 'Would you like to take a swig of this? It's not sea water.'

Whatever it was, something that smelled of rose water and almonds she didn't want it even though her throat was dry. For whatever reason, she shook her head, refused to take a drink and pushed the glass away.

Now she knew the voice was not that of Lydia, it was a male voice, but she couldn't place it, not Dr. Maloff's, not Josh, certainly not George, who then'?

Whoever it was undid the snaps at her side and got her completely undressed. Now she shivered in the cold.

"Whyever are you doing that?" she asked.

There was no answer.

Now she had nothing on at all, not even her maternity undies, somehow they had been stripped from her as well. There were other women on the boat, her mother for one, pointing her finger, calling her a naughty girl, saying no Winthrop had the right to make love to another woman. Lydia was there and argued with her; then she saw Vladg and Hikey and felt better. She knew they would protect her from danger; next she felt something wet on her lips, she figured some of the sea water had sloshed over the gunwale, she tried not to swallow, but a little must have gotten down for her throat was no longer so dry. Then she saw Josh and Phoebe, Joost with Greta, Geri and Dusty, and Jennifer. They were all mixed in with one another. How could they all be on this little boat?

Now the waves seemed to settle down, the boat was off course, then she was no longer in a boat at all, and everyone was gone, they had simply disappeared. She was in someone's arms, someone was carrying her, perhaps two people, she wished that Jeanne d'Arc wasn't still at the clinic, but there was no way the dog could stay at home when there was no one to supervise her care, so at least she had company at the clinic; that made her heart feel good, only what was going to happen to her? At once Phoebe, looking like a Siren, appeared before her, large as life and said that she had just had an orgasm, not from Josh but from Jeanne d'Arc who had been licking her down below. 'You are not my sister' she wanted to shout, but the words stuck in her mouth and the next thing she knew she was in a large ballroom at a cocktail party and when the Siren offered her a drink, this time she took the glass and gulped some of it down, but didn't drain the glass. A strange drink she thought, odd but exciting.

She opened her eyes and saw that it was a surprisingly beautiful glass that appeared to be pure crystal. Expensive she thought. A man was there and he removed the glass from her hand, and offered her a cup that was filled with what smelled like pomegranate juice, it was awfully red and she took a small sip, but she gagged, it didn't agree with her. The man dipped his finger into the cup, drew the dregs across her lips, she didn't want to be rude but pushed his hand away. Now he took the point of his finger and drew it across her heavy stomach, not scratching but making some kind of red marks with it. He was very sepia eyed and had a wry grin, wore a thick moustache, yet she could not recognize him. She felt as if she were awake and asleep at one and the same time.

Someone else, a woman's sweet voice, said: 'She can't see. She can talk, but she can't see.'

'Perfect,' the man with the moustache said, and then she realized that he had removed her St. Joseph's medal and crucifix before making the marks on her belly.

Now she felt paralyzed all over, especially her legs felt as if they were bound together, shutting off her groin so that no one could violate her pouch.

Next she heard music, soulful wild music, then more melodious, someone holding her hand.

She opened her eyes but could not see.

It was Lydia's voice for sure this time.

"I'm home," the voice said.

"Lydia, I'm blind," she said. "I fell on the floor and had terrible wild dreams and now I'm blind."

"No, you're not blind, I put a cold compress on your forehead and slipped your sleeping mask over your eyes because you were shaking and shivering so."

Phoenix was grateful, but still frightened. She needed to know.

"Tell me the truth Lydia. Was Bram here?"

"Yes, I believe he was. I sensed his essence. I think he made those marks on your belly. I recognize them as demonic signs; they are symbols of fertility, to preserve life but in the form that will move your child toward Satan and away from the Christ."

"What can I do?"

"I don't believe Bram accomplished everything he wanted. You didn't drink anything while he was here?"

"I don't know for sure, maybe I did."

Phoenix takes a finger and tests it on her tongue.

"I can't tell."

"Well it couldn't have been enough; you would have had to drink his entire potion and in addition some of his blood for the concoction to be effective."

"I remember now; I saw the cup. It was full of some red stuff, but it was really full to the brim, I may have tasted it, but I didn't swallow any, none at all."

"Good, that's why you're not blind. You see, if you were blind there's no way you could possibly influence your baby after the birth. A child needs to see his mother's eyes for imprinting to occur."

"And his mother's smile," Phoebe added.

"Yes, and his mother's smile," Lydia said, giving Phoenix another warm hug.

"Listen love, I've called for Dr. Maloff to make a house call. I've already exchanged our GPS coordinates with his over the T-cell. You'll have to move from the bedroom to the living room. His hologram should arrive in a few minutes, as soon as he gets set under his Projecto-FAX.

Dr. Maloff's Hologram then appears and he says: "Good evening. What seems to be the trouble Ms Winthrop?"

"I've had a big contraction and a bad dream and I may have drunk something I shouldn't have, I'm not sure."

"Well, I'll do a total body scan first with the Y-Brane ray and we'll see. Please lie down on the sofa right there, no, move a little more to your right, ah, yes that's perfect. Now lift your knees about an inch or two, yes good, are you comfortable?"

"Yes doctor."

"Okay. Don't move. I have a replica of your form here that I'm following."

The hologram of the doctor takes out a small instrument from his breast pocket, one that resembles a physician's type flashlight for examination of nose and throat. He turns it on and a slightly divergent amber ray shoots out from the head of the instrument. He slowly runs it vertically and then horizontally over Phoenix's supine body. Then he has to wait for a brief moment to get the readout.

"All the systems and organs record as normal for both you and the baby. Let me switch the instrument over to toxicology and see if there are any abnormal values."

The Doctor's image twists the head of the instrument two notches to the right.

"Ah, there we are, right on the Tox-ray."

Now, after playing a bit with the fine focus, as one would with a microscope, the Doctor's image makes a grunt of satisfaction. At once the device emits a rather dull bluish beam, a much less divergent ray than the prior one. He scans her entire body, especially each quadrant of her abdomen which he checkerboards, snapping the ray on and off to create a contrasting effect, but covering the entire area effectively.

Again he waits for the readout.

"The manganese and magnesium are slightly elevated in your blood, as is the ferritin and transferritin…"

"What do those stand for?"

"That's your total body iron, the greatest percentage of which is stored in your marrow, spleen and red blood cells, but you don't have to know all that, the important thing is that all of your baby's values are completely normal."

"Oh, thank you doctor. I'm so glad you could make a house call."

"No problem. All my colleagues in the OB department do so, long as they have the Projecto-FAX technology that is."

"I do appreciate it."

"Well, that's nice of you to say, but in this last week before your due date I want you to make a visit to the office every day. If you are having contractions as big as you say, you might suddenly dilate and that means I want you in hospital."

"Yes, I'll come every day, and I know you've explained it before, but I still don't get it, that part about dilation."

"I'll tell you more about it in the office, but for now just think of your cervix as a gate, a gate that has to open for the baby to enter into the garden…"

"What garden?"

"Eden, the Garden of Life."

"Oh Dr. Maloff you are so poetic."

"Goodnight Ms Winthrop. Get some good sleep."

"I will. What time tomorrow?"

"Office hours begin at two P.M. You may have to wait a bit since you are unscheduled, but I will let my nurse know you're coming, okay?"

"That's fine. Thanks again."

"See you tomorrow. Goodnight."

"Oh Lydia, my love, isn't he wonderful. I'm so glad he'll be the one to deliver my baby."

"Well, don't forget I'm a midwife. If it happens suddenly, I'll be right there for you."

"I know, and that's comforting. Please don't be jealous that I think so highly of Dr. Maloff. Take me in your arms. I need you so right now."

Lydia leans over on the sofa, and hugs her for all she's worth.

Chapter XXX

Palm Sunday

As soon as Lydia and Phoenix heard of Vladg's marriage to Hikey they knew that he would not be returning to his old room. So in their congratulatory note they mentioned that they had started in on the makeover of the room for the baby.

Phoenix got into several games of T-cell tag before she got the electronic-paperhangers to come to the house. When they finally did show up, after several feeble excuses, a waxen faced salesman tried to sell the girls a bill of goods. He was pushing Smello-Vision (an old process, out of fashion) and Animal Miniaturization (a new product of Pyrell's) where the little animals jumped right out of the wallpaper and into a preset series of holograms lined about the baby crib. Phoenix thought this set-up was too drastic and might scare the baby, so she held her ground with the aggressive sales type, (fingering her newly acquired St. Thomas medal for courage) and bought neither of these items. She did purchase the standard Dial-In wallpaper which was quite picturesque with an English garden and 'water' fountain and could be set for scheduled intervals, such as every fifteen minutes, or for longer periods, each hour up to twelve hours at a time.

The music was also programmable and could be dialed in for extended or shorter segments. Phoenix chose Handel's water music which followed the color changes of the fountain, several of Chopin's nocturnes, a few Mozart sonatas and certain of Haydn's pieces which she found soothing herself. All this was electronically built into the wallpaper and came with a manual, which she had no qualms about reading, on how to operate the animation.

The men did some patching, some spackling, primed the walls with an anti-proton base, grumbling and moaning all the while, and then they sprayed the electronic adhesive and finally, with great care, they papered the walls with multi layered paper, closely following the sample designs chosen by Phoenix, and which held the internal circuitry in the middle layer. After the workmen finished their job and were ready to leave the house, she tipped each one ten New Dollars. They seemed grateful, wished her well on the delivery.

Then she tested the Dial-In remote and watched as bunny rabbits hopped, puppies scampered and fawns gamboled and frolicked across the pastel colored walls. The old room was now enchanting with a mixture of apricot and light mauve colors mixed in with sky-blue and sun-gold that Vladg would have hated but would be lovely visions for an infant whenever he opened his eyes to the world about him.

Lydia and Phoenix were excited. The room was filling up rapidly with all the presents from the baby shower. Placed in the center was an old fashioned wooden crib that rocked. It had been a gift from Phoenix's Mom who had inherited it from her grand mom. And though Phoenix hadn't had a chance to remove the colorful outer packaging at the time of her baby shower, she had guessed what it was from the outline of its form. Once they got the bubble wrapping off, Phoenix saw that the crib had been newly sanded and varnished. She knew how much work went into a job like that and that her daddy had done this labor of love. She sent him a very special thank you note and meant every bit of what she wrote. He was off somewhere in the

Carolinas hiding in a duck blind and couldn't make it for the delivery but nothing could hold back Phoenix's Mom and she was going to arrive the next day, Palm Sunday, April the 18th.

Lydia's baby shower gift was a softly tufted wide easy chair, which they installed to the far side of the crib. It was fashioned such that there was a specially fitted housing cut right into the armrest into which the wallpaper remote nestled snugly. Phoenix would be able to feed the baby-she wanted to breast, not bottle-and listen to Haydn or Mahler while she nursed. It was during the placement of this chair, to get it set just right, that Phoenix had a true contraction, a fairly big one. The baby had settled nicely after he dropped and had been quiet for some time. This sudden pain must have awakened and disturbed him, for he started moving and kicked for the first time in quite a while. It was this kick that reawakened Phoenix to the meaning of her dream.

She told Lydia she had to have a break before they hung the curtains, that she wanted to test out the chair and needed a little 'sit down'.

The insight came to her like an epiphany. Now she knew why Bram had been there, why he wanted her to drink the potion. She believed the potion was designed to hurry up her contractions, to speed up the birth. She told herself she wasn't a crazy woman, that her beliefs on all this were really true. Bram's plan was to get her to deliver earlier. He didn't want the baby to be born on Easter Sunday, no, that would make things much more difficult for him and his boss. Undoubtedly he wanted the birth to occur on Holy Friday, the day of Jesus' greatest suffering, when Satan was triumphant. She told herself she would prevent that from happening; would fight against his wish with all her soul. She would hold the baby in her womb until the Day of Resurrection, and on that day her baby would enter the world.

When curtains were finally hung, all the closets, bureaus and dressers stuffed full of baby things, folded neatly, they retested all the fancy gadgets, which worked like a charm. The rheostats controlling the indirect lighting set in the floor and ceiling proved reliable as well, so the lights were dimmed and then Lydia and Phoenix stood back and admired their handiwork. They were both pleased, a grand feeling of accomplishment came over them and they gave each other a soft hug and a sweet kiss for a job well done.

∞

In his own way, Bram had been reminiscing as well. After all these many years the fulfillment of his dream was fast approaching. He had lived long enough without an heir, a child of his own to carry on the Alucard name, to promote the traditions he so firmly held dear, to advance the 2nd Reformation he had recently initiated. His reflections brought him back to an earlier time, when maidens who were brought into vampirism were virgins; when men, once indoctrinated, could be trusted to become slaves based on their devotion to the Master.

All that was in the past, mere history, but he did not intend to become a victim of history; certainly not at the whim and fancy of Phoenix or Lydia, two women who had proved themselves untrustworthy; neither of which satisfied the longings of his soul.

He began to mull over his purchase of the mountaintop house with the great sea views of the Channel Islands. It irked him no end that legally this house was now Lydia's. He obsessed about it; just thinking of the fact that Lydia now owned the house stuck in his craw, but he had a plan for her. As to the farm, he was confident that during his absence the Kincaid's, Judd and Edna, together with the now well trained Sextus Duplicants, could run the farm efficiently, and that the number of converts to Satanism would keep things rolling.

It was true that the infiltration of vampirism had not taken root as quickly as he had hoped, the people in Seneca Falls were especially independent minded, but otherwise he felt while he was in Santa Barbara there was little to worry about on the home front.

He had no intention of making the same mistakes that caused Drakonius's precipitate demise. Drakonius had been done in by his own foolishness, distracted by young flesh. Bram had no such problem. Before he left Oneonta he had feasted on the blood of two young converts, maidens who worshipped him and bragged about their conversion when chatting at school as girls once did about losing their virginity.

They willingly offered their throats to his fangs and he partook only of enough blood to satisfy his needs, never overdoing it such that they became ill, although their skin had taken on a rather Gothic pallor. No, that one drink should hold him for a month. Neither was he going to loiter about his old house and try to scare anyone. His intent was to capture his child, put Phoenix in a trance which he felt should be relatively easy right after she gave birth on Good Friday, reduce Lydia to a member of the undead, and immobilize anyone else with his spray, a potion which would destroy corneas, causing blindness even in Duplicants like Vladg, should he be present at the birthing.

He was staying with an old acquaintance, a Siren who had a Greek name, which she translated as Doris. He had met Doris years ago when he first came to Santa Barbara and was struck by the sweetness of her voice. He had tried to put her under a trance and drink of her blood only to discover that her resistance was so strong that she easily evaded his powers. She simply read his mind and would not submit. Then and there he learned that she was a Siren with a lineage even longer than his own. On her maternal side she stemmed from a true nymph and paternally her genealogy was said to go all the back to the Argonauts who sailed with Jason in search of the Golden Fleece. In her younger days she lured sailors at sea to their death, but now was content to help Bram in any way she could.

She owned a small cottage near the Mission and controlled several slaves who would do her bidding. He intended to assign one of these to a task to help in his plans to thwart Lydia. Doris recommended one of her low level slaves, a delivery boy nicknamed Freak, who worked at a local nursery. Bram had some trepidation over this boy as he did not trust anyone who had a nickname of any sort, but he went along with her choice.

Doris was the one who had accompanied him to Lydia's place and helped to undress Phoenix and carry her to bed. It was her voice that announced: 'She can talk, but she can't see'. And, copycatting the form of her twin sister Phoebe, she did get Phoenix to drink some of the potion, not enough to cause regular contractions, but perhaps a sufficient amount to hurry things up a bit. The only fly in the ointment was the fact that Phoenix did not drink Bram's offer of a cup of his blood. Doris knew the rules; this tradition had to be accomplished by him, not her. So this was Bram's failure, not hers.

Bram was satisfied with the work that Doris had accomplished, she had been helpful and now the rest was up to him. The baby would not have a sufficient amount of vampire blood in his fetal circulation to allow him to exert immediate control over the child but with careful and consistent upbringing he could remedy that. All was not lost.

The most important symbols had been set, his blood embossed onto her belly, spelled out in Hieroglyphics, promoting her fertility and readiness to deliver the boy on the day of the crucifixion. The delivery would be accomplished, not by Dr, Maloff, but by his own choice of Dr. Abraxas, a superior physician, a member of the brotherhood in evil standing, one who represented a deliverer of life to the luminous world, meandering between the sanctioned cult of god and the unorthodox cult of the devil.

Once born, he would hold the child in his newly appointed fatherly arms and rock the baby into the rhythm of life, giving him the blessing of all the demons and submerged forces of the world as directed by Lucifer in the Black Mass. There would be no arbitrariness on the question of devotion, no equivocation on his future, no ambiguities with other humans as to who was master and who was slave.

Then, after Dr. Abraxas brought forth the placenta and handed it over to Doris, he would allow the Siren to squeeze out the afterbirth. Doris was instructed to smear the bloody mess all over Lydia's face, careful to stuff the membranous fibrils up her nostrils so that she could not breathe. Doris would take great pleasure in carrying out this ritual, in rubbing the 'fire of the belly' into Lydia's face, anointing her as the Anti-Godmother.

Then it would be his turn. He would gouge out her eyes, sink his fangs for the last time deep into Lydia's throat and exsanguinate every ounce of blood from her that she possessed, transforming her into a diaphanous form, a member of the undead Sisterhood.

He smiled inwardly, not with a sense of satisfaction or revenge, but merely with a sense of prophecy: *'What an enjoyable thought'.*

∞

On Palm Sunday morning Phoenix met her mother at the airport. She was deeply startled when she first saw her. Her mother was not disheveled, but everything else about her was unusual. For a woman who generally presented herself as self assured, her mother had lost her fine bearing. Her face seemed lean and gray, her eyes inflamed, her cheeks drawn in, which slackened the features of the rest of her face.

All in all she was a far cry from the stylish appearance she evoked at Christmastime or even the upscale casual she had made an effort to pull off at the baby shower. The colorless dress she wore made her look older. For a woman who prided herself on having the Jones's in Holdrege keep up with her, she seemed crestfallen, as if her spirit had been strained by a force beyond her ken.

Phoenix put on her best face and greeted her warmly.

After hugs and cheek kisses, regards from daddy and her brother Phillip, her mother suddenly announced that she wanted to go to church. Phoenix was a believer, but clearly not churchy; even so, she did not want to miss a ritual during the week before she gave birth which might be significant to either of the deities whom she now felt were in control of her destiny. Accordingly, following her mother's wishes and in spite of the fact that she felt somewhat woozy, she went willingly to church services. She watched the procession of children on their way into church, carrying palm leaves and singing celebratory songs, which represented Jesus' entrance into Jerusalem.

She listened attentively to the passionate sermon.

What she heard provoked her into a greater state of reverie, one that required a reply tucked deeply within her like a hidden jewel. The pearl she 'took home' from the pastor's words was, "Who would be born again, must first fly into the arms of God." Phoenix did not believe this was coincidence, but that the reference was to her pregnancy, to the birth of her child fighting its way into the world, to worship against the uniting of godly and devilish elements. Her interpretation was that the soul adheres to God's laws and his name on earth is Jesus, not Satan. Yes it was up to the mother to direct the baby to God, to make certain her son sought his embrace.

After church her mother said she wanted to have a 'heart to heart' that at Christmastime, with all that was going on, and at the baby shower with its vile misadventures, she had never really had a chance to have a moment alone with her eldest.

"Only by seven minutes!" Phoenix exclaimed, unable to prevent herself from   repeating what she had said to Feeby.

"Yes, but that still makes you my first born, you'll see soon enough it makes a difference."

"What are you saying?"

"Not here, take me to a place where we can talk. I really need to spend some time alone with you before we go up to Lydia's."

Phoenix thought she knew what was coming, more inquiries about the fatherhood of her child, but there was nothing else for it; she had avoided the subject as long as possible. So, on purpose, she drove her mother to an old style watering hole, a sort of dive with sawdust and spittoons on the floor. The place was located on the outskirts of the city, near Goleta and the university. She figured if her mother was uncomfortable enough, she might not reproach her for the pregnancy out of wedlock which she thought was on her mother's mind. She was wrong on this.

As soon as they were seated Phoenix asked for a strawberry iced tea but her mother promptly ordered a scotch on the rocks. When Phoenix questioned this, saying drinking hard stuff so early in the morning was unlike her, her mother said it was to get her courage up.

"Courage for what?"

"Before I let it all out I want to toast you and the baby."

They clinked glasses, said skol.

"All the luck in the world this weekend," her mother said and she started right in.

"Well you can probably see from the redness of my eyes that I've been crying every day since the baby shower. Of course most of your guests thought it was some sort of spoof, a designed holographic game for entertainment to throw a scare into everyone. I knew better. It was real wasn't it? A world of madness thrown at you full face, own up."

Phoenix had no hesitation, her mother had suffered enough; she told the truth.

"Yes mother it was real; all three were vampires, members of the undead sisterhood, out to convert me and the baby in the name of Satan."

Her mother nodded, not understandably, but it was a gesture that meant 'thank you for being straight with me'.

"My first concern was for your health and that of the baby's, but when I finally got back home to Holdrege, knowing you were okay, I realized a lot more had happened than met the eye."

"Such as?" Phoenix said warily, hoping against hope that she wouldn't have to go into the Iphigènie thing.

"It was all abnormal wasn't it? I mean the strength of that one woman lifting the heavy food table; and the sudden appearance of that giant bat and the crazy woman who seemed to jump right into you. Feen, I saw all that. It happened so quickly that it just didn't register, but now I know it wasn't some high tech illusion, it was real wasn't it?"

Phoenix knows there is no sense in furthering the deception, of trying to convince her mother as she had done to so many others that it was all an elaborate techno-game, a hoax that went wrong.

"Yes mother, she repeated, it was all real. I told you they were vampires."

"But until now I never believed in vampires!"

"It's all very complicated."

"Are you still in danger? That's what I've been crying about, every day, and I can't eat, I'm so worried."

Now Phoenix takes her mother's hand, clasps it warmly.

"I don't believe there's much to worry about now. The creatures involved in all this have been taught a lesson and I've got all sorts of protection if they try anything again. Now that you're here; with Phoebe and Josh coming, and you've seen how strong he's become; and Vladg the Duplicant will be here with his wife…"

"They're married?"

"Yes."

"Heavens to Betsy, what's this world coming to?"

Phoenix doesn't really like her mother's rather bigoted query, but thus far it is the first spark of life she has seen in her, so she doesn't go into it any further.

"The world is evolving mother, and is just getting ready to make you a grandmother for the first time."

Now her mother smiles more pleasantly.

"Don't misunderstand. You already know how pleased your daddy is at becoming a grandfather. Well I am too, I desperately want to be a grandmother and I am very proud of you. I love you and I want you to know that the circumstances mean nothing to me, I've gotten over all that."

"Thanks mom, I know you love me and I appreciate the way you just said that…"

"But the only thing is the father. If you could just see your way clear to tell me something about him, not his name or anything like that, you've already said you want to keep that a secret, but something about his heritage, what kind of man is he? What type of blood? What are we to expect? Anything along those lines would please me and your father as well although he would never pry like I know I'm doing. Don't you see Feen, it's not just curiosity, if something ever happened to you, heaven forbid, I'd know better how to help my grandchild."

"Mom you don't need to know. Lydia will always be there for me."

"But can't you give me some idea…does he have good genes?"

"I can tell you that the father of my baby comes from royal blood, I know that will please you. He is foreign and in his country he is a count, 'so there'. Does that satisfy you?"

"It helps. Just tell me if there are any defects…"

"Like what? Social defects or physical ones?"

"Whichever."

"I had a scan from my OB just yesterday and everything is perfect. You know if you go on like this I'll get upset, and my 'pains' will start in. You don't want that to happen do you? I mean you should know what it's like, you've had three pregnancies."

"You're wrong there."

"Wrong how? There's me, Feeby and Philip."

"There was Pauline before you and before your father. I never told anyone but I got pregnant; my high school boyfriend raped me and I subsequently had an abortion. Your father doesn't know. I'm confiding in you and no one else. This is not even for Feeb to know."

"Yes, mother."

"I was four months along but I wasn't yet showing, no one knew. I went alone to the doctor who did an amniocentesis and some other stuff. He told me the baby had a congenital heart problem, probably would be a blue baby. I didn't know what to do. The boy I was with wanted nothing to do with it, he abandoned me completely. My parents were not the modern types, still living on the farm; we hadn't yet moved into town, they would have killed me for getting pregnant and not carrying to term, so I had an AB…"

"Oh mother…I never thought…"

"That's why I'm so worried. After the abortion I had a period in which I regarded myself with disgust. Every morning I awoke with nausea, a raging thirst, fits of despair and terrible headaches. At last I moved away from my parent's house. I couldn't bear to face them. A year later I met your father, everything once again became godly pure and I knew that I had been forgiven. So you see, I'm not just a nosy woman with a social name to uphold, although I am that as well."

Phoenix had to mull over all this. She decided to tell her mother some, but not all about Bram.

"He is an older man. There's nothing wrong with him physically, you can rest assured on that score. He's recently divorced and retired from the Foreign Service. And just like you I was raped, ravaged and damned, so we do have that in common. When I first came to believe that I was truly pregnant, and that took a while, everything that you and daddy had given me was vanishing, laid waste, trampled upon as if the ground was slipping away from under my feet. Mother, I was living in an orgy of self-destruction. Yes, thoughts of suicide came to me, but then I would destroy not one life but two. I couldn't do that. The two deities that rule the world were fighting over me, one to move me to darkness, the other to light…"

"Don't talk like that…it's weird."

"It was the way I felt. You see I wanted to drive away his portrait from myself; I was trying as best I could to sacrifice everything within me for the baby, to banish his darkness and evil from us. My sexuality was in shambles, a torment from which I was trying to run away. When Lydia came along and put me back together I was no longer in flight, my goal was not happiness but stability, a spirituality that resonated with Lydia. I had never felt anything like it before, certainly not with any man. A new image of life had risen up before me in that slender and boyish figure of hers that I came to love."

"Talking with you like this does bring back memories, incidents, and secretive pastoral conversations. Yes, even after my symptoms stopped, I too had a terrible time for a year or so. I remember feeling sexless, but eventually, when I met your father I settled down within myself, I decided never to be a loser again…it was a sober reality."

"That was your way of handling it mother, and it worked for you, my situation was different. I continued to pursue my memories, my haunted thoughts and dreams and kept my secrets hidden within me. It wasn't until Lydia, not by probing but by creating that harmony I spoke of which put me back together again. My quivering heart finally relaxed and I could live again, don't you see mother what I was going through."

"Yes, I think I do. Maybe not in as eloquent a manner as you put it, but I do remember that for a year after my rape and abortion I hated myself. Still there are practical matters to deal with. Don't you want the father of your baby to have some influence on his upbringing; nowadays they say the presence of a masculine identity is necessary."

"No, I don't want the father to have anything to do with my baby, nothing at all. That is something you must promise mother. If anything does happen to me, trust in Lydia, do not try to contact the father."

"You won't tell me his name."

"No mother. Believe me, it's better that you don't know. He is a very powerful man who will stop at nothing to gain control over the boy, I can guarantee that you are better off not knowing."

Phoenix's mother stared at her daughter long and hard.

"Can I ask just one more thing?"

"Okay, last one."

"You told me were going to marry Lydia. But why? How do you know this will last after you become a mother, I mean no father hanging about, you know what I'm getting at?"

"I'm not sure I do, but no one knows for sure how long a marriage will last, not even one between a man and a woman? You and daddy are exceptions so you think everyone is like that…"

"No, I'm not that naïf. I just think it's more likely that a child will grow up healthy with a father and mother…"

"Lydia and I have a gentle life with each other, a presentiment that we are linked; my inner self and hers are bound together, as are our fates. Can you understand that mother?"

"I'm not sure, she's older than you isn't she?"

"Some of your bridge friends have husbands who are much older than their wives and I never hear you raise the issue."

"Yes, but in that case we know who the wife is and who the husband."

"Lydia and I are not in that box."

"Well how old is she?"

"She is as old or as young as ever…does it matter?"

"I think it does. All those things matter, you need a man around the house."

"The statistics don't bear that out mother. Marriage between same genders has been going on for over thirty years now and there's less cheating, less betrayal and the kids are giving their parents more respect. And their school grades are getting better too."

"Is all that so? I mean what's going to happen if everyone did that?"

"Everyone is not going to 'do that', as you put it. Mom, people fall in love with other people regardless of gender; that's all you've got to remember. Anyway, you won't have to deal with a son-in-law you don't like, how about that?"

"All right. You may have a point there."

Her mother slugs down the rest of her drink, stares at her daughter long and hard, decides not to pursue the issue any further at this time.

"Let's go up to your place; I've had a long morning and it's been hectic for you as well. Are you ready?"

"Anytime."

Phoenix is pleased that she had gotten through the ordeal relatively unscathed, breathes a sigh of relief.

They split the bill.

∞

Jeanne d'Arc, meanwhile, was at home playing with Lydia. She was still somewhat lame in her left forepaw, but was otherwise healthy and powerful as ever. It was the first day in many that she had had the chance to relax and essentially not have to go to the clinic and pretend to socialize with the other dogs, none of whom seemed wise, alert, or challenging. Of course, most of them were either too sick to play or so stuck up, (especially that one poodle with the crazy haircut) that she was either bored to death or simply exhausted from listening to the din of their barking.

So she hoped Phoenix and her mom stayed away for as long as they wished. Yes, she listened when Lydia told her human things, like why Phoenix was off to pick up her mom on a special day like this. She didn't understand the Palm part, but was enthusiastic over the fact that she had Lydia all to herself. Loving Lydia was the second great event in her life. The first being the discovery of fear, which she had learned from that man Drakonius, who, astoundingly, had sliced a hunk off her leg from which blood had trickled for many days.

Had it not been for Lydia's talent, she would have been left with just a stump like that Golden Retriever at the clinic. Yes, Plato was an exception, a brave and beautiful dog who made sense and never complained from dawn to dusk.

Just thinking about that day raised a quiver on her neck muscles, made the fur on her muzzle tense up. Not that she felt sorry for that devil of a man getting burned to a crisp, certainly he deserved it, but what a horrid way to go, gyrrh.

Lydia still sensed the essence of Bram's presence. All of her instincts told her that he was somewhere in the neighborhood, planning, scheming, perhaps in collusion with the Siren, Doris, that he had introduced her to when she first came to live in Santa Barbara. But what he was specifically up to she had no idea. She idly petted Jeanne d'Arc's muzzle, and then scratched her behind the ear, a stroking action the dog loved.

Lydia felt the tension rise in her dog, continued to stroke her behind the ear, when the doorbell rang. Jeanne d'Arc immediately sprang up and ran to the front door barking like all get-out. Lydia, in turn, hardly had to move an inch from where she sat on the floor, but grabbed the universal remote off the coffee table and snapped it at one of the plug in fixtures, a hybrid alarm fastened on the near wall.

The system was newly installed, after the baby shower episode, and its video feature was automatic, on 24/7, but the projecto-FAX had to be initiated manually, either by pushing a button, or by using the remote.

The holograph came on in the middle of the living room and Lydia spoke to it:

"Identify yourself!!" she demanded of the image, which was still a trifle indistinct, as this particular security model, set permanently into the system, took more time to come on, to create a finely outlined image, than the transportable ones.

"Flowers," the image said and Lydia could now make out that the person was a youngish type in a delivery uniform. She manipulated the remote to adjust the outside video camera to the street setting, zoomed out, and saw that a van was parked there whose sign read "STAR FLOWERS" on the side panel. She recognized STAR as a legitimate flower delivery service, as many of the grateful dog lovers sent flowers to her staff at the clinic, as well as to her.

Also, a good many cut flowers and plants had been delivered to the hospital during Phoenix's stay, mostly from friends who had attended the baby shower, so this in itself was not remarkable, but Phoenix had been home for some time now and that was surprising, making Lydia suspicious.

So Lydia got up warily and went to the door, cautiously opened it a notch, keeping the safety chain on.

"Yellow and red roses," the delivery boy said without being asked.

"Just leave them by the door…"

"Can't…someone has to sign."

"Who sent them?"

"I just deliver, most people leave a card inside…c'mon lady, I don't got all day."

"Just hold up what needs to be signed in front of the camera, I'll sign electronically."

"No can do. That way they'll think I faked a delivery, this needs a real signature."

Lydia hesitated.

"Open it up. Show me they are really flowers."

"Geezzus lady, I can't do that, my boss will kill me if I opened people's packages; strictly off base; not allowed!"

This plea sounded genuine to Lydia so finally she opened the door. What she had failed to notice were the delivery boy's boots, they were not in keeping with the rest of his outfit which was designed to move fast. He should have been wearing running shoes, Sketchers or New Balance or some such, instead he had on a pair of heavy clodhoppers. He was an expert kick boxer, and as soon as there was a clear shot, he snapped one off which landed directly on Lydia's jaw. She flew backwards a few feet while Jeanne d'Arc sank her teeth viciously into the boy's other leg, tasting human blood for the second time.

Without hesitation the delivery boy, who was youthful but did not have young boy's eyes, tore open the box and took out a spray bottle, the concoction prepared by Bram. He squirted it directly into the dog's eyes, causing Jeanne d'Arc to howl from pain, and to let loose of her jaw-hold on the boy's calf. He, in turn, was about to use the spray on Lydia when Phoenix and her mother pulled into the driveway, stopping their car with a screeching halt.

The boy kicked at Jeanne d'Arc with his other leg, another powerful blow, breaking two ribs, causing her to whimper. Then he stumbled quickly to his van, blood oozing on the driveway from the deep bite in his leg. The delivery boy, nicknamed Freaky, got into the van, gunned the engine, jerked it into gear and took off as fast as he was able. On the way to Doris's place he wondered half-aloud what punishment would be forthcoming from Doris.

Phoenix ran immediately inside to tend to Lydia who was just regaining consciousness. She nestled her head in her lap while Jeanne d'Arc, in pain herself, licked at Lydia's cheeks.

Before running off, Freaky had dropped the package on the stoop, a long rectangular box, which indeed contained red and yellow roses, one dozen of each. A flower lover, Phoenix's mom couldn't help herself...Phoenix yelled at her, but before she could heed her daughter's warning, she stuck her nose into the package, wanting to smell the fragrance, took a whiff and immediately fell into a trance. She now appeared as immobile and statuary as George.

There was little Phoenix could do for her at the moment, so she concentrated on Lydia. Blood was oozing from the corner of Lydia's mouth and dripping down onto Phoenix's, maternity apron. In a way she interpreted this as a good sign, Lydia's blood overcoming Bram's, but she discarded this notion when Lydia spit out half a molar which had broken off from the force of the kick.

"I think my lower jaw is broken," Lydia said, barely able to eke out these words, falling in and out of consciousness. Her state of lucidity was such that she could not yet employ her mind properly. Instead she saw vague images of Ireland, of the pub she had worked in as a waitress so long ago. Then a ghostly spectre of Bram appeared as she had first met him so many years ago. At once she realized this was his doing, again he was up to his old tricks, sorcery he had learned from his mother.

The memories had an effect, she regained her faculties somewhat.

The anemic sounds emanating from Jeanne d'Arc were so unlike her, so agonizing, that Lydia knew right off she had been wounded severely. At once her professionalism took command; she palpated the dog's sides, determined that at least one of the ribs was cracked; then she saw the unusual stare, the opaqueness of her dog's corneas. She knew immediately that her dog was blind.

Lydia was still barely able to stand erect, she feared that the concussion might have more lasting effects, so she asked Phoenix to call 911 and then she lay back down on the carpet.

Phoenix placed the call, but when the emergency service answered she didn't quite know what to say. As she surveyed the scene she could hardly believe her eyes. There was George with a poker stuck through his torso, her mother in a trance, a blind dog with cracked ribs, the owner with a concussion and a cracked jaw and a near term mother who was now having heavy contractions.

She asked for an airbulance for Lydia and her mother, called the veterinary service for Jeanne d'Arc, and placed a call to Dr. Maloff, leaving a message with his service.

Then the baby started to kick again.

∞

The police arrived within twenty minutes, but by that time Dr. Maloff's image was already present, doing a holographic house call. Phoenix had to obey his instructions to the letter and remained quite still while the various rays the doctor utilized did their thing. So the two officers had to twiddle their thumbs until the doctor finished his examination.

Once she was pronounced okay and told she did not need to be admitted to hospital, she was allowed to move around. After a few minutes of dangling and careful stretching she turned to the uniformed policemen and devoted herself completely to telling the story of the flower delivery boy.

An immediate review of the outside front video camera showed the Star Nursery van parked on the street, then a long period of nothing at all as Lydia had forgotten to refocus the camera. There were no signs of a struggle, no kicking or fighting on the tape, nothing malicious going on. This void was followed by a driveway scene of the delivery boy struggling as he limped hurriedly to the van, dripping blood from his lower leg. In the next section it did show him getting into the vehicle and taking off.

After a few more questions, which included Phoenix's rather extensive description of the boy's clothing and vital features, the officers told her there was nothing more they could do as the Star Nursery was already closed for the day.

"We'll hand in our report to the detectives and tomorrow they'll head up to the nursery and check on the kid's identity, see if he has a rap sheet and such."

Phoenix nodded her understanding.

Then, with an almost obligatory set of phrases, reminiscent of the words of the wallpaper hangers, they wished her well with her delivery.

Up to now they had addressed her as Ms or Ma'am but in making their goodbyes they called her Mrs. which made her feel legitimately maternal.

Chapter XXXI

Holy Week: Monday to Wednesday

Freaky thought that his life would be hanging by a thread for failing miserably to accomplish his task, but on Fig Monday, at Doris's place, he was pleasantly surprised to hear Bram say: "As long as Lydia is in hospital, the dog is out of the way and Phoenix was not hurt, I can take care of that Dr. Maloff and Dr. Abraxas will be free to deliver the baby."

Freaky interpreted this to mean he had 'done good'.

Indeed, as a token of accomplishment, he was meted out a cheek reddening spanking by his mistress given with his own leather belt and finished off with a few slaps from her bare hands. This was quite an honor. He relished the spanking, anticipated the thought of bragging to the other slaves of his reward.

∞

Tony Gentile, the single detective assigned to the case was a large vital man with a ready smile and a mirthful laugh. However, when it came to police work, this aspect of his character was deceptive. He was instinctively suspicious when dark doings were afoot and he pieced together associations that others might term a coincidence.

He had made it to the Star Nursery rather early that Monday morning and was comfortably settled in, drinking a hot cup of coffee and munching on his donut in the company of the owner. The office door was closed, and they were holding court in rather clandestine fashion, as if the case had high priority.

"Normally we wouldn't be so interested in a dog biting one of your delivery boys, but this is the third time a criminal act has occurred at the same address. So tell me about this kid, how long he's worked here, is he reliable, whatever you may think is important."

"Well his real name is Jimmy Gottlieb but everybody calls him Freaky. Been with us close to a year, today is the first day he's missed work in three months. The other time was from a joy ride he took up the coast to Santa Maria…"

"We know about that, he stole a reconditioned Maserati, an Italian sports car from early in the century, and the kid couldn't resist driving something with an old fashioned engine that ran on gasoline. His parents made amends and really, aside from one episode of smoking Ubiquity on a public bus, he hasn't got much of a rap sheet, truancy in grade school, dropped out at sixteen, that's about all."

"Yes, he doesn't seem to be the criminal type, and quite a few of our delivery boys are warned about watchdogs, they know it's a risk, part of the job."

"I talked to him on T-cell. He says he never even got the lady to sign for the flowers, left them on the stoop. The video confirms he was running away, bleeding."

"That's my understanding, not unusual in this business."

"So who is this guy who ordered the roses?"

"We know him fairly well. In his fifties I'd say, quiet type, a retired federal employee of some sort. Used to be a fairly regular customer, then, if you can imagine this, he lost his wife not to another man but to a woman…"

"Happens a lot lately, what with Duplicants in adequate supply, the women are looking for something novel to stir up their juices."

"Whatever the reason, he divorced his wife who apparently got the house, which has one of the best locations in the city…"

"Yeah, I know the area, as I say I've been there twice on investigations."

"Yes, that's right you did say there were troubles there before…"

"That's putting it mildly. The place is earning some reputation as a haunted house of sorts."

"Really?"

"Yeah, but getting back to it, what's he doing? Why would a man who got cuckolded by his wife with a woman send her flowers?"

"Beats me. Shit happens. We just grow and sell plants and flowers. Why the customers buy them, and for whom they're intended, is their business. But you've heard of divorce parties haven't you?"

"Sure, but wouldn't it be unusual to send flowers to a wife who mucked you up and to top it all off got the house in the bargain?"

"Takes all kinds Detective, you see more weirdoes than I do."

"Yeah, well you got any more on this guy Alucard?"

"Not that I can think of at the moment. As I said, he's a quiet type. He's staying with an old friend who lives near the Mission. This is the address he gave when he purchased the roses."

The detective picks up the Post-It on which the proprietor had written the address.

"Yep, this jives with our info on him. Okay, if you can think of anything else let me know, you've got my card."

"Certainly."

∞

At LAX, Josh and Phoebe were hurriedly leaving the Sub-Orb when Phoebe's T-cell started to vibrate. It was Phoenix on the line. She had checked the arrival time and synced her call perfectly.

She told Phoebe all that had happened on Palm Sunday; that Lydia had a fractured jaw which was scheduled to be wired shut today; that their mother was in a trance, due to be released from hospital any time now and that Jeanne d'Arc was blind, waiting in the veterinary eye specialist's clinic for cornea transplants from a matching dog donor.

"My God! How did all that happen?"

"This delivery boy brought two dozen roses ostensibly from Bram and Jeanne d'Arc got suspicious, bit him in the leg and the boy sprayed some sort of poison into her eyes. I didn't see it exactly, mother and I were just driving up when the kid went running off, but Jeanne d'Arc must have been right because when we got inside, Lydia was on the floor, knocked out and her jaw was broken. The doctors say she had a concussion."

"Well how did mother fall into a trance if you two arrived after the fight or whatever was going on?"

"You know mother. She couldn't resist the fragrance of the roses, took a deep whiff and went right into a trance. Most likely the flowers were impregnated with one of Bram's concoctions."

"So he's still hanging around?"

"Definitely! He won't give up. I have my own theory on his plans, I'll tell you when you get here, it's too long over the cell."

"Okay, but aren't you frightened out of your flimsies?"

"Not so much now that I know you and Josh and Vladg are coming. I feel safer."

"You want to say hello to Josh?"

"No, that's ok. Just tell him what I said and that I love him. I'm going to pick up mom from Cottage and spend some time there with Lydia."

"You got it. Luv'ya."

"Ciao, luv'ya, c'ya in a few hours."

∞

Josh goes over to hail a Basic III with a tractor beam wand. He hands him his thin metallic-alloy claim check and the Basic pulls their four bags out of the air. Then he asks the Basic to wait a moment while he fetches a nearby ground transporter. The Basic does just that, and on a signal from Josh leads the four bags through the air and deposits them in the back of the transporter. Josh tips him two New Bucks and the Basic seems satisfied.

Phoebe climbs in the front of the vehicle and they head over to the cocktail lounge as they have to call Vladg and make sure that their timing will dovetail.

Josh fingers his touch pad, finds shipping, a pic of the Queen Victoria appears, ready to dock in San Pedro. He waits until they finish their drinks, then makes the call.

∞

Love can be limp and love can be strong. On rare occasions love can be both at one and the same time.

Aboard the Queen Victoria, during the South Atlantic part of the voyage, such was the case between Hikey and Vladg. As chance would have it, a small clique of students from Ecuador and Peru, all teenage girls, were assigned to the same dining table as the Duplicants. They were making the return trip to South America after a year of study in England. One of them became enamored of Vladg and flirted openly with him. At first it was nothing that Hikey took seriously, but when the girl tried

519

to play footsie under the table with Vladg, Hikey could no longer ignore the matter. She asked the purser to grant them a transfer to another table and this was arranged.

It was then that the teen started to call Hikey 'Big Head' and shouted out that she needed an operation with a can opener to reduce the size of her skull. Some of the other girls got into the 'fun' and continued to heckle Hikey, riddling her with jibes every chance they got, usually on the promenade deck or in the lounge when no crew or staff were around. Hikey checked herself in the mirror, scrutinized the size of her head, powerless to change herself.

Vladg tried to tell her that teenagers were lower forms of life whose youthful impulses were disengaged from the rest of the world, but this didn't work. Hikey had always thought that the large dimensions of her head were a physical blessing, beauteous in their own way, and for Vladg to dismiss teens' opinions as mere low life garbage didn't keep the anger from rising in her head nor shame from descending to her tummy.

Hikey really felt devastated, her 'trip of a lifetime' became miserable. She had never been so insulted by a human before and didn't quite know how to handle the situation as all of her training was designed to be diplomatic with TH's. She asked Vladg to speak alone with the girl, which was exactly what the teen had hoped to accomplish. When he confronted her she flew into his arms and told him in Spanish how much in love she was with him. He managed to push away from the girl, holding her off at arm's length and admonished her for the insults to his wife, but the girl only laughed and went to the Captain with the complaint that Vladg had tried to kiss her. One of her compatriots supported her in the story, but luckily, the Captain saw through the ruse and chided the girls, moving them to another sitting for the dinner hour and warning them not to make contact with the Duplicants under any circumstances.

Somehow the agitation stayed with Hikey. Even with all the delectable foods on board to stimulate the palate, she lost her appetite. It took until the ship passed through the Pacific part of the Panama Canal that she felt somewhat better. There the girls disembarked to make their separate travel plans to their own countries. But the incident remained imprinted in Hikey's mind; she had learned there were two levels of existence and experience, one of which was basically evil for passion's sake. She began to ask herself why she had always longed to rise to the level of a human, to be humanoid. She knew that most of this desire was related to Cynthia, who had been her mentor and idol, an ideal to emulate. Yet none of this type of harangue and harassment had occurred in Holland.

Yes, she had been called names before because she was a Duplicant, but no one had ever ridiculed her construction, challenged how she was put together. Now this had become an issue. In her mind, she reviewed the successive levels of awareness that she had undergone; first a vague sense of life, then consciousness, then education and rationality followed by the development of an ethical sense and a moral compass to judge feeling for others in the world. All this was capped off by meeting Vladg and experiencing love.

She decided to give up all thoughts of becoming humanoid, that she had to remain exactly what she was; faulty construction? Perhaps not, perhaps she was purposely made such to lie in between two extremes of excess and defect, for she knew inherently that the ways of some humans were also defective, designed at the beastly level, a bottomless pit of hurt to others in the name of passion.

Upon disembarking at Cunard Line's mooring in San Pedro Harbor on Tuesday, Vladg and Hikey rent a Ford sedan from the Wheels-Plus Rental Agency. The one they pick has the largest trunk available as they need to stow all their voyage baggage in it and still find room for Josh and Phoebe's stuff.

Vladg is a practiced driver, derived from his time serving as Bram's chauffeur, and he has no trouble finding his way out of the harbor maze.

The distance from San Pedro to LAX is just short of twenty miles and once under way they find the traffic not to be particularly heavy. The only glitch to be concerned about is if the Sub-Orb from Kennedy is delayed, then they would have to wait in the airport which Vladg hates. This worry is resolved when, half way there, he gets a call from Josh; they make arrangements to meet in front of the LAX Sub-Orb building in twenty minutes or so.

This works out well and when Josh does the introductions, Hikey is struck by Phoebe's pagan beauty. Hikey extends her hand in expectation of a formal shake, but Phoebe has no such intention; without hesitation she gives Hikey such a sincere hug on the natural level, that Hikey's sour estimation of humans is immediately revised; returned once again to the more universal principles of human ethics and love that she had held before the teenyboppers made assaults on her construction.

At once Hikey's appetite returns. Her tummy ache is gone and she feels hungry.

They all had agreed in advance to take the old scenic route #1 along the coast, rather than the inland highway, so that Hikey could get a good view of the Pacific Ocean and the writhing coastline. So, after loading the car, they get underway with Josh driving, Vladg in the front passenger seat, Hikey in the back behind Josh with Phoebe sitting next to her. Phoebe starts out with a running commentary on the California coastline, but, as they hit it off so well, the talk quickly shifts to their individual taste in shoes, bras and blouses while they speed by the blueness of the ocean and the billowing waves biting at the wild coastline.

During a lull in their chatter, Phoebe tells Vladg the sad tale of Lydia's attack, her broken jaw and that she is still in hospital with the aftermaths of a concussion. Vladg is stunned. At certain times he is capable of highly rationalized thought and this is one of those times. His hope had been that Bram would forgive Lydia, not be vindictive for the divorce and her love of Phoenix, but he knew in his heart that this was wishful thinking, that Bram would never give up until he got his way, no matter the harm to others, even to those he loved.

∞

When they leave the Old Coast Highway and hit Salina St., entering Santa Barbara, a decision needs to be made. The four of them have some misgivings about splitting up, but there is nothing else for it. Vladg really is pressured to see Lydia to whom he remains devoted although now the entirety of his love is directed to Hikey. Phoebe is busting at the seams to see her sister Phoenix. Hikey is beginning to feel the effects of her hectic voyage as well as the eight-hour time change from London.

She wants to get out of her travel duds and take a good afternoon nap and she is confident that Josh will take care of all the little things that have to be done at the motel as he and Phoebe had done the booking arrangements. So Josh drops

Phoebe and Vladg off at Cottage and Hikey goes along with him to the motel which is not much of a drive down the hill from the hospital.

∞

At Cottage, as soon as Tony Gentile the detective leaves, Vladg enters Lydia's room. She says, "Hello Niner" using her nickname for him as if they were still lovers and he was her companion. She speaks with a slight hissing sound, superimposed upon her light Irish brogue, as her teeth are clenched together from the device immobilizing her jaw.

Vladg has to smile; he moves his bulk towards her, avoiding the wire contraption that holds her jawbones together, kisses her on the cheek very gently so as not to disturb the healing process.

"Well, being an Irish lass it must hurt not to be able to open your mouth very far!"

"Ah, be off with you," Lydia whispers through her teeth, loving his remark.

Vladg fakes it; as if he takes her phrase concretely, makes as if to go: "Your wish is my command, mistress."

Lydia tries not to smile which would hurt her face.

"Come, sit by me, yes that chair, draw it up close there's something I want to ask you."

Vladg knows when Lydia is serious; this is undoubtedly to be one of her 'significant conversations".

"Vladg, look closely at me, forget the broken jaw, do you see anything different in my face?"

Vladg studies her face seriously, she does look more fragile and there are small oval pouches under her eyes, not very heavy, but yes, there is something else.

"I think I do. Those crinkly crows' feet at the edges of your eyes, they're steeper, perhaps a little longer as well."

"Yep, and look at the fold between my nose and the outer edge of my lips, that's more tunneled than it was, isn't it?"

Again Vladg takes his time, he is not about to make light of this, especially when it comes to Lydia's face, he wants to be accurate.

"Yes, it is…"

"You know what this means don't you?"

"Not exactly…"

"It means I'm aging. No more eternity on earth. New wrinkles, dryer skin, deeper folds; don't you see Vladg, I'm losing all my vampire powers, I'm becoming human again, I can finally make my goodbyes to the memories of my youth, and eventually I will get old and weaken like everyone else."

Vladg is stunned.

"How did this come about?"

"I'm not certain, but I believe when I found my love, my true love in Phoenix, that my soul was in God's hands and it just wasn't worth the effort for Satan to fight over, so he decided to abandon me. Of course I had lost Bram's protection long beforehand, and a vampire without a male protector is easy pickings."

"You know, I never would have said this when I was living with you, but considering what I've seen the last few months, that seems as good an explanation as any. You haven't been vampiring around for quite a while, have you?"

"That's right, and I haven't felt the need to drink blood at all, fact is my diet has been very similar to Phoenix's as she is striving to keep her weight gain to a minimum during the pregnancy, so I've mostly been eating like her, low on starches and fats, fairly high on protein, but not particularly bloody meats which she doesn't like."

"Amazing. So you will die eventually?"

"Yes, and I'm looking forward to it in a way. I've spent so much time here on earth already. The only thing is I don't know how long I have…"

"No human knows that Lydia. If you believe in God that seems to be his secret…"

"I suppose. It's just that I'd like to spend enough time here with Phoenix to see Joseph Christian grow up to be a man."

"Is that the baby? The name you've given him."

"Yes, we intend to baptize him right off, almost as soon as he takes his first breath…"

"Well watch out you two don't drown him right off as you say, the poor thing has been imprisoned for nine months in a watery world and now you are going to dunk him again…"

"Got to make sure we're secure before 'you know who' gets into the act…"

"All right! Hope you know how to do it."

"Oh no. We're not the ones. Phoenix has already spoken to the chaplain here at the hospital, he'll be doing the job."

"A professional, eh?"

"Only way to go, this baptism has got to be done right."

"Look Lydia, do you mind if I change the subject. I do have something important to ask you?"

"Sure and it's high time too."

"You know what I'm going to ask?"

"Don't forget I can still read your thoughts a bit, though I'm out of practice."

"Well, I know you've given me my liberty but the magistrate in London wants to see the title you hold over me; he wants it signed over by you granting my independence and freedom to conduct myself as a freewheeling Duplicant in society. In other words, he needs proof that you have no holds on me whatsoever in perpetuity."

"Of course, I understand. The title is in the wall safe at home. I should be out of here by Wednesday, and then I'll see to it, okay?"

"That's fine. It will have to be notarized."

"We'll get it done, satisfied?"

"Yes. Then, and only then, will my marriage to Hikey be really complete. As of now we are hitched for what the British call a six-month trial period. They do it with humans as well…"

"When did that start?"

"A few years ago I guess. I'm not certain exactly when, but Hikey might know, she's in to all the legal-political stuff."

"Speaking of which, where is she? When do I get to meet her?"

"She was dead tired, time jag and all. I'll bring her tomorrow, she had one terrible episode on board ship."

"Oh, what was that?"

Vladg tells her all that went on with the South American teenagers, and while he is talking, both Phoenix and Phoebe come in dragging their mother along who is being discharged.

The mother is animated and immediately sticks her foot into it when she is introduced to Vladg.

"Oh, you look so human," she exclaims.

"Is that a compliment or an insult?" Vladg retorts.

The mother realizes at once that she has committed a social error, but Phoenix comes to her rescue.

"You have something to talk about which interests all of us, namely, the feelings and dreams you underwent while under the spell you suffered from smelling the flowers." She does not mention the fact that the 'spell' was really a trance like state which came about from one of Bram's potions.

The mother begins by stating how surprised she was that the ordeal lasted well over twenty-four hours.

Lydia tries to explain that some trances last so long because they provide an escape. An escape to a different reality, to a world that seems more pleasant than the one the person is living.

"This wasn't like that," the mother interrupts, "please listen to my story."

Her plea pays off; all four give her their attention.

"I was walking toward the wharf here, I believe it is called Stearns, anyway the weather was all different, driving rain, much wetter than it is now. It was close to midnight, and as I approached the smell of the sea, I could hear the church bells booming the hour. The tones were half-smothered by the marching rain, when a man with an odd figure and a wolf-like head, glided past me like a ghost in the gloom. He made directly toward the wharf beckoning me on. I felt that some dreadful tragedy was about to be enacted, but somehow I was forced to do his bidding. I sped after him, actually more in pursuit than following, as he seemed to be moving very fast. He was like a shadow that I couldn't catch up with but out along the deserted wharf I ran to its farther end. Somehow I felt like a fugitive, as if I had stolen something, but the mysterious figure appealed to me, as if he were a guardian of sort. No matter how hard I tried, my efforts were in vain, I simply could not overtake him.

I called out to him, asking him to wait, to hold up, as I was now at the extreme end of the pier, in the scourging rain which lashed fiercely at me., nearly blinding my eyes. It was then I realized it was not just the rain, but my tears of grief, of loss. I suddenly knew I was in mourning, that my daughter Phoenix had lost her child to this shadow of a man who was now far out to sea holding a baby, chuckling and coo-cooing while he seemed to glide over the waves.

"The night wind caught at me, threw me wildly into the air and tried to toss me into the blackness of the sea, I came near losing my balance but somehow I kicked off my shoes and this saved me, as I landed on my bare feet, back on the wooden ties of the wharf, struggling to stand erect. At this fearful moment I stumbled and fell! I was badly bruised and felt angry and stupid that I had allowed this to happen. I got my Midwestern grit together, sat doggedly up and began to check out the chafing of my skin. I cast my eyes far out to sea, but the spectral figure of the man with the baby had evaporated, not heavenward, but apparently into the dread waters of the sea plunging down to oblivion.

"Now I was desperate. I felt that my entire life was a failure. The voice of the gale picked up in my imagination, but I moved forward a few paces over the piles, and gradually I picked up my stride and got off the pier.

"When I came to I was here in the hospital, I felt more secure but my entire body was bruised and my feet were indeed chafed, how do you explain that?"

Lydia and Phoenix exchange knowing glances.

They surmised that the magic potion prepared by Bram had been initially destined for Phoenix. His intent was to show his power over the pregnancy, and to make Phoenix feel that any resistance to his control was useless. But through the intercession of fate, the mother's simple desire to smell the fragrance of the roses, she had received the brunt impact of the concoction. This caused her to have the dream like sequences that were really a display meant for Phoenix.

Obviously Phoenix could not tell her mother this, so she simply said that the dream probably had something to do with their conversation on Palm Sunday, in the saloon where they had had a drink together.

This mollified the mother somewhat, as she certainly didn't want to go into her 'secret' in front of Phoebe, let alone Vladg and Lydia, so all she said was:

"Yes, I suppose that could be it, but how do you explain the abrasions to my skin and feet?"

"I've scratched myself on occasion pretty badly while having nightmarish dreams," Phoebe throws in.

"True," the mother says, "That could be the explanation; I have done that myself in the past."

Even so, the mystery her mother described has aroused Phoebe's curiosity. She intends to talk to her sister later and get the true skinny on all this at a more appropriate time.

Vladg also recognizes the meaning of the tale. He concludes immediately that the mother's story was a consequence of Bram's concoction as it was very much like others that he had prepared in Holland and bragged about.

Phoenix was undaunted. Actually the captive-like story her mother had told under the trance influence made her more confident that she could defy Bram. 'If he had to resort to such low down treachery as this to accomplish his goal, then undoubtedly his powers over me are becoming less and less intense'.

Lydia too was unalloyed by the entire event. She knew Bram better than anyone and hinted to Phoenix that this kind of action was a relief that it meant his powers as a Dhampir were indeed waning, that a true Vampire, like Drakonius, would have been much more direct and violent.

When her surgeon arrived, Lydia was overjoyed. After a rather thorough examination, he told her she could be discharged this very day as long as she really took things easy and stayed at home. Lydia promised to do exactly as he said, but secretively she planned to visit the special eye clinic for dogs and see how Jeanne d'Arc was doing.

∞

On Wednesday afternoon, the entire group was at Lydia's, ooohing and aaahing over what Lydia and Phoenix had done to Vladg's old room. Even Vladg was impressed and he was not easily captivated by anything that represented a remodeling of something that had once been his domain.

This was followed by a late lunch of spinach salad prepared with Greek yoghurt, low-salt Portuguese anchovies, a sprinkling of crushed Mediterranean pine nuts and a hefty dose of Russian vodka mixed with fresh lemon juice and eaten with chunks of Italian ciabatta bread. Then everyone lay back, digesting and gossiping.

The twins huddled together over their frenzied times with jocks in the one bedroom in Manhattan; Vladg and Josh tried to figure out what they could do to repair George who, it seemed, was staring at them; Emily, the mother, got off her high horse on Duplicants and sat together with Hikey. She was giving Hikey a rundown on some political trends in Nebraska; how the Green and Independent parties had overwhelmed the combined Demopublicans and CPP (Corporate-Peoples Party) in the last election of 2058. This was all familiar territory to Hikey and helped her to put the Queen Victoria episode out of her mind and come into her own. She was gradually taking more of an active part in the conversations, absorbing American ways and generally getting acculturated. She told Emily that after the birthing she and Vladg intended to take the air shuttle up to San Francisco and tour the bay area, especially the new Duplicant factory that was being built in San Jose, primarily designed to create female Duplicants of high calibre.

Phoenix, who recently had become quite dominant, had impressed on Lydia the necessity of following doctor's orders, so Lydia was resigned to the fact that she had to stay home. She was by herself, watching a 4-D movie, a mythical romance between Zeus and Diana, taking place on the moon Ganymede which, in reality, had recently been terraformed.

The men were really relaxed, when suddenly Phoenix broke off her chat with Phoebe and announced that she had to make her daily trip to Dr. Maloff's office for a check-up. She mentioned that the office was only a block from the hospital and wanted to know if either of the men would like to go with her.

Vladg hesitated as he did not wish to leave Hikey alone again; Emily was dying to go, but she knew it was safer for Phoenix to have a man along, so she relented and said nothing. Josh volunteered after he received a grim look from Phoebe, who wanted very much to tag along, but knew that she had better not leave her mother alone after what she had been through. Then there was the fact that Bram, who was undoubtedly in the neighborhood, was up to his old tricks. 'Yes, they had better stick together'.

Phoenix was always a bit high strung prior to her doctor's visits, especially now that the time was so short to her expected day; she urged Josh to hurry-up, said she did not want to be late for her appointment. He was surprised at this as neither of the twins had ever been punctual before the pregnancy, and Feeby still never made it on time to anything. But he swallowed the 'hurry-up' and they took off quickly while all the rest stayed put. The 4-D movie was still on, but no one had the patience to watch so Lydia got out the Hickory sword-cane and handed it over to Vladg who went right at it, showing off his antics with the stick and the foil which peeved Hikey no end as it reminded her of the evening in Holland when he had failed to watch her political speech against Rümke.

∞

Late in the afternoon Bram stood outside the office building on Pueblo Street where Dr. Maloff's group of OB's leased space. He was waiting for Phoenix to come out, wanted her to see him, wanted her to know that he was unchanged from his customary ways, and that, in public, he was not a threat to her in any way. When she finally emerged, accompanied by Josh, he straightened himself up with a jerk, lurched heavily to his better side so that she could get a good look at his profile; then he rocked critically on his heels for a few moments, his fiery heart pumping madly. He greeted her as if he was still her master and she his slave. Her now ample breasts twinged at his power; he was still able to throw fear into her heart, but he no longer had any control over her. She would do the unthinkable if it came to it.

Josh would have none of this; he barely acknowledged Bram's presence.

Then, with a flourish, he hooked his arm into the crook of Phoenix's elbow, protected her waddling gait and ushered her off to the parking lot where he helped her get into the car.

But Bram had accomplished his purpose. Now all he had to do was wait for Dr. Maloff.

The parking lot is situated about a hundred yards from the building and Doris was stationed there with another one of her flunkies. She made a point of it; never to use the same slave twice on a mission.

This one was even more remote than the other. He toyed with a dangerous looking hand axe sitting on his lap as if it were a plaything. Actually, these two served only as insurance since Bram intended to do the dear doctor in all by himself. Much as he preferred female blood to men's, his preference in this case was to exsanguinate Dr. Maloff in the old style. Then the slave could split him like a fish and send him to his eternal repose.

So they waited until darkness set in.

But so did Tony Gentile who had remained staked out in the selfsame parking lot for hours and now was running out of donuts.

Chapter XXXII

Holy Week: Wednesday Evening and Maundy Thursday

As soon as dusk descended in earnest, Tony Gentile, his stomach growling, called for back-up. Then he ambled over to Doris's car and flashed his shield. He glanced briefly at her, but otherwise wasted no time on formalities:

"Get out of the car and give up the weapon," he tells the kid holding the axe, "be careful how you do it!"

The kid takes his time, sidles out of the car and rolls the axe handle over and over in his hands. He is thinking about it, decides not to, and grudgingly hands the axe over to the detective.

"Officer, he's a minor…" Doris starts up.

"Detective," Tony corrects. "My name is Detective Gentile. On the street this kid is called Hatchet Jake and I want him to put both his hands on the roof of the car right now!"

Reluctantly the hatchet kid obeys.

"Whatever for?" Doris asks. "He's my ward, I run a foster home for runaways, and the police know the types of kids I nurture along."

"No matter! He's been in trouble before…. I'm hauling him in for questioning. What's your real name kid?"

"Jake, is all," the kid says, sullen as hell.

Tony kicks his legs farther apart.

"Full name," Tony demands.

"Jake Wilson," the kid sulks out, barely audible.

By now it is getting much darker and the flood lights in the parking lot snap on.

A few moments later two uniformed patrolmen, both SWAT trained Basic IV's, arrive. They pull up right behind Jake brandishing billy clubs. They hustle him into the back seat of their black and white. Tony cautions them on the axe, tells them to book the kid for openly carrying a dangerous weapon in a private vehicle and loitering with intent. He hands the axe over to one of the Basics and they burn rubber taking off.

Once they're gone he turns all his attention to Doris.

"You see that guy hanging around just outside the Medical Building?"

"Sure. That's my old friend, Mr. Alucard, he's staying at my place while he's here. No law against that is there."

"I know who he is. What I don't know is what he's doing here or why."

"He's waiting for his old girl friend to come out…"

"Don't give me that, I saw her leave with the Humilicant over half an hour ago. What's he sticking around for, what's he up to?"

"I have no idea what you mean. If the girl's already left, then I missed her. I been talking up a storm to Hatchet Jake, so no wonder I didn't see her come out, and I certainly didn't see any Humilicant."

"Then you're not as observant as I thought, and anyway, you're feeding me horse manure, you know what that is don't you?"

"I'm not going to answer that. I have half a mind to report you to your supervisor for insolence…"

"You do that lady…but we'll find out what we need to know from the kid."

"Oh no you won't, he'll keep his trap shut all right."

"Naaah, we'll offer him the equivalent of thirty pieces of silver, he'll talk for his freedom, all these kids are gutless Judas's. Then you and that Alucard fellow," he points a finger at Bram, "will be up the creek."

At that moment Dr. Maloff comes out of the building, descends the front steps of the entranceway and is immediately accosted by Bram.

Bram speaks forcefully, but there is a certain amount of respect in the way he handles his words with the doctor.

"I want to introduce myself; I'm Phoenix Winthrop's significant other, the man who fathered her pregnancy."

Dr. Maloff stares at him; he can hardly believe that this somewhat dapper man, at least in his fifties if not more, could be involved with Phoenix sexually. On the other hand, in his many years of delivering babies he has seen some strange couples. His medical mind turns on; he tries to treat this odd occurrence professionally.

"She has never mentioned you to me sir, but if you wish to make an appointment to have your spermatic DNA checked out, I would advise you to run up to the office and do so before it closes."

Bram's patience is at an end; he is ready to charge. He moves forward lithely, uncoiling his jaws like a cobra, his long furrowed tongue slips out, his fangs come into view and he starts to drool voluminously.

The doctor's feelings transcend expression. He is more fascinated than frightened by the astonishing display. Not a syllable does he utter, but with a deep-drawn sigh he turns his broad back upon Bram and makes ready to get away to his car.

The detective senses something strange going on, abandons Doris and runs over the hundred yards or so to intercept Bram with the doctor. Unfortunately, his hustle is too late to have heard the initial confrontation.

Bram's peripheral vision and acute hearing perceives a trap. His snake-like features recede to normal just as Tony arrives in a huff, flashing his shield.

"Is this man bothering you?" he asks Maloff, standing between the two and pushing Bram backward, holding him at arm's length.

"No, I don't think so. He claims he has fathered the pregnancy of one of my patients and I have simply advised him to get a DNA check so that he can prove his involvement in the matter."

"That's all?"

"Well, for a moment there, he did seem to get his dander up. I thought he looked ferocious but I'm already late for dinner and I may have been somewhat hypoglycemic myself. I'd appreciate it if I could head on home; my wife has everything on the table."

Tony's stomach is audibly growling. He wants to ask the doctor what his wife had prepared for dinner, but he automatically suppresses the impulse, returns at once to his professional self.

"Of course, you can go. But if he makes any further attempts to contact you, other than at your office, I expect you to report it immediately. Here's my card. If you call that number, you can avoid the station's registry."

"Certainly detective," he glances at the card. On the inside of his side pocket there is a smaller linen pocket sewn in. It is made for the purpose and he offhandedly sticks the card into this opening.

"Ah? Did you want my card?"

"Well, I'm a bachelor, but we never know what fate has in store for us do we? Maybe there is a woman somewhere out there hunkering for my genes."

"That's right, you never know. By the way, my name's Paul Maloff."

"Gentile. Anthony Gentile."

He shakes hands with Maloff who jogs over to his private space in the parking lot and gets in the back seat. His Basic II starts the car and they get underway.

Doris watches carefully, and when Bram comes back, having been released by the detective with a firm warning, she says:

"We've got to go to Plan B with Dr. Abraxas."

Bram nods in agreement. He is royally pissed.

∞

At Lydia's, Phoenix and Josh were eager to tell everyone, about the occurrence outside the medical building, except that Phoenix did not wish her mother to know about Bram. So she and Josh skirted around Bram's identity and just said that this strange man with 'uneven eyes' had accosted her menacingly. Phoenix mentioned how Josh had saved the day, his presence and manner protecting her. Phoebe's eyes glittered with pride, this news scoring brownie points for Josh with her. All the rest caught on to what really transpired, except for Hikey. She was let in to the secret afterwards by Vladg, when they were alone at the motel.

To a degree Phoenix felt guilty about deceiving her mother, but in actuality Emily remained convinced that prayer alone could resolve every nasty situation. Emily did not, would never, admit to the existence of vampires. Even though she had seen strange things, savage things, at the baby shower and while she had been instrumental in rescuing her daughter from the invasion of Iphigènie by the singing of biblical hymns, she still ascribed these happenings to the devil alone, not to vampires on earth carrying out his bidding. Neither did her mystifying dream sequences, during her trance, lead to any convincing proof other than the existence of 'bad faeries'. She saw no correlation between the two events.

As long as her mother thought this way, Phoenix was convinced if she opened up to her, it would start the ball rolling, her mother asking all kinds of questions going back to the initial involvement with Bram which led to the pregnancy and her own excursions into vampirism. All this just might destroy the way she had traditionally bonded with her mom. No, it was better to hide certain parts, at least until after Easter when she became a grandmother. Phoenix was certain the baby would change her mother's attitude on a horde of monstrous mysteries.

In private she told Lydia how the sight of Bram, suddenly appearing before her at the base of the steps, hit her with such a terrible force that her knees began to tremble when his fiercely vibrating voice spoke as if he were still her master. Yes, there lingered an excruciating, but tantalizing, feeling of having your own life's blood drawn away by such a powerful man, but no, she no longer felt he could victimize her. 'That submissive obedience is no longer a part of me'.

As she said this, a deep quiver of vindication went through her, and a faint tinge of color stole back into her pallid cheeks, reassuring Lydia that she spoke the truth.

"He can wander where he will," Lydia said, "as long as he makes no attempt to subdue you…"

It was then that Phoenix drew a long deep breath and told Lydia the part that she had left out, that she had experienced murderous thoughts, homicidal thoughts for the first time in her life. If it came to it, if he tried to dominate the birthing, or her, or the baby she would put her plan into effect.

Curious as she was, Lydia didn't ask. She could see that Phoenix's eyes were hot and tired, and that a good hug expressing their closeness and love superseded and made faint all other feelings.

∞

That same Wednesday evening, at Doris's place, she and Dr. Abraxas were huddled together with Bram contemplating the plan that would be put into effect on Holy Thursday morning.

"You see," Dr. Abraxas was saying, "Dr. Maloff covers for all the other physicians in his group on Christian holidays. That's a lot of work. I am sure he will not want to miss breakfast after his extensive hospital rounds. I'll meet him in the doctor's dining room."

"You can be sure of this? A good deal depends on it. Phoenix's office appointment with the good doctor is at eleven."

"I've done my due diligence carefully; know his ways like the back of my hand. My salve should do the job. That's all I can say. Nothing is for certain, but if he doesn't show up, we've still got Doris as backup. Her voice alone will entice him, and then you shall have to take over with your potion."

"Yes, I have the selfsame elixir I used on Eiselman, and I was able to direct him to do my bidding for months at a time with that one trance and a little reflex brain conditioning."

"Good. It's settled then. I'll use my sorcery to convince him to induce Phoenix to deliver on Good Friday. Should he not appear in the dining room, you and Doris must catch him as he leaves the hospital and then do your thing. Agreed?"

"Absolutely."

541

"It will be my pleasure to lure him into your arms," Doris says to Bram, as if she were reminiscing on ancient times.

"If this works as planned Satan will be pleased," claims Dr. Abraxas.

"And so will I," Bram agrees.

∞

At two a.m. on Maundy Thursday Dr. Maloff was gently awakened by the house Basic II who answered all after hour's hospital calls and doubled as his valet and chauffeur when he was not in service of the wife who commanded most of his daytime activities. He was informed by the Basic that there was a threatening premature delivery and that it was most likely a set of twins.

The doctor surmised who it was; one of his questionable colleagues for whom he was covering made a habit of not giving full information on the status of his patients. Understandably he was upset, and not just at the hour, but the fact of the multiple births; surely that should have been told to him by some member of the staff.

The doctor was only half-awake as the Basic sponge bathed and dressed him, carried him down the stairs and placed him in the rear seat of the large Buick sedan. He continued to snooze on the way, but needed a cortical stimulant of 5-hetoxy methamphetamine to awaken properly and get all his professional faculties in order. This was done quickly and carried out without issue such that by the time the doctor reached the delivery room he was in shape to fulfill his duties adequately.

He found the young mother already suspended above the delivery table by the anti-gravity beams and explained that her own OB was off for the holiday. Although disappointed, she accepted Dr. Maloff's assistance. The two Basic IV's, classified as registered nurses, had done a good job, she was in the proper obstetrical position for Maloff to get to work.

He first spread the labia, the lips of the vulva, with the use of two opposing, funneled tractor beams. Then he was able to complete the dilation of the elongated cervix and enlarge what had been a small aperture to an extensive opening which could easily accommodate the head of an infant, especially a premature one. This procedure obviated the need for an episiotomy which had been so necessary early in the century before the advent of spread-beams and anti-gravity rays.

He delivered the first baby head on with no problem. He handed the crying infant to one of the Basics who aspirated mucus and phlegm from nasal passages and the baby's mouth, cleaned off the lanugo hairs and oils and after swathing the newborn in swaddling clothes, handed it over to the other Basic to be put through its checkpoints for organ size and quality and metabolic codes.

The second baby was another story. One foot was already visible, partially sticking out of the mother's vulva. Dr. Maloff adroitly pushed the foot back in, manually rotated the infant one-eighty until the baby's head was foremost, and then, when the mother pushed on the next big contraction, the baby practically delivered herself.

Once respiration and heart rate were checked out traditionally, the twins were passed through several different radio-magnetic scanners, pronounced organically intact and returned to their mother, who was now resting in a special post-delivery bed, so designed as to keep her legs slightly suspended and rotated above the bed's surface for adequate return of circulation to selected organs that were detected to be in need of more blood flow.

Each baby, a boy and a girl, weighed less than five pounds, so after the mother did her soft cuddling embraces and exclamations of wonder, the neonatologist took over. He was a pediatrician who traditionally worked nights and had witnessed this procedure well over a thousand times.

After saying a few congratulatory words to the young mother, Maloff had to make a practical decision. By the time he was finished and out of delivery it was well past four. Should he return home for a few hours or stay here? He chose to go to the Doctor's lounge and grab a couple of hours' sleep. He T-celled his Basic II and told him to wait in the parking lot with the car, but if the Mrs. called for whatever he was free to go.

The couch in the lounge was lumpy but soft and comfortable. He downed a two-and-a-half-hour soporific and in minutes he was fast asleep. He awoke precisely at seven a.m., took a shower, drew on fresh whites and after a quick cup of coffee started out to make his rounds.

Chapter XXXIII

Hutspot to the Rescue

Dr. Paul Maloff was not so professionally mechanical that he failed to note the almost superhuman creativity of motherhood. He was in awe of the delivery of the twins and was pleased with the hospital rounds that he had just completed. The satisfaction of a job well done and the happiness expressed by the majority of mothers with their babies was evident, although there were one or two who seemed to be suffering from post-partum depression and for these he called in the psychology experts to remedy the bond between mother and child.

All this activity left him famished and he was now seated comfortably in the hospital cafeteria chowing down on crisp bacon and scrambled eggs, wheat toast and strong coffee. He had thrown caution to the winds as far as his cholesterol was concerned and was just about ready for another mouthful when Dr. Abraxas approached his table and asked, very politely, if he would like some company. Dr. Maloff had always thought that if he ever grew a beard, he would keep it trim and tidy. This man's beard was ill kempt, largely a dull black color with rude patches of gray, and the overall growth was uneven. Then too there was something beastly about this particular colleague's face, with his pointed teeth and wide smelly nostrils, but there was no way in the world he could refuse the man's request, so he said: "Please, have a seat."

Abraxas set down his tray and true to form, in his guise as a gentleman, he forced Maloff to lay down his fork and shake hands. Maloff immediately felt a soft gooey film spreading quickly over his palm. The feeling was disgusting and as soon as he was able to disguise his action, he made as if his napkin had fallen to the floor, bent down to 'retrieve' it and wipe his hand dry. To his surprise his hand was already free of the 'sweat'. What he didn't realize was that the neurotoxic potion, formulated as a salve, had already been absorbed and was now at work, penetrating his brain and entire central nervous system. Maloff tried to return to his food, but his appetite had left him. He cautiously downed the rest of his cup of coffee but even caffeine seemed not to do the trick.

Dr. Abraxas, rather monotonously, appeared to be going on and on over an article in the Lancet regarding sexuality in Duplicants, but his voice seemed to be coming from very far off, as if from a distant land, and for some reason Maloff readily accepted this state of affairs. Indeed, he now felt closer to Abraxas than earlier when he had wanted to be alone to enjoy his breakfast, when he had thought the man's presence to be a nuisance, a deliberate intrusion into his solitude. Now he admonished himself for feeling this way and at once he felt terribly lonely. For some reason Abraxas passed his hands back and forth before his eyes and this gesture seemed perfectly reasonable to Maloff. Certainly there was nothing wrong with anything the man did.

Maloff did not sob, but tears actually came to his eyes for thinking such morbid and selfish thoughts.

The tears were Abraxas's sign that his potion was working adequately and now he announced firmly, "You have an appointment with a certain Ms Phoenix Winthrop at eleven this morning, do you not?"

Maloff did not see this question as intrusive to his professional privacy.

"Yes, certainly I do. She was having early contractions, most likely Braxton Hicks. False or not, I have asked her to come to the office every day this week. Just a precaution until her due date, probably on Easter Sunday…"

"Or sooner!"

"Yes, or sooner," Maloff repeated.

"I want you to induce her to deliver tomorrow, on Good Friday. I will be there to assist you."

Maloff's eyes were no longer moist.

"Certainly, if that is your wish, I will do as you suggest."

"You have the necessary twenty-four-hour induction pills?"

"Of course, my office has the latest of everything…if its high tech, we purchase it. That's our group's motto so to speak."

"Good. Remember to give her the pills, two should do the job, tell her they are for her overall wellbeing."

"I suppose that is true."

"Do not suppose. Nothing I say to you is to be construed as supposition, do you understand?"

"Yes, I understand."

"I am not admonishing you, but I must be absolutely certain you fully grasp my intent. I will be there to assist you in the delivery."

"Of course."

"Good. There is one more thing."

"Yes."

"Ms Winthrop has a lady friend; a certain Lydia Alucard I believe her name is."

"Yes, I'm familiar with her. Over the weeks and months that I have treated Ms Winthrop she has confided in me. The two plan to marry soon after she gives birth. The child is to be named Joseph Christian."

Abraxas winces visibly when he hears the name pronounced.

"Enough. I want this Lydia to attend the delivery. I have a present of sorts for her."

"That is possible. The hospital makes no distinction between women and men when it comes to the delivery room. A proper aseptic gown will be provided for her by one of the Basics."

"Good. Then I am going to leave you now. When I say goodbye to you, you will respond by saying: 'Have a great day'."

Abraxas stands up, gives Maloff one last eye shattering stare.

"Goodbye."

"Have a great day."

∞

Phoenix is not a woman to be late. She has had to hustle Vladg up a bit in order to be on time for her appointment with Dr. Maloff. Vladg has offered to serve as her protector on this day just as Josh had done the day before. Vladg shakes off his morning doldrums and they make it to the office right on the stroke of eleven.

They do not have to wait but are immediately called into the consulting room.

Dr. Maloff is still quite observant in spite of the trance he is under. He sees immediately that Vladg is a Duplicant, but Phoenix simply introduces him as if he were mortal. Although he is curious, Maloff makes no fuss, skips the issue.

Phoenix too inhibits an urge to ask Maloff something. She sees that his eyes are somewhat glazed over, but makes no mention of it.

"Have you had any further labor contractions?" he asks.

"No doctor, none at all. In fact, I'm getting a bit worried that I may be overdue, I do so want to deliver on Easter Sunday."

"Understood. Let's do the tocodynamometry test in the examining room."

He asks Vladg to excuse them but first explains that the instrument's purpose is to test for labor contractions and is useful at times in avoiding premature birth.

Vladg is scientifically interested, he had really wanted to be present to observe the instrument in action, but Maloff seems to be treating him with the same respect he would accord any human, so Vladg does not persist.

After about fifteen minutes they return. Maloff announces there are no signs whatsoever of uterine contractions.

"If you wish I can provide you with induction pills, they will insure that your labor begins on time." He hands two pills and a glass of water over to Phoenix.

She accepts them, plays back and forth with the pills in her hands, but doesn't drink them down. "They won't provoke me earlier. I certainly don't want to deliver tomorrow, not on Good Friday."

"Nothing is for certain, so I can't promise, but usually it takes forty-eight hours or so to really stimulate the womb, so I doubt you have anything to fear. As it is now, the uterus appears relatively dormant; the test shows minimal signs of uterine activity."

Phoenix thinks this over. She really does not want to be overdue.

"What if this does not work?"

"We can always start an induction infusion on Easter Sunday, that way you can be assured…"

"Why take these two pills then?"

"Because you said you wanted to deliver as naturally as possible, an IV infusion of oxytoxin is not natural, but will do the job if that is your preferred day."

"I see." She is still pondering what to do. "I want to talk this over with Lydia, you don't mind that do you?"

"I'd prefer you take them now," he says assertively.

This is the first time he has ever spoken so forcefully to her.

She is offended, gets her nerve up and decides to say what she feels.

"That doesn't sound like you Doctor; you've never talked harshly to me before."

Maloff realizes he has committed a faux pas; that this statement was very unlike his natural approach to patients and certainly not in keeping with the relationship he had cultivated with Phoenix over the time he has known her. As a way out, he decides to make a joke of it.

"It has to do with Matzos."

"Matzos?"

"Yes. You see it is our Passover and all week I have not had any bread to eat, just these unleavened matzos, I believe it is getting to me." He burps. "Sorry."

Now he feels doubly guilty as this is an outright lie since he has had wheat toast for breakfast with bacon, the last surely a religious no-no. Nevertheless, the lie is effective, both

Vladg and Phoenix chuckle at his gastrointestinal plight.

Somehow the laugh relieves the tension; Phoenix swigs the pills down.

"So there," she says, imitating Lydia once again.

"Good so," he yuk-yuks. "I don't think you have to come in tomorrow," he lies again.

"Let's skip a day and make it for Saturday, how's that?"

"Fine," she says, "I could use a day off before the fireworks start."

Now they both chortle in turn, but for different reasons; Phoenix to relieve her nervousness over the forthcoming 'pains' of childbirth and the doctor because he has gotten away with the scheme. He was worried over what harm Abraxas might do to him if he had failed to complete the required task.

She shakes the doctor's hand, as does Vladg. They both leave in good spirits.

Maloff breathes a sigh of relief.

He reports immediately to Abraxas.

∞

That evening the entire clan is seated comfortably at table for a group supper. Emily, in her glory, is reciting grace, a passage from Romans, and all the rest are holding hands. Vladg and Hikey, both non-worshipers, are respectful of the beliefs of humans in prayer. They too bow their heads, as if in reverence, so as not to disturb the mood created by the special occasion.

All seven are gathered together to memorialize their presence in anticipation of Joseph Christian's birth, not to do an imitation of the Last Supper. But since it is Holy Thursday, religious thoughts were clearly on their minds. One stumbling block was what to eat? Other than unleavened bread and wine, which was nixed by all, no one could come up with a good idea except Hikey, so they took her up on her suggestion.

She had offered to prepare a country Dutch meal, going as far back as medieval times, called hutspot which she had picked up from Cynthia. (In addition to the potatoes and onions, Cynthia had revamped the ancient Dutch recipe with a variety of

Indonesian herbs and spices including Dong Quai and a small amount of Valeriana to quiet down the intestinal gurgles).

Since it is unknown what type of wine was served at the Last Supper Lydia made her best guess that the climate in southern Sicily now paralleled that of Judea back then. A very dry, 2037 bottle of red Italian wine from Sicily was uncorked and served. This particular vintage happened to be very stimulating to the tongue and as such tended to pick up the flow of conversation. Since Phoenix was forbidden to drink any alcohol whatsoever Hikey made her a cup of tea steeped in very hot water, but not simmered, with the Dong Quai leaves she had left over from her preparation of hutspot.

Once the meal was finished, and the onions and spices had done their work (evidenced by all in the rumbling sounds of borborygmi unsuppressed by the Valerian) the murmurings and chatter of the group foraged into the greater scheme of things, the political and economic problems of the world. As is often the case, the talk became more general and eventually philosophical. Questions were asked such as why is there life at all, on which Josh held forth. Hikey, naturally, had a different view. This led to, 'Why is there a universe'? Vladg spoke out on this one. Then the discussion got more specific, almost exclusively related to the subject of childbirth and the miracle of creation. Emily had strict views on this issue.

Then everything changed again from the general to the specific and the immense size of Phoenix's belly. She tolerated the jibes with good cheer, but it was obvious that Phoebe was deadly afraid to have her body distorted in this way. She took a stand and expressed her opinion. It seems the scientists were contriving a new incubation tool of sorts which was designed to take over the fetus at three months' gestation; women would no longer have to go through such radical bodily transformations. Once this subject was milked for all it was worth the conversation got back around to Phoenix and her due date on Sunday.

"What if you give birth on Holy Saturday? That wouldn't be so bad would it?" the mother asks.

"No, that would be okay, it's still a holy day in anticipation of the resurrection; I just hope it's not tomorrow, not on Good Friday."

"But Jesus did give up his life for us on that day," Josh says fervently…

"The Devil doesn't look at it that way," Phoenix says abruptly. He thinks he's won out over the Lord by the crucifixion and all that that entails."

"You know sis," Phoebe says, "I know where you're coming from, but if I were you, and I'm closer to being you than anyone else, I wouldn't worry so much about the Devil in this. I'm sure God has things well in hand for you."

"That's a comforting thought Feeby, and I hope you're right, but just to be on the safe side I'd rather not deliver on Good Friday which to me is really 'Sorrowful Friday'."

There follows a prolonged silence, not provoked by anyone in particular, just hanging in the room like a shroud over the ambience.

Vladg senses the meaning of the moment, changes the subject, as he doesn't want things to get sour.

"Enough on that. What about you Lydia? When are you going to be allowed to leave the house?

"Tomorrow, I have an appointment with the Neurologist. I was hoping you could drive me? Afterward I'd like to visit Jeanne d'Arc if that's all right with you?"

Vladg checks with Hikey who nods in assent.

"I don't have to visit with Dr. Maloff tomorrow, so I can stay here with Feeby and mother. Josh can go hit golf balls if he likes," Phoenix says.

"That's perfect," Lydia says, you three haven't had a chance to be together as of yet; the only glitch is security, what if that delivery boy comes by or you know who?"

"We could hire the Basic III Georgette's again; they weren't too bad at the baby shower."

"Not too good either," Phoebe chimes in, looking sadly at George.

Now Emily pipes up, she is definitely peeved.

"I wish you wouldn't beat around the bush like that she says. I know there's danger, why don't you just name it for god's sake!"

Phoenix finally realizes that this style of avoiding mention of Bram is insulting to her mother, puerile in the extreme. She decides to open up.

"Mother," she begins, "you're right. I've told you some things about Bram, the man who is the father of my child. In the tavern…"

"That was no tavern, you took me to a lowdown saloon, it was awful, but I didn't say anything then because I had hoped you would quit all the deception…I confided in you but it didn't do any good as far as this is concerned!"

Phoenix knew her mother was in her rights to say all this. She decided to get everything off her chest. Her bosom actually heaved violently as she spoke:

"I did tell you that the father of my child is a powerful and dangerous man, but I didn't say that he is a vampire which he is, and not just any vampire but the head of the brotherhood that exists all over this world. You said you could never believe in vampires so yes; I hid this from you. So now you know."

"All I know is that you believe in all this and that is good enough for me. It doesn't matter what I believe or do not believe, you are my daughter and I am prepared to fight for you in any and every way I can."

"You may have to mother. It wouldn't surprise me at all if he was the one behind the poison in the roses that put you into the hospital. So here goes: he is capable of anything and yes, he is a danger to us all, but probably not to me, at least not until I give birth. He is very dangerous to Lydia to whom he was married for some time, so she is in catastrophic danger from him as well, so is Josh and Vladg and to a lesser extent Phoebe and Hikey.

So that's why everyone has been tiptoeing around the subject. I just didn't want you to think of him this way because I thought you would believe that if he is a madman the baby will have his genes and be like him. So that's it. We're all living in fear and with good reason. Now you know."

"Daughter of mine," Emily says, giving her a great hug, "no demon or vampire or any other creature of evil can defeat a Winthrop. Why your father would tear them limb from limb."

With that said, with optimistic mood, they all have a nightcap, Phoenix downs the last dregs of her tea, and everyone decides to call it a night.

∞

Sometime in the middle of the night Phoenix has to get up to go to the bathroom to poop and pee. While she is in the Johnny, she habitually feels her belly. There are a few twitches here and there, but no signs of contractions, not even the false labor pains she has, over time, learned to distinguish from the true ones.

When she finishes her toilette she thinks of Dr. Maloff. 'Yes he has done right by me. I doubt very much that anything significant will happen this day'.

At Paul Maloff's house the situation is quite different.

Maloff has told his wife all that had transpired with Abraxas including his suspicion that Abraxas had somehow poisoned him. He goes on to reveal what he did with Phoenix, the two pills, the first time in his professional life he has ever knowingly told an outright lie to a patient.

Muriel, his wife, happens to be a good listener. A day before, she had also been told the story of her husband meeting up with the detective in the parking lot. Now she advises him to call the detective in the morning and explain all that took place with Abraxas.

"Maybe there's some connection?" she intuits.

"I don't see how. The man that claimed he was the father of my patient's baby was never mentioned by Abraxas…"

"True," Muriel admits, "but the connection is your patient; for once in your life tell me her name!"

Maloff doesn't hesitate.

"Her name is Phoenix…"

"Well if she's as beautiful as in mythology that may be all there is to it, two men interested in the same woman, fighting over her. But there is one thing more…another connection."

"Really, what's that?"

"Some time ago, in the Santa Barbara News-Press, you know how avidly I read the gossip, there was a divorce announcement of a couple named Alucard. The strange sounding of the name stuck with me. Isn't that the moniker this Abraxas gave you when he requested that you ask Phoenix to have her friend attend the delivery?"

"Why yes, I think it is, I'm almost certain…"

"See there, that's the connection…call that detective in the morning! Now go to sleep and for the rest of Passover you had better eat matzos for forgiveness."

Maloff has to snicker, the first time he has broken his solemnity since Abraxas poisoned his system.

∞

In Tony Gentile's small apartment, he too is unable to sleep.

He is toying with his gin and tonic, taking occasional sips, not doing any serious drinking. What concerns him most is a decision he had made earlier in the day. Because of the holidays, he had let Hatchet Jake go free, withdrawing his request to send the juvenile to 'Outskirts' a boy's home in Alaska for wayward youth.

The boy's mother had come to the station and pleaded for his release. She said he had been an altar boy and was quite religious as a child but after he was molested by a priest he seemed to go bad in every way, taking up with the wrong crowd, doing drugs of all sorts, ditching school and not listening to his mother. She went on and on until from sheer exhaustion of listening he gave in. He did withhold the axe as evidence, but he knew how easy it was for the boy to get another, any hardware store would sell him one.

He had a bad feeling about his decision and he thought it had something to do with the lady in the car whom he had given a warning. Why? Where did his itch come from? She claimed that the man who had frightened the doctor was simply a guest, an old friend. Something didn't add up. The man claimed he had fathered a child for one of the doctor's patients. He was certain of that, the doctor himself said so.

The computer readout revealed he was a retired Foreign Service worker; recently divorced from the woman who lives in that hillside house where the murder of the two teenagers had taken place. Then there was something odd that had happened at a baby shower at the same house, but not for the life of him could he put it all together.

∞

There was one other 'person' who couldn't 'sleep'.

The growling and peculiar intestinal movements striking the walls of his abode were affecting his surround, shaking up the fluid in which he floated. He didn't quite know he was 'upside down' because he was full of abysmal ignorance. All he knew was that this shaking was a major event and that the membranous walls of his nest were trembling in a manner that was unlike anything that had happened to him before. And yes, he could hear sounds, the drum-drumming from above somewhere in that bony cage that he couldn't precisely locate, that he had previously seen, before he had somehow reversed position.

What he didn't like was the drinking. He had to take in the fluid, sometimes breathe it in, and yet it always seemed to replenish itself. He wasn't aware enough to figure that part out, so he just continued to pee and poop in it and hope for the best. There was no use kicking anymore, not since he had been denied the joy of space, all that did was hurt his toes, so he just had to play the waiting game. He quivered and swerved unexpectedly, struggling to quiet down the stump of tissue that seemed to elongate on its own whenever it needed to pee. He had no control over that whatsoever and it bothered him some. If he couldn't control the stump, there might be other things beyond his control. He didn't like that idea at all.

Finally, his oversized eyes closed, he gave way to stillness and fell asleep.

Chapter XXXIV

Good Friday

The weather was unseasonably warm in Santa Barbara on Good Friday. Since the stock market, banks and many other businesses were closed including the doctor's office of Paul Maloff, traffic was scant and what cars there were did not appear to be in much of a hurry. One of these vehicles, however, contained a rather strange grouping; two wayward looking teenagers, an aged nymph with time limited ability to transmogrify and two vampires, one of whom had enormous powers of sorcery, the other a Dhampir, burdened with human emotions derived from his mother.

They were on their way to Lydia's where Doris intended to sneak into the house, dissolve into the animated wallpaper and portray herself as an angelic young nymph standing by the fountain. Once this was accomplished, Doris telepathically let Bram know that she was securely in place, essentially invisible.

Then the rest headed for the Star Nursery to drop off Hatchet Jake and Freaky who needed to pick up his van. He had a great number of flower deliveries to make on this day of days, both at the hospital and otherwise. The idea was for Hatchet Jake to accompany him, help with the deliveries, and as soon as the work was done the two boys would drive over to Maloff's Montecito house and serve as lookouts in the event things didn't go off according to schedule.

"I don't want to be disillusioned," Bram said to Abraxas, who was driving, now on their way to Cottage.

"Everything has been foreseen. I have heard with great clarity the voice of Satan in my ear and he looks forward to this conquest."

"Hail Satan," Bram quipped ritually, more or less to assure Abraxas of his loyalty. Actually, there was very little dedication attached to his routine response; the human part of him was skeptical. And he had a vague notion that something, somehow, would go wrong.

"I hope that all goes following the plan, including my strategy for Lydia's demise…"

"If it happens that the baby delivers at home, Doris is there, she will suffocate Lydia with the placenta following your wishes."

"And if the baby comes into our world at the hospital?"

"Then you and I will be there along with the doctor and you can carry out the deed yourself."

"What if there are no contractions today, what if the pills don't work?"

"The only possible adversity is the inaction of the pills themselves. If, for some reason they were inert, had undergone some type of physical or chemical decomposition, then the contractions will not start today, but Maloff has assured me that the date on the bottle of oxytocin was very new and the pills should be vitally active. In fact," he hastily checked the time on his high powered T-cell, "your lady should be getting 'pains' just about now."

∞

In actuality Phoenix was not having any 'pains' or 'panic' whatsoever. Thanks to the inhibiting action of the Dong Quai, of which she was totally unaware, all she suffered was some minor visceral shudders of her large intestines and to a lesser extent of her womb, but these twitches were more due to the heavy onions and spices of the hutspot than anything else. Other than this minor discomfort she was really in good shape to carry on the events of the day. It was still early morning, and as she had no need to visit Dr. Maloff, she remained in bed, a picturesque woman, her whole body radiating a vapor of good health, naked in repose, a position she preferred in spite of the rounded size of her belly.

Other than this natural protrusion she had no fat whatsoever, none of the flabby and sour ravages of the last weeks of pregnancy that embitter so many women; a bitterness which some mothers project onto their newborns as the cause of their gross bodily malformations.

No, the world was not her enemy, yet Bram and his atrocities were still a threat to be taken seriously. Yes, it took some months to anaesthetize her mind against the sinkhole of her past, to calm her wild passions against the recurring images of the time spent in Bram's power, when she was grateful to him for impregnating her, for being her master. Back then she was encamped in a Hades-like abyss, reticent and silent until Lydia came along. Since then she passionately devoted hours and hours yielding to her love of Lydia. Even though they were different characters, with different upbringings, they had suddenly found themselves living together, committed to sleeping in the same bed, to sharing their affinities and their destinies.

Lydia had taught her something important that she had failed to learn from men; that the physical act was only one part of the feat of attaining deep love. Over time the strength of their love had managed to burn out the nest of vipers that had been poisoning both their souls. And now she looked forward to something seductively maternal, an anticipation that she did not want to cause any separation in the fate of their love or to allow it to go off in the wrong direction. She stretched her arm out to feel for Lydia, but then remembered that she was long gone, off to see the neurologist accompanied by Vladg, and then on to the special veterinary clinic to see if there was any progress made in the search for a set of corneas for Jeanne D'Arc.

∞

It was like old times between Lydia and Vladg, he acting as chauffeur and she making 'significant conversation'. In this case telling old tales of Parisian culture, the shops along the Saint-Germain-des-Près doing big business, her love of Pierre August Renoir and his art, sharing a drag on a Turkish cigarette with her friends, eating onion soup at a favorite café after a night out dancing, and then returning to their little flat to make love. As she spoke with such animation, Vladg got the 'feel' of Paris in the mid nineteenth century. Then he turned his head and focused his attention on the almost silent streets of the day, comparing them to the vividness of the sidewalk cafes and the teeming street life that Lydia was exalting. He wondered which century was actually a better one in which to live. Then he realized that without the technology that created him he would never have experienced anything at all. He decided not to criticize what, for him, had been a great technological breakthrough.

With the exception of her recent concussion and the limits it had placed on her working life, Lydia was happy with her newly found mortality. She was no longer shocked by her sudden wrinkles, her fading lips or the gray like ashes in her hair. The evil in her had been pulled out by the roots. The sediments of vampirism that had eroded her soul over the course of her many years of life had been sucked out by the vortex of aging and had been carried far downstream by the flow of Phoenix's love. Her soul was at peace.

Miriam Maloff was not big on Jewish mysticism, but she did like to make life interesting around the house. So in the laundry room she had two ersatz hollowed out tree stumps, made from all natural materials, which served as hampers. Paul didn't want her to label anything in the house since he felt that such markings blemished the character of an object; so she called them ToL and ToK. This was done so that Paul could distinguish one from the other, hoping that the Yiddish sounding acronyms would help him to remember which one was for dry cleaning and which for the washing machine, a new unit that used absolutely no soap or water. It cleansed by running first through a neutrino cycle which bombarded the dirt and fuzz out of the fabrics, then a second cycle of cleansing rays which also removed wrinkles in the process.

This was followed by a third 'rinse' of folding beams which ordered and 'packaged' the entire load at the bottom when the machine was ready to be emptied. There remained some proper folding to be done afterwards, especially of silk blouses and smart hoodie pants, but it was nice to have a coordinated bundle of clothes at the ready when the washer finished its program, rather than a jumbled mess that had to be untangled piece by piece.

Of course, certain items still had to be dry-cleaned and pressed. Miriam thought that the Tree of Knowledge hamper would signify this to Paul. The Tree of Life hamper designated the clothes of day to day life that they wore routinely, and though this reasoning worked for her, it generally failed for her husband. Mostly she bore this with good cheer, but on this day they had to dig deep in both hampers, searching to the very bottom in order to find his yesterday's suit jacket where he had inserted the detective's card in the little side pocket. Naturally, the suit jacket had been placed in the wrong hamper. Once again Murphy's Law prevailed.

Miriam scrutinized the card, asked her husband to repeat the story of the sorcery that had been practiced on him by Abraxas. Then she decided to take over.

She immediately called Tony Gentile's private number, and related all that her husband had told her about Abraxas. For a man who had slept very little during the night, the detective sounded sharp and alert.

"Tell your husband not to answer the phone under any circumstances. If that piece of filth can cast such a powerful spell over a man like your husband, the probability is that he has a conditioning *signal*, a word or phrase of some sort that will restart the trance. So make sure he has no electronic or personal contact with the man whatsoever."

"I understand detective, but he is obligated to make his hospital rounds…the patients have to be seen."

Gentile thinks this over, comes up with an idea.

"Okay. Tell him to drive straight to the station house, no stops, and pick me up here. I'll accompany him to the hospital and cover as his security. In the meantime, in case Abraxas or that guy Bram he hangs with decide to invade your place, I'll dispatch two of my best for your protection. They're Basic IV's, SWAT trained, and you can rely on them. I doubt the perps will come up there, but you never know when it comes to whackos, so let's cover all the bases. The likelihood is they'll want to intercept your husband at the hospital, get him back into a trance and carry out their mischief, whatever it may be."

"Sounds good, but wouldn't it be better if I went with him, straight to the station."

"Yes and no; when your husband comes here to make his statement that will give me the legal right to post the two Basics at your home to protect you. I like to work with them, they're almost like partners. If you come here, then I have no legal call to use them for your safety, the chief would say it's a waste of personnel's time."

"I see," Miriam snickers, "so you want me in danger just so that you can have these two on the job."

"No, I know it sounds like that, but when you're working with inadequate data, as is mostly the case in this business, more's the better. You never know what the perps will throw at you."

"Okay, I'll go for it your way. Do these officers have names?"

"Sure, the taller more solemn one is Ollie IV, and the other, with more of a sense of humor is called Rollie IV. They're both two stripers, so their rank is the same."

"Why do you say they talk strange?"

"They're originally programmed by an Aussie, speak a bit of slang, but don't pay any attention to that. I can assure you they are as honest as the day is long. They pay their taxes, neither one steals stamps from the desk sergeant's drawer and they both pay their Police Union dues on time."

"How about you Detective," Miriam asks undaunted, "do you pay all of your income tax?"

Gentile snorts a bit.

"I've been known to wiggle a little."

Miriam skitter laughs.

"I imagine Rollie and Ollie will be hungry when they get here, I'll prepare something tasty for them, do you think they like latkes?"

"What're they?"

"Potato pancakes, mine are delicious and I'm dying to cook for someone. My husband is still on Matzohs, a Mitzvah of sorts."

Gentile doesn't ask what a Mitzvah is, but he wonders whether he should have done things the other way around, have the Basics protect the Doctor while he himself covered up at Miriam's.

"Give them anything. Basics aren't particular long as they get fueled."

"All right detective, but it's a tradition in our house to serve guests properly."

"Save some for me. I'll come up there after your husband does his rounds."

"I'll keep them warm. And I do wish to thank you; you've been very attentive to our distress. I want you to know we appreciate the service."

"No problem, it's what you pay taxes for. Just stay vigilant."

At the neurology clinic, the doctor made short shrift of his examination of Lydia, saying that he wanted to get home by noon for Good Friday. He pronounced her fit enough to return to work after the holiday and wished her a Happy Easter. His release raised her spirits. For the first time in days she felt like an independent woman again.

Their next stop was over at the specialty vet clinic where they received both good and bad news. Yes, a pair of corneas had been donated to Jeanne d'Arc, but they were from the owners of the Golden Retriever named Plato, with whom Jeanne d'Arc had struck up such a deep friendship. After a long illness, Plato had succumbed to non-Hodgkin's lymphoma and when the owners heard of the blindness in Lydia's dog they readily made the corneas available. Lydia was very grateful and immediately sent them a thank you note and stated that Plato would always be remembered by her. The transplant operation on the right eye was scheduled for the next day, Saturday, and the eye surgeon said that if all went well they would do the left eye about a week later.

Lydia couldn't help but reflect on how different life would be in that one week; a new arrival at home, Phoenix nursing, no more worries about Bram, and the departure of all the guests with Hikey and Vladg going on with the rest of their honeymoon trip and Josh and Phoebe returning to work in Manhattan. The mother had already made some noises about sticking around to help with the baby but Lydia hoped she would head back to Nebraska to be with her husband who was due to return from his duck hunting jaunt in the Carolinas.

When they got home they were both surprised to see Josh. He had thought the better of leaving Phoebe and Phoenix unprotected, alone with their mother, and had decided not to go to the driving range to hit balls. Instead, he was working on George, while the twins chatted things up in the bedroom. He had most of the front panels removed and was waiting for Vladg to help with some of the circuitry work and to see which parts could be repaired and which had to be ordered anew.

Vladg was eager to help as he had been idle for some days now. He knew something about the internal workings of Duplicants, not at Josh's scientific level, but from his own experience with his 'sweat' gland and nipple features. Then again, the poker embedded in George's frame would have to be removed, and not even Josh's Humilicant arm strength could do that alone but perhaps with the two working together it might be accomplished.

What they found was that George's spine was not involved. The reason for his immobilization was that his heart had been pierced completely by the lance like point of the fireplace poker. Then too, most of the liver and kidney circuitry was beyond repair, while all the other organs, including the lungs, pancreas, stomach and intestines looked intact. However, the logic boards controlling the gastrointestinal, plumbing and circulatory systems would also have to be renewed. As the poker had gone straight through the mechanical heart, that too would have to be ordered, but not all the way from Pyrell's in New York. The former Silicone Valley was now known for its production of Duplicant parts and circuits, in some instances their bio-nanotechnology was more advanced than Pyrell's.

So the first task was to remove the poker without causing further damage.

Vladg went out to the garage to check on the oxyacetylene torch he had used when he lived here as Lydia's companion. Pyrell's had first given him lessons in regular and electric welding, before they decided he could earn more for them as a teacher, and most of the knack of welding was still in his mind. Even so, he reviewed the old welding manual from the initial disk programmed in his brain circuitry before attempting to cut off the end of the poker which stuck out of George's back by a length of about three inches.

His dexterity was adequate, good enough to separate the pointed edge of the poker from George's torso. He did have to be careful not to burn George's tissue which would easily burst into flame if touched by the fierce heat of the torch, so he took his time and was successful; the pointed end dropping off into an iron cup held in Vladg's insulated gloved hand. Josh had held his breath during the procedure, and now let it go with a deep whoosh. He glanced at Vladg, a look that signified a job well done.

While Phoenix palavered with her mother, Phoebe had come out to watch, and she too breathed a sigh of relief when George was not set afire by the welding torch.

The next step was the hardest part. Both Josh and Vladg grabbed hold of the handle of the poker and pulled together with all their might, no success. The poker would have to be hooked up to a winch of some sort. This time Josh solved the problem, fastening a steel cable from the garage around the handle of the poker and, while he and Vladg pushed on George, acting as counter weights, they managed to lead the cable through the window and out to the car where they attached the other end of the cable to the front axle. Phoebe started the car and put it in reverse. Slowly the poker began to move a few inches, and then, when Phoebe applied more battery power, the rest of the poker emerged all at once and in one piece.

"Now I'll have to go up to Palo Alto," Josh announced. "I need to get a disk for a Basic III which was George's originally manufactured design, until Phoebe talked Eiselman into status upgrade, giving him a few advanced features in keeping with the secrecy attached to his job."

"What good will a disk do, there's no place to insert it? And we have no access to an H-W wheel?"

"Maybe that's not necessary Phoebe. Remember the old plumbing system he had?"

"Of course I remember. He peed and defecated all over our new carpet in Manhattan, how could I forget that?"

"Well after that fiasco you talked Eiselman into giving him Sextus type plumbing and a GI system for defecating. But the old disk space is still there. I think I can jury rig the old waste receptacle on his right side, where the filter was, that slides open. If I can get a disk in there, then it should be a piece of cake to set it up so that it connects to the learning and logic boards."

"You think that'll work? Really?"

"If I can adapt the old system to hold the disk I can add new circuitry to the logic board to juice up his brain. Once we activate it, a good deal of what he knew beforehand should come back if his memory bank is still in existence."

"If that were so he'd still be able to speak; at least to say the basic seventy-five words which were originally programmed at construction."

"Not necessarily, the brain may be dormant, not dead…"

"It won't work. You just want to get away, to take an Air-Scoot and be with your Palo Alto friends and out of here…"

"That's not true! I thought George was dear to you. Do you want me to try and fix him or not? It will cost money, you know. I have to buy circuitry for the lungs, liver and kidneys. We can't afford a new heart, but if this one doesn't begin to fibrillate when we start things up, it probably will leak, but it should be adequate until we can get him back home."

"What about the lymph he's lost?"

"Unlike blood, Duplo-lymph is plentiful, cheap to make and holds more oxygen per fluid ounce than blood. No, that shouldn't be a problem."

Phoebe is still skeptical, but somewhat sheepish at the suggestion that she would stand in the way of Josh's attempt to rejuvenate George.

"Okay, when will you be back?"

"If all goes well, maybe tonight, more likely on Saturday."

"You will be here for Easter. In addition to the birthing we plan to go on an Easter egg hunt."

"I promise."

Lydia interrupts, breaks up the little squabble, tells Phoebe she will have to drive Josh to the airport.

"They don't have strobe light signals to hail the shuttles here like they do in Manhattan, but the Scoots are frequent, at least one an hour."

Phoebe grudgingly agrees to drive him.

"Great. I'll call one of my nanotech colleagues on the way to explain the problem, see what he thinks of the situation."

∞

Almost as soon as Dr. Maloff gets in his car to head for the police station, his T-cell goes off. Following the detective's advice, reinforced by Miriam's repeated warning of danger as she kissed him goodbye, and said, "Remember, '*Don't answer the phone! Not under any circumstances*'."

Maloff allows the message to go to voice mail. He dares not check it for fear of a conditioned response which would throw him back into a trance, so he just munches on his matzos and lets the phone remain on the passenger seat, unanswered and with the screen totally closed. He is pretty sure the call was from Abraxas and the way his phone was rigged, even when the call went unanswered, the picture of the caller would appear as long as the screen was open.

When Abraxas realizes his call has gone unanswered, his rage is so great and deep, so murderous and bloody, that his arms ache to strangle Maloff. He turns to Bram and says:

"When we get to the hospital, you cannot go on rounds with me. I had thought of giving you a white Doctor's lab coat, but it's not worth trying to pass you off as a physician. If I come across Maloff, and I'll be looking for him, you can rest assured on that score, I intend to put him under a trance from which he will never recoup, the bastard will be brain dead. But first things first; you must contact Doris; get her to induce Phoenix to come here. I don't care what ruse you use, but get it done! Then I myself will deliver the baby!"

"Why don't you take this spray with you, it is a concoction I have prepared which will put over ten people to sleep in the event they try to interfere..."

Abraxas interrupts him in mid-sentence.

"I'm afraid you are unaware of the extent of my powers as a sorcerer. I can abort as many as twenty mothers at a time if I so wish. I thank you for the thought, but I do not need concoctions of any kind, when it comes to pregnant women, they are putty in my hands, they are at my mercy by a simple wave of my hand accompanied by the correct incantation."

For once in his life Bram is the subdued one. If Abraxas truly has the power, he speaks of then there should be no glitch in the plan. If he can abort full-term women, he should certainly be able to induce normal contractions and labor. All that is necessary is to get Phoenix here. He immediately cocoons himself into the required telepathic stance and contacts Doris, gives her the proper instructions.

∞

By the time Phoebe drove back, with Josh well on his way air-scooting north, her mood was more settled and she was ready to get into domestic stuff.

She and Hikey adjourned to the kitchen to prepare a veggie lunch, a mixed salad with Melba toast starting off with small cups of vichyssoise. Hikey was handy with the large cutting knife so she did most of the chopping, cleaning the leeks and cutting onions while Phoebe saw to the peeling of the potatoes for the cold soup; getting utensils ready, setting napkins out, and positioning water glasses on the kitchen table.

Vladg remained busy studying just how to repair the damage to George's mechanical heart. He was thinking theoretically. 'Perhaps the hole in the ventricle might be filled up by an emulsion of pentagonal toroidal nanotubes dispersed within the heavily carbonated Buckyballs (Fullerenes) then mixed with contractile tissue derived from mammalian muscular fibers. This would simulate both functionality and performance, but the heart so constructed would have to be workable with the circuitry already installed in George, and that could be a problem. Nano-technology responds to a different language'.

While he is thinking along these heavy lines, Phoenix, Emily and Lydia step into the baby's room to play around, here and there, adding a few more refinements to the already finished product. Emily keeps busy selecting different doo-dads and frou-frou to put on the corner walls. Phoenix doesn't like half the ornamentation, but sees that her mother is having such a great time, that she doesn't put a stop to it. At a later point, after her mother is back in Nebraska she can always take down what she doesn't like. Lydia, on the other hand, is hand painting creative color designs in oil on the dresser drawers (which contain pampers and such) and the armoire, which holds the entire wardrobe of baby things.

What all this busy activity portends, Vladg in deep thought; Hikey and Phoebe preparing lunch; the three women doing their thing in the baby's room, is that no one in particular is on the alert; no one is at hand to look out for intruders, no one at the ready to check on security.

Phoenix is relaxed, sitting in the wide tufted easy chair, the gift from Lydia. She has the hickory stick by her side and every once in a while she has to use it as a cane when she is wobbly. At the moment she is studying the manual's instructions, how to operate the remote to change the activity of the flowers and fauna in the wallpaper. A graphic design in the manual, labeling each animal with a letter, and each flower or plant with a number, causes her to look up at the tapestry and compare what she is reading with the actual wallpaper. She sees an angelic little girl standing in the decorative mosaic.

One hand placed gently on a fawn's neck the other touching the 'water' fountain. This seems strange to her although she knows that the wallpaper changes itself automatically at certain times. What confounds her is the absence of the representation of the little girl by the fountain in the manual. She begins to wonder if the brand of wallpaper she ordered was not the right one, not the properly designated factory product. She goes to check this out with the original catalogue from which she had made her purchase. All this checks out accurately. The little girl in the wallpaper is staring directly at her with large black eyes, trying to influence her thoughts, she seems to be saying that it is all right to have contractions, that she must go to see Dr. Maloff at the hospital right away, but Phoenix fights these thoughts off. 'What business of hers is it anyway?"

Then she does something she definitely, absolutely, has no business doing. She comes across the special section in the manual designated for experts. It shows how to add or subtract animals and flora from the wallpaper, but in order to do so, one must know and be capable of handling several nano-tech languages, one of which is involved in drawing, in this case it is NTGD (Nanotech Transposition for Graphic Drawing).

Phoenix is not equipped to do any of this, but somehow, staring into the eyes of the little girl in the tapestry, she becomes convinced that she can accomplish anything she wishes. On the projecto-pad (part of which is a TI-84 PLUS Graphing calculator) she draws a graphic representation of what she conceives as a mother doe. Her design does have four legs and a head and tail, but unfortunately she decides to 'pretty it up' with a few strokes to represent stripes. The resulting illustration is supposed to accompany the fawn standing by the little girl, who, it seems, no longer appears so angelic and is obviously trying to get her attention, yes, to captivate her.

Actually Doris is receiving telepathic messages from Bram to induce Phoenix to come to the hospital. She has already convinced Phoenix that 'she can accomplish anything she wishes' but for some reason she cannot get her to listen to the part about leaving the house and going to the hospital. The only thing left for Doris to do is to abandon her position in the tapestry. She decides to change herself into a viper, slithers out of the wallpaper and coils herself in front of Phoenix with a hypnotizing stare, just as Phoenix connects the projecto-pad drawing to the remote and presses the 2nd PRGRM button, which, of course, is entirely wrong.

What results is not a doe, but a tigress, who emerges in, what to her, is the body warm and stuffy air of prey. She spots the viper immediately, crouches and springs at it and with one tremendous bite from her massive jaws and sharp teeth, snaps off the viper's head. Then the tigress turns its yellow eyes toward the transfixed Phoenix and is about to spring once more when Vladg suddenly appears, alerted by the roar of the tigress, and presses the Complex Reverse Probability Button on the remote and the tigress disappears back into the illustration that Phoenix had designed on the projecto-pad.

All this has happened so fast, that Phoenix is now having contractions, coming every minute or so. Lydia runs to her and says: "We've got to get you to hospital immediately!"

"No," Phoenix shouts, "that's the one place I should never go." And she tells them all what had transpired with Doris, who has reverted to her original shape, but is now headless, only a small amount of blood oozing from the stump of her neck, trickling slowly to the floor.

∞

Unlike Abraxas, Gentile sails a different tack. He talks Maloff into introducing him as an associate, giving him a fresh white doctor's gown. Maloff takes an extra stethoscope from the nurse's station, wraps it around the detective's neck and they start off on hospital rounds. Gentile is glued to Maloff as tightly as the deception will allow. He has both a taser pistol and a 357 Ruger revolver with a short barrel hidden on his person, stuffs a pair of handcuffs in the side pocket of the white lab coat.

Luckily there is no activity in labor and delivery and there are only ten or so mothers on the floor, three post-delivery and the rest close to, or right on their due dates. Maloff visits the mother of the twins he had delivered first, she is in a private room, and once he is assured that she is doing well, no hemorrhages or other complications he moves on to the next room, which is semi-private. Neither of these women are his patients, he is merely covering for a colleague, but he gives them as much attention as if they were his own.

Then they go on to the third room, and there is Abraxas talking to one of the patient's, inquiring about Maloff. He pays no heed whatsoever to Gentile, but jumps at Maloff with hands at the ready to strangle the doctor. The mother-to-be in bed screams, Maloff pivots to avoid the onrushing threat, but Gentile is cool. He takes out his taser, puts it on full phaser strength and fires it directly at Abraxas's midriff. Abraxas stumbles backwards from the blow to his solar plexus, ten times as lethal as that of a professional boxer, and slumps to the floor, Gentile cuffs him immediately and unceremoniously pulls him out of the room. Maloff goes to the frightened patient and tries to calm her down, but his explanation is ineffective, so he orders a mild sedative, soporific enough to stop her screams and hyperventilation but not so strong as to cause the fetus any problems.

While Gentile is out in the hall he gets a call from Vladg at Lydia's house who gives him a quick summary of events, going over the main points one by one. The only recourse the detective has, since he is stuck with an unconscious Abraxas, and Maloff still has to complete his rounds, is to pull one of the SWAT IV's from Miriam's and send him up to Lydia's to investigate the death of Doris and take depositions.

He calls, chooses Rollie and leaves Ollie, now without wheels, with Miriam. Then he contacts the desk sergeant at the station and asks to have a uniform come to haul Abraxas in and drive him up to Lydia's where he can investigate the death scene.

Dr. Maloff decides to finish rounds later. He wants to go to his wife immediately. Gentile agrees. He tells Maloff to 'hurry up and get home'. He will get a ride from the backup, not to worry.

Maloff breaks all records speeding over to his Montecito house.

∞

When Hatchet Jake and Freaky see Rollie drive off in his black and white, they decide to move in on their own. One Duplo copper and one helpless housewife should be easy pickings.

Hatchet Jake uses the hammer end of his axe to knock off the lock to the back door. They storm in to the house whooping it up to scare Miriam, not even pretending to hide their intentions…Ollie draws his Beretta…shouts a warning, but Hatchet Jake throws his axe like a tomahawk. There are no winners. The hatchet splits the skull of the Duplicant causing immediate brain death, but Ollie had gotten his shot off, aiming directly for the heart but hitting Hatchet Jake in the throat, the bullet totally destroying the boy's breathing apparatus. Jake suffocates and drowns in his own gurgling slime, blood and saliva.

Freaky sees the chance of a lifetime. He is sexually aroused by all this, cares not a whit for Hatchet Jake's demise, but rips off Miriam's blouse revealing the soft globes of her full breasts; she struggles to get away but cannot fight off the now overly excited rapist who has found great strength in his perversity. He subdues her arms and legs, lifts her skirt and tears off her panties and takes out his schlong and is about to insert it into her vagina.

He gasps.

A rubber tube is choking him.

He falls off Miriam.

Paul Maloff has the tubing of his stethoscope so tightly wound around Freaky's neck, the predator cannot get away. His neck is horribly swollen, a circle of black begins to appear where the tubing has bruised it. Maloff twists the metal parts of the scope tighter, in effect creating a tourniquet of sorts encircling Freaky's neck, the boy twitches once or twice, then slumps into a coma from which he will never recover.

Chapter XXXV

Holy Saturday

In the morgue, at the pathologist's table, Gentile was scratching his head at the findings. Not only did it seem that Doris's severed head was indeed the result of several bites by a tiger, or some other wild cat, but the autopsy showed definite evidence of a great cat's saliva mixed in with blood…and that blood was non-human…actually turned out to be the blood of an adder or viper.

One reason for his confusion came about the day before when he had taken Phoenix's declaration. She had said flatly: "Doris was first an angel in the wallpaper, then a viper and lastly, after she was mauled and beheaded, she returned to her old self, an aged nymph who had lured sailors to their death eons ago." Because of the impending birth of her first baby, and on the advice of Dr. Maloff he said nothing back to Phoenix on this, but acted as if he swallowed the story whole and believed every word. In actuality, he thought she was having pre-natal delusions or some such insane pregnancy phenomena as her story sounded so weird, so far-fetched.

When it came to his picture of the decapitated old woman lying on the floor, in the baby's room of all places, and the story of the viper creeping out of the woodwork, he had serious doubts. Even though the pathologists agreed with the finding of tiger bites, he had to admit he was unsure of the facts. There was no way in the world he could ask a prosecutor to present this rendition of what went down as admissible evidence to a sober

Grand Jury. What was really piling up was that either Lydia's house was haunted or Phoenix's story was true as told.

Now, muddling things over in the morgue he didn't know what to believe; what was real, what was fanciful or what was an outright lie.

Later that afternoon, the local precinct became an exceptionally busy place for what was usually a quiet holiday.

A high powered criminal attorney had come up from Los Angeles to represent Abraxas. He was a member of the brotherhood who doted on innocent starlet's ambitions, luring them into his lair with promises of small parts in 4-D demo productions and then feasting on their young blood. While this part of his character was not common knowledge, he was reputed by those in the know to be a 'tough cookie' to go up against in court.

Needless to say, Gentile had his work cut out for him.

In spite of the detective's personal opposition, Maloff was charged with manslaughter, and, as it turned out due to the L.A. lawyer's cleverness, Abraxas got off relatively easy. Of course, Gentile was not totally aware of Abraxas' three-part plan: to artificially induce the birth of Phoenix's baby on Good Friday, to use Doris to strangle Lydia with the bloody placenta, and finally to aid Bram in the possession of the baby and whisk the child away from the mother. Even without this knowledge, every bone in his body told him the man was up to no good

Accordingly, he had asked the prosecutor to charge Abraxas only with one count, an unwanted and unjustified presence in the hospital room of a patient for whom Abraxas held no authority. But the accusation was so ill defined, so fuzzy, that Gentile could not bring to bear any of the other plotting details related to Abraxas's ill intentions against Phoenix or Maloff. The charge devolved essentially into a case of exploitation; using a pregnant woman for selfish purposes to such a degree that it constituted a criminal act. The prosecutor told the presiding commissioner, who was assigned for the holiday by the absent judge, that it was Maloff, not Abraxas, who was the covering doctor for the weekend. That he was the only physician legitimately allowed in the patient's room and that Abraxas 's presence was a violation of every medical and hospital code in the books.

In legalese, the commissioner responded that the evidence the prosecutor had transmitted all sounded too vague for presentation to a sitting judge; that the charge, in his opinion, should be reduced to a misdemeanor. All the other accusations went by the board.

"That sucks," Gentile told his prosecutor in police parlance.

Oddly enough, after Abraxas's charge was reduced to a complaint, the clever L.A. attorney was able to secure his release on bond, pending indictment. Then he immediately threatened Metro with a civil law suit, alleging Gentile had used unnecessary and excessive force, putting his taser on full phase, in subduing the accused, his client. Once the status of the crime had been reduced, the lawyer knew full well that the prosecutor was not likely to go further with the case. Most likely there would be no indictment, no presentation to a Grand Jury. In effect, he had used the threat to sue as a bargaining chip to secure Abraxas's outright release from custody.

Neither could Gentile make his accusation for Bram's stalking and harassment against Phoenix stick. He did mention to the selfsame commissioner that Bram, in his opinion, was a co-conspirator of Abraxas, but no legal credence was given to this connection.

His chief wouldn't go for it either, insufficient evidence.

So Bram walked.

Maloff, on the other hand, was in deep doo-doo. He was arrested, accused of aggravated Manslaughter, a capital crime, and had to remain in jail until indictment occurred in the presence of a sitting judge, not a commissioner. That meant he could not possibly deliver Phoenix's baby as it would take at least until Monday morning for a judge to be in attendance. This left Phoenix without an OB to deliver her baby and Bram and Abraxas free to roam the streets at will. Maloff used one of his phone calls to let Phoenix know the situation. He offered her the services of one of his clinic colleagues, one whom he recommended highly, but Phoenix said she would have to think it over. She just might give birth at home, using Lydia, who had prior experience in deliveries, as her midwife.

Maloff didn't like this idea but said nothing against it since he had so many troubles of his own.

He had no supporting eye witnesses to his strangulation of the young flower delivery boy. His wife's testimony, was not relevant, could not be introduced as evidence. The support of Detective Gentile, who had told Maloff to 'hurry up and get home' because of his suspicions that a catastrophe might occur, was not of much value since he was not an eye witness to the alleged rape scene.

After much searching on the attorneys' web, Miriam finally found a good local attorney to represent her husband but his release could not be obtained until a judge was found to preside on Monday next.

∞

Gentile's next move was not without focus. He was excited about getting up to Miriam's. He took a Projecto-Fax along with him, one he had signed out from the storage room of captured articles. Johnson, the Duplo-custodian in charge of the room didn't ask why he wanted it, but he did give him a quizzical look; this detective was in homicide division, not case research. Gentile didn't care, if things worked out there should be no problem. What he planned was illegal, or in his way of thinking, 'wriggling' a bit. After all Ollie was still police property, but he couldn't use the experts on the force to accomplish what he wanted, the chief would nix it. He wracked his brain to come up with someone as trustworthy as those in the department. Someone who had the expertise to take an IV apart and put it back together again.

He found Miriam busily cooking. She was wearing slacks, a breezy blouse with a brassy type belt, no apron, and comfortable wedgies.

All this kitchen activity surprised him. What little he knew of her indicated that she likely would be in a sullen mood, in a funk over Paul's situation, probably sitting around doing next to nothing. He was very wrong.

In the past, whenever she was embroiled in some state of nervousness Miriam had developed the habit of keeping herself busy to reduce her anxiety. The activity itself seemed to take away some of the strain and her mind was consequently freed up to explore exactly what was causing her worry. In this case, she knew everything revolved around the manslaughter accusation and how it would affect her life and that of her husband and his reputation as a physician in Santa Barbara. In fact, the news of the doctor's arrest was already in print, on the second page of the morning News-Press.

She was in the process of making beef kreplach, dumplings made out of noodle dough that she usually put into soup, but now served them as a kind of appetizer to Gentile as she really wants to talk; kitchen table style.

She sits down directly across from him.

Between bites they make pretty good eye contact. He strikes her as a man with a dreamy type of loneliness. She wonders if his work has made him this way or if detectives are inherently lonely dreamy people who are drawn to the profession?

Then she abandons these thoughts, seeks a more practical connection.

Once again the two of them go over the entire story.

All the emotions at once, how she defended herself, how angry she was, so frightened she hadn't even seen or heard her husband come in, she was so busy fighting off the rapist that she was unaware of everything else. But when Freaky spun off of her she immediately recognized that it was her husband pulling tight on the tubing around the kid's neck. Before she could stop things from going any further the boy was already limp as a wet noodle.

"He had a thin pulse, but that was all. Paul said he was probably brain dead, but called immediately for an airbulance and then called you."

"Right, that listens," Gentile said, then he goes back to chewing and gulping morsels of kreplach. He is a rather slow eater when at table, savors every bite, and takes his time swallowing.

Miriam watches his Adam's apple go up and down. She can tell he likes the food, and in spite of her worries this pleases her. She thinks: *'As a woman sees, so the man is'.*

She never even considers that her vision might be corrupted.

There is a weighty pause.

Gentile is sympathetic to any woman who goes through a rape attempt. He knows that intrusive thoughts and flashbacks are even more lasting in rape issues than murder cases.

Suddenly he breaks the silence, changes the subject completely, says: "What we have to do now is very tricky."

He goes on to explain: "Because of all the police work that had been going on with the corpses of Hatchet Jake and Freaky at your house, no professional had paid very much attention to Ollie. Yet, in my view Ollie may be an important eye witness. Like all SWAT trained IV's in service, he was outfitted with the latest gadgets. One of these is a miniaturized built in TRU (Time Retrieval Unit). It was thought to be of no help now because its retraceable time function is limited to two hours. However, if it was hooked up to a Projecto-Fax there might be some data that could be retrieved from his circuitry."

"How do we do that?"

"Not easy. Ollie will have to be taken apart before Monday. That's when the transport people will undoubtedly come to take him, he's an expensive item, and they will want to get him back, for parts if nothing else."

Miriam shudders visibly; Ollie was so alive to her that she cannot possibly think of anyone taking him apart, merely using him for parts.

"It's the bottom line," Gentile says, "that's the way these people think, all they're interested in is what they can get out of you, me included." He is trying his best to relieve her tension, as a moment ago he saw her shiver, but he is not very good at this sort of thing; so he just goes on with his ideas.

"We have to find an expert quick, someone who can go in and capture the mini-TRU mechanism without disturbing anything else."

"That sounds difficult."

"Do you mind if I have one more dumpling?"

"Help yourself, I like to watch a man eat."

"I don't have the know-how or the mechanical ability to attempt this procedure. But I think I know who does…"

"Who?"

"This Humilicant is a friend of the Duplicant from Holland, the one who called me up from Lydia's when Doris went down. His name is Josh and he does this type of work for Pyrell's in New York."

"How do you know all this?"

"Rollie. He was the one who went up to Lydia's right after he left you and I got the call from Vladg. Rollie interrogated everyone before I got there, as I had no wheels. He learned from Vladg that Josh was in Palo Alto searching for parts for an immobilized Duplo named George. When I finally made it there I saw George still standing like a large upright piece of petrified wood in the living room. He's nothing compared to Ollie and Rollie."

"But isn't this illegal detective, I mean Ollie is owned by the police department, right?"

"Yes, but it's the same as wriggling a bit on your income tax. I mean it's not like Ollie was human, the law takes wide sweeps around end when it comes to Duplos."   "I don't get the football analogy…"

"I mean the judge will simply look at the data itself, not how we got it off a Duplo."

Miriam thinks this over. On the one hand it is against her principles; on the other she will do anything to get her husband off as quickly as possible. Ordinarily she would ask the rabbi for counsel, but as it is Shabbes and time is of the essence. She says to Gentile: "Do what you have to do."

He nods, grateful that she did not make a fuss. He likes this woman's grit as much or more than her cooking.

∞

Later that evening Josh returned from Palo Alto, getting the skinny from Vladg on the details and manner of Ollie's demise. At once an idea starts sloshing around in his head. He realized that Ollie's heart had to be intact. Of course he was completely brain dead, getting your skull split with an axe like that totally disrupted the rest of the nervous system, but there was no reason for his heart not to be capable of reactivation. And when Vladg told him that his garage experiment, preparing an emulsion of Bucky balls and mammalian muscle fibers, had failed to result in regular and consistent contractility for more than thirty seconds, he became more resolved than ever in the probabilities of success.

He knew that if this scheme worked out he would score brownie points with Phoebe, who hadn't been high on him lately, or so it seemed. And they would be out from under with Eiselman financially as far as George was concerned. Of course he still owed Pyrell's for his transformation and testicular operation, but he didn't really count that so much, as every two weeks that debt was withdrawn from his paycheck automatically.

The problem at hand was legal, not surgical. It would actually be quite easy, though time consuming, to remove Ollie's heart and replace it in George's body, but the fact of the matter was that a Duplicate donor for a heart organ had never been done privately. Pyrell's did it on a few occasions, but all of those transplants were under heavy quality control of factory personnel. A privately owned Duplicant, in this case by the Metro Police Department of Santa Barbara County, would require a good deal of legal procedure, complicated by governmental involvement for a transplant request.

The thought occurred to Josh to simply talk Miriam into allowing them to steal the heart, substituting George's spent organ in place, but then he realized that involving her, especially at a time when her husband was accused of manslaughter and was still in custody, was out of the question.

This dilemma was solved when they received a call from Detective Gentile, on speaker, suggesting that they might be helpful in securing Dr. Maloff's release if only he could do some data retrieval with the mini-TRU and a Projecto-Fax. He told them time was an urgent factor, it had already been over sixteen hours since the murders, but sometimes it was possible to regain some data, especially with a miniaturized TRU that was connected internally to the nervous system of a Duplicant.

Josh acted as if he wasn't 'certain' he could do the job, hinted he might not be 'capable'; waited for the detective's response.

After he received every confidence from Gentile, he asked: "Is it legal and all that?"

"On the fence; not exactly legal, not really illegal," Gentile said. We are authorized to seek the truth in every murder case and sometimes we have to take extreme measures…"

Vladg interrupted.

"We have a proposition for you. We need a viable donor's heart for George. You must have noticed him when you were here last night."

"Sure. How can you not notice the size of that Duplo, he's standing like a statue in the middle of the living room. What is he a III?"

"Originally yes, but he's had a lot of upgrades…"

"Well IV's are smaller; their hearts aren't built to support a working III's body. I don't think it will work."

"Let us be the judge of that! Ollie was taller than Rollie."

"So your proposition is that if I let you exchange hearts, you'll go inside Ollie's thorax and retrieve the mini-TRU."

"Essentially yes, that's it. But in all honesty I doubt you'll get anything. Even if the mini-TRU is in good working condition, I doubt you'll get much data of value. A mini-TRU has to be supported by a viable brain and central nervous system. From what I understand that's not the case here."

"I figure it's worth a try. This guy Maloff is a good egg. Any man that has feeling for a woman being raped would have interfered, and if it's your own wife, I can see how he might lose it and kill the guy."

"That's for a judge to decide," Josh says. "Why not allow him go to court? Let justice be served."

"Because I've seen what so called Justice can do, it can ruin a life at the same time it's saving it."

"Look Detective," Vladg barges in, "I don't want to get into the ethics of this. We've made a proposition to you, do you accept?"

"Absolutely. On one condition!"

"And that is?"

"That Josh brings the mini-TRU straight to me at the station house right after you've made your exchange."

Josh and Vladg agree, nod positively to Gentile on screen.

"Okay, get your asses over here ASAP!"

∞

Bram and Abraxas are holed up in Doris's cottage, huddled together, planning their next move. Bram's frustration and disappointment on the miserable results of Good Friday show visibly on his face. All he is interested in now is getting control of his baby; weaning him from bottled milk to blood as soon as the child's digestive track can tolerate it; giving him the proper lore and knowledge that every Alucard for centuries has been taught by their parents, all members of the clan. If he is able to destroy Lydia along the way, so much the better, than Phoenix might consider joining him in his Carpathian retreat once she has lost her lover. However, another thought springs out at him? Will he really be able to control a woman whose love for other women was greater than that of a man? He didn't know the answer to this question, but he hoped that once Phoenix was returned to true vampirism, he could master her again.

Abraxas's agenda is somewhat different.

Having lost Doris and the two teenage slaves, all three of whom had aided him for some time in his work, he wants revenge, to avenge their deaths yes, but also to satisfy Lucifer by the destruction of Maloff and that juicy wife of his along with the idiotic detective who had tasered him and treated him as if he were a low class mortal.

They discussed strategy and tactics, drew up plans to go into effect the next day, Easter Sunday.

Chapter XXXVI

Easter Sunday

A little after sunup there were as yet no manufactured sounds to be heard, none of the noises made by humans, only the murmurings of nature awakening in the early scattered sunlight. A few hundred yards or so beyond the wooded area that Drakonius had used to hide himself, a fast moving brook ran down the foothill through the forest toward the Montecito area and then, curving, was lost to view. At first glance nobody was in sight, but on closer examination, on the far side of the narrow stream, Bram was slowly, steadily, climbing up to his old house via this back way, his blood lust stirred. With much effort he reached the crest, stealthily crossed the gentle down slope topped with a few vertical eucalyptus tree trunks, and then found open ground.

He had lived in the house even longer than Lydia and knew every nook and cranny of the dwelling, so he had little difficulty sneaking into the the main house through the garage. He kept out of sight, stepped behind the statue of George, using him as a convenient shield to conceal himself. There was no sign whatsoever of the presence of Josh or Vladg. This was not a surprise to him for he knew the play by play from contacting Abraxas who said that those two had been busily engaged in carrying out some trivial task with George. Indeed, the front of the Duplicant's torso was already stripped and bare.

He stared stonily at the group of five chirping women in the other room, gathered in a small semicircle, all of whom were engaged with a holograph projection of a phone call from Greta and Geri coming out of Holland, apparently a wish-well call to Phoenix. These two had been on his mind lately, especially Greta, and as soon as this business was finished he had every intention of sucking her dry, bringing her back to Dolno Katore where she belonged as one of his mistresses. As to Geri, he would feed that piece of excrement to the wolves, she was worth nothing more, but she was not the focus of his concentration.

Hikey was especially striking, her large head standing out amongst the others. She was going on and on about their honeymoon trip on The Queen Victoria, how awful the teenagers had been to her and, in contrast, how much she valued the way Phoebe and her mother treated her, taking her shopping to buy a hat for Easter and now inviting her to church.

"Of course I am a total atheist, I want you to know that," she was saying, "but I am looking forward to a resurrection sermon here, I'd like to compare it to the ones I've been to in Holland."

"But why do you go to church at all?" Emily asked, "I mean if you are a non-believer?"

"Because I'm a politician, a member of the upper house in Holland, and if I didn't go I'd lose the votes of my constituents."

"Isn't that hypocritical?" Phoebe asked.

"Certainly it is! Hypocrisy is the way we explain things; the better we are at it, the better politician we become, its how we keep getting voted in."

Now they all laughed.

"At least she's honest about it, that's more than I can say for some of ours," the mother said.

Just then Phoenix got a small cramp in the back side of her womb, said she wanted to go to the bedroom and lie down for a little while.

"You're sure you don't want us to stay with you, I mean if the pains start coming regular, we want to be here with you," Emily said motherly, but in a good way.

"They're far from that. I'm sure you can go and be back in plenty of time."

"Yes, if you're anything like me and my pregnancies, it'll be awhile yet."

Then Emily went on to describe the subtle differences in her very own pregnancies, glancing every now and then at Phoenix to assure her that she was not, by mistake, going to mention her abortion. The others asked questions back and forth about the stages of labor, chattering on and on about babies' needs and motherhood feelings.

Bram listened patiently to all this prattle. He saw Phoenix check her watch, press one hand to her belly, the other to the small of her back. As yet not much seemed to be happening; apparently she was having some contractions, but not rhythmic ones. Much as he enjoyed watching her, he dared not tarry. He moved quickly, silently, into the back of the hall closet where he remained motionless and, folding his arms, secreted himself completely from view. All he had by him was a pressurized spray can of venom that he intended to use on Phoebe, Hikey and the mother as soon as they were isolated from Phoenix and Lydia. Then he would fog them completely with the vapor.

He looked forward to his role; saw himself more as a deliverer of death to be treated with some formal manifestation of respect following the proper etiquette of vampirism. After all, he was providing a service as a dignitary from Satan, not as an executioner.

He remained silent and fixed in position, he would defer to time, subordinating himself until Phoenix showed definite signs of labor, then he would observe the birth and carry out his destiny serving as a simple lynch-pin to the greater goal of the 2nd Reformation.

He also knew that Abraxas was positioned in a similar manner to his own, hiding in his car just outside the Montecito home of Dr. Maloff. Apparently the detective, along with Rollie the Duplicant, planned to stay and bodyguard the wife all day. If Abraxas intended to go ahead with his plan to destroy Miriam, he would be sorely tested.

∞

At Miriam's, Vladg and Josh had worked all night and were taking a break for breakfast. There was a hot discussion going on.

Rollie spoke more Aussie slang than Ollie. Both had originally been programmed to go to Australia to serve on the force there, but the contract fell through and S.B. County Metro had picked up the two for a song.

Rollie didn't like the idea of a Humilicant and a Duplicant taking his partner apart in front of his eyes and said so:

"It's Gawd awful Mate, allowin' these two blokes to take my old matey apart, whyfore?"

"Don't get your dander up Rollie, they know what they're about and they've been gentle, not to worry."

"I could take it if they was human, honest I could, but this way is shameful, embarassin' I call it."

"Well you don't have to watch. Mrs. Maloff wants to visit her husband in the holding cell at the precinct. I called the desk sergeant and what with Easter and all he's given permission even though it's too early for visiting hours. So I'll stay here with these two and you make sure you guard the lady real good, agree?"

Rollie is somewhat mollified.

"Fair dingum Mate, but the lidy is cutting brunch and has the billy boilin'."

"You can take the sandwiches with you and the Mrs. will put the tea in a thermos, howzat hitya?"

"Good oil. We'll visit her gyno and if we run into that dickhead, I'll protect her right enough. She ready?"

"Just about," Miriam says, shucking off her sandals, sliding into three inch heels, and slyly slipping Gentile the keys to her car.

"Goodbye, take good care of the Mrs." Gentile says.

"Won't come a gutser…"

"See that you don't, I'm counting on you."

"Hooroo, then."

"Hooroo too", Miriam says. She likes the way to say goodbye in Aussie slang.

As soon as Rollie and Miriam took off in the black and white, Abraxas followed in his car. He was surprised to see that the two left without the detective. He had expected both of them to bodyguard her. The separation made his plan easier to carry out, casting spells and creating illusions on two is much easier than three, even for a sorcerer with his powers.

Gentile waited but a moment, told Vladg and Josh they had the place all to themselves and to finish up doing their thing. He remembered to take the Projecto-FAX along with him, then he opened the garage door and jumped into Miriam's car. He strapped himself in, gunned down the driveway and after a few quick turns, got onto the coastal highway. He spotted the Black and White first, then squeezed his way through traffic, speeded up and was quickly on Abraxas's tail heading for the precinct on Castillo Street.

∞

Vladg and Josh were making good headway, the tedious work was done. Now they had little trouble extricating the mini-TRU from its myriad of inner fiber optics, but the heart itself was another story. In order to remove it from the great lymph vessels (which it connected to lungs, liver, limbs and head) in such manner that they could replace it with George's heart they had to make certain that all the lumens were patent, nothing clogged, at least not on the Ollie heart side. The other problem was that George's heart was indeed larger, but the absence of the TRU helped create more space in the thorax and after some maneuvering they were able to fit it in properly. Unlike humans, there was no suturing necessary, but a gluey substance that Josh had brought back from Palo Alto, and was standard for this sort of work, did the trick. The entire procedure had taken over twelve hours not counting the time spent with George.

They finished buckling up Ollie's front panels, double checked that he looked none the worse for wear and encased his heart in the aseptic container that had previously contained George's heart. Then they packed the mini-TRU in the special case left for this purpose by the Detective.

They made sure all the household items they had used were returned to their prior condition. Next they did a final check to ensure that everything was in proper order, that nothing was disturbed such that the fastidious Miriam would become upset. Before they locked up they agreed on one small change to the plan. Vladg would first drop Josh off at Lydia's to install Ollie's heart into George, while Vladg would continue on his way to the station house to hand over the mini-TRU to the Detective.

∞

Bram was just about ready to exit the stuffy closet and show himself. He was intent on befogging the three women with his vapor can, when all at once he realized they were set on going to church and were making ready to leave. He smiled sardonically to himself; sometimes the Jesus-God came in handy. Once the three women finished dressing, did some more primping and preening, got all decked out in their capricious Easter bonnets, he waited patiently until (after what seemed like several hundred cheek kisses and goodbyes to Phoenix and Lydia) they finally left. Now that the house was clear of those three all he had to deal with was Lydia and Phoenix. He watched as they adjourned to the bedroom and overheard Phoenix say that she was in need of a nap. He stayed hidden for another half hour or so, but then saw no reason to conceal himself any longer.

Just as he entered the hallway, Lydia emerged from the bedroom.

She feigned a lack of surprise, spoke legally.

"What are you doing here? This is my house now and you're in violation of the injunction."

Bram paid no attention whatsoever to this remark, instead he replied as if he were still her master.

"You look older," he said by way of greeting.

"So do you," she snapped back, going for her T-cell.

Bram was quicker, snatched it from her and struck her an open handed blow across the face, knocking her sideways, a sensation of evil delight filling his desire for vengeance, but he controlled his canines, did not allow his nails to turn into claws.

She recovered quickly, not wishing to give him the satisfaction of knowing how much pain that one slap had caused her freshly healed jaw.

"You'd better get out of here," she said flatly, an immediate bruise appearing on her cheek. "Josh and Vladg should be here soon, and now that Josh is a Humilicant, it won't be the same as when you lost your thumb trying to get at him and Phoenix in the Manhattan apartment."

"I don't want to 'get at' Phoenix as you put it. I accept the fact that she's yours," he lied, "all I want is to observe the birth, to see my son breathe his first breath, and then I'll go."

"Who do you think you're fooling? I can tell when you're fibbing Bram, be off with you, get away while you're still in one piece, go practice your vampire routine somewhere else. We're ready for you here; you have no chance if you stay!"

Bram roars with laughter.

"What do you think, I came unprepared? You know me better than that."

He takes out his can of pressurized venom, sticks it under her nose.

"Now that you're mortalizing, I could kill you with a few whiffs of this, but I need you for the birthing. There will be plenty of time afterwards to take care of you…"

"Go to hell!"

"I intend to…"

At that moment the door to the master bedroom, bursts forth, Phoenix appears, shocked to see Bram, but more concerned with her pains.

"Lydia," she screams, "it hurts so bad, they're coming every three to four minutes now. I think I'm dilating."

Lydia forgets all about Bram. She acts as if he is not even there, goes to her love and embraces her, leads her back into the bedroom.

Unabashed, Bram follows.

∞

Rollie has left the highway, switched over from Cabrillo to Carillo Street and is heading for Castillo still traveling at breakneck speed, flashing lights spinning, amber, red and blue. Abraxas, following closely, knows it will require every bit of his sorcerer's power to cast an illusion of the type and complexity he desires which will fool Rollie the Duplicant, and Maloff's wife. He gets himself set, calls upon the Delphic Oracle to send Pythia, the Priestess of wind, heat and fire of the Temple of Apollo, to assist him. He appeals to her, concentrates fiercely, steps his mind down to the very marrow of his bones, opens both windows and shouts out his incantation, drawn from the Apocrypha, a variation of the Letter from Jeremiah:

"Set the offering of the burning boy before them! They cannot protect themselves. The dust of death lies thick upon their faces, let them be enveloped by the burning boy. They cannot protect themselves; let them be enveloped by the burning boy!'

The south east wind immediately carries his magic spell forward at infinite speed.

At once there appears, before their very eyes, not thirty feet in front of the onrushing police car, a beautiful blond curly haired boy of about six years of age. Rollie and Miriam are mesmerized.

The boy wears a whimsical smile on his face and holds a small Grecian urn filled with flammable fluid. He nonchalantly douses himself with it and sets himself afire. The blaze is torrid and the innocent face of the boy remains smiling amid the flames as Rollie swerves away at high speed to avoid hitting the child and the car rolls over once, but ends up on its wheels in a ditch at the side of the road.

This particular car is outfitted with the newest safety features, including the automatic release of two force fields upon impact. One of the fields is anti-centrifugal, to prevent momentum from thrusting the passengers forward and striking the windshield; the other acts sideways to hold them in position. Unfortunately, like a lot of new gizmos, the second force field over pressurizes and immobilizes Rollie and Miriam to their seats as if they were fixed images of themselves. As the force field increases the molecular friction against the bodies of the two, the heat increases exponentially and Rollie and Miriam are left sweltering. They cannot catch their breath in the hot air, are beginning to asphyxiate, when Abraxas manages to open the door and the two are released from the power of the force field.

The sorcerer lets out a long ghoulish laugh, his wide smelly nostrils dilating to the extreme.

"Abraxas to the rescue," he opines, totally sarcastic.

"Get us out of here," Miriam demands.

"What's with the burning boy? Is he alive?" Rollie asks, still not realizing that the apparition was a total illusion.

Abraxas merely grunts, totally pleased with himself.

"Well this worked out better than I had hoped. I should never have opened the door, but I wanted you to see me with your very own eyes before I incinerate you both."

He starts to chant another incantation, but doesn't get very far.

Detective Gentile is right behind him, holding a wide angle video camera in one hand and his taser in the other. This time he has recorded every word, every action and expression that Abraxas has uttered. With glee, he sets the taser on full phase and pulls the trigger.

By now two more B&W's have arrived, paramedics have landed and several bystanders have gathered about the scene.

Gentile points to the prostrate Abraxas who is being lifted off the ground by two uniforms, then handcuffed by the patrolmen and carried away.

"This recording should get me off the hook," he says to Miriam as he helps her out of the car and the paramedics come over to check on her. "Now we've got to get right over to the station and secure your husband's release if the TRU works like I think it will."

Miriam is slowly coming out of it, nods in agreement.

"How ya fairin'?" Gentile asks Rollie, striving to imitate the lingo.

Rollie smiles big time.

"None the worse for wear, 'twas a boil over Mate; Ya aced it, got the bounce; right clever. Had this all set out aforehand in that mind' a yours?"

"Ya betcha," the detective says, offering him a helping hand out of the now totaled car.

∞

After Vladg dropped him off, the first thing Josh heard upon entering the house was Phoenix's screams. His immediate reaction was to go to her, but then he realized that she was having labor pains, that it was a privacy thing, and maybe it would be better if he stayed out of her bedroom. So he went right to work on George, became focused on what he was doing and purposely masked out the sounds from the bedroom. After a while the screams stopped and he heard talking sounds that he could not make out. He was so busy, so engrossed in replacing George's heart, that he did not even notice Bram leaving the bedroom.

He had just completed the transplant and was about to give the new heart an electronic starting jolt, when he heard a deep sigh behind him. He turned his head to see what was going on, and was met with a toxic blast of venom. In spite of his new-found Humilicant power, his reaction was very similar to that of Vladg, who had been sprayed with a comparable dose at the Van den Valk factory in Amersfoort. The vapors knocked him out immediately.

George remained as immovable and still as ever, his front panels still unbuttoned.

∞

In the master bedroom, which is now the labor room, Phoenix, who has been in labor for almost three and a half hours, accuses Bram of raising a welt on Lydia's cheek.

"Did you do that to her?" she asks sternly, as if she were talking to a little boy.

Lydia is nervous, she expects a harsh wrangling response from Bram, but such is not the case.

Bram mumbles unintelligibly to himself, starts to say something, derails his answer, finally says he's sorry, submitting temporarily to Phoenix's will.

"Don't ever let that happen again!" she tells him threateningly. She seems, for the moment at least, to be the one in charge of the situation. Then a cramp comes on, the head of the baby presses against her lower spinal cord, she grimaces, and draws in a quick breath; now her entire demeanor changes, her facial expression reflects her suffering, her body bends over, folds inward, and she returns to bed to lie down. After the spell subsides, she relaxes some in the period between contractions.

Lydia goes to her, kisses her cheek, massages the small of her back, then puts on fresh gloves.

Watching her labor, suffering the pain of each contraction, shakes Bram into a new dimension, awakens more of his human qualities. The counter-agency to the powers of evil sends him into a different mindset. He feels that the world has begun to play tricks on him, that his mind has become a battleground for the forces of good and evil. His senses are beginning to accuse reality of inconsistency. He strains every nerve in his body to return to the task that he has set before himself, but through the bay window he sees Edna Kincaid leading Daisy to the grassy area by the Eucalyptus trees; then a bat-like creature with a devilish head, flapping its great wings appears, but it is chased away by an angel in a flowing white gown, an angel with ultra-blue eyes. He realizes at once that he is in peril of a mental overthrow.

He begins to feel a modicum of compassion when he sees Phoenix writhing in pain, striving to find a more comfortable position as her cervix dilates and continues to thin out. Suddenly he notices a mucus plug pop out from her vagina and Lydia, immediately wrapping it in a tissue, orders him to throw it in the waste can.

"Make yourself useful!" she commands.

He is startled, does not like the idea of being ordered around by anyone, certainly not by Lydia, but after all, he is the father, the one who initiated this entire process. He starts to experience fatherly concern, a feeling for the well-being of both mother and child, not just his selfish desire to secure the baby for his own needs.

"What else can I do?" he asks, eating humble pie.

"Go to the garage. There are dozens of ancient newspapers there, mostly from Ireland. Bring as many in here as you can carry. And set the tea kettle on, I have to boil my instruments."

"She wants a natural birth. She told me so when we were together. No cutting. No episiotomy."

"Don't be a dunce," Lydia says more gently than the words sound. "Anyway, I may have to tweak open her membrane if her bag of waters doesn't let loose by itself. That has to be done with a sterile instrument, so there. Be off with you."

Bram heads out to the garage, does as he was told.

On the way back he checks once on Josh, sees that he is still out cold. He places a sofa cushion under his head, making him a bit more comfortable. He feels guilty doing a good deed, but rationalizes that he will have to postpone his other plans until after the birthing.

He glances at George who appears as immobile as ever, his sightless eyes staring straight ahead.

Then he goes back to the kitchen and sets the tea kettle to the boil.

∞

At the station house, Vladg has already made acquaintance with the desk sergeant and a few others, both human and Duplicant officers. They appear fascinated, watching him set up the mini-TRU. This is an instrument that, under normal conditions, is rarely seen, as in regular usage it is housed in the body of a Duplicant where it runs 24/7. However, to display data it must be connected to the Projecto-FAX. Ordinarily this is simply done by neutrino-laser beam, which can penetrate to the exact location of the TRU in the body of the Duplo and make an internuncial connection to the P-FAX machine.

Vladg doesn't have to wait much longer; he has barely finished the preliminary work when Gentile arrives with Miriam and Rollie. Together they complete the n-l beam connection and everyone sits back to watch the holograph.

What they see is not in color; the number of color pixels extant over the extended time period is clearly not sufficient to produce an image. But the black and white projection begins to convert into visible shapes and forms. It shows Hatchet Jake throwing his axe straight at Ollie's skull, and a nano-second later, the bullet from Ollie's gun penetrating the throat of the murderous youth.

Then, although it is fuzzier, one can still make out that Freaky jumps Miriam, rips off her blouse and takes out his schlong. The holograph then loses clarity, but it is evident that a dark form has sprung at the rapist and is applying a tourniquet of some sort to the boy's neck. Then the projection slowly evaporates and nothing more is to be seen.

"Well that's better than I expected," Gentile says.

"Do you think it's enough to convince the judge?" Miriam asks anxiously.

"Depends on the judge, who we draw and all that, but I'm fairly certain with all the witnesses we've got here to verify what they saw, there should be no problem in securing your husband's release."

"Really? Do you really think so?"

"That's my professional opinion. The TRU shows the act was justifiable and excusable, an act of passion in defense of your rape. We've made copies. It's rare these days for any judge not to admit TRU data into evidence."

Miriam gives Gentile a grateful hug with plenty of squeezy oomph in it, turns to the jailer, and asks if she can see her husband now.

The turnkey's face is filled with a taciturn expression, as these are not proper visiting hours, but he begrudgingly leads her to the holding cell.

For the first time since all the troubles began, her step has lightness, her hips swivel in their old rhythm, moving in harmony with her gait.

Gentile watches closely as her rear end moves provocatively away from him. His bachelor thoughts are searching: 'This is certainly one special woman', but when he thinks long term of intimacy, a deep relationship with a woman, he gets scared. He rationalizes back to his yearning for serenity, believes it is to be found in solitude.

He turns to Vladg and asks if he would like to stick around, have some donuts and coffee, and tell a few lies with the boys, but Vladg says he had better get up to Lydia's, that Phoenix is due to give birth any hour. They shake hands for a job well done and Vladg takes off, wishing all a Happy Easter.

∞

On the return drive to Lydia's, Vladg thinks back to how much his life had changed in the last year and a half, to how remote he had been from all of life's contingencies. Like any other Sextus IX he had been assigned to Lydia as a designated companion, to meet her sexual needs, to be her chauffeur and to do chores around the house. Yes, he had gone through the usual phase, common to the average Sextus who was outfitted with a sensual system, that of falling in love with his owner, but then he traveled to Holland, found a new mode of experience and the true meaning of love in Hikey, something that was not in the manuals, or in any of the training modules at Pyrell's. And now he was a married Duplicant, still on his honeymoon, a teacher by profession with everything in life in front of him, a new culture and a new freedom.

When he reached Lydia's he was startled by what he saw, an unconscious Josh, lying on the floor in an awkward position, a sofa cushion placed rather neatly under his head. This bothered him. If Josh had simply fallen from exhaustion, or whatever, why would a cushion be there at all? No, logically someone had to have put it there and most probably after Josh was already dead to the world. He bent down to feel Josh's pulse, which was strong and regular, but as he leaned forward to stand back up he got a whiff of Josh's breath and this smell he recognized immediately. The odor was not pungent, but characteristic enough to be one of a kind. He had experienced it himself when Bram knocked him out in the lab of the factory in Amersfoort, where de Boer was murdered.

At once he was on the alert, Bram had to be here, somewhere in the house. He went to the hall closet, swung the door open, at the ready for a confrontation, his ATP already surging like a cyclotron in his lymph and musculature. No Bram, but what he spied was the hickory sword cane that he had given to Lydia as a present. He grabbed it, remembered that Lydia had silver coated the last six inches or so of the foil. If it came to it, he would have no hesitation using it on Bram, not after all that Bram had shown himself to be, even if this violated one of Pyrell's fundamental laws: *'No Duplicant is ever to cause willful harm to the purchaser or the owner'.*

He saw the empty heart case on the floor, glanced at George, whose panels needed to be closed. This he did, carefully hinging them up. Apparently Josh had been able to insert Ollie's heart in George's chest, but there were no signs of life at all. Better to wait. He knew it would be some time before Josh came around. As curious as he was to know why the transplant had failed, he did not want to examine or manipulate George any further without Josh on hand.

Then he heard screams, Phoenix in labor. He went over to the bedroom; got into his old eavesdropping stance and put his ear to the door. Now he detected another more calming voice, Lydia. This was followed by a somewhat gruffer tone, he could not make out the words, but he was sure it was Bram's voice. He drew the cane from its hickory sheath, tested the doorknob, twisted it full around and swung open the door.

As he busted in he saw Phoenix, in the delivery position, lying on a bed of newspapers in the old fashioned manner; Lydia at the ready, holding a long pair of pointed forceps in her gloved hands, about to snip the membrane of the bag of waters. This she did and the fluid came gushing out, flooding the papers, sloshing everywhere.

Lydia turned to Bram: "Clean up this mess," she orders.

Bram refuses adamantly, pulls his venom can up to a spraying position.

"I've had enough of your claptrap, let the Duplicant do it now that he's here."

Vladg is perplexed, does not know what to do. On the one hand he wants to run Bram through with the foil, on the other his deep training and roots of service are calling on him to help in every way he can. He has never had a headache in his life, but now the tension in his skull is very similar to that malady.

He chooses to abandon the sword cane, and starts to clean up the mess while Bram, conceding for the moment that he needs to impress Phoenix with his desire to be helpful, places some fresh newspapers under her butt.

Once the bag of waters has been broken, the thinned out cervix is dilating almost to the maximum and is fast approaching that transition state where the baby descends further in the birth canal. Now Phoenix's contractions are lasting almost a minute long and are coming every one or two minutes.

"I want to push," Phoenix says, taking a deep breath, but Lydia tells her: "No, no. Not yet. You are not yet fully dilated; hold back a few minutes more."

"But it feels like I need to go to the bathroom…"

"That's the baby's head pushing on your rectum through the back of the womb; please don't push yet love, not until you're dilated the full ten centimeters."

"I feel nauseous."

At that moment a bloody discharge emanates from her vagina, Phoenix barfs, Vladg catches the puke in a paper bag he has been handed by Lydia. Bram mops up a bit and Lydia continues to measure the dilation, waiting for the full transition, the second stage of labor when she can tell Phoenix to push. After a few more minutes in which Phoenix is shivering and shaking, Lydia announces that she is ready, that she has attained the full ten centimeters and that she can push.

Phoenix makes a few grunting sounds, but she has lost the energy to push that she so wanted to do a minute beforehand.

In between contractions there is not much activity, very little progress in the birth canal, so Lydia asks Vladg to massage

Phoenix's back, and his powerful kneading strokes appear to give her some relief.

She tells Phoenix this is the most intense stage of labor; that once the pains start coming every minute, instead of every two to three minutes, her baby will come forth. Phoenix tries to smile at this news, but she is unable; she wants to cry, but recovers and puts on a brave face.

At that moment the three women (colorful as tropical parrots in their dresses and bonnets and chirping nearly as loud) return from church, banging the front door open, shouting their arrival. They are in a joyous mood, talking about the sermon which was taken from Paul's First Letter to the Corinthians. Apparently, even Hikey was impressed with the pastor's delivery.

But when Phoebe spies Josh on the floor of the living room, she lets out a horrid scream which is seemingly echoed by a scream from her twin sister, who is now in dire pain, fully dilated and pushing with all get out.

Phoebe feels her allegiance is with her twin, leaves Josh on the floor and rushes to her sister. She goes to the side of the bed, holding one hand while Emily goes to the other side to comfort her.

"We've got to get her to the hospital, you can't let her suffer like this," Emily screams at Lydia.

"I am getting ready to give her an epidural if that is what she wants," Lydia replies tartly. She hates the interruption; paradoxically, she feels that she is the only one who has any rights in the decision, the matter of hospitalization.

Hikey has gone to Vladg, holds him close. She too has never attended a birthing; she is taken aback by all the amniotic fluid mixed with spots of blood and mucus that are still visible on the newspapers, which she finds gross.

"Let's get out of here," she says to Vladg.

"I can't. I'm needed, but you should leave…"

"And the rest of you too," Lydia says.

Now Phoebe turns to Bram, her face red with anger.

"You did you this to her you know, look what you've done to my sister you selfish oaf!"

Bram refuses to respond to her, controls the urges of his body, to turn fang and claw against her, but his anger is rising.

"And Josh on the floor in the bedroom, out cold. What on earth have you done to him?" she demands to know, snapping her fingers right under Bram's nose.

Vladg is aghast at the chance she is taking, sees that Bram is about to erupt. He grabs Phoebe bodily with one strong arm wrapped around her waist and hauls her kicking and screaming through the air and out of the bedroom. Like the trooper that she is, she shouts her contempt of Bram at him reeling off every Manhattan epithet in the book, one right after the other.

Emily and Hikey, at Lydia's urging, also leave the room and Lydia is finally able to start Phoenix's epidural.

She lavishly brushes on an antiseptic solution over the skin of Phoenix's lower back, and then covers this area with an aseptic cloth that adheres to the skin. This piece of cloth has a three by three inch cut out in the center; she places this square space below the fourth Lumbar. This is the area she intends to use to puncture the skin and to direct the infusion needle. She then injects a small amount of lidocaine to the area so that Phoenix won't feel the prick. Bram assists her, helping Phoenix to maintain a sitting position, bending forward from the waist in order to increase the curvature of the spine.

Lydia guides the special needle through the layers of tissue and as the needle passes through the covering ligament into the intervertebral space she feels a 'pop' and knows she is in the epidural space. Then she threads the catheter through the special needle and starts the infusion of pain killer.

Phoenix cannot hold this position very long, but she doesn't have to, as Lydia is very adept at this procedure, having performed a good many epidurals in operations on large dogs as well as earlier in her career as a midwife. As soon as the needle is properly set, so that it cannot move around, Phoenix is allowed to lie on her side for a time. After twenty minutes or so she gets relief from the pain. She is still able to sense the contractions, however, and with Lydia's direction knows when to push.

"You see Bram, a good deal can be done at home, in some ways it's less risky than in a hospital."

"You didn't have a scanner to guide you, but you got in right away. Risky, it could have been otherwise."

"True, but this is what she wanted and you too, right."

"Yes, but I had no idea what went on, how complicated it all is. I've never been to one of these deliveries before."

"You sound almost human, Bram."

He tries to manager a smile, but it doesn't come off.

She glances at Phoenix who is having a respite, a short relief from pain, as the transition proceeds and the baby's head inches downward, ready to make its turn in the birth canal toward the cervix. Then the baby seems to stall, almost as if it is uncertain whether it wants to go further and take the final pathway to the end of its journey. The contractions stop.

Phoenix becomes anxious, asks Lydia if she thinks something awful has happened: "Maybe the cord got tied around Christopher's neck?"

Lydia doubts this, but to placate her she puts on a new pair of sterile gloves, enters the birth canal, her fingers find the baby's head, then the neck and she pronounces that all is clear and ok.

Phoenix is relieved. Her head is swimming; she is fatigued but not exhausted and decides to rest, to take advantage of this second lull in her delivery. Then too, she is much more confident now about becoming a mother, about a good result for Christian. The only glitch is Bram; she is still unsure over how she feels about his presence. Yet she is less afraid of him than ever before. Finally, she drops off, taking a light catnap.

The situation is such that Bram and Lydia find themselves essentially alone. It's not that Bram has had an alteration of his beliefs, certainly not. His exploration of the domains which lay unexplored within him has had its effect this day. He is still an unpredictable figure of moods and silences, but he is now at least willing to discuss the many years of their lives spent together. They actually have much to say to one another, words that need to be said, but have been postponed for some time because of circumstances.

They speak almost as if they were still partners.

"You were cruel to me in many ways," Lydia says, "my heart always sank upon hearing your derisive laugh, but I must admit you pulled me out of a death trap in Ireland, I wouldn't have made it in those days without you."

"Well I got into the habit of evading the subject of your inability to produce a child, an offspring of which I could be proud. It was absurd in a way. I should have talked to you about it.

"Yes, you should've."

"On the other hand, we did have many a good time drinking blood together at the Cabal of the brotherhood."

"That was truly many lifetimes ago. I am mortal now; none of that type of partying would be pleasurable for me."

"More's the pity."

"And may I ask, whether you are being truthful; whether you will leave us alone with Christopher?"

"Yes, I think so, yes. I have seen how hard Phoenix has fought for the birth of the boy, how she has nearly shredded herself to pieces to preserve his life. I do want to see him take his first breath, and then I shall go, but I cannot promise what I will do afterwards to Phoebe, nor to anyone else. The alchemy that my mother has taught me, the vampire ideals from my father are firmly entrenched in my soul. You can only view this Easter birthing as a one-day aberration, a mere postponement of my plans. I promise nothing further."

"But for the present you have an interior hold on yourself, nothing else will happen here today."

"I will not initiate any mischief, no, but I will not tolerate anything from Vladg or that Humilicant Josh if he awakens while I am still here."

Lydia nods, she knows that is the best compromise she can hope to get out of him.

Just then

Phoenix awakens, calls to her.

It is time to push again.

∞

In the living room, Phoebe is traipsing back and forth working herself into a frenzy. She is nervous about her sister, worried about Josh and concerned over George. She is keeping up a steady roiling chatter to herself that is beginning to put everyone else on edge. She doesn't trust Lydia's ability at this point and wants Phoenix to be sent to hospital. In spite of Vladg's reassurance, she thinks a doctor needs to be called for Josh. Vladg has repeatedly told her that he knows exactly what is going on with the venom and that if Phoebe is patient time will heal and Josh will come out of it. This she doubts. She also wants to call Eiselman and seek his advice, tell him what went on with the transplant. Then she begins her entire spiel all over again.

Emily is about to say something to her when the accident takes place.

No one knows for certain exactly what happened, but the presumption is that Lydia was already upset, pissed over the stoppage of the baby in the birth canal when his head was so close to the cervix, to the end of the tunnel. The conjecture is that she spied the foil of the sword cane on the floor where Vladg had left it to help with clean-up and must have kicked it, intending to merely knock the rapier out of her way, but that it somehow took flight at exactly the moment Phoebe was traipsing in front of the open door.

Emily attests that she saw Phoebe raise her arm offensively, as if she wanted to swipe at the missile that was headed for her, like an athlete swinging a forehand return in tennis. Phoebe doesn't know why she did it, only that her peripheral vision caught a glimpse of something metallic flashing toward her at the speed of light and she reacted defensively. In any case, whatever the reason that Phoebe swung at it, the result was that the sharp end of the foil pierced her palm and went right through her hand.

Phoebe let out a sharp scream when she saw the lengthy foil stuck in her hand, and it is this scream that apparently animated George, whose sensory apparatus had always been very much attuned to Phoebe's needs. His eyelids flashed open and his visual sense came on board, coordinating with his brain; his hearing became acute, and though his motor systems were not yet functional, all of his sensory apparatus appeared to be in working order.

But George commanded no attention, everyone was busy with Phoebe, especially Vladg who was getting ready to pull out the foil from her hand but was studying the best way to do this so as not to injure more tissue when he withdrew the sword.

In the labor room things were happening very fast.

Phoebe's contractions had restarted, she was pushing to beat the band and a portion of the head was visibly emerging from the vulva, slowly to be sure, but definitely coming through. Bram had taken up a position directly behind Lydia, who was standing between Phoenix's legs, slightly bent over, making ready to help deliver the head. Bram was only a spectator, but he could see everything, and to his astonishment, as Lydia grasped the head and guided it free from the vulva, the newborn's eyes popped open and the angle was such that Bram's face was the first image of life outside the womb that the baby visualized.

The shoulders were no problem, first one and then the other glided free and both lower legs followed easily. Lydia squeegeed the cord with a small forceps so that the maximum amount of fetal blood, containing all the good stem cells, circulated back into the baby's system.

At the exact moment that Lydia cut the cord, Vladg managed to withdraw the foil from Phoebe's hand and George, who assumed that Bram had done this to his beloved Phoebe, finally became animated, his motor system coordinating with the rest of his body functions.

The first thing he did was to grab the poker from its place at the hearth, and with a determination that knew no bounds headed for the bedroom where he heard Bram's voice praising Satan for delivering a son to him.

Bram was very excited, breathing hard now, his inspirations and expirations accompanied by a soft audible wheeze.

Lydia was still very busy. She did not slap the baby on his bottom, nor did she turn him upside down, but first sucked out all the phlegm and fluids from his mouth with a piece of rubber tubing specified for the purpose so that he could not aspirate, as he had yet not taken first breath. She cleaned his eyes and put a drop of silver nitrate in each one. She was so focused on what she was doing that she did not see George enter the room. Neither did Bram. But he heard something behind him and made to turn, but it was too late. George thrust the poker savagely, from back to front, straight through Bram's heart.

Just as Christian drew his first breath, Bram drew his last.

He expired with a long slow wheeze as his features withered, shriveling into the tight lines of the gray mask of death.

Lydia wanted to go to him, she saw faded lithographs of their ancestral life together, but at once, reality hit her and erased these pictures. She needed to clean the baby of all the oils and lanugo hairs that remained on the skin and then she had to deliver the placenta. So she called for help and Hikey came to her aid, Emily being busy comforting Phoebe.

Hikey said nothing whatsoever about the prostrate body on the floor. After the rape and mutilation of Cynthia at the hands of a vampire she had little sympathy for Bram, but her face still showed dismay and despair at the appearance of death.

Lydia pulled herself together; pointed out where the swaddling clothes were, and Hikey was glad to be of help. She wrapped the multicolored soft cottony material firmly around the baby and then set him gently on Phoenix's chest where the baby's cheeks felt the warmth of his mother's breasts and smelled the essence of her scent.

It was to be a little while yet before Phoenix fully realized she was no longer gravid. The baby had been so long in forming inside of her, that she was still unprepared to hold his precious body, but now that Bram was no more, she was no longer scared of motherhood. Indeed, she felt as if the world had given her a nudge in the right direction.

The first thing she did was to lift one of the baby's eyelids. She wanted to check the eye color. It didn't matter to her whether all newborn babies' eyes were blue. She had to see for herself. Indeed, Christian's eyes were not just blue, they were ultra-blue. To her this meant more of her genetics were in Christian than Bram's. Now she was satisfied. She was so joyous, she felt as if she were in heaven, and for that matter, the baby probably did too now that he was free of the chamber in which he had been lodged for so many months. Of course he did not yet suckle, that might take a day or two, but he nestled his head by her left breast and went to sleep, the image of his father's face firmly imprinted in his mind.

Both Phoenix and Lydia were totally exhausted, physically and mentally.

Phoenix realized she was in great debt to Lydia for all that she had done for her, but she also was aware that this gratitude was not to be verbalized, that it would somehow be demeaning to their love, that the words themselves could never embrace the deep feelings she felt for what had been accomplished.

Lydia had but a moment or two to come to her before she had to deliver the afterbirth. She stood by the bedside and they clasped hands, feeling the warmth course through their veins. They said very little to one another, but they each knew, with Bram's passing, that the primeval state of their love was over, that they had transcended to a new beginning.

After Lydia delivered the placenta, she handed it over to Hikey who wrapped it in newspaper and put it in the trash. Then Hikey started gathering up all the old papers that had served so well to prevent the blood and other fluids from seeping onto the bed-sheets or anywhere else. Next she spread a fresh bed-sheet over Bram's body, covering it completely so that the unsightly corpse was less disturbing to everyone.

"Did you think he was going to come back to life," Lydia asked, confronting her in a strange way.

"No," Hikey said, thinking of what Drakonius had done to Cynthia and how he had disappeared, "but I have certainly seen vampires do some strange things."

This response seemed to mollify Lydia, who had not yet settled her mind over the loss of the man to whom she was attached for so many years.

"Yes," Lydia agreed. "Yes that's true," she repeated.

Now Emily and Phoebe made their way in to see the baby and to congratulate Phoenix.

Lydia, resolute in her doctoring mode, told Phoebe she had to undergo first aid before allowing any visit to the baby. Phoebe pouted some, but gave in.

Lydia first stanched and cleansed the drips and clots of blood from the puncture wounds in Phoebe's hand with alcohol soaked sterile gauze pads. Then, she spread the same antiseptic she used on Phoenix's lower back over the palmar and dorsal surfaces of her hand. She finished up the bandaging and told Phoebe to get a tetanus shot within twenty-four hours. Phoebe, much more settled down now that the baby was born, promised to do so the very next day.

Finally, Lydia allowed her to go over to hug her sister and see the baby.

"He's truly an Easter Sunday gift of joy isn't he," Phoenix says to her sister.

"Yes he is," Phoebe answers lovingly, just as a woozy Josh walks in, held up to some degree by Vladg who is lending a supporting arm. They immediately head over to the bed to congratulate Phoenix and perform their 'coo and aah' flirtation with the baby in the awkward way that most men have.

After admiring the newborn, Vladg calls Detective Gentile, tells him there's been another murder at Lydia's place and asks him to come over.

On the small screen the detective says:

"What's with you people? Who's the victim?"

"The man you were so suspicious of, Bram Alucard."

"Oh, that sleazebag. Yeah, you're right, not one of my favorites."

Vladg doesn't know what else to say about Bram, lets it go.

Tony Gentile sighs; says he'll be right over.

"And detective…"

"Yes…"

"We have a new life as well…"

"The lady delivered?"

"Yes, a newborn, a boy named Christian."

"A new Christian, eh? Well break out the …never mind, I can't drink on duty, but give her my congratulations. I'll be right there."

Josh meanwhile is feeling stronger. He is careful not to fall, walks gingerly over to Phoebe. He holds his lips close to her ear, whispers:

"I want to make one just like that."

Phoebe throws her arms around him.

"I do too," she says. "This is a new beginning for us, isn't it?"

"Yes, it is," Josh says right back, his certainty clarifying a good deal of the friction between the two.

Now Hikey, doing clean-up, spies an Irish headline from one of the news pages. It has three little drops of blood on it, but is otherwise clean. She starts to read. The lead article refers to the St. Patrick's Cathedral and discusses the historic construction of the twin spires and their recent renovation. Two of the drops are settled in one paragraph and emboss the words *'he has'*. The other drop is situated in an entirely different paragraph and highlights the word *'risen'*.

Hikey calls Emily over to show her.

"Look," she says. "What a coincidence. If you put together the three drops of Phoenix's blood that spot the words, it reads: He has Risen

Emily sees what Hikey means. She calls out to Phoebe, and wants her to read the words as well.

HE HAS RISEN

Phoebe brings the paper over to Phoenix, who is finally relaxing with her baby in a way she has not done in ten lunar months. She too puts the three drops of blood together that spell out the words: HE HAS RISEN

Phoenix is content. She has Lydia and she has Christian.

Now she knows there is no beginning and no end, only the cycle of life, both good and evil.

About the Author

F. Eagles Pope

As an enterprising 'hard-studying' medical student at the University of Amsterdam, I necessarily felt the need for a refreshing pilsner a couple of times a week. I discovered, in a side street of the Leidseplein, the most wonderful bar, called 'Eijlders'. There I met many mystical and mysterious people from the Dutch Antilles who, over drinks, regaled me with stories of voodoo and vampires. This was the basis for upcoming paranormal novel '*The Robot and the Vampire*'.

Tell-Tale Publishing would like to thank you for your purchase. If you would like to read more by fine TT authors, please visit our website:

http://www.tell-talepublishing.com